Two-Dollar Pistol

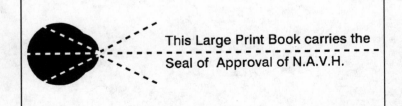

This Large Print Book carries the
Seal of Approval of N.A.V.H.

Two-Dollar Pistol

Brett Cogburn

THORNDIKE PRESS

A part of Gale, Cengage Learning

GALE
CENGAGE Learning·

Farmington Hills, Mich • San Francisco • New York • Waterville, Maine
Meriden, Conn • Mason, Ohio • Chicago

GALE
CENGAGE Learning®

LIBRARY OF CONGRESS CATALOGING-IN-PUBLICATION DATA

Cogburn, Brett.
   Two-dollar pistol / by Brett Cogburn. -- Large print edition.
      pages cm. -- (Thorndike Press large print western)
   ISBN 978-1-4104-7112-3 (hardcover) -- ISBN 1-4104-7112-8 (hardcover)
   1. Outlaws--Fiction. 2. Large type books. I. Title.
PS3603.O3255T96 2015b
813'.6--dc23   2015006073

Published in 2015 by arrangement with David Brett Cogburn

TWO-DOLLAR PISTOL

CHAPTER ONE

*"I generally avoid temptation
unless I can't resist it."*
— Mae West

Claude Miller sat with his back to a big sycamore trunk and scanned the timber for any sign of something to shoot. The morning sun was straining down through the thick canopy of hardwood limbs overhead, and the fog that had lain so thick over the bottomland earlier was burned away until nothing of it remained other than smoky tendrils hovering above the muddy water of the river. He watched a pair of wood ducks paddle by in silence, and he frowned when a police siren sounded in the distance.

Nothing of much consequence ever happened in his country, and the howling siren promised something perhaps out of the ordinary. Most young people in that neck of the woods would have been excited to hear anything that blared excitement and novelty, but not Claude. He was a hunter by nature as much as by practice, and liked it when the woods were quiet. Any kind of noise made it harder to hear a whitetail buck crunching through the oak leaf bed, or the scurried rustle of a gray squirrel in the trees. The wind passing through the timber, the hammer of a woodpecker on a dead snag, or the cawing of crows coming off their roost was usually the only noise that hampered his keen ear. Needless to say, a blaring siren was especially irksome.

The awful wail grew louder as it came up the county road, and it set Claude's teeth on edge. Whoever was driving finally shut the thing off, but they must have stopped on the river bridge upstream. He couldn't see the trestle bridge from where he sat, but he heard the rattle of timbers on the iron joists, and the sputtering idle of an engine. Several other cars were coming behind the first one, and somebody shouted from near the bridge.

Claude guessed that the ruckus would eventually pass, but he was already out of the mood to hunt. There wasn't much game stirring anyway, and he had work waiting on him at home. He rose to his feet and gathered his gun and the single squirrel he had managed to kill. He put his feet to a narrow trail at the edge of the high river-bank, and worked himself upstream. Cattle hooves had beaten back the green briars and churned the black earth into a soft, cool pad beneath his bare feet.

More cars stopped on the bridge, doors slammed, and he could barely make out the voices of several men. Lots of folks put in their boats at the bridge to run trotlines, or to cast a baited hook into the Kiamichi River. Be that as it may, he had never heard so many arrive at once, nor with police sirens, either. Something had the country-side stirred up, and he couldn't help but wonder if the bridge had fallen in, or if maybe somebody had drowned. He remem-bered when little Eddie Folsom dove into the river and broke his neck on a sunken snag, and how the men of the community dragged the bottom of the river with giant treble hooks to find his body. He hadn't been there when they fished Eddie out, but folks said he was swollen up so that he didn't look like a boy anymore, with his eyes and nose full of mud and his skin as white as a fish's belly.

The trail led through a thick canebrake, where the hollow green and yellow stalks grew higher than Claude's head. He waded through a shallow bog in its middle, careful to keep a lookout for snakes. A beaver slide made a narrow break in the cane that led down to his boat, and he turned into it. The warm mud oozed between his toes and he strained at the suck of it as he pushed his way through the thicket with his left forearm held in front of his face.

He busted through the canebrake in time to see two strangers preparing to steal his boat. The man and woman whirled about at the sound of the switch cane cracking beneath his feet. Despite their fancy clothes, Claude knew them in an instant for what they were. The hard, hunted look on their faces, and the .32 Colt automatic that appeared as if by magic in the man's hand gave them away.

"Give me that gun, boy." The man leveled the automatic on Claude's chest.

Claude looked down at the single-shot rifle in his right hand, as if remembering it for the first time. The dead squirrel, with a sharpened piece of green stick run through one back foot for a carrying handle, hung limply in his other hand. Claude studied the squirrel, the rifle, and the tops of his filthy, bare feet in the silt of the riverbank. He could hear a sizeable party fighting through the dense thicket of briars and flooded sloughs that lay between where his boat was and the bridge a few hundred yards upstream.

"That's my boat," Claude said quietly.

"Come on, just get the kid's gun and let's get out of here before the coppers show up." The young blonde woman talked around the Lucky Strike cigarette dangling from her lips. She sat in the back of the boat with one very long, slender leg revealed by her hiked-up skirt. She seemed more concerned with the tear in her nylon stocking that she was examining than the barefoot boy with a dead squirrel, or the lawmen plunging through the woods after she and her man.

"Kid, I'm not going to tell you again." The man's eyes were shadowed by the brim of his fedora, and all that was visible of his face was an oversized, scarred nose and a mouthful of crooked teeth.

Claude studied his boat and then the blonde sitting in it. He tried to get his mind wrapped around what was happening, and a part of his brain was screaming at him to give in before he got shot. He watched the man's thumb reach up to flip off the toggle safety on the .32.

A bad man in a twenty-dollar suit with a diamond tiepin should have known to have his safety off. The rifle came up in Claude's hands and a bullet punched into the man's forehead and out the back of his skull before the squirrel had time to hit the ground.

The dead man fell at the edge of the water, and a slow, oily trail of blood was already floating downstream. Claude stood confused and mesmerized, until it slowly dawned on him that he had killed a man. There had been no time to think, and the rifle had almost jumped in his hands of its own volition. But then again, guns had always come natural to him.

He turned his attention back to the blonde, and caught her searching frantically for some sort of weapon. The sounds of the manhunt were getting closer. He dug another cartridge from his shirt pocket while she stared at him. The look she gave him reminded him of the time he jumped in the creek and came up face to face with a poisonous cottonmouth snake. He was almost as hypnotized by her as he had been by the snake.

He broke away from her gaze and his vision wandered over the short, summer dress she wore. She immediately noticed, and the hard anger and panic on her face gave way to something else akin to instinct. She ignored his gun and shifted that long leg before her and tucked a strand of hair behind one ear. His eyes were slowly drawn from the earring dangling from that earlobe down to the braless breasts almost visible beneath the thin fabric. He blushed at the hardening of her nipples beneath his gaze.

"What'cha gonna do now?" She shifted that leg again, and he could almost see what he knew he shouldn't be looking for.

The brush was cracking not far up the river bottom, and he tore his eyes away from her long enough to gauge how far off the pursuit was. His eyes went back to her as quickly as they had left. She seemed to know where he was looking and what he was thinking, but wasn't at all bothered by it. In fact, she seemed to invite him to stare. He never imagined there was a woman like that.

"There's at least ten thousand dollars in that bag." She kept her smoky gaze on him.

He studied the leather satchel in the bottom of the boat as cautiously as he did her. "I guess that's the Law I hear coming after you."

"Finders, keepers. I suggest you take me down the river." Her voice was huskier than cigarettes had any right to make it.

"You would have killed me a minute ago."

"That was Mike's idea."

"We'll wait here until the Law shows up.

I'm pretty sure they're looking for you."

"What's the matter, don't you like to have fun? I bet you haven't ever had more than two bits in your pocket at one time, or more than a pair of shoes a year."

"I've got shoes. I just don't want to ruin them wading around in a river bottom." He didn't tell her that he had just one pair to go to school in. He wondered if she was lying about the money. That was a lot of cash if she wasn't.

"You don't have to be poor if you've got enough sense to take advantage of the opportunity. You get me out of here and I'll show you things you've never even imagined."

"I could just take the money if I wanted it." Claude was shocked at how easily the idea came to him.

"I bet you could." She dabbed at the sweat on her white throat with the back of her curled fingers. "Good things don't come around often. You've got to be man enough to take them as they come."

Claude was torn between the hunger the woman brought over him, and what he knew he should do. The bag she claimed was full of money tempted him almost as much as her pale flesh. He'd never been a thief, but he'd never had that much money

14

laying before him for the taking either. He was sure that he could eventually fight off the wicked urges he was feeling, but he already knew that the situation wasn't going to give him the time it took to be good. Doing what he felt like was always much easier than doing what he ought to do. He bent quickly and picked up the .32 automatic and tucked it in his waistband. He started to shove the boat off, but paused long enough to take up the dead man's fedora lying on the sandbar. He set the hat on his head and it fit him perfectly. He tugged the brim down low over his eyes and took a quick glance at the water to see how it looked on him.

"Get up here in the front of the boat." He untied the boat quickly, lest he change his mind.

His mother always told him that nothing people did should come as a shock, but he didn't know she meant even him. She didn't have a clue how right she was. He found himself wondering what had come over him. His mind was saying "no" to temptation, and his body wasn't listening. More than the fact that he'd killed a man, he felt that he was on the brink of something, and even more, that he was helpless to refuse the Devil whispering in his ear.

She smiled thinly and took the front bench facing the stern. A heady, sweet smell of perfume hit his nose and slowly settled down through his shoulders and into the pit of his stomach. He studied the bare flesh of one of her shoulders and the nape of her neck as she pulled her hair up and over to one side as if the morning were hotter than it was. He pushed the bow of the boat free and turned it broadside to the bank. One long step into the boat and he sat quickly to steady the rocking hull. He was already half wishing she wasn't facing him. There was something about her that made him twitchy and too aware of himself, and it would be much easier to look her over without her looking back at him.

"You just be still, and don't do anything sudden. I'll be watching you." A hard shove of his paddle against the mud started them toward midstream.

She reclined back against the bow of the boat with an arm resting on either side of the hull. "I know you will."

The boat was a homemade job, cobbled together out of thin oak planks caulked with tar, and its handling was heavy and slow where it rode deep in the dark water. He paddled, his rifle propped against his side. The blonde was studying him with a look

16

on her face he couldn't interpret. He stared back at her, lest he forget what had tempted him enough get in the boat with her.

The sluggish current wouldn't carry them downstream fast enough. He paddled at a steady pace, and tried not to think about the bad thing he was doing.

Nobody living in Pushmataha County could remember such a terrible drought, much less one that lasted three years and showed no signs of breaking. Moisture was such a scarce commodity that people in those parts had ceased to look at the sky for thunderclouds — a sure sign of hard times when hope died of thirst. Rather than a real river, in places, the old Kiamichi was more like a chain of potholes linked together between the high flood banks of a yesteryear when it had actually rained.

"Do you know who you shot back there?" She tapped her cigarette pack on the heel of her left hand.

"No." Claude's mind was swimming so that he couldn't latch on very long to any one thought, and he kept pushing away the image of the bad man's brains splattering into the river.

She shook out another cigarette and tucked the butt end into her full lips. The red of her lipstick was bright against the

17

white paper. "That was Murder Mike Holley."

He shrugged. The name meant nothing to him, other than a sickening realization growing in his gut that he must be wicked — not just wicked, but a killer too. He tried not to think about that either. He was good at pretending things were better than they were. He wished the woman would quit talking so much and give him time to work things out.

"You haven't heard of Murder Mike?" She looked at him over a lit match.

He could tell by her incredulous tone that maybe he should have been more impressed with her former partner. "All I know is that he was slow."

She gave that careful thought. "Mike robbed banks from Iowa to Texas, killed a couple of policemen among others, and did hard time in places you don't even want to imagine."

"If he was so tough, how come he went to prison in the first place?"

"You think you're a little bit salty, don't you?"

"I'm the one paddling the boat, ain't I?"

She studied his broad shoulders, and the muscles of his legs where they stretched the thighs of his jeans tight. "Maybe you're

18

right. We'll see."

"My daddy always said, don't ever give up your gun, because you'll probably just get killed anyway."

"Easy enough to say, but I don't know anybody but you foolish enough to put that into practice when somebody's got the drop on you, much less with a peashooter like you're packing." She jabbed a finger in the general direction of his rifle.

"That Mike didn't give me time to think about it. Maybe I was lucky. I've always been good with guns."

"There's lots of men these days that are good with a gun."

"Maybe. I'm not bragging, but there are folks that say I'm better with a gun than anybody they ever saw."

"Real modest, aren't you? I can see that all your talent has made you a fortune." She gave his ragged attire a scornful once-over.

He tried to tuck his bare feet back under him and out of sight. "Well, I reckon that's my money in that bag."

She didn't like his mentioning the money, but her voice grew husky again. "You learn quick. I like a man who knows what he wants."

He watched the tobacco smoke roll slowly out through her red, pursed lips and

19

wouldn't have been surprised if little horns had sprouted from her head. "If you think you can con me, you've got another thing coming. I didn't fall off the tater wagon yesterday."

She stretched that leg out again and rested it on the satchel. The wind pulled her skirt higher up toward her hips until he could see a patch of soft white inner thigh below the lacy edge of one garter. "You're the man."

"I might leave you on the riverbank somewhere. Or maybe I'll turn you in to the Law. There's probably a reward on your head."

"I don't think so. Bad boys always go for all the loot."

"What kind of woman are you?"

She laughed loudly. "The bad kind. The best kind."

He tried to focus on the river ahead and behind her, but his eyes kept following the inside of that lovely leg up and up. What he wanted to do right then wouldn't steer the boat. It was about more than he could bear. Facing down Murder Mike had been easy compared to paddling down the river with that woman.

"I'm Myra Belle Hooser, but the lucky ones call me Sugar."

His clenched jaw and the lump in his

20

throat almost kept him from answering. "I'm Claude Miller. Folks just call me Claude."

"Claude, what a dreadful name. We're going to have to change that."

"It's always been good enough."

"Are you Indian? You've got the prettiest dark skin."

"My mother's Choctaw." He didn't know how she could talk about his skin with her former man bleeding in the river still in sight. And it was bothersome, her looking at him that way while she was talking. He was already as hard as a rock, and he felt uncomfortably sure that she had noticed his fever. He tried to focus on paddling the boat.

"What kind of an Indian name is Claude?"

Before he could defend his given name a bullet splashed into the water beside them. More guns were going off by the time he twisted around to look back upriver to the shoal they had left behind. He could see at least ten men aiming rifles from the sandbar, and leaned his back into the paddle. He wished the Law had shot at him earlier, and maybe he wouldn't be in the boat.

"What the hell did you and that Mike do?"

Myra licked her upper lip and smiled up at him from where she had hunkered down in the floor of the boat. "We robbed the Antlers Bank."

Claude let that rattle around for a bit. "Well, that's no worse than I expected."

"You aren't shocked?" She seemed a little put out.

He couldn't tell her how shocked he really was. He'd been on many a morning squirrel hunt, but he hadn't ever had a day like he was having. And never had he expected that he had so much bad in him as was showing itself right then.

Another bullet came way too close for comfort. They were a good three hundred yards down the river from the shoal, but that didn't stop the shooting. Most men couldn't hit anything offhand at that distance, but there must have been some optimistic sorts in the posse.

"Can't you paddle faster?" she asked.

"Why don't you shut up? Can't you see I'm kind of busy here?"

Another bullet smacked into the bow of the boat, knocking a splintered hole only inches from Myra's head. She peeked over the side at the riflemen. "My Lord, but those country boys can shoot!"

"That might be the Sheriff. Everybody says he's the best rifle shot in Push County. Him and old Joe Oklahombi shot more

Germans in the war than you can shake a stick at."

"How can you tell with your back to him?"

Claude dug his paddle deep in the water and smiled a crooked smile. "I ought to know him. He's my daddy."

CHAPTER TWO

"In other periods of depression, it has always been possible to see some things which were solid and upon which you could base hope, but as I look about, I now see nothing to give ground to — hope."
— President Calvin Coolidge
on the Great Depression

Claude listened to the sound of a car passing along a road on the riverbank above where he had banked the boat earlier that afternoon. The night was pitch black, but he could feel Myra close to him nonetheless. He almost jumped out of his skin when she laid a hand on his elbow.

"Go ahead up there and get us a car." She shoved him gently.

He jerked away, but could still feel her touch on his arm even with distance between them. "I'm not stealing anybody's car."

"We've gone about as far as we can in that boat of yours. You either walk down to the crossing and stop that car, or the Law's going to catch us." The frustration was plain in her voice.

"I haven't done anything for the Law to want me." He still hadn't gotten his mind wrapped around how he had come to be where he was.

"Do you want to keep the profit, or don't you have any idea what that kind of money means?"

He had been thinking about the money a lot, especially after he had taken a look in the valise. Every time he thought of that much cash he pictured old Roy Burkhalter down at his cotton gin with his fancy suit, new car, and fat cigar clenched between his teeth. Everybody wished they were as rich as crooked Roy, even if they said they didn't. Claude had long imagined himself as a high roller like Roy. That money could buy a lot of things, and up until the instant he laid eyes on it, his dreams all seemed to cost too much.

"Take your gun down to the crossing and stop that car," she hissed.

He thought about the fancy automatic

Remington rifle he'd seen in the Sears and Roebuck catalog, a new set of clothes, and maybe one of those Ford coupes with a flathead V-8. In the midst of all his dreaming he remembered his family and how little they had. His mother making do with what little his father made as sheriff and the meager offerings of a garden during a two-year drought made him ashamed.

"I ain't robbing poor folks."

"If they were poor they wouldn't be able to afford a car. If you're going to be an outlaw, you've got to forget all those silly notions you're packing."

"Who said I'm going to be an outlaw?"

She snickered in the dark. "You're an outlaw, honey, or you wouldn't be here right now."

"You keep your distance. I don't trust you close to my guns."

They could hear the car slowing to cross downstream from them, and its headlights showed faintly on the river. They listened to it until the sound of its motor faded in the distance.

"Now you've done it. There probably won't be another car by here the rest of the night." It was plain that she was pouting.

"You can go off on your own anytime you want." He was proud of his willpower. It wasn't too late to set things right. He hadn't robbed any banks; all he had to do was to turn the money and the woman in and he could go back to his life.

"I should have known better than to team up with a boy, and a hick at that."

"I'll be eighteen come January. How old are you?"

"You don't ask a woman her age."

"How old are you?"

She waited a long moment before she answered him. "Twenty-five."

"Well, that doesn't make you any smarter than me." He crouched down at the water's edge with his rifle between his knees and resting against his shoulder. "I ain't the one with the Law after me."

"If I had the gun, I'd have been smart enough to go stop that car. I think you're scared."

"Think what you want. Think it all night, for that matter. Come morning, I'm going to take this money and turn it in before I dig the hole I'm in any deeper. It's a wonder nobody has headed us off yet." Claude was worn-out from paddling the boat and dragging it over one dry stretch after another.

"What about me?"

He gave that some thought. "Don't know what to do with you. I think the best thing

27

would be for me to get as far away from you as I can."

Her feet rustled in the leaves as she eased up to him. She was so close he could hear her breathing. His hand found the rifle and gripped it tight.

"You don't want any such thing," she said.

"You don't know what I want."

"Why don't you build us a fire? It's a little chilly."

"We're going to have to go without one. Somebody looking for us might see it."

"I'm getting real cold." She sounded as if she were freezing, even though it must have been at least seventy-five degrees.

Her hand reached out of the dark and rested on his thigh. He gripped his rifle tighter. "You ain't getting my gun."

"Just cold." Her shoulder brushed against him. "You won't mind if I lean up against you, will you? I need to get warm."

He tried not to notice the soft push of one of her breasts against his arm. He could smell her perfume mixed in with tobacco smoke and some other scents foreign to him. He didn't turn his head, but he knew she was looking up at him just the same. He could feel her blue eyes on him, even in the dark.

"You like me, don't you?" she whispered.

When he didn't answer, her hand slipped up his thigh and his grip threatened to break the forearm on his rifle. "You wanted to kill me not so long ago."

"I've seen the way you've been looking at me."

"I guess you're pretty enough."

"Don't be shy. There's nothing wrong with a man looking at a woman like that." Her hand wandered in the dark. His legs quivered slightly and the gunstock was the only thing propping him up. His grip failed him for a moment and his hand slid down his rifle and he almost fell over.

Her mouth was close to his ear and her breath was hot as she whispered to him. "You can touch me if you want."

"You don't care that I shot your man?" Claude's voice came out an octave higher.

"We were just business partners, nothing more. I never really wanted a man until I saw you." Her tongue nipped at his earlobe as she pressed against him.

He untangled himself from her arms long enough to set the rifle aside, and laid the pistol with it. His mouth found hers and they melted into the soft bed of rotten leaves and sand behind them. She took one of his hands and put it to her breasts.

"Are you my man?" she whispered.

He thought her the softest thing in the world. She was like one of those hot, sweaty, summer-night dreams he used to have sleeping on the screened-in back porch, tossing and turning on sheets sprinkled with drops of cool, cool water. He fumbled and then tore at her dress, but she grabbed his wrists and gently shoved him over onto his back. She straddled him and placed his hands on the small of her back. Her kiss brushed his forehead and her hands pulled him free of his fly. He raised his hips from the ground and a gasp escaped his lips as she clutched him with one hand and slipped his jeans down to his thighs with the other.

Her hand was almost more than he could stand, and the warmth that wrapped around him when she slipped him inside her was heaven. She moaned and swayed, her hair swinging wildly as her hips ground into him.

"Are you my man?" she cried out softly.

"Lord, yes." He shuddered and dug his fingers into her back. Wicked, sweet heat — she was as hot as a two-dollar pistol.

He didn't know when he fell asleep, but the sun was streaking the sky when he awoke. He reached out hungrily for her, but found nothing. He rolled to his side and rubbed at the sleep matting his eyes. The first thing he saw was her sitting facing him with the .32 in her hand. The pistol was resting on her lap, and pointing nonchalantly in his direction. She stared blankly at him, and he wondered how long she'd been sitting like that. For the first time he realized he was naked, and tried to ignore the pistol while he turned his back and struggled into his jeans. When he faced her again he thought he saw the trace of a smile at the corners of her mouth.

"How long have you been up?" he asked while his eyes found the rifle in the leaves.

"Since before daylight," she said.

He wondered if she was going to kill him, why she hadn't already done it. He watched her out of the corner of his eye as he went to the river and dipped himself a handful of the muddy water. She seemed to be looking right through him.

He stood slowly and walked by her to the rifle as nonchalantly as he could. He had to turn his back to her again when he bent to pick it up. When he turned around the pistol was still in her lap. He held his hand out to her, and after a moment she took it and let him pull her to her feet. He wanted to kiss her, and she didn't resist. Her lips were colder than the night before, and she didn't kiss him back. His hand found the pistol and he pulled it gently from her grasp.

31

He didn't know what to say to her, and his mind wouldn't seem to stay in any one place. "I'm hungry."

"You go get us a car and something to eat," she said.

He tried not to think about her body, or what had happened during the night. Everything in him wanted more of her, but he hadn't forgotten the money bag in the boat either. "Come with me and I'll see what I can do."

"You don't trust me with the money, even after last night?" Her lower lip jutted out a little.

Maybe he'd already gotten more of a reward for his sins than he'd ever imagined, but he kept reminding himself what he could do with so much money. He realized that somewhere during the night he'd decided to keep the loot, and the woman too — if he was man enough to hold on to the both of them. He didn't know how to go about it, but was sure he would think of something by and by.

He'd never known he was so bad. It was the damnedest runaway feeling that ever came over him, and he didn't know if he could do anything about it if he wanted to. The only thing he could compare it to was the time when he and a friend had smashed up his father's car. Claude was driving, and the throttle cable hung wide open just as he was coming down the mountain. He was doing ninety to nothing before he had time to think, and mashing the brake pedal darned near through the floorboard trying to stop. The brakes were screaming, but the motor kept on pushing it downhill, fishtailing full-throttle from one roadside ditch to the other. He'd smashed up that car pretty bad against a big old oak, and had the feeling that the only thing that was going to stop the runaway with Myra would be another wreck.

They walked down to the road cautiously, with her carrying the money and him carrying the guns. Surprisingly, there were no lawmen waiting for them at the crossing, and he led her to a giant water oak on a small hill overlooking the road. He sat down against the trunk, and motioned her to join him. She frowned, but sat down beside him. He could tell she wanted to fuss, but he ignored her and kept a watch on the road for traffic.

From their vantage point they could see about fifty yards of road each way where it came out of the hardwood bottom to the river crossing. After a half hour wait they heard a wagon coming from the north. The rattle of its wheels on the rocky, rutted dirt road was plain long before it came into sight. He set the rifle behind the tree, and pulled at her elbow as he rose to his feet.

"Oh, no, tell me you aren't going to steal a wagon." She pulled back against him and refused to rise.

He let go of her and took up the satchel of money. "Stay here if you want."

He started down the hill, and smiled smugly to himself when he heard her following. He had been feeling that she was in control the whole morning, and it was good to have the upper hand again.

"Why'd you leave the rifle?" she asked.

"Wouldn't you be leery if you were driving down the road and some fellow came up with a rifle?"

She didn't have an answer for that. "I'm not stealing a wagon."

"Suit yourself."

He led them to the edge of the road as the wagon passed below them. It wasn't much of a wagon with its rotten sides and peeling paint. The black man driving it pecked at the skinny team of mules harnessed to the rickety contraption with a long persimmon switch. Neither he nor his wife on the seat beside him noticed them until Claude stepped out into the road.

"Hello there." Claude waved and tried his friendliest smile.

The black man looked to his wife nervously, and then back to Claude. "Good morning."

Myra stood sheepishly. She kept her eyes down, but stole a quick, questioning glance at Claude. The elderly couple on the wagon looked at him suspiciously, and Claude didn't have a clue what to say. He kicked one big toe into the dirt and tried not to panic.

Myra saw that he was hung up, and came to the rescue. "Could you give my husband and I a ride? Our car broke down up the river a ways."

The black man passed another look to his wife. There was a single-shot shotgun leaning against the seat between them, and Claude saw him glance at it before he looked back to them. If the man seemed cautious, it was no wonder. Hard times had lots of men wandering the roads, and many of them weren't to be trusted. Hobos and vagrants with empty pockets, growling bellies, and nothing to lose made a lot of good people nervous.

"You say your car broke down?" The man's eyes looked up the faint trail that led in the direction of where they'd left the boat.

35

"Yeah, we were doing some fishing yesterday evening and it wouldn't start when we went to leave. It's just an old worn-out Star," Claude said.

"Where do you live?"

"Aw, a ways up past Dunbar." Claude hated to lie like he was doing. It seemed like he was getting worse by the minute. First he had killed somebody, then he had stolen a bag full of money, and now he was looking a man in the eye and lying. At least he hadn't felt near so guilty sleeping with Myra. Sinning was easier when it felt real good.

"Well, we're only going down the road another five miles or so." The man tugged at one gallus on his overalls.

"That'd be fine, if you don't mind. Maybe we could find somebody to take us on to Rattan, or know where we could find a mechanic."

"You two climb up in the back." The black man motioned to the empty wagon bed.

Claude pitched the money into the bed and helped Myra over the tailgate. They both sat down on the wooden floor and took a hold as the wagon started bouncing along. They crossed the river at a shallow gravel shoal on logs laid crossways against each other and imbedded into the riverbed, what was called a "corduroy road" in that country.

Once on the other side, the driver cocked his head around and smiled at them. "Name's Clarence James, and this here's my wife, Adel."

He scratched at the graying curls on the back of his head while he talked. His wife turned on the seat long enough to nod at them and smile politely.

Claude started to introduce the two of them, but Myra beat him to the punch. "This is my husband, John Smith, and I'm Betty."

"Good to meet you," Clarence said.

"Same here." Claude was already repeating his new name over and over in his head, lest he forget it. Once a man got started lying, he could get tangled up pretty easy.

Clarence shoved a corncob pipe into the corner of his mouth and chuckled through clenched teeth while he loaded it with Prince Albert tobacco. "Lordy me, I was a little scared when you folks came out of the brush like that. There's no telling what kind of people you might have the bad luck to run across these days."

"You've got to be careful who you pick up," Claude agreed.

"Yes, indeed. We passed the High Sheriff

and a regular posse coming up the road this morning."

"Oh, yeah?"

"They're all stirred up looking for bank robbers, but I told them I hadn't seen anybody on the road."

"Bank robbers?"

"A man and a woman held up the Antlers Bank yesterday and got off with all the town's money."

"We'd best be careful, honey." Myra grabbed Claude's forearm to get his attention, and gave him a wink.

"Lord yes, be careful. There's folks getting robbed and killed right and left these days. It's hard times, I tell you." Clarence nodded his head sagely and puffed on his pipe. "The papers say Pretty Boy Floyd will shoot you just for the fun of it, and there's worse than him traveling the roads."

"I thought you looked a little scary about giving us a ride. Can't say as I blame you," Claude said.

"Don't pay me and Adel any mind. We're just getting old and silly."

"Where're ya'll headed?" Claude asked.

"The government is having a cow killing this morning."

"Your cattle?"

Clarence chuckled again. "We ain't got

but one old milk cow back home, and I wouldn't let the government shoot her no matter how much money they offered. No sir, I like my cold milk of a morning."

"I never could see the sense in killing good livestock," Claude muttered.

"They say there's too many cattle and that's what's got prices down so far. They claim it puts money in people's pockets and is going to bring prices back up."

"It just doesn't make any sense, killing perfectly healthy stock."

"I ain't arguing for the government, I'm just after a little beef," Clarence said. "They ain't supposed to allow it, but nobody'll stop a man from cutting a little meat from the carcasses they're going to bury and leave to rot."

"Will there be a lot of people there?" Myra asked, the slyness in her voice evident to Claude, but seemingly lost on Clarence.

"Yes, ma'am," Clarence said.

Myra nodded to Claude and smiled. "Maybe we'll go with you. We're bound to find somebody to help us in such a crowd, or to give us a ride north."

"Sure, that's a fine plan. There'll be lots of folks there with cars. Maybe somebody will have the know-how to help you get yours fixed up."

Myra grinned and winked at Claude again. "Lots of cars, he says."

"Won't the Sheriff be there? Maybe we could catch a ride with him up to Antlers," Claude said.

"I asked Sheriff Miller that very thing, but he said he was too busy chasing after those robbers. Do you know the Sheriff?" Clarence asked.

"I've met him a time or two."

"He's the best sheriff we've had in my memory. He's honest, and don't stand for any foolishness from anybody, black or white. Of course, there are folks who say he goes easy on the Indians on account of the fact that he's married to one." Clarence pointed to a trail cutting across the pasture to the right of the road. "Down there's where they're having the killing."

A gunshot broke the stillness of the morning, and both Claude and Myra flinched. Another shot cracked across the pasture.

"They're already at it," Clarence said.

The wagon topped a slight rise, and Claude looked down on a ring of wagons and cars encircling a set of wooden corrals. Clarence guided the wagon along the wheel tracks mashed into the wispy-thin and sunburned grass. He pulled up at the edge of the crowd of people gathered around the corrals.

"I'll let you folks off here," Clarence said.

Claude and Myra climbed down from the wagon and Claude held his hand up to Clarence. "Thanks for the ride."

"It's good to meet you." Clarence shoved his frayed straw hat back on his head and shook Claude's hand.

"Same here," Claude said.

"I can't say that I've known many, but you two are about the nicest bank robbers I ever met." There was a slight twinkle in Clarence's eyes.

Myra stiffened like a board and she looked like she was about to run. Claude stammered and tried to force his mouth to form a coherent denial, but Clarence held up one calloused, immense hand as if to save him the trouble.

"Me and the missus won't tell nobody," he said with a wink that was no way in keeping with the creases and lines of his weary face. "If I had the gumption I'd rob me one or two myself and retire to my rocking chair and sip ice tea on the porch and flirt with the young ladies that passed by."

Adel elbowed her husband in the ribs, but had to cover her mouth with one hand to hide her smile. "You old devil, you can't

41

keep up with no young girls no more."

"Hard times I tell you." Clarence chucked to his team and drove off.

"Good folks." Claude was thinking that he had once unjustifiably thought of himself as one of those.

"They're liable to rat us out the first chance they get," Myra said.

"You don't have much faith in anyone, do you?"

"Let's get us a car," Myra said while she frowned over their choices. Most of the automobiles there were battered and patched up old Model T's, Stars, Pioneers, and cast-off military Dodge touring cars not far removed from nor better than the wagons and horses more than half the crowd had arrived in.

"I told you, I'm not stealing anybody's car. There's good people here, and I ain't taking from them."

Myra sighed and stomped her foot. "I was looking for a Clyde Barrow, and all I got was a boy squirrel shooter."

Claude studied the crowd. At least fifty men were gathered around the corrals in little clusters, and nobody was smiling. The place had the feeling of the funeral it was. Some folks were giving up prized animals they had worked hard to raise, in order to get some money to see them a little farther into the year.

"I'm going to go down and check things out," Claude said.

"You know you aren't wearing shoes," Myra said.

Claude stopped to study her. "You must be a city girl. Nobody around these parts is going to think anything of me not wearing shoes. Don't you know we're in a depression?"

"Everybody else may be in a depression, but I've got a bag full of cash and I need a car to take me out of the backwoods so I can spend it."

"Am I your man like you said last night?"

"I'm having second thoughts." Her lip was sticking out again.

"You just hang around and smile at folks while I get us a ride." He left her to go down amongst the crowd at the corrals, toting his case full of money and smiling like he was wearing shoes.

The men he passed merely nodded and went back to their angry conversations. Claude stopped at the corrals and hung his elbows over the top rail. A good set of Hereford cows and a few young calves crowded the pen in front of him. A stooped, weathered old man in overalls and a white shirt was arguing with a government man at the gate. The government man seemed out of patience, and the old man looked tuckered out. He nodded his head wearily and went back to his wife and children watching from the bed of his pickup. He said something quietly to them, and Claude heard the woman sobbing while her husband hugged her.

The government men drove a couple of cows out of the pen, and with help, walked them down to the gully a few yards away. A man was waiting with a surplus Springfield rifle and shot them as they neared the gully. The .30-06 would crack, followed by the metallic slide of the bolt and the glassy grate of a fresh round sliding into the chamber, and then another crack. The cattle didn't seem to have the sense to know they were about to die, and began grazing or simply stared blankly at the shooter as if they were waiting for him to feed them. With every roar of the rifle one of them would fall limply to the ground as if a bolt of lightning had struck it. Some of them grunted in a great gust of their lungs as the spitzer bullets shattered their foreheads and turned their bovine brains to juice. The process was repeated until the entire pen was empty and dead cattle covered a fifty-yard square, some of the bodies still twitching and releasing their bowels into the grass. The whole pasture smelled like death.

Claude watched the shooter for a while with his teeth gritted and his stomach muscles flinching with every report of the rifle. He couldn't take any more, and forced his attention to the old man who he presumed was the former owner of some of the cattle. The man had loaded his family into his pickup and then gone back and climbed up on the fence to watch his livestock murdered. The men gathered at the scene made an effort not to watch him, and nobody but Claude saw the tears streaking down the man's leathery cheeks. Claude understood why the man stayed to watch, even though it was obviously heart wrenching. It was simply a matter of seeing things through until the bitter end. You knew the world was in a depression when a man had to watch things like that. He was impressed that the old rancher never flinched as he saw what might have been his life's work and savings brutally wiped out in the matter of seconds.

Somebody started up the bulldozer and the big blade scraped up the bloodstained grass and shoved the carcasses into the gully. The heavy thud of the lifeless beeves

45

hitting the bottom carried in the quiet afternoon. One of the government men walked up to the edge of the gully and put a second shot into an animal that refused to die and bellowed pitifully. Claude cursed under his breath and thought that the government ought to hire a better marksman. The clank of the bulldozer's cleated tracks set his teeth on edge.

The rancher climbed down off the fence, and passed slowly behind Claude, muttering as he went. "Hell of a thing."

People were gathering to leave. Claude could see Clarence and his wife with their wagon backed up at the far end of the gully behind a thin honey locust thicket. The thorny brush didn't hide their efforts, but it was enough to give the government men an excuse to act like they couldn't see the old man and woman butchering beef and loading it into their wagon.

"That's a shame to waste so much meat," somebody behind Claude said.

"You're damned right it is, but nobody with any pride is going to take money for their cattle, and then eat them on the sly. Nobody but niggers and white trash," another said.

Claude watched Clarence and his wife struggling bloody-armed to load a hindquar-

46

ter into their wagon. He knew that it didn't have anything to do with pride. A poor man who would let his family starve for the sake of pride was a poor man indeed. It was the damned government that was to blame for such a day, and maybe for the hard times of the last several years.

There were two kinds of people in Claude's country. There were those who cried for the government to help them, and those who blamed the government for everything and wanted no part of it. Although, he did have to admit there were even a few that did both. Claude didn't understand what had led to a time that men couldn't find work, but watching the government kill cattle and then bury them with a bulldozer when so many were going hungry reinforced the fact that the government must be to blame.

The crowd was just about gone, and he feared he'd waited too long to try and catch he and Myra a ride. His eyes latched onto a man in a khaki shirt and a gray hat standing beside a brand-new Ford sedan. The man was sipping iced tea from a jug sitting on the roof of the car. He smiled at Claude when he walked up. Claude knew he must be a government man, for nobody else would be smiling like that at a cow killing.

"Fine day, isn't it?" The government man was eyeing the noon sun and acting like he was thinking about going fishing later.

"Pretty sad one, if you ask me," Claude said.

The man's face straightened quickly. "I didn't mean to sound happy about what we had to do here today. I know how hard this is on people to watch their livestock killed, but it's a good thing in the long run."

"My wife and I's car broke down, and I was wondering if you might give us a ride."

The man pulled at his chin and studied over the matter. "You look a little young to be married."

"Tell that to her." Claude pointed up the hill to where Myra was standing.

"Yeah, they know how to latch on to you." The government man passed Claude a conspiratorial smirk. "I guess I could give you two a ride as far as I'm going if you're headed south."

Claude walked up to Myra swinging his satchel and whistling merrily. "Come on."

"Where are we going?"

Claude pointed down at the man waiting for them by his car. "You said you wanted a car, and I've always wanted to drive a new Ford."

She gave him a curious look, and then did

her best imitation of his twangy, country accent. "I thought you weren't taking any poor folks' car."

"I'm not taking just anybody's car. That one belongs to the government, and I reckon a little comeuppance would serve them right."

She cocked an eyebrow and rested a hand on one hip. "Why, Claude, you're a regular Robin Hood."

CHAPTER THREE

"I have drove Fords exclusively when I could get away with one. For sustained speed and freedom from trouble the Ford has got ever other car skinned. . . ."
— Clyde Barrow in a supposed letter written to Henry Ford

"Please don't shoot me," the government man pleaded.

Claude wasn't going to shoot him, but the pistol he held against the man's cheek concealed his intentions. He thought the whole thing would probably go over better if he acted mean enough. And it seemed to be working. His hostage looked like he was about to cry. Normally, that would have bothered Claude unless it was somebody he was mad at, but the fellow was a government man and that made Claude feel a little less guilty for scaring him so badly.

"You just ease out that door," Claude said.

"I've got a wife and three kids."

"That's what they all say." Myra came back out of the woods on the side of the road from where she had pretended to go pee.

"Get out." Claude shoved hard on the pistol.

The government man stepped from the car slowly, and his legs almost failed him. He looked from Claude to Myra, fearing the worst.

"You just keep walking right out into those woods. You turn around once to look back and I'm going to shoot you," Claude said as he climbed behind the wheel. "Anybody that would shoot livestock deserves a hell of a lot worse."

The government man started slowly toward the timbered ridge leading up from the road. Myra looked from Claude to the man, and then back again. She seemed about to say something, but changed her mind. She went around to the far side of the car and climbed in.

Claude didn't pay her any mind. He was busy watching the government man. "Hey, stop."

His hostage froze, holding his arms high and wide. Claude climbed out of the Ford and came up behind him. "Take off your boots."

"What?" The government man's voice cracked. "You aren't going to kill me, are you?"

"I said give me those boots."

The government man started to turn around, but Claude poked him in the small of the back with the .32. "Don't turn around. Just get your boots off."

Claude had been admiring the boots the whole time driving south from the killing grounds. Claude figured they were Tony Lamas or maybe Justins.

The government man held out the boots in his right hand without turning around. "Here. Please, don't shoot me."

"I already told you I ain't going to shoot you if you cooperate." Claude took the boots and was disappointed when he looked inside their tops for a label. He'd thought for sure they were Tony Lamas just like old Roy Burkhalter wore when he propped his feet up on the shoe-shine stand down in front of the pharmacy back home. Claude had often watched Roy there with his cigar clenched between his teeth and growling at the shoe-shine boy about how to polish those boots until they shone like a silver dollar. It was just his luck that the government man couldn't afford Tony Lamas, but at least they were size tens like he wore.

"I had those boots custom made in San Angelo. They're M. L. Leddys and cost me forty dollars."

Claude didn't know anything about Leddys, but wasn't about to believe that any kind of boot was that high-priced. Roy wore Tony Lamas, and they didn't cost near that much. The government man was full of it, because everybody back in Antlers knew Roy wore nothing but the best. The fact that the man was a damned cow killer proved that you couldn't believe a word he said.

"You get to walking up that hill and don't look back," Claude said while he tugged on the boots. They fit perfectly. He left his jeans tucked into the tops so he could admire the fancy stitched and oak-leaf-tooled tops of his new boots. They might not be Tony Lamas, but he'd be damned if they didn't look good on him.

He took one last look to see that the government man was still headed up the hill before he trotted back to the car. Myra was looking out the open driver's door with a smile on her face.

"You're learning." She patted the seat beneath the steering wheel. "Get on in here and let's drive."

He put the car in gear and gunned the motor. They spun around in the road in a shower of dust and flying gravel, and were soon speeding south. Claude liked the feel of the wind blowing through the window, and the vibration of the V-8's power coming up through the gas pedal to his foot.

"Slow down, you're going to kill us," Myra said as he slid around a curve.

"I always wanted to drive one of these." Claude couldn't keep his eyes on the road for very long at a time. Despite the car, he couldn't help looking down at his new boots every so often. He wiggled his bare toes against the leather and smiled.

"Drive slower." Myra had the wind in her hair and one hand on the open window post.

"I'm going to get us out of Oklahoma."

"Where are we going?"

"I've got a cousin down at Sherman."

"Why don't we just go on to Dallas? I've had about all of this hillbilly stuff I can stand."

"I don't know anything about Dallas." He wouldn't have admitted it to her, but he'd never been out of Pushmataha County. He knew about as much about a big city as he did the moon. The mountains of southeastern Oklahoma had no metropolis.

"I do. I know lots of people down there,"

she said.

At first that sounded good, but then a little bell began going off in his head. The kind of people a woman bank robber was likely to know might be the kind to help her get her money back. Despite their lovemaking the night before, she hadn't shown the slightest interest in him since. The puppy dog feeling he had earlier was slowly being replaced by caution. Pride made him want to think she was attracted to him, and ignore the fact that a good-looking woman like her could have about anybody she wanted. Claude may have been young, but Sheriff Miller didn't raise any fools.

"I think we'll just go to my cousin's."

She immediately started pouting. "I'm filthy and hungry, and my clothes are about in rags. What a way to treat a woman."

Claude didn't see her looking out of the corner of her eye to judge his reaction. When she got no response from him she swiftly changed tactics. She scooted across the seat to lean against him, and her hand was roaming around his lap again. The speedometer climbed to sixty-five on a road that wasn't safe to travel at thirty-five.

"If we go to Dallas, I can show you where to get some really nice clothes for the both of us, and a haircut for you." She was running her hand through his thick mop of black hair. "I can take us to all the good places to eat, and I know just the hotel we can stay in. Think, we'd have a bed."

He couldn't help thinking about it with her rubbing all over him. He was rapidly learning that caution was only a warning, and that heeding that warning was the challenge when you had a woman like Myra tempting you. He tried to focus on his driving, and to keep his foot from mashing any farther on the accelerator. They were already doing seventy-five.

"I want to take off all my dirty clothes and climb in a tub of hot water." Myra dragged her hands across her breasts as she stretched and yawned like a cat. "Would you scrub my back?"

As hard as he tried, he couldn't get that picture out of his mind. The thought of watching her take a bath outweighed any danger that went with it. "I guess we could go to Dallas."

"Thank you, honey." She smiled sweetly and kissed him on the cheek while her hand plucked at the buttons on his jeans.

His foot came off the gas and the car lurched. Myra clucked her tongue and wagged the pointer finger of her free hand under his nose. "No, no, you keep driving, lover man. We've got to get to Dallas."

Claude groaned and clenched his lower lip in his teeth. He couldn't make his foot stay steady on the pedal, and all he could do was go faster. "Lord Almighty!"

Myra looked up to him from his lap. "My, my but you're excitable."

Claude mashed the accelerator to the floor and leaned his head back over the seat to stare at the ceiling. The car could have been racing to hell or Dallas either one with a demon in his lap. He didn't care.

Sheriff Miller stopped the car in the middle of the crossroads at dusk, and drew heavily on the cigar clamped in his jaw teeth. It had been a bad two-day stretch for him. He eyed with equal disdain the four directions he could go, not having a clue where to find his bank robbers or his son.

"We'd best go on home for the night. They're probably long gone out of the county by now," the tall deputy beside him said.

"Burke, do you think he's a prisoner, or has thrown in with them?" Sheriff Miller wasn't sure he really wanted an answer.

Burke Wilson had worked for Jim Miller for a lot of years, and knew how much store the man set by his son, so he was cautious with his answer. "You've asked me that at least twice an hour for two days running, and I still don't know what to tell you. All I know is what I saw, and that was him paddling that woman down the river."

Sheriff Miller took off his Stetson and pitched it on the seat beside him so he could run his hands through his gray-streaked hair. The brown eyes above his heavy mustache were red-lined, and his haggard face made it plain that he hadn't slept the night before. He leaned his head back against the door and studied the whippoorwill sitting in the middle of the road. The night bird's eyes glowed in the weak headlights of the car.

"He's always been a good boy. That woman must've had a gun on him," he said.

"Could be, but it doesn't fit in with the dead man."

"Maybe she got the drop on Claude. Two against one is pretty rough."

"Why didn't she shoot him then? He'd just shot her partner."

"Hell, I don't know," Sheriff Miller said. "Maybe she needed him to handle the boat, or to guide her downriver. And besides that, we don't even know that Claude killed her partner."

Burke shifted his bony butt in the seat and tried to remind himself that if it were his son he might be acting the same. "All I know is that we've got an empty .25-20 case from his rifle, and I don't see any mean-ass bank robber, even a woman, taking the time to figure out she needs a guide during the middle of a gunfight. The simplest answer is usually the best. I've got to assume that Claude killed that man, and I'll let the rest of the story work itself out."

Sheriff Miller slammed his hand down against the steering wheel. "Damn it, Burke, you've known Claude since the day he was born!"

Burke couldn't say how much that accounted for his thoughts on the matter. Claude wasn't an only child, but he was the Sheriff's only son. He was a polite boy with a quick smile, but everybody except the Sheriff noticed that he was a little wild. He wasn't a sneaky kid, nor dishonest, but he never seemed to let good sense get in the way of something he wanted to do — like setting fire to the school outhouse, or painting Mrs. Anderson's cat red, white, and blue and tying firecrackers to its tail on the Fourth of July. Then there was the time the boy stole the Sheriff's car for a joy ride with his friend and wrecked it. Maybe it was just the harmless mischief of a growing boy, but his antics had raised the eyebrows of the community more than once. Burke had even caught the kid hanging around Baxter's beer joint a time or two, but had kept it to himself.

And the Sheriff knew what a bad temper his boy had. The kid had whipped about every boy in school, and if rumor had it right, he'd walloped a grown man or two. In Burke's experience young rascals could turn quickly into bad men, even the little Claude that he used to bounce on his knee at the jailhouse. And the boy had always been gun crazy.

"I'm worried for him too," was all Burke managed to say.

"There's got to be some explanation for all this. Kids don't go off on a morning squirrel hunt and end up running with bank robbers. Did you ever think that the robbers may have gotten the drop on Claude, disarmed him, and then the woman shot her partner with Claude's gun so she could get all the money? And then she made him take her in the boat?"

"I'm not the detective you are, but I've considered that." Burke had also considered that maybe the robbers had recruited Claude before the robbery, but wrecking their getaway car near the bridge made it look like they simply happened on the boy

60

by chance.

Sheriff Miller started to say something mean, but caught himself. He sighed and looked an apology at Burke. "I don't know anything. I'm just worried about my boy. He might be dead right now for all I know."

"The Law is looking for him in three states, and they're bound to find him."

"That scares me even worse. I almost shot him by accident yesterday morning before I recognized him. With the kind of bandits running around these days, the Law is apt to shoot quick and ask questions later."

Burke hoped the boy turned up soon. He'd never seen his friend so shaken, not even in the war. The man could climb out of a trench under machine-gun fire with a grin on his face, and look down his rifle barrel at a swarm of Germans trying to kill him without batting an eye. The Sheriff rarely wore his pistol on his hip, usually leaving it in his car. Burke had seen him walk up on Willard Stephens' porch unarmed when Willard was holding his whole family at gunpoint and threatening to kill them all and anybody who got in his way doing it. The Sheriff had walked right in the house and had taken Willard's gun from him without ever raising his voice, or so much as a bead of sweat forming on his forehead.

He claimed that the county didn't hire him to shoot people. He was nervy like that.

"What am I going to tell his mother?" Sheriff Miller asked.

Burke had no good answer. Mrs. Miller thought as much of the boy as the Sheriff did. "Tell her you don't know."

Sheriff Miller put the car in gear and started back to Antlers. The whippoorwill fluttered away before his headlights. "Lord, he's just a boy. He's got a baseball game tomorrow night."

Burke didn't say it, but he was thinking that the Antlers high school baseball team might have lost its star pitcher for the rest of the season. A little voice in the back of his head was telling him that nobody was going to find Claude for a long time, dead or alive.

The Dodge touring car rattled down the dirt road in a glowing cloud of dust. Burke tried to keep his hat from being smashed against the canvas top by placing his left hand over the crown. They hit a big bump and all he got for his trouble was his knuckles smashed against a roof strut. The Sheriff always drove fast when he was upset. Although Burke had known the man since they were schoolboys and gone to war with him, he'd worked so long as his deputy that he never thought of him as Jim anymore. Somewhere along the way, he'd simply become "the Sheriff" in Burke's mind.

"I've seen about every kind of crime you can imagine in my career, but I never expected this," Sheriff Miller muttered.

"No, I don't guess you did."

"I was riding with Joe Leflore once. You remember Joe? He was a Choctaw Light-horseman back before statehood and later a US deputy marshal."

"Yeah, everybody knew Joe. My daddy used to point Joe out in a crowd and tell me what a man hunter he'd been back in the old days."

"Well, I was working as a county deputy with him when he was a deputy marshal, and we were after a bad bunch. They had tortured a man and wife to find out where the couple's money was hid, and when they got the stash they killed them with a hatchet and burned them up in the house. Now, Joe was an old man by the time I worked with him, but when he was in his prime he was about the toughest lawman this country ever saw. Back in the old days he didn't have any real jurisdiction over white men, but he made a living catching them and turning them in for the bounty put up on a lot of them. I guess Joe saw about everything there is when it comes to crimes." Sheriff Miller cut off short to swipe at the cigar ash that had blown onto his white shirt.

"I reckon he had," Burke said.

"I asked Joe if he'd ever seen such an awful murder, and he told me to find comfort in the thought that the killers granted the family enough mercy to whack them with a hatchet so they didn't have to burn to death."

"My daddy used to tell me that if you could ride through Indian Territory without getting robbed at least once a month back in Joe's day you were one tough SOB."

"It's about as bad now. If the economy doesn't turn around, it's going to get worse."

Burke shook his head solemnly. "The whole damned world's gone crazy. Everything seems turned upside down and inside out. Good folks starving, men wandering the roads begging for work or food, killers and stickup artists as thick as flies on a cow patty."

"I don't know anybody who understands what's going on. No matter how many times I hear how folks overspent and the stock market crashed, and the banks failed, and droughts, and . . . Hell, I just don't know. Sometimes it almost seems like we're being punished for something."

"Hard times," Burke muttered. "I don't think it's ever gonna rain again."

"Times are bound to get better. This depression can't last forever."

"The newspapers are saying the government's going to repeal Prohibition. At least there's that." Talking about liquor made Burke remember the bottle beneath the seat.

"That'll stop a lot of the bootlegging, but it won't put an end to all the trash robbing stores, banks, and such. Maybe you're right, and the whole damned country's going to hell."

"Damn it." Burke was having a hard time finding the bottle with the Sheriff driving so fast.

"Are you looking for your bottle?" Sheriff Miller asked.

"Yeah, this seat's killing my back and I thought I could use a snort."

Sheriff Miller rolled over on his left hip and pulled a pint bottle from the hip pocket of his khaki pants. "Here, I borrowed it."

The label on the bottle stated that it was Canadian bourbon, but the original contents were long gone. Burke used it to carry his moonshine in, because a quart mason jar was too hard to conceal. The bottle felt light and he shook it to gauge its contents.

65

It had been full when he put it in the car that morning, but it seemed that the Sheriff had been nursing on it pretty strong.

"At least there's one good thing about this job. Raiding moonshine stills keeps me in sippin' whiskey." Burke took a slug and waited out the hot fire that hit his stomach.

"I ain't never totally trusted cat whiskey since I saw my brother go blind on a bad batch of it one time." Sheriff Miller held out his hand, wanting the bottle back in spite of what he said.

The Sheriff rarely drank, at least since he took office. Folks said it was because his father was nothing but a worthless drunk, and they were correct. Burke remembered when the Sheriff was drinking pretty regular right after they came home from the war. He was wild and reckless back then and the booze was about to ruin his marriage. He also remembered when his friend finally came to his senses and swore off the stuff. He walked up one day and told him he wasn't walking down his father's path anymore. He hadn't had more than a snort here and there in the years since his vow. Watching him take another slug of whiskey, Burke was sure that the stress over his son was getting to him.

"What's that in the road yonder?" Burke

pointed out the windshield.

An instant later they both recognized the thing in his headlights was a man walking down the road. Sheriff Miller slammed on the brakes and the car skidded wildly from one bar ditch to the other. They came to a stop with their bumper just inches from the man's knees, and with him waving his hands wildly over the hood for them to stop.

Sheriff Miller righted his Stetson on his head and glared over his steering wheel. "Is he drunk?"

Burke watched the stranger hobble and wobble tenderly around the hood of their car toward his window. "Naw, I just think he isn't used to walking barefoot on a gravel road."

"I'd swear that fellow looks like he's been robbed or something." Sheriff Miller didn't have a clue how right he was, or that his long day was about to get worse.

CHAPTER FOUR

"You can go a long way with a smile. You can go a lot farther with a smile and a gun."

— Al Capone

It was almost noon when Claude came back to their hotel room after a walk around the neighborhood. He hadn't intended to be gone longer than it took to get breakfast, but after two weeks of city living he needed some fresh air and a stretch of his legs. Myra wouldn't mind, she never got up before noon anyway.

The bellboy smiled at him as he walked to the elevator, and Claude knew that wouldn't have been the case had he seen him when he first arrived in town. The barefooted boy that had captured Myra on the banks of the Kiamichi River had little in common with the dapper young gentleman staying in room 305 of the Adolphus Hotel in downtown Dallas.

Claude's mane of unruly hair was clipped and greased back in a style that Myra assured him fit his face, and the suit she'd picked out for him was supposed to flatter his long, lanky frame. The jacket she'd suggested had at first felt confining on his shoulders, but he was getting used to it. He didn't know what felt better on his feet, the soft wool socks, or the new Tony Lama cowboy boots he'd bought for ten dollars. He'd liked the government man's boots, but Roy Burkhalter wore Tony Lamas. The boot salesman had even given him five dollars in trade-in value for the used footwear. He didn't seem to know any more about good boots than that government man had.

His hat he'd picked for himself, and he'd shaped the three-inch brim to a slight downturn over his eyes that he thought made him look older and mysterious. He couldn't help but fondle the big gold ring on his right hand. It was one just like the one Roy flashed around to the locals at the cotton gin. Yes, indeed, it was good to be rich.

One of the cleaning girls wolf whistled as he got off the elevator and walked by her on the way to his room. The dark skin that was a leftover from his Choctaw mother couldn't hide the blush on his face. Even so, he didn't feel like the dirty, poor kid he'd been only weeks before. The clothes made him more confident than he'd ever been, like somebody entirely new and different from Claude Miller, born on a little farm in Oklahoma, son of a Choctaw woman and a war-hero sheriff.

Myra wasn't in the room when he opened the door, but the radio was turned up loud and Louis Armstrong was singing "Ain't Misbehavin'." He poked his head inside the bathroom looking for her. She was in the tub, and rapidly covered herself with a towel and scowled at him.

"Get out of here. Don't you have any manners?" She acted truly offended.

"What's the big deal? It isn't like I haven't seen you naked before."

Myra reached for a hairbrush beside the tub and hurled it at him. "You act like I'm a tramp or something!"

He ducked back barely in time to avoid the projectile she aimed at him. The brush struck the door with a violent thump as he closed it. He leaned against the door and tried to understand the two Myras he was coming to know. The Myra who would play with his pecker while he drove and the Myra who didn't want him to see her bathe seemed too different to occupy the body of one woman. He walked to the window and looked down on the street below. Seeing Myra naked made him wish the slutty Myra would show back up.

His mother had always warned him to stay away from bad girls, but Momma wasn't a seventeen-year-old young man with Myra either. His mother was pretty smart about canning, gardening, and raising babies, but Claude already knew that Myra was about the most fun he'd ever had — sometimes.

He felt a little guilty thinking about Momma. He would have liked to send some money home, but the Sheriff would know where it came from. The Sheriff would be right to frown on stolen money, but Momma Miller could use a little cash to free her from her worries. He wondered if he could slip her a few bills in a letter. The Sheriff hardly ever looked at the mail. He usually sat at the table of a morning sipping his coffee. If there were any letters from family, Momma would read the good parts to him and occasionally he'd grunt or comment on this or that.

Myra came from her bath wrapped in a towel, and Claude grabbed her in a hug as she passed. He only intended to pick at her, but the feel of her body against his gave him other ideas. His hand slipped of its own volition inside her towel.

"Quit it. I need something to eat." She turned her head away and held his hand at the wrist.

"You can wait a little while for supper."

"I'm hungry." She pushed away from him and walked to the coffeepot with a swish of her hips. "And by the way, we're going to have to work on that 'little while' thing."

Claude didn't have a clue what she meant. He waited patiently for her to have her coffee and two cigarettes. Myra had a two-pack-a-day habit, like cigarettes didn't cost fourteen cents a pack.

"What do you say we go for a drive after supper, I mean breakfast?" he asked.

Myra didn't seem interested. "I'd think you would've worn the new off that car by now."

They had ditched the stolen car — Myra's suggestion — but Claude had bought a new one just like it. Riding around town in his black '33 Ford was all he wanted to do for days.

"How about we go downtown and buy you a dress?"

"I've got dresses." She jerked a thumb at the pile of expensive purchases on the divan.

"Well, there's bound to be something

you'd like."

Myra sighed and tobacco smoke rolled out of her mouth in a cloud. "Listen, Sport. You're going to run us out of money if you don't slow down."

"We've got plenty, don't we?"

"We're paying ten dollars a day for this fancy room and we've spent better than four thousand on clothes, jewelry, and that car of yours."

"How much have we got left?"

"At this rate, we can live like we're doing for another week or two."

"That doesn't add up."

"You're forgetting the protection money we're paying to the coppers, and the local bad boys."

Claude hadn't liked that one bit, and he still couldn't see that it was necessary. "Nobody would've even known we were here."

"You've got a lot to learn. Some country bumpkin and his floozy come into town and start flashing cash around, and folks put two and two together pretty quick. We would've been in jail in a couple of days, or perhaps hijacked by the local toughs."

"I guess we can go somewhere else and I'll get a job."

"What job? It's pretty slim pickings out

there, in case you haven't noticed. I know all this is fun, but you'd better get out of the fairy tale you're living in and face the facts. Money doesn't last forever."

"I'll figure something out." He knew how lame that sounded as soon as he said it. Half the country was starving, and the other half was standing in soup lines and wondering how long it would be before they were too.

"Just what kind of outlaw are you? Neither one of us is going to live like we want to without sticking a gun in somebody's face. We've got to take what we want right out in front of the whole world." Myra was almost spitting her contempt. "I promise you, a thief isn't the worst thing in the world."

"I don't have to stay a thief."

"You've got at least three things going for you, and don't you dare screw it up."

"What's that?"

"You're damned quick with a gun, and the Law isn't after you yet."

"Those are only two things. What's the third?"

"Me."

"I don't know if I'm cut out for all of this," Claude said.

"Don't play the angel with me. You tell me you didn't like running off with all that bank money? And you shot Murder Mike without even flinching."

"That doesn't make it right."

"For the life of me, I don't know why I teamed up with you."

"You didn't pick me. I was the only choice you had."

"Believe me, honey, I chose you. Don't you forget it." Myra picked up one of her outfits and started back to the bathroom. "You just forget all that choir boy stuff if you want to keep hold of the good things in life."

"Meaning you, I suppose?"

Myra stopped in the bathroom door and looked back over her shoulder at him. She let her towel drop to the floor and blew him a kiss. "I'm worth every penny."

Claude started across the room for her, but she quickly shut the door in his face. He stood there with his cheek pressed to the cool wood, knowing the power she held over him and unwilling to fight it. He needed her like he needed that flathead Ford and the fat diamond ring on his finger. She was a hot, sweaty dream that he didn't want to wake up from.

"You drink yourself a cold glass of water. As soon as I get ready, we're going to take a little business trip. I'll introduce you to some of the boys I know, and maybe we can find some work," she said from the other side of the door.

"You mean robbing something."

"That's exactly what I mean. Fun is expensive, and the overhead in this business is high."

An hour later she came out of the bathroom looking like the fortune they'd spent on her. Her short blonde hair was curled neatly about her shoulders and the tight skirt and blouse clung to her like a glove. She noticed that Claude seemed depressed. He was sitting at a little table by the window and staring out of it while he played absentmindedly with the necklace he wore. In fact, he did that a lot when he was thinking about something.

She walked over behind him and rubbed his shoulders. "What are you beating to death?"

"Aw, I was just mulling over what you said. Do you think I was born an outlaw, or came to it lately?"

"You worry too much." She looked down over one of his shoulders at the necklace in his hands. She'd never paid much attention to it, but reached down and gently took it out of his hands. It was a set of military ID tags with the Miller name stamped in the little tin plates. "Where did you get this?"

"The Sheriff gave it to me. He wore them in France. Got a lungful of mustard gas and a German trench knife in his leg wearing these." When he saw the funny look on her face, he added, "I quit calling him Daddy back when I was a button. I don't know why, somehow he became the Sheriff to me like he is to everybody else in the county."

"You must think a lot of him if you're wearing his dog tags."

Claude seemed to give that a little thought. "He's the best man I've met so far. He's just hard to live with."

"Did he whip you a lot?"

"No, but it's real easy for him to do what's right. Comes natural to him, like his badge, and he can't understand folks who don't see things as straight as he does. Mixed-up people bother him some," Claude said. "Never has been that easy for me. I didn't get his common sense, I guess."

"Everybody's different," Myra said softly. "He sounds better than most, but you don't have to be him."

"That's what I was really thinking when you walked up." He stood to his feet and turned to face her with her shoulders in his hands. "It'd be easier if I was him."

"Don't think I'm going to feel sorry for you just because your daddy is a sheriff."

Myra put her hard face on. "I was raised dirt poor — the hungry, hopeless, withering-away, too-tired-to-cry kind of poor — with a father who beat me, and a mother who didn't care what he did."

"I don't have any excuse for my mean-ness," Claude said.

"Come on, Tiger. Let's go paint the town." She checked herself one last time in the mirror by the door, and smacked her red lips together.

He laid her fur wrap on her shoulders and kissed the nape of her neck. "I bet you're the best-looking woman in Dallas."

She frowned halfheartedly. "Have you got your gat?"

"No." He'd been leaving his pistol in the dresser.

"Well, get it. The boys I'm taking you to see won't pass for Boy Scouts."

He tucked the .32 behind his waistband at the small of his back. He'd had no reason to go armed about the city, but the weight of a pistol pulling at his pants was a good, reckless feeling. He stopped to look in the mirror to see if the pistol was noticeable beneath his suit jacket.

Myra stopped in the hallway outside the door. "The guys we're going to see won't care if you're packing a heater. In fact, they

78

expect it."

Instead of hunting for a new restaurant to dine at, Myra gave him directions to a little café on the south edge of town. The seedy-looking diner was doing scant business, and the only customers were a small group of men gathered around a radio at the end of the long counter fronting the kitchen. "Rye Whiskey" and Tex Ritter's twangy voice came quietly from the speaker.

Claude and Myra passed by the line of stools at the counter and took seats at a table at the far end of the room. The ceiling fans that hung below the molded tin ceiling clicked rhythmically while they waited for service. A skinny little man in a suit left the radio and walked over to their table with a pencil and a book of what looked like tickets in his hand.

"You folks want to buy some insurance today?" he asked with a wink.

"Insurance for what?" Claude asked.

The man looked at him like he was a little off in the head. "Where are you folks from?"

Before Claude could answer, Myra cut him off. "Don't mind him, he's new in town."

She took ten dollars from her little beaded purse and handed it to the man. "We'll take ten policies."

The man scribbled with his pencil and handed her ten small sheets of paper. "There you go. It pays to be protected."

"What do we need insurance for?" Claude asked when the man was gone.

Myra laughed. "You hick, it's a lottery. You know, gambling, a raffle."

"Well, why did he call it insurance?"

"It's a racket. It wouldn't do to rub it under the coppers' noses, so they call it insurance. They give you a little policy certificate with a number on it, and those numbers get put in the lottery."

"How was I supposed to know that?"

Myra was still laughing at him. "Relax, you're in the big time now."

A waitress came by, but Myra declined the menus she offered. "We're friends of Diamond Joe."

The waitress studied them carefully and then motioned them to follow her. She led the way down a hallway past the restroom and to a closed door. She knocked on it and a gruff voice from the other side answered her.

"I've got two friends of Diamond Joe's out here," the waitress said. She went back to the dining room without even waiting for a response.

The door opened a crack, and the single

eye staring at them soon widened in recognition. When the door swung wide, a short, squat man of the dimensions of an icebox stood there with his arms held wide. "Myra, doll, where've you been?"

Myra pressed herself against his broad belly and returned his hug. "It's good to see you, Bull."

Bull patted the mass of stomach hanging over his belt with a club of a hand. "This sitting around is putting too many pounds on me."

"I've got the remedy for that," she said.

"Oh?"

"I need to talk with Diamond Joe about a job."

Bull nodded at Claude. "Who's this with you?"

"Claude Miller." Myra grabbed Claude's arm and hugged close to him.

Bull didn't try to hide his suspicion. He stepped aside and followed them as they passed. There were three men playing poker in the center of the dark room. Their faces were lit by a single lightbulb dangling from a cord above the table. They all nodded to Myra, but gave Claude the cold treatment.

Myra ignored all of them but the big man with his back to the wall and a fancy ring on every one of his fingers. She leaned over and kissed the man's cheek as he puffed on his cigar and studied Claude through the smoke. Myra took the empty seat beside him, leaving only one opening at the far side of the table. She motioned for Claude to sit. He looked to the men on either side of the empty chair, but they neither offered nor denied him a place.

Myra gave Claude a small frown and nodded her head to the vacant chair. He sat down stiffly, eyeing the two pistols he could see sticking out of the ring-fingered gangster's waistband. Claude knew without asking that the man must be none other than Diamond Joe, the king of the Dallas underworld, or so people around the city said. He was also the man to whom Myra had been paying protection money.

Diamond Joe's face was unreadable, and he seemed to stare straight through Claude. "Myra, whatever you've got had better be good. You've interrupted my game when my cards are hotter than they've been in months."

"You'll think your luck is just starting to gin when I tell you about a couple of jobs I've cased," she said.

Diamond Joe hooked his thumbs in the armholes of his vest and leaned back in his chair. "I'm all ears."

"Me and Mike never got to finish the round we'd planned. There's two juicy plums still out there for the picking," she said.

"I never got the straight of what happened to Mike. You come back here flush with cash and toting this Indian around with you."

"Mike got himself killed."

The look on their faces made Claude think she'd made a bad, bad mistake.

"I already know the Law didn't get him," Diamond Joe said.

"He tried to double-cross us, and Claude killed him." Myra had a poker face to match any of theirs.

Diamond Joe studied her for a hint of a lie and then looked Claude over again. "You killed Mike?"

"Mike had the drop on him, but it didn't help any," she said.

"I don't believe you," the slim little man to Claude's left said. "Mike was the best hand with a rod I ever saw."

Claude met the man's glare and was acutely aware of two things. His .32 was pinned behind him against the chair back, and Bull was standing behind him. He couldn't imagine why Myra had brought him into a den of Mike's cronies and then told them he killed Mike. She was unpredictable to say the least.

"Mike was fast," the man to Claude's right said behind his brush pile of a mustache. There was something about him that was a little off that Claude couldn't quite put his finger on. The man's unblinking, bloodhound eyes sagged down halfway to his cheeks, giving him a highly unsettling stare.

"You're damned right he was fast, Ernest," the little guy was working his temper up.

"What'd you do, kid, shoot him in the back?" Bull asked from not a step behind Claude.

"Mike wasn't quick at all." Claude smiled and looked to each of them at the table in turn.

The little guy almost knocked his own hat off scooting back from the table. His hand swept back his jacket on his left side to expose a revolver in a shoulder holster.

His hand was almost to the butt of his gun when Claude said, "You do that and I'll have to kill you."

The little guy stood to his feet, but the gun stayed in his holster. "What the hell did you just say?"

Claude relaxed in his chair and slowly placed both his hands on the edge of the table, willing them not to shake. "I don't want to have to kill you."

84

"Did you hear that, Dink? He doesn't want to kill you," the mustache they called Ernest said with a chuckle.

Dink laughed too, but his eyes were working back and forth from Claude to each of his friends. Claude kept his hands on the table and continued to stare at him calmly, noticing Dink lick his upper lip and the nervous quaver in his laughter.

"If you make me pull my pistol, it's going to hurt," Claude said.

Dink cackled again, and Ernest had turned slightly to take in both Dink and Claude at once. Claude could hear the soft shifting of Bull's feet on the hardwood floor behind him. He listened closely for the sound of a gun sliding against cloth or leather.

"You must think you're some kind of Billy-Bad-Ass where you come from," Dink sneered, but he still didn't pull his gun.

"I was better than Mike," Claude said. "Think on that."

"You cocky son of a . . ." Dink was going to draw.

During the whole proceedings, Diamond Joe had watched with almost disinterested amusement. He reached out and grabbed Dink's gun arm with one of his big fists. "Sit down. Now!"

Dink sat slowly, but his eyes were firing shots at Claude. "You ain't a pimple on Murder Mike's ass."

Claude kept his watch on Dink, but he noticed out of the corner of his eye that Ernest had his hand under the lapel of his coat. Diamond Joe put both of his elbows on the table and lifted his hat and ran his fingers through his blond hair. The diamonds and gold on those thick digits flashed brightly under the light above.

"Claude, or Bob, or whatever you call yourself, you aren't even dry behind the ears yet." Diamond Joe stared across the table.

Some instinct told Claude that Diamond Joe was tougher than all the rest of the thugs in the room put together. "Age ain't all that matters when it comes to shooting."

Diamond Joe's eyebrows lifted. "What else matters?"

"Talent," Claude said.

"Talent?" Diamond Joe didn't laugh, but one side of his mouth parted just enough to reveal his front teeth. Those perfect white choppers weren't sharp, but there was something about the smirk that reminded Claude of a mad dog's snarl. "Kid, if you're half as tough as you let on, we can use you. And if you're all bluff, well, you've got nerve enough. A hell of a bluff can sometimes be as handy in a fight as a gun or a fist."

"You've got to be kidding," Dink said. "This damned hillbilly kid don't know nothin'."

Diamond Joe looked at Dink like a man about to squash a bug. "You weren't anything but a damned cotton picker yourself when I first put you to work. I think you and Ernest had better get back to collecting. We've got a business to run."

Ernest immediately rose from the table, but Dink lingered long enough to let Claude know that it wasn't over between them, but not long enough to get cross with Diamond Joe. The two thugs left the room and Claude heard Bull take a seat back by the door. He turned his attention to Diamond Joe.

The crime boss looked to Myra. "What have you got for us?"

Myra was visibly pale, and it was the first time Claude had ever seen her lose that cool shell she wore like armor. She gathered herself with a deep breath, and then that old smile spread across her nymph face in a swath of red lipstick.

"Have I got a sweet deal for you," she said with the devil twinkling in her eyes.

When Diamond Joe had heard her out he smiled at her with something almost like fondness. "You always were a bright girl."

"Are you in on this?" she asked.

"Count me in. You can hit the road tomorrow."

"Aren't you coming?" Claude asked.

Diamond Joe frowned patiently. "No, Myra's the brains, I'm the power, and you boys are the muscle. You and Myra will take Dink, Ernest, and Bull with you. I get ten percent of the cut, you split the rest even between you two and my three men."

"That's kind of steep, ain't it? Myra's the one who did all the footwork." Claude was immediately cursing himself for opening his mouth. He wanted nothing more than to get out of the room with his skin intact.

"Then you and Myra can work by yourselves," Diamond Joe said. "I'm supplying the car and sending some muscle with you. I'll put you up when you get back and see to it that the coppers lay off of you while you're here. I'll fence anything you steal for forty cents on the dollar, my appraisal."

The take-it-or-leave-it look on Diamond Joe's face was obvious for what it was, and Claude read even more into it than that. He was sure the kingpin was still deciding what to do with him.

Myra shook her head at Claude. "Sounds like a deal to me. We can't work this trip ourselves."

"It's done then," Diamond Joe said.

"Do you think taking Dink and Ernest is a good idea?" Myra asked. "If I was you, I'd send somebody else."

"Well, you aren't me. They'll mind their 'p's' and 'q's' if I tell them to. Bull, you make sure they understand to lay off Claude here. This is business, and I don't let anything get in the way of business." Diamond Joe stretched and made a show of adjusting his pistols behind his belt. "And besides, I never did like Murder Mike anyway. He wasn't anywhere near as good as he liked to let on."

Myra headed for the door, and Claude started to follow her before Diamond Joe leaned across the table toward him. "What would you have done if Dink had pulled his gun?"

Claude counted six of his heartbeats before he answered. "I'd have killed him."

"Maybe you would've. Maybe so."

Claude rose and crossed the room to Myra. She gave him a big-eyed look and breathed a sigh that ruffled her bangs. Bull started to unlock the door, and Claude thought they had made it out alive.

"Kid," Diamond Joe said.

Claude didn't turn around, but he did pause his stride.

"Next time, you better not wear your gun behind your back when you set down at a table. Talent isn't everything, and that's a good way to get killed."

Claude could still hear Diamond Joe laughing when they walked back out into the diner and the door closed behind them. He was certain of one thing, and that was that an amateur could get himself killed real quick in Big D.

CHAPTER FIVE

"Frankie drew back her kimono. She took out a little forty-four. Rooty-toot-toot, three times she did shoot, right through that hardwood door. Shot her man, he was doing her wrong."
— "Frankie and Johnny"

Diamond Joe gathered the cards and shuffled them while he considered things. He always thought better when he had something for his hands to do. People who didn't know him were amazed that a man with hands as massive as his could be so dexterous with the pasteboards. He soon pitched the deck back onto the table with a deep sigh and studied his knocked-down knuckles and the scars of many an alley brawl. In his youth, those meat hooks had been his bread and butter. Somebody was always willing to pay for a little muscle that wasn't afraid to crack heads. There had been a time when everyone knew that if you needed somebody to pay up or to vote a certain way, you could call Joe and he would handle your little problem for a price.

But that was back when he had been plain old Joe and not Diamond Joe. However, as the underworld of the city soon learned, Joe had ambitions, a lot of them, and a mind as intricate as a Swiss clock ticked inside that thick skull of his. It was his wits and cautious cunning that had gotten him where he was, and not his brawn. Of course, it didn't hurt in his business that he had less mercy than a housecat with a mouse when it came to knocking off those who got in his way.

"Hey, Bull," he said when the door was closed and he was sure his recent guests were out of earshot.

"Yeah, boss."

Diamond Joe absentmindedly polished one of the jewels on his fingers and glanced up at his immense bodyguard through his eyebrows. Bull had the brawn, but he wasn't especially bright — he wasn't really dumb, just unimaginative. However, he possessed two attributes that his boss valued more than anything. The man was loyal and he never got too excited. If you spelled a plan out to him he could be counted on to get the job done with a minimum of fuss.

"You keep an eye on those two. Myra's a sharp dame, but she assumes that the rest of the world is stupid."

Bull merely stood there and nodded. It came to Diamond Joe that maybe Bull did have another good quality. He never interrupted, and was a good sounding board to bounce ideas off of. Sometimes hearing himself talk was Diamond Joe's best way of working out strategy.

"And I wouldn't put it past her to be hiding something up her sleeve," Diamond Joe said.

Bull waited until he was sure the Boss was through and expecting a reply. "What about the kid?"

"You've got to admit he's got balls." Diamond Joe turned his palms up and curled his fingers as if weighing an enormous pair of testicles above the table. "I'm still thinking about him. I don't know. Something about him bothers me. No kid should be as calm as he is. He looked us all in the eye and basically told us to go hell or shoot him. What kind of little cotton picker does that?"

"You just say the word." Bull didn't know he did it, but unconsciously his hand went to the lead-weighted leather slapjack in his right front pocket.

Diamond Joe was damned aware of the habit, and he watched him carefully. He had once been a pretty good poker player, and a man couldn't make money if he couldn't read the subtle habits that gave away an opponent's hand. Few people didn't have a "tell." Maybe it was a facial expression, or a repeated way of betting when they had a good hand or didn't.

One of the prerequisites to living a long life in Diamond Joe's chosen profession was to never trust anybody completely. There was always somebody who wanted to knock you off of your hill. Despite Bull's long and loyal service, he'd told himself for years to watch out if it were just he and Bull alone and the man went to rubbing his bung for no good reason. In that situation, he'd best go ahead and shoot Bull — better safe than sorry. There was more than one body feeding the catfish in the Trinity River that had its skull caved in with that weapon. And Bull didn't give any warning other than that one little tell. He could kill you with the same straight face he wore when he sat down to his breakfast.

"You keep a close eye on those two."

"And if they cross me, or start acting fishy?"

Diamond Joe had already lost interest in

the conversation. It dawned on him that all of his rings were looking a little dingy and could use a good cleaning and polishing. There was a little jeweler in the neighborhood that was behind on his payments and the interest points were climbing. It wouldn't be hard to get him to do the work for free. As a bonus, they could do a little business on the trip. There was some damned cowboy gambler running a dice game out at the old wagon yard who wasn't paying Joe his 25 percent of the game. The man was small potatoes, but stuff like that couldn't be ignored. Gambling in the city was Diamond Joe's racket; it was a matter of principle.

"Bring the Cadillac around. I need you to drive me down to Oak Cliff."

Bull had heard him plainly, but he continued to stand there with a question on his face. Everyone knew that the Boss usually had a lot on his mind, and tended to get off the subject from time to time.

Diamond Joe kept frowning at his rings. They were really dirty, and he liked them to flash. Half of keeping the old neighborhood scared of you was looking like you were The Man. He rose to his feet, and his fifty-year-old knees popped and creaked beneath his weight. He was six foot three and still reasonably fit-looking considering that most of his adult life had been spent drinking too much whiskey, smoking cigarettes, and staying out all night. But his waistline had been growing steadily the past few years, something that was beginning to bother him. He'd always taken pride in the fact that he was a hard man, both in mind and body. The bad thing about having men like Bull to do your dirty work was that a man could go soft in a hurry, and soft didn't have a place in the operation he ran.

He clenched his right fist and felt the strength in his own grip and the massive bulge of his forearm. In the blink of an eye he pulled one of the hammerless .38 Smith & Wesson Safety revolvers from his waistband and he aimed at a pinup girl calendar on the far wall. He sighted down the little snub-nosed barrel and put the front sight right between Mae West's big tits.

"Pow."

"You're still as fast as greased lightning, boss," Bull said.

Diamond Joe couldn't suppress a little smile. He might be a little softer around the edges than he used to be, but Dallas was his town and he was still more than enough to handle anybody who thought otherwise.

He finally realized what Bull was waiting

for and waved an impatient hand at him. "Just kill 'em both if they become too much of a bother."

Normally, Myra wasn't an early riser, but the morning sun spilling through the window was too much for the gin headache she was nursing. She propped herself up on one elbow and studied Claude's still face. Sleeping, he looked even younger than he was. She asked herself what she'd asked a thousand times since hooking up with him. There was no good reason to stick with the kid now that all the loot was about spent, but there she was waking up with him again.

She thought of him as a kid even though she lied about her own age. She wasn't twenty-five like she claimed, nor even twenty. Myra was nineteen going on one hundred. Hers was an old mind and an ancient soul. Life had taught her one hard lesson, and that was that you looked out for yourself. You took, as you were likely to be taken from, and you never trusted anyone so you wouldn't ever be let down.

Maybe that was why she hadn't ditched Claude. He was as plain and simple as an open book. She had known that about him from the instant she laid eyes on him back on that riverbank. She knew the things men

97

were capable of when liquor stripped them down to their raw quick, or when they thought nobody was looking and they could get away with it. But Claude wore his desires and weaknesses on his shoulders for the world to see. When he was hungry he ate like he was starving and smiled at her with his mouth stuffed, as straightforward in his appetites as when he woke her in the mornings with his stiff cock pressed against her bottom. He wanted money and a woman, but felt guilty for the taking of them. She knew he was in love with her, but he never said it. She liked that he never asked for more than she could give.

Claude was too good for the life he was leading, and she was too smart for him. That was the simple truth of the matter, and she prided herself on being realistic and practical. There would come a time when he would hesitate too long while he tried to talk himself out of doing wrong and that would get him killed. She didn't intend to be around to see it, nor to die with him either.

She told herself she was through with him. Once they pulled off the jobs she'd planned she would cut herself loose. She'd taken from him, but she'd also given as good as she got. He would have to settle for that.

He stirred and stretched with his white teeth revealed in a sweet smile. His hand untangled itself from the sheets and found one of her breasts without even opening his eyes. Her body stirred under his touch and she couldn't help taking him for just a little more. His kind of man died young, and a woman like her was more than he had any right to expect.

CHAPTER SIX

"The trouble with being a criminal is the company you have to keep."
— unknown

It was a long drive into Louisiana, and most of it on bad roads. Claude leaned his head against the window and tried to let the hum of the tires put him to rest. He couldn't get his mind to slow down, much less go to sleep, no matter how hard he tried. He kept thinking about the fact that, come morning, he was going to commit armed robbery.

The dust from the road was leaking into the car, and his stomach felt so jittery that he was afraid he was going to get motion sick. Myra had her head tilted back over the seat on the passenger side in front of him and was sleeping soundly. He reached up and rubbed a strand of her hair between his fingers and studied the soft glow of her cheek in the dim dash lights. Ernest and

Dink were trying to out-snore each other on the backseat beside him, and Claude felt absolutely alone. The night outside the car was so black that the only thing of the world that was left was the pale streak of road ribboning out in front of the headlights, and that didn't feel real. It was if he were floating along in a bad dream.

Occasionally, he would look up into the rearview mirror and see Bull looking back at him, nothing of his face visible but his shadowed, measuring eyes. He couldn't tell what the bruiser was thinking, but it made him feel lonely anyway. He had nobody other than Myra, and she was asleep and couldn't talk to him. The car felt like it had him trapped and he didn't have the courage or the goodness to make it stop and let him out. He closed his eyes and tried to put his mind into neutral like he always did when there was something bothering him that he couldn't seem to work out. Just sleep and maybe things would be better in the morning.

They didn't get better, but the sun finally peeked over the rice paddies alongside the road. He shoved the night's worries away like he always did. Being bad wasn't so terrible if he could keep from thinking about it, and the coming of daylight helped. His mother liked to say that the sunshine could chase away a lot of hurts.

Myra yawned and stretched until her little fingers brushed the roof. She twisted in the seat and smiled at him with sleepy eyes. She looked like a little kid, or maybe an angel. He'd dreamed about angels before, and they had always looked like her right then.

"I wish I had a cup of coffee." Ernest was awake and he scowled at the countryside showing itself through the windshield. "I hate swamps."

"Look at all those damned birds." Dink was picking his nose and pointing a finger with the hand that wasn't busy at the little cloud of wings that were lifting off the rice field and framed in his window like a picture. "I hate birds. They aren't good for anything but shitting on cars and making a racket. The state people ought to do us a favor and kill them off. Save a lot of work washing cars."

Claude wished Dink didn't curse so much in front of Myra, but she had already told him to let it slide. Foul language was just part of the trade, along with a lot of other things he was having trouble getting used to.

He watched the birds until they climbed so high that he couldn't see them for the roof of the car. He twisted his head around and pressed his face against the window glass beside him, waiting until the flock reappeared on his side of the highway. The sun cast them in dark silhouettes, but an occasional flash of green caught his eye. He liked watching the world come to life in the morning, and thought them a beautiful sight.

"They're ducks," he said.

"What?" Ernest asked.

"I said 'ducks.' " Claude pointed out his own window at the "v" of the flock disappearing on the horizon. "Mallards. It's kind of late in the summer for them to be around. They ought to be far north this time of year."

Ernest glanced at the ducks, but turned away quickly as if the sight of them horrified him. He tugged at one corner of his mustache and studied the road ahead.

"The kind that quacks and all that shit?" Dink asked.

"No, the other kind." Myra twisted around and laughed at Dink. "Like there's some other kind of duck. You're such a moron sometimes."

"And you need slapping around a little to knock some of that sass out of you," Dink said. "There's nothing worse than a mouthy dame."

Claude straightened in his seat, but Myra held up a hand and took a deep breath. Her mouth trembled as she stared right through Dink. "That's been tried before."

Dink attempted to laugh her off. "Yeah? What'd you do?"

"He didn't try that again."

Myra seemed to have lost it a bit. She was always moody, sometimes more like five different people than just one girl, but it was as if she had grown a new face right then. She looked paler, and very, very mad. She kept staring at Dink, and her eyes were all but on fire. Maybe the long trip in the car with Dink had finally gotten to her, but Claude guessed there was more to her anger.

"Yeah, whatever." Dink waved a hand at her to blow her off, but made a studious effort to look out the window, as if something in the rice fields had become interesting.

Myra finally turned around and flopped down in her seat with a flip of her hair. She drummed her fingernails against the armrest on the passenger door panel and nobody said a word for miles. The silence in the car was making them all edgy.

"That's kind of wasteful to be killing all

104

the ducks. What would you do with them?"
Claude sought to lighten the mood. He
thought Dink stupid and callous for suggesting that the state kill all its ducks, given
that market hunters half a century before
had almost done that, but any kind of
conversation beat listening to the maddening drum of Myra's fingernails on the door.
He'd seen her do that before for hours when
she was only a little bit mad at him, and
there was no telling how long it would go
on as fired up as she was at Dink.

"What?" Ernest looked startled, even
though Claude had aimed his question at
Dink.

"Maybe they could make some stew out
of them and feed those poor bums standing
in line down at the soup kitchens every
day," Bull said.

"I don't eat duck, or goose," Ernest threw
in with a little more excitement than the
subject called for.

Dink kept his gaze out the window.
"They'd stink like hell if you killed them
all. You ever had to handle a dead body after
it's laid around for a week? That's some
nasty stuff, I promise you."

"Birds aren't like people." Ernest wasn't
the sharpest tool in the shed, and he looked
almost as disturbed about something as

Myra was. His mustache nearly covered his mouth, and was usually unkempt to say the least. Bits of food, dried beverages, and other unimaginable things clung to it. He tugged at one corner of it so firmly that it sagged his cheek and eyelid down, as if he were trying to pull his whiskers out.

"You ever killed chickens, Ernest?" Dink asked.

Ernest looked at him like he was offended. "No, I never."

"Ma used to wring their necks, but Pa would use an ax," Dink said. "He'd whack their heads off and let them go, and the damned chickens would run around like crazy for a while."

"Without their heads?" Ernest asked.

"Yeah, squirting blood and running around like they still had them. My sisters used to ask Pa not to let the chickens go until they quit moving so that they wouldn't run around like that. It made them cry."

"The chickens?"

"No, you dunce. My sisters would cry."

"You remember Paul?" Ernest asked. "That kind of bothered me some."

"Paul just flopped and twitched."

"He had six bullets in him."

"That's different than being up on your feet and running around, and besides, he still had his head."

"Well, I thought it odd," Ernest said.

"Paul was always stubborn like that. He wouldn't even die easy," Dink said. "I liked him before that, but I ruined a brand-new suit hacking that bastard up. I ought to buy myself a hound and track down the pieces of him just so I could piss on them."

"No, he didn't want to die at all," Ernest muttered.

"You boys need to shut up. The kid doesn't need to hear your stories." Bull didn't attempt to hide his hint. "Give him nightmares."

Dink and Ernest both looked at Claude suspiciously.

"Kid, you better forget anything we say," Dink said. "You know, business talk."

Claude nodded. "What business?"

"You got it," Bull said.

Claude tried to focus his attention on the gun section in the Montgomery Ward catalog on his lap. He'd brought it with him for something to pass the time. The sight of so much blued steel and oiled walnut usually made him happy. He avoided the prices like he usually did when he was window shopping and wishing, and tried to read the specs of each firearm offered by the company. However, he could find no enjoyment

107

in the catalog. The car was too stifling, and he felt as if the gang was watching him all at once.

He glanced at Bull behind the wheel, and then to the two beside him on the backseat. He had determined earlier that Ernest and Dink were killers, but he was just then beginning to appreciate how bad they were. He cursed his luck that he couldn't have thrown in with some plain old, honest robbers. He'd heard that Bonnie and Clyde gave poor folks money from their robberies, and Pretty Boy Floyd supposedly paid people for their cars when he had to take them during a getaway. The criminal life wasn't turning out like he expected it to be. Before he had taken to the bad, he'd assumed that armed robbers had to be something exceptional.

"I could use some breakfast," Dink said.

Bull reached onto the seat beside him and held up a metal thermos and a brown sack that smelled like food. Grease had soaked through the paper at the bottom. "Here, you sleeping beauties missed out when I stopped to get gas in Beaumont."

"What's that?" Ernest asked, the prospect of some food taking his mind off of ducks and dead bodies.

Diamond Joe often asked Ernest to do

some unpleasant things, even though he paid well. And he could always do without any mention of birds. His mother once had a parrot, but he tried hard not to remember that. It was an evil bird that would bite your finger off if it got the chance. It had a huge, hooked beak, and would flap its wings against its cage and bite the bars anytime he walked nearby. She would make him hold it even though he cried, but his fear just grew worse until the point that he wet himself every time she set the parrot on his arm. He kept that hid for a while, but one day Mother finally smelled him and then noticed the pool of urine staining her wood floor at his feet. She told him what a sissy he was, and doubted that she had really given birth to a boy; made him drop his trousers and show her his little dingus and laughed at how small it was. She laughed at him and coughed cigarette smoke and threatened to let the parrot bite It off.

And then she moved the parrot's cage to his room. He would lie facing the wall and feel those beady bird eyes looking at him, even in the dark — nobody but him and the awful parrot in the room and thinking about the feeling of his dingus in her cold, smooth hand, and the taste of her mouth like oily bourbon and grease. He wanted to kill the bird, but he was too afraid of it. Besides, Mother might catch him if he got up enough courage to try. She often came to him in the night without warning, slipping under his covers even though he clenched them tight to his chin.

He always looked out the window to check for birds before going outside. At a distance, they made him a little uncomfortable and gave him bad thoughts, but he couldn't breathe when they were in close proximity to him. Even the fat city pigeons littering the sidewalks terrified him. He'd once accidentally scattered a bunch of them on his apartment steps, with their wings flapping against him and attacking his face as they cooed evilly and took flight. It had taken a fifth of scotch and a pack of cigarettes before he could make himself go back outside, and he still dreamed of Mother that night, even though she'd been dead for many years. But he was never to tell, or the parrot would bite It off. Mother said so.

"Eat up. Lady at the café said it was *boo-dan,* or something like that," Bull said, noticing that Ernest was just holding the sack and staring out the windshield. "Are you all right, Ernest?"

"What?" Ernest became uncomfortably aware that the thought of birds had caused him to break out in a sweat, and that he had an erection. He lifted his hat and mopped the perspiration from his forehead with his handkerchief. He was sure that Myra knew how hard he was. She probably wanted him to show It to her. He was glad he couldn't see her hands.

"What the hell is the matter with you, Ernest? You're acting strange. Let me at that breakfast." Dink reached in the sack and frowned at the pale link of sausage he pulled forth before biting off a chunk. He puckered his mouth and acted like he was about to spit it out.

"It's boudin. Just rice and pork sausage with a lot of spices." Myra reached over the seat back and took a link out of the sack while Ernest held it for her. "It's Cajun."

"Well, those swamp donkeys will eat anything." Dink rolled down his window and tossed his portion out. "Tastes like those ducks shit in it and then they soaked it in vinegar."

"Fucking birds," Ernest growled, but ate the boudin anyway while he studied Myra when she wasn't looking his way. He didn't want to, but he kept looking to see if she raised her hands above the back of the front seat where he could see them. If he remembered correctly, they were very white and slender.

Claude took a piece and ate it while Myra got up on her knees facing the backseat and poured them all a cup of coffee. She gave Dink one last dirty look like she might pour his coffee in his lap. "Drink up and wake up. We won't be here long enough for you to have to eat much Cajun food."

Dink winced at the sound of pouring coffee. "We've got to stop. My eyeballs are floating."

They barely had time to eat before there was a town showing itself ahead. It wasn't really a town, but a combination grocery store and filling station and a few houses and barns sitting at a crossroads. They met one farmer driving a tractor along the edge of the road and he smiled and waved at them in passing.

"Friendly people down here," Claude said.

"Is that it?" Bull pointed at the store.

"Yeah," Myra said. "The owner sleeps in the back and they open early."

Bull pulled over into the muddy parking lot and stopped the car at the single gas pump. Claude couldn't see anything with the pump in his way.

"Shit, here we go." Dink downed his coffee in one gulp and climbed out the back door with his pistol in his hand.

"Get your ass out of the car." Ernest was going out behind Dink on the driver's side, but waited to make sure Claude was coming.

Claude staggered out on stiff knees, and stopped on the far side of the gas pump looking at the little store. A tin Wonder bread sign was nailed to the back of the bench along the front wall, but it was way too early in the morning for anyone to want to spit and whittle and tell tall tales on it. Beside the bench was the door painted with red paint smeared so thinly that the wood showed through, and with a closed sign hanging on it.

"Looks like they aren't open yet," Claude said.

"We're fixing to open them up." Dink had stopped to take a piss at the back bumper.

The sound of urine splattering into the mud was almost more than Claude could bear, and he realized just how bad he needed to urinate himself. He hadn't gone since the night before when they'd stopped along the roadside for just that. He was afraid he was going to wet himself, but he was too nervous to go in the parking lot when they were about to rob the place. And those same nerves were weakening his ability to hold his bladder back.

Ernest was standing beside him, and Claude wrinkled his nose at the strong odor coming from him. It smelled just like tomcat pee, and he thought maybe Ernest had accidentally walked through Dink's puddle. Then he noticed that one leg of Ernest's slacks was soaking wet. It bothered him that the man would wet himself, but maybe he was a veteran. Sheriff Miller had a friend who'd been shot in the war, and the Mauser bullet he'd taken in the guts had done something to him where he couldn't control himself anymore. He was apt to wet himself at any time, even at the supper table. Claude's mother tried to act like she didn't notice, but it was hard to eat with someone urinating during supper. He had once caught the man dressing in the morning and saw that he wore some kind of diaper. It had shocked him greatly at the time that a grown man would wear such a thing, and he wondered if Ernest wore one too.

Claude had never considered the complexity and logistics involved in a robbery, and the simple act of urinating during one. Bull seemed a poor leader to have overlooked such a basic body need. He vowed that if he were ever running the show he would plan for ample time to pee prior to a holdup.

Dink passed him on the way to the red door. The little bandit stepped out into the muddy parking lot and raised one Italian leather shoe up beside his knee to look at it. "I hate swamps."

"Get your ass in gear. You can buy a new pair of shoes when we're done," Bull said.

Dink took a few ginger steps, scowling at the mud. He tried to hold up both pant legs while still holding his pistol. Claude found the scene decidedly comical, and he would have liked to tell Dink how silly he looked tiptoeing with his gun against one knee and strips of his bare, white legs showing above his socks. He turned his knees way out when he walked, and looked like some kind of ballerina frog.

"I hope you know what you're doing, Claude." Ernest racked the bolt on the Thompson submachine gun. "This isn't a business for amateurs."

"I'll hold up my end." Claude pulled his pistol from his waistband and followed Dink. In truth, he didn't have a clue how he had ended up in front of the store, but life seemed to keep dragging him along to unexpected places.

Dink was already at the door, and Claude knew that he was just seconds from his first robbery. It wasn't just the need to urinate that had him dancing from one foot to another.

CHAPTER SEVEN

"All we wanted was the money. Robbing banks and trains was our way of getting it. That was our business."
— Willis Newton

Claude had envisioned his first big-time robbery a lot of ways. In fact, he'd worried about it as they drove through the night into Louisiana. He hadn't been sure what to expect, but he would have never imagined what he was looking at. The store appeared to be a shotgun-style sharecropper's cabin with a lean-to add-on at the back. There was smoke coming out of a stovepipe in the rusty tin roof of the little living quarters. A small shed lay about ten yards from the store. It was sided with cypress, but the gaps between the rough-sawn lumber were so big that you could almost see inside except where the big Coca-Cola sign hung on the wall. Somebody was pounding on an anvil

117

or something in there. Several broken-down cars and farm equipment littered either side of the open front, and Claude guessed that it was a makeshift garage. The whole place didn't look like it had the dollar bill it would have cost to build the setup, and robbing such an establishment seemed kind of silly.

"I'll keep an eye on that shop." Bull had climbed out of the car and was dragging the gas hose over to fill the tank. "Myra, you slip over behind the wheel in case we need to leave in a hurry."

"I've got to go pee first." Myra was already heading for the outhouse behind the garage.

Claude was a little surprised that Bull would be so bold as to pump gas in the middle of a robbery. The fact that Myra was taking the time to go to the outhouse was risky if not crazy, but who was he to say? He guessed that professionals like them didn't sweat the little stuff.

"Come on, Claude," Ernest said.

He and Dink were already at the door and waiting for him. Claude ran to catch up. He looked back at the car as he was running and saw Myra wave him on as she headed for the outhouse. He gave her a halfhearted smile that he hoped looked dangerous.

"Scoot over out of sight." Dink motioned to one corner of the store on the opposite side of the door from the single window beside it. He tested the doorknob and rapped on it with the butt of his pistol when he found that it was locked.

Ernest and Claude waited out of line of the doorway. Claude heard somebody walking across the creaking wood floor inside, and sensed rather than heard that someone was looking out the front window. He watched as Bull waved at whoever it was. Dink crossed his arms and hid his pistol under one armpit. Claude thought the man was a fool if he believed his pose looked harmless. Any smart storeowner would take one look at him and slam the door shut.

The front door creaked on its hinges and Dink smiled at whoever opened it. Bull was walking slowly over to the dilapidated garage.

"Morning, ma'am." Dink followed that immediately by whipping out his pistol and storming into the doorway.

Claude heard a little croak that sounded faintly feminine as he followed Ernest into the store. The place was dark and a little elderly woman in a faded housedress stood in the shadows of the cash register counter with both her hands in the air. Dink had his pistol barrel inches from her quivering chin. She never noticed when Ernest stepped to the register beside her, because she was studying the pistol bore so intently that her eyes were crossed.

"Watch the window, kid," Ernest said.

Claude did as he was told, but he couldn't keep his eyes off the woman. The sunlight pouring through the window was too bright to see outside anyway. He stood feeling like some kind of imbecile in the pool of brightness it threw on one spot on the stained hardwood floor. "You don't need to scare her so."

"Shut up," Dink said, but he did take a step back and lower his pistol a little. "Old lady, you keep your trap shut and give us your money and you'll be okay."

The woman was crying, and that seemed to make Dink mad. "Are you deaf? Just open up that safe and we'll be out of your hair before you know it. You don't, I'm going to shoot you in the face."

The woman kept crying, and her jaw was shaking so bad she could hardly talk. "There isn't but twenty dollars in the register."

Claude noticed that it hadn't been the pistol that had her looking crazy-eyed. She was really cross-eyed. There was a dark snuff stain at the corner of her trembling mouth and tobacco juice was leaking out of it. He felt silly when he looked at her and his fellow criminals with all their guns. Three grown men with two pistols and a Thompson machine gun just for one little cross-eyed granny with shaking knees and tobacco juice running off her chin.

Ernest opened the register drawer and pocketed a tiny wad of bills and a couple of handfuls of coins. "Yep, about twenty dollars, give or take."

"Don't give me that sass, Granny," Dink said. "We done know you've got a safe in back. You've been loaning money around here for years."

The old woman turned her crazy eyes down to the floor, but spouted something out in what sounded like French. She was too scared and talking too fast for Claude to be sure. He wasn't an expert by any means where foreign languages were concerned. He could speak a little Choctaw, but that was it. And he was sure she wasn't talking Choctaw or English either one.

"Shut that Cajun shit up and show us that safe," Dink said.

When the old woman didn't respond, Dink gave her a hard poke in the belly with his gun. "You look at me when I'm talking to you."

"She's cross-eyed," Claude said.

"What?"

"He said she can't see good." Ernest leaned an elbow on the register and made a show of crossing his eyes.

"I heard him, but it don't mean she can't hear me." Dink gave her another poke with his pistol.

"No, cross-eyed people probably hear fine." Ernest was squinting his eyes to get them to feeling normal again after staring at the tip of his nose for too long.

Dink wasn't going to wait for the old woman to snap out of it, and he pushed her toward the back room. Ernest followed him and stopped, blocking Claude's line of sight into the doorway. There was a thump of furniture and then the woman squeaked again like she had when Dink had first barged into the store. Claude started forward, but Ernest turned to him with his Thompson pointing at the floor between them.

"You watch that window and let Dink tend to this," he said.

Claude glanced at the window and then back to Ernest. "There's no need to rough that old woman up."

"She'll be fine. It sometimes takes a good scaring to get some of these people to loosen up and let go of their money. Dink will have her seeing straight in no time at all." Ernest laughed at his own pun, and didn't seem to mind that Claude didn't find it as funny. He went over to the soda cooler and pulled out a bottle of Dr. Pepper. He popped the cap off with the opener on the side of the cooler and walked back over to the door to the bedroom.

The old woman was jabbering something crazy again, but Dink's threats were too muffled for Claude to hear. In what seemed like hours, but was actually only minutes, Dink came out of the room with the old woman in front of him and a pillow slip hanging from his fist.

"You sit over there and keep your mouth shut." Dink motioned her to a seat on top of a few sacks of dog food in a corner.

Ernest nodded at the pillow slip. "We good?"

"You're damned right. The old bitch had a little square safe back there at the end of her bed," Dink said, making a show of hefting the sack. "There was enough cash in the thing to choke a horse."

Ernest sipped his Dr. Pepper and chuckled and looked at the woman. "How long have you been hoarding that back?"

She didn't answer him, but gasped and started to get up when Bull barged in the front door with an old man on the end of his gun. Claude hadn't been watching the window like he was supposed to, and Bull's entrance surprised him so that he almost let his gun go off into the floor.

The old man was wearing overalls and a filthy hat with grease and oil stains all over the crown, probably from crawling around under cars and tractors working on them. He wasn't cross-eyed like the old woman, but he didn't act like he was all there either. He looked at the robbers like he still wasn't sure what was going on.

"Sit down with her," Bull said.

Maybe the old man didn't hear well, and Bull gave him a gentle shove toward the dog-food sacks. The old man sat down and put his arm around the woman and muttered something to her that sounded like he was trying to comfort her. It was plain to Claude that the two were husband and wife.

"Are we done?" Bull asked.

Dink held up the pillowcase. "We got it."

Bull studied the old man looking up at them with hound dog eyes and his thin, scraggly white hair jutting out over his ears from under his greasy hat. "You just sit there and hold onto your woman while we get out of here. I'm going to leave the front door open, and if I see you getting up I'm going to send somebody back in here. Do you understand me?"

The old man continued to stare dumbly, breathing through his mouth. Dink raised his pistol above his head like he was going to hit him, but Bull held out an arm to stop him. "You better answer me."

"He doesn't speak good English," the old woman said.

"Well, you'd better set him straight," Bull said. "Do you understand what I'm saying?"

She chattered something to her husband in the French-sounding tongue, and he nodded quickly. The two of them hugged together and looked down at the floor.

"Let's go." Bull started out the door.

"They could call the cops or go for help," Dink said. "We ought to at least tie them up."

"Come on. There isn't anything to tie them up with, and hunting for something to use would take too long. Besides, they don't even have a phone, and there isn't a soul showing themselves around here to tell," Bull said.

Dink frowned, but shrugged his shoulders. He motioned for the door and Bull went out with Ernest on his heels. Claude stayed at the window waiting for Dink to pass, but the little robber remained in front of the old couple with his pistol hanging beside his leg. He kept cocking the gun and letting the hammer down, only to cock it again. The crisp clicks of the rotating cylinder and hammer spring were loud within the room, and he stood that way for a long time, clicking his pistol. Claude started forward, afraid Dink was going to shoot the owners.

Dink looked over his shoulder and saw how close Claude was to him. "What the hell are you doing?"

"Nothing," Claude mumbled.

Dink laughed. "Did you think I was about to put one in their heads, or are you wanting for me to leave so you can tap the old woman?"

"No." Dink thinking he might want to rape the old woman horrified Claude. He was also sure that Dink was toying with the idea of shooting the couple. "I was just going to tell you we'd better hurry out of here like Bull said."

"Well, hero, it just so happens that I ain't in the shooting mood," Dink said. "When I am, you'd better be careful, cause you're working hard to get on my list."

"I was just afraid you were going to shoot them." Claude was vividly aware that he and Dink were both holding pistols and only a few feet apart. At that range a gunfight was going to be deadly for both of them. "I don't think I could let you do that."

"Kid, I'm going to enjoy myself when I finally get to put a bullet in your mouth."

"How long do you think Bull's going to wait for us?"

Dink turned back to the old couple. "Today's your lucky day. Claude here likes you."

Claude remained where he was, not liking it that Dink had used his name in the presence of their victims and not trusting Dink enough to turn his back on him going out the door.

"Do-gooder, huh? Damned pain in the ass is what you are." Dink worked the hammer on the pistol even faster. "You want me to go first so you can have some alone time with this old bitch. Won't no young woman give a half-breed like you the time of day."

Claude remained where he was.

Dink finally lowered the hammer on his pistol and left it there, followed by a shrug of his shoulders. "Suit yourself. It's your pecker, but that ugly old bitch is going to be as dry as sandpaper. You'll have to put a sack over her head so you don't have to look at her cross-eyed ass."

"Let's go." Claude was squeezing the grip of his automatic so hard that his hand was hurting. Everything about Dink disgusted

127

him. He might be bad himself, but he was learning that he couldn't hold a candle to some people in the world.

"All right, hero." Dink ducked out the front door in two long strides.

Claude was left alone, and he stood there for a count of five. The couple finally got their nerve up enough to look at him, and Claude immediately recognized that they believed he was left behind to kill them. He tried to think of something to say, because the pitiful looks on their faces made him feel it necessary to speak. He couldn't say why, but it did.

"You folks stay where you are and you'll be all right. I ain't like him." He turned on his heel and went out the door.

His comrades were already in the car, and Myra ground the transmission into gear and revved the engine. He ran and practically dove into the backseat on the driver's side as she spun mud in a big rooster tail behind the car. His legs were dangling out the door and he fought to get a hold on the slick vinyl seat as she cut a donut around the gas pump. The rear end of the car slid easily in the slimy, dark mud, and the car spun its tires and inched its way toward the highway. Myra gripped the steering wheel with both hands, as if she could keep the car from getting stuck by willpower alone.

A black Studebaker sedan with a county sheriff's emblem on the door eased through the crossroads and turned into the parking lot. Claude could see one driver behind the wheel. It was just a face beneath a campaign hat looking out the windshield at them.

"Damned coppers," Dink said.

"Get us out of here, babe," Bull said.

"I can't get any traction," Myra all but shouted.

The deputy was going to pass them on the passenger side. Dink took Ernest's Thompson and shoved the barrel out the window. He let off a long burst into the grille of the patrol car. Claude watched as the line of bullet holes and sparks climbed up the hood toward the lawman's windshield, but the Thompson's magazine ran dry before it got there. Dink was cursing and fumbling with a spare clip Ernest was trying to hand him, and the deputy cut his wheel hard and accelerated. He crashed into the side of the garage just as Myra found a little traction and shot them out onto the highway. Claude looked out the back glass at the deputy staggering out of his car and tugging at the pistol on his hip. He slipped in the mud and fell down and then Myra drove out of sight of the store.

"Damn, Ernest, why don't you get a drum magazine? That county stooge almost had us, because I ran out of bullets."

"Diamond Joe gave me that gun. He might not like it if I changed it," Ernest said.

Claude was trying to get his mind wrapped around what had happened. He had no doubt that Dink was a killer, and Ernest was acting creepier by the minute. The man was squeezing himself through his piss-soaked pants like nobody in the car would notice.

"What are you staring at?" Dink asked.

Claude noticed that Dink's hands holding the machine gun were shaking wildly and his eyes were lit up as crazy as the cross-eyed old woman's. "There wasn't any need to shoot at that deputy."

"You can kiss my ass, schoolboy." Dink tried to clear the barrel of the Thompson between his knees and the back of the front seat so he could point it in Claude's direction. "I can give you some of the same."

"You do, Dink, and I'm going to do some shooting myself." Bull had turned halfway around in the front seat and had his revolver casually pointing at Dink. His voice was calm, but he said it like he meant it.

Bull only carried a Smith & Wesson .38 Short, and Claude wondered if the man knew how light the caliber was for man shooting. At the close range the little bullets would permanently mess up Dink's forehead, but a .45 bore staring over the seat would have been more intimidating, not to mention that it would make bigger holes if it came to a shooting. Claude had already vowed that he was going to replace his .32 with a .45 the first chance he got. Watching Bull and Dink staring hatred at each other with guns in their hands emphasized the importance of caliber. Why carry a little gun, when you could have a big one? He wished somebody made a .46.

"That was a stupid stunt you pulled. That deputy didn't have a clue what was going on, and we would've been long gone before he did," Bull said.

Dink didn't argue, but he was glaring at Claude. He pitched the machine gun onto the floorboard and flopped back against his seat. "Claude is going to push it too far one of these days."

"How about we get our asses out of here before they get the posse rounded up?" Bull turned back to study the road ahead. "Keep calm, doll, and follow the plan."

Myra nodded. She still had both hands on the wheel, and her knuckles were gripping it so tight they were chalk white. The car

131

must have been going eighty over the slick gravel highway, and every mud puddle they crossed splashed and thumped against the floorboard like a hammer.

Bull pulled a map out of the glove compartment. He started to unfold it, but Myra shook her head.

"I don't need that. I know the roads," she said.

Bull studied her carefully. "Are you sure?"

Myra sighed and blew her bangs out of her eyes in one quick gust. She took one hand off the wheel and tried to relax against the seat back. "I'm good. That was a little tense."

"Stay calm and keep your mind on the road. There aren't enough bridges in the entire state for all the water they've got, and these damned roads around the bayous are easy to make a wrong turn on," Bull said. "I don't want to end up at a dead end in the middle of some swamp with some coon-ass John Law right behind us."

"I know the route like the back of my hand," she said. "Hasn't everything gone just like I told you?"

Claude had to agree. Almost everything had been exactly like she said, give or take a few things, like the old folks getting roughed up and Dink shooting at a cop. But as smart as Myra was, there was no way she could have planned for a cross-eyed woman or a county deputy showing up right in the middle of the robbery. Claude was sure that was a little out of the norm. He wanted nothing so much as to get him and Myra away from Diamond Joe's men, but he thought it worth storing away that you could never plan for everything when it came to a robbery. If stealing money was easy and risk free, probably lots more folks would be doing it.

Myra had explained to him that the reason for hitting little country enterprises was because big towns were too hard to get out of ahead of the cops. With proper scouting, a good team of bandits could lose the cops among the rural back roads and slip out of the area without hindrance.

So far so good, but Claude knew he'd better keep his eye on Dink. Every time he looked over that way the little killer was staring back at him with a smug look on his face. Anybody that would shoot a cross-eyed woman couldn't be trusted.

Claude unconsciously reached for the dog tags around his neck like he always did when he was deep in thought. He dug around under his collar and checked inside his shirt to see if the chain had broken and fallen down to his waistband, but the necklace wasn't there. He searched the seat around him and the floorboard to no avail.

"What are you looking for?" Myra glanced at him in the rearview mirror.

"I lost my dog tags."

"You're too young to have been a soldier," Bull said.

"Look around for me. They were my daddy's and I'd hate to lose them."

Ernest let go of his crotch and lifted his backside up off the seat and looked under himself and then between his feet.

"It ain't over here," Dink said.

"Maybe it's under here." Ernest sat back down and bent over to feel around under the bench seat.

Claude kept looking, but found nothing.

"Maybe you lost them back there at the store," Myra said.

"You better hope the cops don't find it," Bull said. "That's like leaving a business card behind."

"I can't remember when I had them last," Claude said.

"Great. This damned amateur kid is going to get us all caught," Dink said. "You wind up in jail, you'd better not squeal on us."

Claude was worried sick about the possibility of leaving the dog tags back at the store. What was almost as bad as leaving something behind that might lead the cops to him was the fact that he'd left the Sheriff's name at the scene of a crime.

"Damn, Ernest, you smell bad." Dink put his face closer to his open window to get some fresh air.

"Is that another patrol car coming?" The panic in Myra's voice got all their attention.

Every one of them leaned forward to look at the car coming to meet them. It was a black dot on the highway about a mile away, but it did look like the car the deputy back at the store had been driving.

"Dink, you get that chopper ready." Bull started rolling his window down. He had his pistol in his other hand.

Dink rested the barrel of the Thompson on his window seal and grinned like a madman. "Shit, I love my job!"

"We're going to have to stop soon so I can pee." Claude's bladder had gone from strained to positively feeling like it was about to burst.

"You tie a knot in it, or if it isn't long enough just tie a string around it," Bull said.

Claude wondered how long the day was going to last. It was a long way out of Louisiana, and there were bound to be a lot of cops between them and the Texas state line. There'd probably be so many of them that he'd never get to pee, and have to wet himself like Ernest. He hated the thought of having to continue his life of crime wearing a diaper. Armed robbery wasn't all that it was cracked up to be.

CHAPTER EIGHT

"Don't look back. Something might be gaining on you."
— Satchel Paige

Sheriff Miller blew on his coffee and stared out the kitchen screen door into the yard. The sun was already well above the eave of the porch, and he knew he should have left for work two hours ago. And yet, his gun belt still hung on the peg beside the door with his hat.

"You can't believe Claude killed that man or had anything to do with the robbery." His wife intended to be shelling peas, but seemed to have forgotten the task. Her hands were unconsciously resting inside the bowl in her lap, and had been for nearly as long as Sheriff Miller had been nursing his coffee. "He's a sweet boy, Jim."

"It doesn't look good for him," he said.

"It doesn't make any difference what he's

done. We know he's a good boy," she said.

"The notion of your sweet little boy and the truth are starting to look pretty far apart."

She was an easy woman to get along with, but he had never been able to keep anything from her. She had an unreadable face, except when she was smiling, and her dark eyes had always cut right to the middle of him. He reached across the table and pulled one of her hands from the bowl and held it on top of the table. A little crease formed between her eyebrows and she pinched her lower lip gently in her teeth.

"You haven't told me all of it, have you?" she asked.

"That agriculture agent said it was a young woman and a teenage boy that kidnapped him, and his description matched Claude to a T."

"I can't believe Claude would do such a thing. Don't you think it kind of preposterous for a teenage boy to be robbing people on the roads?"

"Well, he did. He held that man at gunpoint and stole his boots and then his car."

"My God, Jim, you make it sound like we've raised another Pretty Boy Floyd."

"He's always been headstrong. I've tried everything, but for the life of me, he just won't listen."

He measured the time by the ticking of the old clock on the wall. Maybe it only seemed like a long time, with such an ominous mechanism in the room. He'd never liked the noisy clock, but it had been a wedding gift from her mother, and the very same timepiece that her grandmother had carried over the Trail of Tears when the government had marched all the Choctaws to Indian Territory from Mississippi and Alabama a century earlier. A good number of Mary's family had frozen to death or had been walked or starved to death along that march, and the old clock was a token of what her ancestors and her tribe had suffered in those years gone by. Even more, it was a symbol of survival and rebuilding.

"Do you think he killed that man on the river?" she asked.

"It looks like he did, but I'd like to hear it from him." In actuality, he wanted to hear no such thing, and saying what he was coming to believe didn't lighten his load any. He hadn't intended to mention it to his wife, because he knew she was already fretting worse than he was. She didn't need him dumping his grief on her. He immediately regretted not avoiding a conversation with her.

"Oh, Lord, I hope it doesn't get any worse," she said quietly.

"Brace yourself, because that's a distinct possibility."

She slipped out of his hand and set the bowl of pea hulls on the table. He watched her as she rose and went to the icebox and stood there with her back to him and one hand resting on its top. She had been about the prettiest girl in the county when he first met her, and he thought she'd grown more beautiful over the years. Bearing two children hadn't changed her willowy frame, other than to round it a little more in a few places. Her jet-black hair was bundled up at the back of her head, like she always wore it when she was working in a hot kitchen. He found himself watching the smooth brown skin at the nape of her neck, but it didn't give him the pleasure that it usually did.

"It's been a bad year," he said, as much to break the silence rather than anything else.

She turned to gaze out the doorway and he noticed the sadness crinkling the little crow's feet at the corners of her eyes. He'd seen that very same sadness take a hold of her more than once over the years. She'd looked like that after two stillborn children, and when he'd told her he was going off to war. Some people said that Indians didn't

140

talk much, but they didn't know his Mary. They didn't know how she woke up chattering and smiling at the break of day, and how her laugh could soothe his soul even when his thoughts flew back to bad things best left behind in the trenches of France. But he feared for her just as soon as he'd seen her hands shaking in the bowl and that haunted look creeping into her eyes. His own mother had once gotten that look, and it never left her. His father had snapped her arms and ribs over the years, and finally her will. It wasn't only his fists that had finally broken her spirit, nor his boozing, but rather that life just got to be too bad and too much. He was afraid that if Claude had gone as bad as he suspected, that Mary might quit. The thought of her losing her laughter was almost worse than the thought that his son, his seed, was no good.

"Where did we go wrong?" she asked.

He'd been contemplating that very thing since seeing Claude paddling down the river with a boatload of stolen money, but he hadn't come up with any explanation. "He knows better."

"Don't you say I spoiled him," she said. "Don't you dare."

"Maybe it's more my fault than yours. Maybe I should have kept a closer eye on

141

him. I wish . . ."

She walked across the room and stopped behind his chair with both hands on his shoulders. "You aren't your father."

"Yes, but . . ."

"But nothing. There's not a thing in the world you can do to control life sometimes. You can't make Claude be you; you've just got to help him as best you can."

He bowed his head and closed his eyes. "I've never understood that boy."

"We'll get through the hard times. We've done it before." Her hands kneaded at his knotted muscles.

"Not like this."

Her hands went still again, and she trembled slightly. "No, not like this."

He scooted his chair around and pulled her into his lap, hugging her close to him. "Well, Mary, our boy always bragged he was going to do something big. The Republicans and the Democrats both couldn't break our little town bank, but Claude did."

"What?"

"Harry called me at the office yesterday and told me to be ready. The bank's broke, and there's going to be a lot of mad people when they find out that their money isn't where they thought it was," he said. "I don't think there will be a bank left open in the country by the time another year goes by."

"I thought Roosevelt gave all the banks a holiday so that they could get their finances straight."

"Well, four days apparently wasn't enough to make up for the fact that Claude or his new woman took ten thousand dollars out of the safe. Our little bank president is good with a pencil, but he can't stretch nothing into ten thousand dollars."

"How much money did we have deposited?"

"Not much, but with the exception of what you've got squirreled away in that old baking-powder can of yours, everything."

She leaned back from him until she could look him in the eyes. "I can survive that. I can live with being broke, but I can't sleep knowing Claude is out there alone with bad people, and with lawmen probably wanting to shoot him on sight."

"Pray for him, Mary." He had given up praying during the war, but still had enough faith to believe that God listened to some folks. He'd always admired his wife's faith.

"I will, but you go find him."

"He's out of my jurisdiction."

"He's your son. He's never out of your jurisdiction," she said. "You're a war hero. The governor held a parade for you; everybody in the state knows Jim Miller, fearless lawman and Medal of Honor winner. You can go where you want and smile at them and tip your hat, and everybody's going to be too busy stepping aside for you to feel like you're stepping on their toes."

He'd tried to tell her for years that he wasn't a hero, and that the only thing special he did in the war was to survive when a hell of a lot of his friends didn't. Luck shouldn't be something that they gave a man a medal for. He wasn't the only one that had sucked up a lungful of mustard gas, or crawled through barbwire under fire because some damn fool had told him that a little stretch of cannon-pitted dirt was worth dying for.

"I'll try. I promise you I'll try," he said.

"And I'll pray."

He listened to her humming an old camp revival song as she walked out the door to water her garden. He waited until her voice faded and her footsteps were gone from the porch before rising to gather his gun belt and settle his hat on his head. What he didn't tell her was that Claude was probably long past helping. He'd do what he could, but his greatest fear was that the boy might come back to Oklahoma and not want any help. He didn't know if he could quit being the sheriff if it came to that.

From the way Dink's legs were squirming around and the way he was cursing, Claude decided that the car was past fixing, at least without somebody towing it to a garage. That wasn't an option considering every cop in the state was probably looking for them already. Short of any better alternatives, Bull wasn't giving up, and he was trying to crawl under the car beside Dink. He had a fistful of barbwire and a pair of pliers in his hands. The jack had sunk into the soft ground to the point that his belly would barely fit under the running board, and he was wiggling his shoulders back and forth and trying to grind himself past it.

Claude sat on a hump of dirt in the bar ditch in front of the clipped section of fence that Bull had salvaged for his repair work. Myra sat beside him playing with the wildflowers she'd picked and laid out on her skirt between her knees. She was braiding the stems together, being careful not to knock off the tiny little blooms. Ernest was pacing back and forth in the middle of the dirt road, nervously scanning both ways for traffic.

"It's a dead-end road." Claude pointed at the sign not ten yards past the car.

"There's got to be a reason they built a road," Ernest said. "Somebody besides us might come along."

Claude looked around them skeptically. Two little farm fields lay to either side of the road, but there was nothing but flooded timber beyond that. It looked like the road sloped down into the water a hundred yards past where they sat. Myra's maps didn't show the road they were on, but it appeared that they were stranded in the middle of a horseshoe of swamp.

"There's bound to be coppers looking for us by now," Ernest said. "But you and your dame there can keep sitting in the ditch and acting like nothing's wrong. I don't give a shit if you're worried or not. What do I care? We can all get shot or locked up in prison and it'd be the same to me."

"Calm down, Ernest. Bull will get the car patched up and none of us will have to go to jail," Myra said.

"Why don't you shut up? I'm tired of hearing what a smart little girl you are." Ernest stopped his pacing to stare at her, and the expression on his face wasn't quite angry or worried. It was stranger than that, and more than a little creepy.

Claude didn't like Ernest looking at Myra like that. The truth of the matter was that he hadn't liked the way Ernest had been looking at her for days. Something was a little off-kilter about the man, and he seemed to be getting worse by the hour.

"Why don't you walk back out to the highway and play in the middle of it?" Myra asked without looking up from the flower bracelet she was braiding.

Claude noticed the little revolver lying beneath the flowers between Myra's thighs. The girlish wrinkle of her freckled nose while she studied the bracelet wasn't in keeping with the pistol she had handy. He didn't know if he was ever going to understand her.

"Dink's right; you're a saucy dame." Ernest was licking his mustache like he loved the sound of his own words. "You want to see It, don't you?"

"Ernest, quit being a nut," Bull growled from under the car. "Leave Myra alone, or crawl under here and help me fix this damned car. Dink doesn't know his ass from a hole in the ground when it comes to mechanicing."

Ernest started down the road, but not toward the highway. He'd left his hat in the car seat and the Louisiana sun and humidity had already plastered his hair to his forehead. The sweat and melted hair-styling grease was pouring down his face, but he didn't seem to have the good sense to fetch his hat.

Claude watched him walk aimlessly down the road. "You be careful around him."

"I can handle Ernest," Myra said. "He's a creep, but you'd better get used to creeps. Stuff like that comes with the territory."

Bull had scooted out from under the car, and was wiping his hands clean with his handkerchief. He'd taken off his jacket to work, and the back of his white shirt was stained from crawling around in the black mud. "Ernest is okay. He just gets a little loony when he's working. The stress gets to him some, but he'll be all right once he's had time to settle down."

"If you ask me, he's crazy," Claude said.

"Nobody asked you," Bull said.

"Is the car fixed?" Myra asked.

"The front U-joint flew apart, but I tied the driveshaft up with barbwire." Bull studied his torn palms. "Dink, get in that thing and see if our patch job will hold. Maybe if you clutch it easy we can cripple it down the road."

Dink's legs wiggled again as he started to squirm from under the car. There was a loud thump and more cursing before he finally reappeared holding one hand to his forehead. He was coated in mud and his face was beet-red. He knelt down and lowered the jack and jerked it out from under the car. "I hate swamps."

"Try the car," Bull said.

Dink didn't attempt to knock any of the mud off of him, and got behind the steering wheel and started the car. He put the transmission into gear and tried to ease it forward. The tires were having problems in the mud, and he goosed the throttle impatiently. Something snapped and clanged, and the rear wheels quit spinning even though the engine was revving wildly.

"Shut it off!" Bull yelled. "I told you to ease into it."

"I was easing it!" Dink yelled back.

"Get out and help me. It's going to take more wire." Bull repositioned the jack. He was soon working his way back under the car with another strand of wire in his hands.

"I don't know why you want me under there. There ain't room for me and your big ass both," Dink said.

"Quit your whining and come on. I'm not going to wallow around in the mud alone while you stand around with your thumb in your ass."

Soon, there was once more two pair of legs protruding out from under the car. A swarm of gnats and mosquitos flittered around in the sunlight above them. The repair work went slowly, and their cursing timed the sun as it climbed higher in the sky.

"We've got to get shut of this crew," Claude whispered to Myra.

She took his wrist and tied the flower bracelet around it. "You should go home. This isn't the life for you."

"I'm not going without you."

"This is all I know. You can go back, I can't."

"Nothing's stopping you."

She laughed sadly and weakly. "Go back to the farm, Claude. I won't say it hasn't been fun."

"I won't leave you." His tongue had suddenly grown thick. "I love you."

She scoffed, but couldn't seem to find the something it took to really pull it off. "I'm just your first piece of tail."

"Is that what you think?"

She looked directly into the sun and Claude thought that must have been what made her eyes misty. He was also distinctly aware that she still held his arm.

"I used to believe in princesses with fairy godmothers and some charming prince to come along and rescue me," she said. "My mother never believed it, but the kids' books were full of that stuff."

"And now all you've got is a half-breed Indian who wasn't even wearing shoes when he came to rescue you."

She laughed lightly, but truly. That little chuckle made him love her all the more.

"The best thing you could do is to get as far away from me as you can," she said.

"You'll have to run me off, and I don't know if that would work."

Her little fingers dug into his arm. "Claude, when are you going to learn that you can't trust anybody, not even me?"

"I trust you, and you can trust me. I'd say it's a sad world if you can't find that simple little thing in it."

"Can't you see I'm just a tramp?"

"Don't say that, not ever."

"I'm no worse than some, and better than a lot of women. But that doesn't make me some kind of angel," she said. "Look where I've led you."

"I came along of my own accord."

"You're a fool."

"A fool that loves you."

"Quit saying that. Do you think you're the first one that ever said that to me?"

"Maybe not, but I mean it."

She stared him in the eyes, and he felt as

if she were trying to find something — as if
she could tell if he were lying or not from
the blinking of his eyes or the pulse of his
heart showing plainly in the rise of his chest
and the throb of the blood vessels at his
temples.

"I'm not really twenty-five. I'm only
nineteen," she said.

"I kind of thought you might be."

The smile came faintly back to her face.
"Getting smarter are you?"

"Naw, I've just been holding out on you."

"My mother ran off with the circus and
left me with Daddy and my two sisters."
She let go of him long enough to wipe at
her eyes.

"What happened to your sisters?"

"They wouldn't run away with me. Maybe
they could take Daddy's drinking better
than I could."

"How'd that turn out for them?"

"Not as good as it should have." She
ducked her head to avoid his eyes.

"I guess you did what you had to do."

"I did a bad thing . . . a real bad thing."

He waited to see if she was going to say
more, but she cut off the memories with a
quick shake of her head. He tried to think
of something to say in the awkward silence.
"The Sheriff always says that it's who you

are that matters, and not where you came from."

"I don't believe that."

"When I look at you I don't see a drunkard's daughter, nor a tramp. I just see Myra, the prettiest, smartest girl in the world."

"Did that stuff work on the schoolgirls back home?"

"I never said anything like that up until now. Never had any reason to."

"You bastard." Her whisper was so weak it was really just a ragged breath.

Myra let go of him and started to stand. Her pistol fell from her skirt into the mud. "See there what you've done to me."

"You can trust me, Myra."

She seemed about to say something else, but her attention shifted down the road toward the highway. "There's someone coming. I hope whoever it is isn't too attached to their car."

CHAPTER NINE

"Murder is always a mistake. One should never do anything that one cannot talk about after supper."
— Oscar Wilde

The car turned out to be a Ford Model A Woody with roll-up canvas windows and a small boat tied on top of it. Claude stayed in the ditch while Myra slipped her pistol into her beaded purse and walked out to meet the latest arrivals. The driver stuck one arm out the window and waved at them as the car ducked and dodged up the rutted road.

Claude was shocked to discover that it was a priest behind the wheel when the car finally pulled to a stop beside Myra. The skinny, spectacled man wore a black coat and one of those white collars like some of the Methodists wore, with a gold crucifix hanging from a beaded necklace over the outside of his shirt. Most of the preachers back home didn't wear such outfits, but the congregation in his mother's church poked enough fun of papists to give him an idea of the man's trade. The Catholics had never really taken a hold where Claude was from, or at least there weren't many of them. The old people said they were idol worshippers, drinkers and dancers, while the protestant denominations seemed to provide just the right amount of promises and guilt for mountain folks.

Claude didn't have any opinions about which church Jesus liked best, but the sight of any kind of preacher was enough to make him uncomfortable. It made him feel like God was paying special attention to him, and as if he was caught in the act of sinning. God was said to always be watching people, but it was easy to get to feeling like you could get away with stuff. Any kind of preacher seemed to have a way of walking around corners and catching you hiding. They knocked on your door, and sat down in your kitchen and asked you too many questions. His mother was a worrier, and she would have the preacher over to talk to him every time he did something bad enough to make her fret. Claude didn't like being asked questions that he didn't have good answers for, especially those that had bothered him for a long time.

"Looks like you could use a Good Samaritan," the priest said.

Myra was giving him a Sunday smile, just like they weren't bank robbers broke down on the side of the road. "Oh, could you help us? We've been stuck here in the hot sun for hours."

"You're a long way off the highway. It's a blessed thing that I happened along." The priest's smile matched Myra's, even though he probably hadn't robbed a store that morning.

"We aren't from around here, and we must've made a wrong turn," Myra said. "I'm terrible with maps."

"Where are you headed?"

Myra glanced at Claude and then at Bull's and Dink's legs sticking out from under the car. "We're going to a family reunion at Beaumont."

"That's all the way over in Texas." A young boy leaned across the front seat to look out the window at Myra. He was maybe twelve or so, with a gap-toothed grin.

"I've never been to Texas. How far is that?" Another boy of about the same age chimed in and stuck his face out of the back window. He was all pimples and dimples.

156

"What are you folks doing out here?" Myra asked.

The priest nodded his head one at a time at each of the boys. "One Saturday a month I take some of the boys from the orphanage out for a fishing trip."

"That's nice of you," Myra said, pouring on the charm.

"I like children, and the orphanage can be kind of tough." The priest paused to push his glasses up his nose. "What's the matter with the car?"

"Busted U-joint." Bull's voice bounced off the bottom of the car, and sounded as if it came from inside a well.

"I know of a good garage over in Orange that has a wrecker," the priest said. "Let me go down to the landing and unload this boat, and then I'll come back and give you a lift to town."

Bull was crawling out from under the car again, but the priest was already waving and driving away. He watched the car leaving with a look of distaste. "Why'd you let him drive off?"

"He's got to come back by us," Myra said. "You guys are the muscle."

"You're going to steal a preacher's car?" Claude asked. "That's bound to be worse than stealing from regular folks."

157

"He won't give us any trouble. All he'll get is a long walk home and a story to tell to his congregation at the next Mass," Bull said. "We need a car, unless you want to be sitting here when the bulls show up."

"I'd rob a one-legged leper and piss on the head of John the Baptist if it would get me out of here," Dink said. "Did I tell you how bad I hate swamps? And I hate coppers even more. Maybe even more than preachers."

"Get your stuff together. We're taking that car when he comes back," Bull said.

"I wouldn't go to digging guns and a sack full of cash out of the trunk. You might make that preacher nervous," Myra said.

Claude wasn't paying them much attention. He walked out into the middle of the road and watched the car disappear into the trees at the edge of the swamp. "Ya'll know Ernest is down there somewhere."

"Shit," Bull said.

"Old Ernest will bring us a car," Dink said.

"Yeah, that's what I'm afraid of." Bull propped his hands on his hips and squinted down the road.

Claude looked at Bull. "I thought you said he'd be better after he had time to settle down."

Bull started down the road. "That can take a while. Dink, you stay at the car and make sure nobody else comes along."

Claude followed Bull, and the shooting started before they walked fifty yards. Pop, pop, pop. One of the kids yelled and then pop, pop again. There was no more yelling.

The road dipped down a little slope to the swamp, and the first thing Claude saw was the top of the Woody and Ernest's head at the water's edge. He took one more step and could see the .45 bucking in the crazy man's hand. By the time they reached the car the priest and the boys with him were nowhere to be seen. Claude searched the murky water for signs of bodies floating amidst the cypress stumps and flooded timber. Ernest was cursing and jumping up and down. He loaded a fresh clip in the government pistol and fired bursts randomly into the swamp.

"What the hell are you doing?" Bull asked.

"They ran on me." Ernest trotted to the other side of the car and shot off another round. "Thought I saw that preacher for a second. I swore I hit him twice, but he kept running."

"Did you shoot the kids?" Claude asked.

"No, they're dodgy little devils." Ernest

was jerking and twitching like the madman he was.

During the pause in gunfire they could hear the boys out in the swamp calling out to each other and looking for the priest who finally shouted back to them.

"Stop shooting, Ernest." Bull had pulled his own gun, but he had it pointed closer to Ernest than he did the swamp.

Ernest shot again, not at anything he could see, but simply sound shots in the general direction of the voices coming out of the swamp. The racket caused a big gray heron to fly up. Instead of weaving through the timber, it curled back its long neck and flapped its enormous wings right over the top of the car. Ernest went positively wild and began shooting at the bird passing over him. As he swung his pistol back up the road, Claude had to duck to keep from getting shot. He couldn't see Myra, but he hoped she had taken cover.

"Damn it, stop shooting. You're going to hit Dink and Myra," Bull shouted.

The heron was flying low and should have presented an easy target, but Ernest had run out of ammo. That didn't stop him from squeezing the trigger crazily, even though the slide on the .45 was locked back in the empty position.

160

"You've lost it," Bull said. "I always knew you were a little off, but you've gone plumb bonkers."

Ernest looked blankly at Bull, and he was tugging at his crotch again. "That thing just surprised me, that's all."

"It was just a damned crane," Bull said. "I guess you hate preachers and kids *and* cranes."

"Don't tease me about birds." Ernest swung around to face Bull with his pistol hanging beside his leg. His finger was still squeezing the trigger of his .45 as if it had a spasm. Both his eyelids were blinking like Christmas lights.

"You're just lucky I don't shoot you and leave you for the alligators." Bull was already headed for the preacher's car. "Get in, kid."

"What about the preacher and those boys?" Claude asked.

Bull jerked the driver's door open and climbed in. "You can look for them if you want to. I'm getting the hell out of here."

Claude ran to the car and slid into the passenger side of the front seat. "Do you think those folks are all right?"

Bull spun the car around in reverse, and the boat flew off and thumped on the ground. "Yeah, Ernest wouldn't have been so excited if he'd hit what he was aiming at."

"Maybe those little boys are wounded out there in the swamp."

"They sounded all right to me. I'm not a doctor, and I don't intend on hanging around and getting caught." Bull slammed on the brakes beside Ernest. "Get in the car or get left."

Ernest jerked open the door behind Bull and folded himself into the backseat. "You don't have any .45 shells, do you?"

"I wouldn't give your crazy ass a butter knife right now," Bull said as he dumped the clutch and lurched the car forward.

Dink had the trunk of the broken-down car open by the time they pulled alongside it. He tossed the Thompson and a pile of other guns into the back of the Woody and jumped in on the far side from Ernest. Claude opened his door long enough for Myra to climb over him to sit between him and Bull. She held the pillowcase full of money in her lap.

"What the hell happened?" Dink asked.

"Ernest decided to have target practice," Bull said.

"That priest tried to put up a fight when I wanted to take his car," Ernest mumbled.

"That little old man tried to fight you?"

Myra asked.

"He grabbed at my gun and told those kids to run," Ernest said.

"That preacher must've loved his car," Dink said. "Or else he must have known how bad Ernest shoots."

"There were too many trees and they were all running too fast," Ernest said.

"What about you, Claude, can you shoot good enough to jump shoot two kids and an old man?" Dink asked.

"It was the crane that got me rattled. I usually shoot better than that," Ernest said.

"A bird? Really?" Dink asked.

"I don't like birds. They'll bite It off." Ernest gave a little groan and reached up to touch Myra's hair.

"Hey, watch it, you creep!" Myra pulled loose from Ernest's grasp and almost hit her head on the rearview mirror.

Claude wasn't sure what Ernest had done, but he twisted in his seat and cocked his right fist, preparing to belt him one. He was too slow, because Bull backhanded Ernest square in the lips with his revolver. Ernest grunted and flopped against the back of his seat, and Bull gave him another one for good measure. Ernest was almost out of his reach, but the blow was still stout enough to bounce his head off the seat once more.

163

"Dink, you shoot him if he so much as moves again before we're back in Texas," Bull said. "If he killed those kids and the coppers catch us, they aren't going to put us in jail. They're going to bury us under it."

"I don't want to shoot Ernest." Dink had his pistol on Ernest, but he had a pouting look on his face that would have been better suited for a child. "Why don't you shoot him, or let Claude do it."

"Ernest won't ever be going with me on a job again, and you might not either," Bull said.

Dink shook his head and got a little more serious with his gun. "Ernest, you sit still or I'm going to have to plug you. Bull is feeling a little touchy."

Blood was pouring out of Ernest's nose and dripping off his mustache, but he didn't bother to wipe his face. He didn't seem to realize he was bleeding, or that his nose was broken and his lower lip cut half in two. He was either strangely tranquilized, or perhaps knocked half senseless.

After a long moment he did manage to answer Dink. "That's all right, Dink, Bull just doesn't understand. He didn't see that big bird."

Claude passed a look to Myra, and he

could tell she understood him. Dink was crazy, Ernest was crazier, and Bull was crazy enough to think he could control them. The scariest thing to Claude was that they had one more job to pull, and he wasn't sure they would survive it. He felt bad things coming, whether he wanted them or not.

CHAPTER TEN

"Under a violent barrage, dashed to the attack of an enemy position, covering about 210 yards through barbed-wire entanglements. He rushed on machine-gun nests, capturing 171 prisoners. He stormed a strongly held position containing more than 50 machine guns, and a number of trench mortars. Turned the captured guns on the enemy, and held the position for four days, in spite of a constant barrage of large projectiles and of gas shells. Crossed no man's land many times to get information concerning the enemy, and to assist his wounded comrades."
— a portion of Private Joseph Oklahombi's citation for the Croix de Guerre medal.

Sheriff Miller eyed the mob surrounding the front door of the bank as calmly as most men put their pants on in the morning.

Deputy Burke was behind him with a pump scattergun, but he was anything but calm. He had already spotted clubs, bottles, and guns in the crowd.

"This ain't looking good, Sheriff," Burke said. "Those are some frustrated people, and I'm kinda glad you're wearing your gun."

Sheriff Miller's town was a small one, and he was a friendly man. You didn't get elected if you weren't willing to brag on babies and say hello to everyone you met. He made it a point to know everyone in town, and there weren't many in the whole county that he hadn't shook hands with at one time or another. Of the forty or so people gathered to storm the bank and kill the president, there were some good, hard-working, honest folks among them. Despite that, Sheriff Miller could barely recognize the faces of those he knew well. Anger did that — anger, hunger, and feeling helpless. They were just good people at their wits' end. He studied Mrs. Jones, who ran the little café at the north end of town. She was usually a quiet woman who got bashful any time she had to talk in front of a crowd, but it was her that was screaming the loudest and egging the mob on. She was threatening to do things to Banker Harry that would have made Sheriff Miller blush if he hadn't been so worried he was about to be run over.

"Sheriff, you get out of the way. We don't want to hurt you, but that thieving Harry Hill is going to give a pound of flesh for every dollar he's stolen from us," Bill Roberson shouted. He ran the funeral home, and led the local Boy Scout troop.

"Harry didn't steal your money. The bank's investments went bad." Sheriff Miller realized how weak that sounded, but he had to say something.

"Well, who was doing the investing?" The preacher over at the Church of Christ flung a ripe tomato at the stenciled glass door, splattering Burke.

"Brother Ted, what do the scriptures say about hurting old Harry?" Sheriff Miller asked.

The preacher shifted his position a little to hide his face in the crowd. Sheriff Miller kept his eye on Roy Burkhalter at the front of the mob. There was a chance he could talk the rest of them down if Roy would keep his trap shut. Roy was gripping his fat cigar in his teeth and growling and cursing about what they ought to do to the banker. Roy was good at getting other people to do his dirty work.

"Banks have been investing our money

since there have been banks. That's why we get paid interest. You can't blame Harry just because those Wall Street boys back East messed up," Sheriff Miller said.

"That damned Roosevelt gave the banks a holiday to give them time to sneak out of town." Those were strong words from the mayor, who was a yellow-dog democrat himself like the president.

"What's Harry paying you to protect him?" someone shouted.

"I see a lot of you out there that Harry has helped from time to time. What about you, Roy? Didn't Harry loan your father the money to put in the cotton gin?" Sheriff Miller asked.

"I had fifty thousand dollars in that bank, and now Harry tells me it isn't there." Roy Burkhalter stepped forward and shook his finger a few feet from Sheriff Miller's face.

Sheriff Miller didn't believe for a second that Roy had that much in the bank. He'd learned long ago that you had to divide Roy's bragging by two, as he usually only had half what he claimed. And sometimes there wasn't even a half-truth in Roy's claims. He loved for people to think he was some kind of hillbilly tycoon. There were folks that swore he owned an interest in every business in the county, and he was glad to let them think that.

Roy had both his thick fists propped on his hips and was chewing on his cigar like he was grinding corn. "We ought to burn down the bank with Harry in it."

"I'll say it once again. Nobody planned on this depression. Go burn down the state capitol if you want to or march on Washington DC with barbwire hanging nooses, but Harry isn't to blame," Sheriff Miller said.

"How about that damned thieving boy of yours? If he was here we could tend to him too." Roy made sure he said it loud enough that everyone could hear him. "Maybe you and that squaw of yours are about as much to blame for raising a thief as Harry is for using our money and losing it."

Normally, Sheriff Miller would have ignored Roy to avoid appearing like he was protecting Claude or playing favorites. But Roy never should have brought Mary into the conversation. He whipped out his long-barreled Colt and busted Roy over the top of the head. He folded a crease in the crown of Roy's little beaver hat, and the steel barrel thumped pleasantly against the man's skull. The local tycoon fell limply at his feet. Looking at Roy's head lolled back and the white of his eyes showing, the sheriff realized that he might have killed the nickel-plated bastard, but he didn't really care at the moment.

Somebody in the rear of the mob threw a beer bottle and it barely missed Sheriff Miller's head. He knew things were about to get out of hand. People had just heard that they lost all their savings, and the nearest bar was only a block away. Not a good combination. He nodded at Burke behind him. The deputy pointed his shotgun skyward and let off a round. The crowd quieted some, and the second boom had them backing up.

"You people disperse, or I'm going to haul you all to jail," Sheriff Miller shouted. "I promise you that Harry is doing everything he can to figure out a way to get the bank back on its feet, and my son will stand trial for running off with your money."

He took two steps forward and Burke found the nerve to follow him. A few more insults and threats were thrown their way, but they were halfhearted. The mob slowly fizzled and drifted off.

"That was close. I've lived with those folks all of my life, and I've never been so scared," Burke said after he let out a big gust of air.

"I'm going to haul Roy down to the jail. You stay here and guard the bank until I can get another deputy to relieve you."

"Maybe Harry should get out of town for a while."

"See if you can talk him into it." Sheriff Miller doubted Burke would have any luck with Harry. The bank president was eighty years old and feeble, but he was as stubborn as a mule. It would take more than mobs and death threats to run him out of the town he helped build.

Roy was stirring a bit and feeling around at the growing knot on the top of his head. "You sumbitch. I'm gonna have your badge for this."

"You promise me you'll either go home to your wife, or to that whore you keep across the railroad tracks. You do that and I'll not throw your sorry ass in jail," Sheriff Miller said.

Roy looked like he wanted to fight, but Sheriff Miller knew better. He was all mouth. Roy had hated him since they were both teenagers, and getting whacked over the head wasn't going to make things much worse than they had always been between them.

Burke swore that Roy was jealous because the two of them had gone off to war when he hadn't. Everybody in town knew that Roy's daddy had paid off the doctor to have Roy determined physically unfit for soldier-

172

ing — something about asthma or the like to keep young Roy from having to join the Army and get shot at by Kaiser Bill's boys over in Europe. Roy was a big-shot high roller and a town tough down at the local bar, but he couldn't hold a candle to the Sheriff and local war hero, no matter how hard he talked himself up to anyone who would listen. Roy felt he was better than any man in town. Listening to people brag on Sheriff Miller's war record and watching him and his skinny deputy marching in the city veterans' parades was bound to bother a blowhard like him. Roy could flash his diamond ring and jaunt around town in his Lincoln with his mistress all he wanted, but he was never going to have any war stories to tell.

"This ain't over between me an' you." Roy gathered up his smashed hat and dusted himself off.

"You know where I'll be," Sheriff Miller said.

"Hey, Roy," Burke said when Roy turned to go. "You forgot your cigar."

Roy caught the smashed stogie that Burke threw him and jammed it in the corner of his mouth. "I'll get you too, you bony bastard."

Burke patted his shotgun. "The Sheriff

173

here will be nice and whip your ass, but I'll put a hole in you that you could drive a tractor through. So, you come on anytime you're ready."

Roy tried to smile like he didn't believe Burke and disappeared into the bar down the street. He would tell his cronies how he was going to whip the Sheriff the first chance he got.

Twenty minutes later Burke showed up in the door of Sheriff Miller's office.

"I take it that Harry's safe?" Sheriff Miller asked.

"Randy showed up and took over. I told him to drive Harry home when he's ready." Burke pitched his hat on Sheriff Miller's desk and took a seat in the chair facing him.

"How's Harry taking it?"

"He scared to death and ashamed to boot, but he's going to stick it out."

"Well, I hate what's happening to him, but he'll have to get by like everyone else."

Burke studied the ceiling fan so he didn't have to look at the Sheriff. "He was asking me about Claude again. Seems he's calling around trying to get a reward put up on him."

"That's to be expected."

"And he told everybody that came in that the bank wouldn't have gone broke if it wasn't for Claude."

Sheriff Miller leaned back in his wooden office chair and propped both his boots on the desk. "That isn't what he told me two days ago. He said that if all his depositors had shown up at once a month ago he couldn't have given them their money."

"He told that to me too, but that isn't the song he's singing now," Burke said. "Claude better never show back up in this town."

"Damn it!" Sheriff Miller gave a fly on his desk a resounding whack with a rolled up newspaper.

"I don't think most folks will blame you for what Claude did," Burke said.

"The only thing that shames me is that I'm afraid I'm more ashamed of Claude than I am worried about him. That's no kind of father at all."

"None of this is your fault." Burke had said that before, actually multiple times since Claude went bad.

"Maybe I was too hard on him. I've never known what you say to a kid, much less a boy who thinks he's outgrown his britches and wants to be a man."

"There isn't a thing you can do for Claude. He's made his own bed, and now he's got to lie in it," Burke said.

Just to prove Burke correct, a big-hatted

175

shadow filled the open doorway. The lanky deputy twisted around to see who was behind him. The shadow was wearing a pale gray Stetson with a wide ribbon hatband, and his cowboy boots were polished until they looked like glass. A pearl-handled, engraved 1911 automatic rode in a tooled holster high on his right hip. What was more interesting to Burke was the badge on the man's shirt. Their visitor was none other than a Texas Ranger.

"I take it that you're Sheriff Miller?" the Ranger asked, stopping in front of the sheriff's desk.

"I am. Should I know you?"

"I was recently informed that some Louisiana lawmen found a set of dog tags with your name on them."

Sheriff Miller didn't know what to say to that.

"They found those dog tags at the scene of an armed robbery," the newcomer added.

"I don't guess you think I did it, or you would have your hand on that pearl-handled pistol," Sheriff Miller said.

"Mind if I have a seat?"

Burke got up and offered the Ranger his chair, and dragged up another for himself. He spun it around and sat in it backwards, far enough away from the desk that he could see both of them.

"I'm Sergeant L. T. Jones of the Texas Rangers," the Ranger said as he seated himself.

"Well, Sergeant, I guess I'm about to hear the rest of the bad news," Sheriff Miller said.

"Somebody in our office saw a piece in the newspaper about your boy, Claude, being a suspect in robbing your local bank. He immediately put your name and his together as soon as he heard about the dog tags."

"And?" Sheriff Miller could tell there was more coming.

"The McKinney, Texas, police department found the car your son stole off the agriculture agent inside their city limits. It seems that a young man pitched the keys to a boy working for a Ford dealership there, and drove off in a brand-new car."

"And?"

"The kid he gave the stolen car said he was with a young, pretty blonde."

"Any idea who she might be?" Sheriff Miller asked.

Sergeant Jones shrugged. "Could be anyone. I've got a list of bad girls and gun molls a mile long. Although, I think we can rule out Bonnie Parker."

"Clyde Barrow shot Deputy Moore over

177

at Stringtown last summer," Sheriff Miller said.

Sergeant Jones shook his head. "Bonnie might have bleached her hair, but I doubt the blonde we're looking for is her. She only works with Clyde, and that wasn't him you found shot dead on the river. I looked over the photos you mailed to your state capital."

"I thought Alfalfa Bill was mad at you Rangers over blocking his bridge," Burke said.

Sergeant Jones laughed. "Your governor is a tough old bird, and sharp as a tack, even if he tries to play himself off as a hick farmer. I thought he was going to have the National Guard shoot us if we didn't let traffic cross the Red River."

Burke well remembered when a bunch of Texas businessmen who owned another toll bridge across Red River had convinced their state government not to allow people to pass on the new public bridge. Alfalfa Bill Murray had marched his National Guard troops down to the bridge, Texas and the Devil be damned. It had been all over the news-papers, but the Toll Bridge War hadn't amounted to much, other than a chance for reporters to take pictures of Rangers and Oklahoma National Guard troops staring at each other across the bridge. Regardless,

178

Alfalfa Bill got his way, and Texas backed down and traffic started flowing.

"Sounds like he's working with you now," Burke said.

"That hayseed politician doesn't like criminals any more than my governor does," Sergeant Jones said.

"Your new governor is a criminal," Burke observed. "I hear Ma Ferguson stole more money the first time she was in office than all the hoodlums in Texas combined."

"Didn't they impeach her husband when he was governor?" Sheriff Miller asked.

Sergeant Jones grinned. "Didn't you hear her campaign slogan? 'Me for Ma, and I ain't got a thing against Pa.' "

"The Sherman newspaper said she's going to get rid of you Rangers." Sheriff Miller was an avid reader, if only to remind him that the world was indeed insane.

"True, but she's also pardoning a hundred prisoners a month. At least she'll keep us busy until she fires us," Sergeant Jones said.

Burke snorted. "Politicians are barely better than child molesters."

"Maybe so, but at least she and Alfalfa Bill aren't feuding," Sergeant Jones said. "His state troopers and justice boys are giving us all the help they can, and we're doing the same for them. The thing is, no mat-

179

ter how we cooperate, our communications are too slow. By the time we get somebody on the scene the crooks are usually long gone."

"If we had more phone lines in rural areas we might stand a better chance," Sheriff Miller said. "Or maybe somebody will figure out how to get a radio to work in a car. We communicated with them in the war, but not in vehicles."

"We still catch a few of them. Time is on our side if they keep up their meanness."

"And you never suspected me when they found my dog tags?"

Sergeant Jones grinned. "Well, I admit we made a couple of calls, but everybody up this way laughed at us when we mentioned you as a thief. Seems like you're some kind of Alvin York up here."

"You can hear all kinds of foolish rumors," Sheriff Miller said. "Deputy Burke here was over there with me, and so were a lot of others. I didn't do anything special."

"I wouldn't call the Congressional Medal of Honor a rumor, nor anything to snicker at either," Sergeant Jones said. "I myself was at Hamel and the Marne."

"I noticed your limp," Sheriff Miller said.

"Shrapnel." Sergeant Jones shrugged.

Sheriff Miller simply nodded. "It was a

bitch, and there are a lot of men who deserved medals far more than I did. In fact, we've got a Choctaw fellow around these parts by the name of Joe Oklahombi. Some folks call him the Indian Sergeant York. They say he and his Choctaw code talkers captured a whole company of Germans."

"You and I both know that there were a lot of brave men over there on both sides, but it still stands that you're a man of some reputation. I read in *Life Magazine* how you caught that hobo killer. There's no telling how many people he murdered across half the country. You did what a lot of lawmen couldn't."

"Old Burke here had more to do with guessing who he might be than I did, but the way it turned out, I happened to be the one who shot him when he tried his knife on me." Sheriff Miller waved off the praise with his hand, as if it were something tangible in the air.

"Regardless, nobody is going to believe for a second that you are robbing country stores and shooting at little kids and priests." The Ranger sounded to Burke as if he was running out of patience with all the small talk.

Sheriff Miller swallowed the Ranger's latest revelation with the last of his coffee. He grimaced, more from the mention of his son shooting at kids and priests than from the strong, bitter brew in his mug. He went over to the little propane stove and poured himself another cup. He reached into his hip pocket and pulled out Burke's pint bottle of whiskey and poured a glug into his coffee, and then another one for good measure. He'd meant to give the bottle back, but somehow hadn't. Burke was watching him and the bottle, but he ignored his deputy. Sometimes Burke was too smart for his own good, and his silent stare was the same as telling him he was drinking too much.

Sheriff Miller looked at the Ranger and pointed at the coffeepot. "Care for some?"

"The coffee or the whiskey?" Sergeant Jones asked.

"Either one."

"I'll have some coffee." Sergeant Jones waited while Sheriff Miller poured him a cup.

"No thanks. Whiskey doesn't set well with my work," Burke said, even though he hadn't been asked. He tried to appear like he was gazing out the window without a care in the world, but he was watching the Sheriff out of the corner of his eye.

Sheriff Miller scowled at Burke, but let the jab at him slide. He turned back to the Ranger. "From what you're telling me, I gather that you think my son tried to kill a priest and little boys."

"Maybe I went too far, speculation, you know. The facts are that the Louisiana boys found your dog tags at a robbery scene. However, the witnesses' descriptions of the thieves matches a bunch who shot at a priest and some choir boys down the road a piece."

The Sheriff gave up on his coffee and took a snort straight from the whiskey bottle. "I gave my dog tags to Claude when he was a little boy. He was wearing them the last time I saw him, but that doesn't mean he's shooting at preachers and kids. I know him better than that. He may have gone bad, but he isn't a killer."

"Your own report says that you think he shot that fellow on the river," Sergeant Jones threw back without any passion, more like he was playing the devil's advocate.

"That might have been self-defense."

"Might have," Sergeant Jones agreed.

"Go to hell," Sheriff Miller said.

Sergeant Jones held up both palms as a peace offering. "Hold on there. I didn't come to argue with you, or to accuse your son of anything."

"What did you come for?"

"I need your help."

"I'm listening."

"Would it be safe to say that you know your boy better than any other peace officer out there?"

Sheriff Miller found that to be a difficult question, but he gave the Ranger the answer he was wanting. "Yes."

"Do you think you could fairly and impartially come to Texas and help us locate him?"

"The boy's mother might tell you I've always been harder on Claude than anyone."

Sergeant Jones reached in his pocket and pulled out a piece of paper and a badge. He pitched them both on the desk. "There's a badge deputizing you. The paper states that your authority extends to every county in the state of Texas, and you're to work with me."

"And you trust me to help you catch my boy?"

"Do you believe he will eventually be caught?"

"Yes."

"Would you rather have some trigger-happy locals shooting at your boy, or a chance to see to it that he might come peaceful?"

184

Sheriff Miller frowned. "Don't lie to me. You need help catching Claude, and don't give a crap how you get him."

"True, but I will promise you that I'll do everything I can to give him a fair shake. Both of us might get what we want."

"What the hell did Claude do in Texas?"

"Somebody spotted a Ford Woody north of Beaumont like the one stolen off the priest. The priest said there were four men in the gang, and a girl. Texas is bound and determined to clean up the thugs and holdup artists that keep the newspapers in business."

"They sicked a Ranger like you on a small-timer like Claude?" Burke asked.

"We've reason to believe that Claude may be working with a man we've been trying to get the goods on for a long time."

"You can't find this fellow?" Sheriff Miller asked.

"We know where he is, but we haven't been able to pin any robberies or thefts on him. He's got the gambling rackets sewed up in Dallas, but we suspect he's fencing stolen bonds and other goods and providing protection for a cut of what his crews steal," Sergeant Jones said.

"If you're right, it sounds like Claude isn't

185

hanging out with the local choir," Burke said.

"Sheriff Miller, you give the sheriff over at Calcasieu Parish, Louisiana, a call and have him tell you about the crew your boy's running with and how they operate."

"I will."

Sergeant Jones stood up. "I'm going to walk to that little café up the street and have me a glass of milk and a piece of pie. That ought to give you time to decide what you're going to do."

"And if I decide to go with you?"

"I'm headed back to Dallas tonight." Sergeant Jones went out the door without another word.

Burke studied Sheriff Miller. "What are you going to do?"

"What the hell do you think I'm going to do?" Sheriff Miller asked. "I'm going with him and hope I can help him catch Claude before somebody else does."

"Don't get grumpy with me," Burke said. "I just thought you were taking an awful long time to decide."

Sheriff Miller laughed. "I was wondering how to tell all this to Claude's mother."

"Mary will hold up. At least knowing Claude's alive will be something."

Sheriff Miller went over to the cabinet

phone on the far wall. He picked up the earpiece, but paused. "You think you can hold down the fort while I'm gone? There might be another lynch crowd wanting Harry's neck."

Burke wallowed the chew of Redman tobacco to his other cheek, and hefted his shotgun off of the floor beside him. "I'll load old Thunder here up with a little Number 8 birdshot just in case Roy Burkhalter gets sassy again and needs his ass peppered."

Sheriff Miller couldn't suppress a grin, and he could tell his deputy was pleased to have lightened his mood, if only for a moment. Burke was more than just his deputy. He'd known the man since they were both kids, and gone off to war together. Burke was only thirty-nine, the same age as Sheriff Miller, but didn't look it. His hair had gone gray early and with his willowy stooped frame he looked a decade or two older than he was. But then again, Burke had always been mature and wise beyond his years, even if it was hidden behind his wit and banter. If Sheriff Miller counted on him more than anyone, it wasn't only because he looked the older of the two.

"Wish me luck," Sheriff Miller turned his back on Burke and rang the operator.

"Call me a sap, but I still believe in happy endings," Burke said as he went out the door to give the Sheriff some privacy. "And don't you let Mary believe any different."

CHAPTER ELEVEN

"Hunger doesn't need much encouragement. It just keeps coming around naturally."

— Will Rogers

Claude stared out the windshield into the night, looking for the shine of passing cars or a light to turn on in the house just up the driveway. He felt like he ought to hold Myra's hand, but she didn't seem as concerned with their predicament as he was. He decided to play it calm and cool, as if he'd ever been parked on the side of a farm-to-market road in Texas in the middle of the night waiting with the headlights out while Dink went to steal them another car.

"He's taking an awful long time," Claude said.

"Don't worry about Dink. He's the best car thief I've ever known." Bull was leaned back behind the Woody's steering wheel with his hat down over his eyes.

Ernest snored in the backseat. He always snored, but it had gotten worse since Bull busted his nose. The sounds coming out of his throat and nasal passages sounded more akin to a choking hog than to a man's breathing.

"Couldn't we have found a car that wasn't parked so close to someone's house? That looks pretty risky," Claude said.

"Quit your worrying. Dink never gets caught," Bull said.

"I seem to recall him mentioning that he spent two years in the big house down at Huntsville for stealing cars," Myra said.

"That was when he was learning," Bull said.

"I hope they don't have a dog," she said.

Claude wished she would quit pointing out potential problems. Stealing made him edgy. "I think I see him coming now."

Bull lifted his hat brim and they watched the shadow of the car backing down the long driveway to them. No dogs were barking, and all of the lights in the farmhouse were still off. Dink pulled alongside them and they quietly transferred their belongings to the new car. Ernest was hard to wake up and had been saying all day that his head didn't feel right. He promptly went back to sleep once he was in the stolen car.

"She isn't a Ford, but she'll do," Dink said patting the steering wheel of the Chevrolet.

"Get in the back with Ernest. I'm driving," Bull said.

"Why can't Claude or Myra ride back there with him? He smells like a litter of pigs," Dink said.

"Ernest is your sidekick. You ride with him."

Dink did as he was told, and they closed their doors gently and quietly. Bull drove more than a mile with the lights off until they turned onto the highway.

"How far is it to Dallas?" Claude asked. "It can't be far."

"We aren't going back to Dallas, not yet," Bull said.

Myra patted his thigh. "I told you I had two little jobs worked out, and this next one's going to pay big."

Claude didn't want to pull another job, at least not with his present company. All he wanted to do was to take Myra and get as far away from Diamond Joe's boys as he could.

"Don't worry, sugar, I'll make Bull stop somewhere along the way," Myra cooed. "We've got a long drive ahead of us, and I positively want to go dancing."

"How do you find out about these jobs?" Claude asked.

Bull and Dink both snickered.

"Why, sugar, that old lady at that store back in Louisiana had a son who got himself locked up with a fellow I know," Myra said.

"You mean her own son told a crook and a convict about the safe she had?"

"Her son was planning the job himself, but he's still waiting for his parole." Myra patted his leg again. "I told you, don't trust anybody."

It was a long walk to Minnow Charlie's, but Mary Miller had never learned how to drive. Her husband would have driven her if she asked, but she didn't want him to know where she was going. He wasn't the least bit prejudiced, but he didn't set a lot of store by Choctaw shamans.

Mary gathered her skirt with one hand to keep it from being torn by the brush on the edge of the trail. It was a hot day, but she much preferred walking along the river and sweating than being swarmed by mosquitoes in the cool of the evening. She was a fit woman, and her slim legs made quick work of the trail. Minnow Charlie's place came into sight beneath a large grove of water oaks.

Minnow Charlie was a widower. He had built his wife a fine house, but after her death he had decided to take the screens off the windows and the screened doors to make minnow traps out of. He made his living selling bait to fishermen, thus the name the locals had given him.

When Charlie's wife had been alive, their home was neat and tidy, but she'd been dead for many years. The once-white picket fence surrounding the house was peeling where it hadn't rotted down, and was almost hidden by weeds and junk he had accumulated in his years as a widower. For some reason, he had removed the front door, probably to burn in his stove sometime when he ran short of firewood. Southeastern Oklahoma was hot and humid in the summertime, and he'd moved some of his furniture out into the yard under a shade tree. He was sitting in a rat-chewed sofa when Mary walked up.

"*Halito,*" Mary said.

"Hello, Mary." Charlie wouldn't wear the teeth his dentist made for him, except when he was eating, and it gave him a little lisp and nearly folded his wrinkled face in half when he closed his mouth.

Charlie had been old when Mary was a teenager, and was at least on the far side of eighty. Like her, he was a full blood. He was barefooted, and the white shirt behind the bib of his tattered overalls was stained to more the color of old ivory. He fanned himself with a wild turkey wing and studied the minnow trap he was building and had laid out before him. As old as he was, he would walk for miles to retrieve old scraps of hardware cloth and various other wire that people were about to throw away.

"How have you been, Charlie?" she asked.

"Shhhh, the spirits are talking to me," he said, holding one finger to his lips.

She waited a polite amount of time, until she was sure that Charlie was thinking about his latest minnow trap and not conversing with spirits. "I need your help."

"I'm not a healer anymore."

Mary hadn't come to see Charlie because he was a healer. At one time he had the reputation as a fine medicine man and seer, but she thought he had gone a little crazy and senile.

"I'm looking for Betty Ludlow." Mary had heard that Betty was living in a cabin in back of Charlie's house.

"Huh?" Charlie was about half deaf, and he cupped a hand to his ear. "Are you wanting to talk to spirits, or your fortune told?"

"No, I just want to talk to Betty." She

leaned far over, closer to the ear he had cocked her way.

"Well, you still might need to consult the spirits. Betty is a much better seer. I can still hear the spirits sometimes, but I can't talk to them anymore," he said. "You'd better go talk to Betty or that gypsy woman in town."

"Is Betty around here?"

Charlie jerked a thumb back over his shoulder. "Just follow the trail."

Mary eyed the wild growth behind Charlie and couldn't discern a trail through it. She stood there for an uncomfortably long time waiting for him to give further directions.

"You wanting some minnows?" He looked up from wiring the minnow trap, surprised as if she'd just walked up.

Mary smiled and shook her head, and walked past him. She did manage to find a trail of sorts weaving through blackberry bushes as tall as her head. Snakes loved berry patches, and she kept a careful watch on the edges of the path. A big rattlesnake might be lying in the shade of one of the bushes. Her bare ankles were no match for a viper's fangs, and she hoped she made it clear of the blackberry thicket with only a dose of chiggers. The invisible little bloodsuckers loved berry patches too, and her skin was already itching thinking about them.

Betty Ludlow was picking dewberries at the edge of her little log cabin. She waved at Mary when she saw her. Betty was shorter than the dewberry bushes and clumps of Johnson grass, and her cabin's roof was barely head-high on a short person. Mary might have missed both of them if she hadn't been lucky enough to wander right on top of them.

Betty motioned Mary to follow her, not asking what she'd come for. It had been years since they had seen each other, but there was a time when Mary often sought her out for advice. Betty was a well-known traditional Choctaw healer, and some even swore that you could throw a rock in a mud puddle and she could read your future by studying the disturbed water. But Mary had never asked her for magic. Betty was simply the most levelheaded person she knew. Sometimes it helped to have someone to talk to, especially someone who would listen. Jim — she might have been the only one in the whole county who didn't think of him as "the Sheriff" — tried to talk with her, but he wasn't much of a listener.

Betty didn't lead her to the cabin, but

rather to a small hut of sticks beside it. A few old quilts and a surplus canvas Army tarp were draped over the pine pole framework. She stripped out of her summer dress and motioned Mary to do the same. While Mary was looking around modestly, the old woman retrieved a bottle from the springhouse and plucked a bucketful of smooth creek stones from a bed of coals beside the hut. She took her gatherings and pushed aside the flap that served as a door and disappeared inside. Mary stripped down and folded her clothes neatly on a large rock. She felt a little girlish giggle building in her at the thought of being so exposed in a strange place. Quickly, she followed Betty inside.

Betty was kneeling over the stones, which she dumped onto a little steel grate that looked like a camping grill. She took a ladleful of water from another bucket beside her and poured it slowly over the rocks. There was a hissing, and steam rolled up thickly, soon filling the hut.

Mary sat on a tanned deerskin laid out on the floor for just that. The room was hot and getting hotter. She smiled at Betty through the steam.

"What troubles you?" Betty was stoking up a little fire beside the hot rocks, and once it was smoldering she placed a pot full of liquid over it.

"Nothing, I just needed to talk to someone."

The old woman raked the sweat from between her sagging breasts with an antler scraper and smiled again. Her eyes were always calm. "Does the Sheriff need a little something to put him in the mood?"

Mary would have blushed if her face hadn't already been so hot. "No, Jim's fine."

"Most women come to me because their husbands think they've grown too fat after having children, and won't look at them anymore."

"Jim still loves me."

Betty nodded slowly. "Yes, he was always a good man, and at least smart enough to marry you."

"He's been a good husband."

"Well, it's plain that you're troubled." Betty poured a little water over the stones again.

Mary started to deny her worries, but Betty was smart enough to realize that there was a reason she had shown up after so long without visiting. "It's my son."

"Have you heard from him?"

"No," Mary said. "Wait, that's not true. He mailed me two hundred dollars a few weeks ago. No letter, just money. I never told Jim, and I left the money in an envelope stuck in the bank's front door."

"You look like you've lost weight since I saw you last. Have you been eating enough?"

"Yes . . . no. I can't quit thinking about Claude."

Betty motioned to the little pot. The liquid in it was simmering and giving off steam of its own. "Lean over this and breathe in."

"I'm not sick."

"Okay, but it will help you relax."

Mary did as she was asked. The stuff in the pot had a strange smell, but she took several deep breaths while Betty wafted the steam toward her face with a cupped hand.

"What's in it?" Mary asked when she leaned back.

"Yellow root, dandelions, and a few other mysterious things," Betty said.

Mary didn't know if it was the potion or the sweating that had her feeling more relaxed already.

"Now, drink this, please," Betty said in a motherly voice and offered a long-necked glass bottle her way.

"More herbs and medicine?" Mary held the bottle up between her face and the little flames beneath the cook pot, and swirled the red liquid around behind the glass.

Betty laughed. "Just some wild cherry wine I made."

"What's that supposed to cure?"

"Nothing, but it feels like we ought to get drunk," Betty said.

Mary started to refuse, but thought better of it. She shrugged her shoulders and took a long drink of the sweet wine. They passed the bottle back and forth between them for several minutes without talking.

"How is the Sheriff taking what Claude did?" Betty asked.

"He's blaming himself for it all," Mary said. "And I've smelled liquor on his breath more than once lately. I bet he hasn't drunk a pint of whiskey since he came home from the war, but he's drinking now."

"Just what has Claude done? You can hear all sorts of things if you listen to the gossips."

"We don't even know what he's done, and the not knowing has been the hardest on both of us." Mary expected a response, but Betty seemed to be waiting for more. "Some people believe that Claude stole all the money from the bank, and that he and some woman killed a man. Maybe he's done some other stuff. I don't know."

Mary took another drink of wine. "Jim

thinks there's something he could have done raising Claude that would have prevented all of this."

"What do you think?"

"Maybe Jim never let Claude make any decisions. He was good to him and looked out for him, but he doesn't understand about letting people make mistakes. No teenage boy likes being considered a boy. Maybe all the little bad things Claude has done over the last few years were a way of rebelling. He's fearless like Jim, and that makes it worse," Mary said.

"Do you believe that?"

"Jim says . . ."

Betty reached out and put a hand on Mary's shoulder. "What do you think? Not Jim, but you?"

"I can't reconcile the boy I raised and thought I knew with the truth."

Betty poured more water on the rocks. The steam grew so thick that her face disappeared and there was only a voice. "Can you stop loving your son?"

"No."

"Is he your son, no matter what he does?"

"Yes."

Betty opened a little hole in the roof to let the steam pour out of the room, and let the sunshine in. "And he's breaking your heart, and the Sheriff's?"

"Yes."

Betty offered the last of the wine. Mary was shocked that they had almost finished the bottle. She realized that she had no clue how long she had been in the sweat lodge.

"Why did you come to me with this?" Betty asked.

"Because you're my friend and because you're a wise elder."

Betty shook her head somberly. "I'm no wiser in these things than you are. I don't have the answers you're hoping for."

Mary sighed. She hadn't really expected Betty to able to heal her misery, but she was desperate enough to foolishly hope for a miracle. "No, I guess you couldn't."

"I do know that you can quit breaking your own heart. The sins of your son aren't your sins," Betty said.

"That's what I've been telling Jim."

Betty smiled and her teeth were as flawless as a young girl's. "Ah, see. You already know the answers."

"But I don't think I can take the worry."

"You and the Sheriff have to find strength in each other. You both tried to show Claude the difference between right and wrong, and all you can do is hope that he comes back to his raising. Until then, just hold on to each other."

"A Texas Ranger offered to let Jim look for Claude down there."

Betty clucked her tongue. "I'll give one other piece of advice. Don't let the Sheriff go. There's nothing but hurt in a father set against his son."

"It's too late. He's already gone, and I'm to blame for pushing him to do something that maybe nobody can."

"You're going to have to be very strong — for yourself, for the Sheriff, and for your family."

"Claude was always my favorite, but his sister never broke my heart." Mary was on the verge of crying.

Betty rolled a small coal from beneath the cook pot, and poked at it with a stick. "See. The brightest coals will burn you the worst. It burns so brightly that you can't keep your eyes from it, but you cannot hold it."

"I thought you said you were no wise woman."

"Age doesn't necessarily bring wisdom, but it does bring life lessons," Betty said. "I've outlived two husbands and raised children of my own."

"And what did you do when they strayed?"

"I prayed, and I hoped, and I drank cherry wine on the worst nights."

Betty cast a set of trinkets on the dirt floor before her. There was a hawk's foot, tiny bones, feathers, colored stones, and other objects Mary didn't recognize. The old woman clutched a little cross hanging from her neck and began to rock back and forth on her knees. She prayed to Jesus both in English and in Choctaw. She looked to the sun and called on gods long since forgotten by their people — animal totems, spirits, and ancestors returned to the dust. Mary was always a little bothered by Betty's blending of the pagan ways of old and Southern Baptist doctrine. She had mentioned it before, but the old woman seemed to see no contradiction or complexity in her strange mixture of faith.

Betty stopped chanting and looked once more to her baubles. "Do you think Claude tried to kill the priest and his children?"

Mary gasped. "How did you know that? Are you truly a seer?"

Betty raked up her trinkets with one hand and put them back in a little buckskin bag. She arched one eyebrow mysteriously and held it a while before she started laughing. "No, one of the Sheriff's deputies came to buy bait from Charlie and told him what the Ranger said."

Mary laughed too. For a moment, she had

been wondering if what many of the elders said about Betty was true.

Once she had regained her breath, she considered Betty's question. "I don't believe that. Claude will fight, but he's no killer."

Betty set the cook pot off of the fire and scattered the embers. "The little Claude I knew had a brave and good heart."

"Yes."

Betty went out the door and motioned her to follow. There was a clear creek beyond the sweat lodge, and they plunged in. The cool water washing away the sweat and grime felt delicious on Mary's skin.

Once they had swum a while, they went back to the lodge and dried off with towels that Betty offered. They dressed and Betty looked at the empty wine bottle they'd pitched on the ground in front of the door.

"I made more of that. Care for another bottle?"

Mary was tempted. "No, I'd better get home before dark."

Betty smiled wryly. "If I didn't know better I'd think the wine had gotten to you, and that the Sheriff was waiting for you at home."

"Betty!"

"What? Do you think I'm so old I've forgotten what it's like to get drunk and horny?" Betty mocked. "I'd find another man if he would only come around when I'm drinking wine."

Mary laughed more, and the pressure that had been filling her chest for weeks seemed to leak away with every exhale. It felt good to laugh again. She promised herself that she and Jim would find things to laugh about when he came home.

"Do you think I'm too old for a man just because my butt isn't tight like yours and my breasts aren't the ripe little plums they used to be?" Betty asked.

"I never said that."

"Well, you're right. I don't have the patience for men anymore, even if I still have the urge now and then," Betty said. "But the love never leaves our hearts, no matter how old we get."

"There's always your landlord," Mary said.

"Minnow Charlie? He smells like an old fish."

"Good-bye, Betty, and thanks."

"Don't wait to come see me when you're sad. Come visit and tell me good stories so I can remember that love."

"I promise I will."

Betty Ludlow may have not been a seer, but she was a healer. Mary's heart felt better than it had for a long time.

The old woman stood there long after Mary had disappeared into the blackberry maze. She watched a covey of quail flutter up on the far side of the brambles, possibly spooked by Mary's footsteps. She watched them fly low into the setting sun as if they were a sign, and listened to the quick flutter of their wings as if there was a message there. Her eyes grew sad. She hadn't told Mary everything. Claude was the kind that liked to live on the edge, and tempt fate. That kind didn't often live to see happy endings, no matter how much their mothers prayed for them.

"Claude isn't a half-bad dancer," Bull said.

"I'd rather watch Myra." Dink couldn't take his eyes away from her swaying hips as Duke Ellington and his orchestra jazzed through "It Don't Mean a Thing."

Ernest glared at the couple dancing by the jukebox under the light of neon beer signs. "I don't like that kid."

"Me neither," Dink added. "Bull, you either get rid of him, or Ernest and me are going to quit you and head back to Dallas."

Bull stared hard at the two of them long enough to see if they really meant it. "We've got a job left to pull."

Dink looked across the bar to make sure that Myra and Claude couldn't hear him. "Myra's already filled us in on the job. We don't need her, and we damned sure can do without the kid. Let me shoot him in the face."

"What've you got against the kid? I admit he's cocky, but no matter if we know Myra's setup or not, we might need an extra gun."

"You already told us that Diamond Joe gave you the go-ahead to whack the kid if he gets in your way," Dink said.

Bull sighed. Personally, he had nothing against Claude, but he had to admit that their take from the robbery in Louisiana had been smaller than what Myra had promised, less than three thousand. There was no telling if their next job would pay any better, and one less man in the crew would mean more for the four of them. They could even cut it to a three-way split, because they didn't need Myra to rob a bank. He nixed that idea quickly. He was secretly sweet on Myra. She was a cute little tart, and as sexy as red silk. And besides, Diamond Joe wouldn't tolerate them leaving her somewhere on the side of the road. Diamond Joe liked Myra too, but he wouldn't care if Bull knocked off his competition for Myra's affection by getting rid of her young beau.

"You want to leave him here?" Bull asked.

"And let him rat us out?" Dink returned.

"I want to kill him," Ernest said.

"I know Dink wants him because he shot Murder Mike, but what's he done to you, Ernest?"

"He's nothing but a filthy, mongrel Indian," Ernest said. "That Myra isn't any better to let the likes of him bed her."

Bull studied the two killers across from him. He wished he hadn't agreed to stop at the roadside bar in the first place, but Myra wanted some music and the rest of them were hungry. Had he kept driving through the night he could have avoided the conversation. He briefly considered letting Ernest and Dink take their cut of the Louisiana robbery and leave him. If Myra was right about the next job, it was going to pay well, and he could pull it off with just her and Claude. He never had liked Dink, and Ernest was insane. That was the thing about working for Diamond Joe — Bull sometimes didn't have any choice in important matters that might get him killed. He wondered if it would have surprised his boss to know how much he'd been thinking of what it would be like if he were the top dog. Diamond Joe was getting old, and a nervy, smart man might take over his whole operation with one bullet. He played with the slapjack in his coat pocket. It wouldn't even take a bullet, not if he kept his eyes open for the right opportunity.

Claude and Myra were coming toward them, laughing and clinging to each other.

Bull made up his mind. As bad as Ernest and Dink were, they were loyal to him. There might come a time soon when he would need some men who could take orders. They were both stupid enough to turn against Diamond Joe, should he decide to go that route.

"Wait until we finish this last job, and you can whack the kid before we get back to Dallas," Bull whispered.

"What are you boys all huddled up about?" Myra asked.

Dink leaned back in his chair and smiled. "Aw, nothing."

Ernest simply stared at the tabletop, and another one of those strange groans coming from his lungs.

"All that dancing's got me hungry." Claude dragged a chair out and took a seat.

Dink shoved a big bite of hamburger in his mouth and talked around it. "Eat up, kid. You've got a big day ahead of you."

CHAPTER TWELVE

*"I rob banks, because that's
where the money is."*
— Willie Sutton

There were only a handful of cars on the street when Bull pulled up in front of the bank — all of them coated in dust and making it impossible to tell if they had been driven to town that morning or had been sitting there a hundred years. The first word that came to Claude's mind was "desolate," but that didn't do the place justice. There was a café up the street a bit where most of the cars were parked, but the sun was glaring on the dirty glass that fronted the building, so that he couldn't see if anybody was staring back at him. The only sign of life in the whole damned town was a hound dog on the sidewalk. That wasn't exactly true. Somebody's milk cow had gotten loose and was picking at the weeds growing around the gas pump at the little station opposite of the bank. It was as if the town was dead, or at least slowly dying and gasping its last breath. Nothing stirred except the veil of dust drifting across the street on the hot breeze. Even the dog seemed affected by the tempo. He kept one lethargic eye on the cow across the street, but lacked the energy or the will to rise and chase her off.

The city limit sign had read "Booker, Texas, Population 435," but even if the dog and the cow counted, where were the other 433? Claude couldn't understand why they had driven a day and a night to the little spot in the road somewhere in the Texas Panhandle. The dog surely didn't have any money, and from the look of the withered bag on the cow, she'd gone dry.

"This town ain't too lively." Claude continued to study it through his window. "Myra, are you sure that this little farmer bank is still open? Maybe it already went broke and shut its doors."

Bull frowned at Claude in the rearview mirror and nodded at Myra on the front seat beside him. "You just tend to business, kid, and leave the thinking to your lady. If she says this job is ripe, then you'd better believe her."

Claude ignored Bull's scowl in the mirror.

"Looks to me like everybody here done went to California or was buried alive."

"In case you haven't heard, there's a damned Dust Bowl going on," Bull said.

Claude had noticed. The drought had been bad the last few years where he came from, but it was nothing compared to what they saw driving through western Oklahoma and the Texas Panhandle. Folks back in the mountains joked that there wasn't anything out west except flatlands and crops. The land was still flat, but there weren't any crops to be seen. It was odd to see not a hint of green anywhere. The countryside appeared as if you were looking at it through some strange, filtered camera lens. There was nothing but dust and more dust. Everything was covered in it, and to breathe was to taste it. In places the powder had piled so high on the barbwire fences along the highway as to cover them entirely like snowdrifts. Claude had never seen anything so horribly surreal. It was as if the whole country they were passing through was no country at all, but rather a desiccated skeleton lying upon the earth and waiting to blow away. Being there felt like lying in a grave with the grit already beginning to fill your mouth.

"I'm ready for some action." Ernest racked

213

the bolt on the Thompson submachine gun and stuck one foot out the door of the sedan. He looked even meaner with his nose taped up and with both of his eyes swollen and masked in one enormous bruise.

Claude smiled nervously at Myra in the front passenger seat. "I'd do almost anything to get out of this rough-riding Chevrolet. I'd think professionals like you boys would steal a Ford."

"Quit talking and go get us some money," Bull said.

"Come on, lover. It's time to make a living." Myra bailed out of the car and Claude and Ernest followed her inside the bank. Dink took a stand at the little brick building's front door with a short-barreled, pump '97 shotgun tucked under his overcoat. It was a genuine, Army surplus trench gun with a steel heat plate and a bayonet lug. Dink didn't have a bayonet, but Claude couldn't imagine a scenario where one would be useful for a bandit. A fellow would look kind of silly marching into a bank with one on the end of his shotgun. He begrudgingly had to admit that Dink had made an excellent choice in weaponry for the day's work.

Bull stayed behind with the car running and his eyes scanning the street. The three of them went in with their guns in the hand, ready for a show of force to get the bank under control if necessary. That was the way Bull had laid it out — go in strong and scare the shit out of the room before anybody had the chance to do something stupid. They wanted the people that saw them going in to know it was danged sure a robbery in progress.

Ernest pointed his Chicago Typewriter at the ceiling, but stopped short of letting off a burst. From the look on his face, Claude assumed Ernest felt as silly as he did. There they were bristling with guns, and there wasn't a single customer in the lobby. One tiny little man in a suit stood behind the counter smiling at them like they were selling magazine subscriptions or something.

"Lock that door behind you," he said.

Claude looked at him blankly, not quite sure what to make of him. The man was way too cool, considering what they were about to pull off.

Myra locked the door. "Hello, Uncle Walt."

Claude guessed any kind of man could have the name "Walt," but somehow he'd always associated it with big, overgrown fellows. But Uncle Walt wasn't as big as a minute. He looked to be somewhere around forty, with a suit and that snappy look people that handle money seemed to have. Myra had told Claude the setup, but the banker was still way too cool. Claude told himself to keep an eye on Uncle Walt. Some of the men back in Antlers who spent all day playing poker in Baxter's bar were tricky calm like that. They might look like they were half asleep right before they took all your money. Diamond Joe back in Dallas had that same look, like he was thinking on how to shake you down the whole time he was talking to you.

"I thought there was only going to be you and one other." Walt gave Myra a hard look.

"You can promise me that we'll have no trouble getting out of your town, but it's a long way back to Dallas," she said. "I thought I'd bring a little extra help to make sure I got back."

"You've no worries here." Walt walked back over to the cashier's counter and reached for something behind it.

"You just hold on there," Ernest leveled the Thompson on the banker.

Walt scowled at Myra. "You could have, at least, brought professionals."

Myra shrugged.

Walt turned his attention back to Ernest. "If you'll put that gun back down, I'll give you what you've come for."

Ernest didn't lower the machine gun, but he nodded for Walt to go ahead. The banker pulled a small canvas duffel bag from behind the counter.

"How much is there?" Myra asked.

"There's twenty thousand dollars, just like I promised you."

"I'm no banker, but pardon me if I still don't understand this deal," Claude said.

Walt looked Claude up and down, and didn't seem to find anything he liked. "It's simple. You take twenty thousand, and I take twenty thousand. You get the blame for robbing the bank, but also an easy heist. I get to pocket a cut and claim that you took everything in the bank. I'll handle any inquiries by the government auditors, and you provide me with an excuse for coming up a little short on deposits."

"That's pretty slick," Ernest mumbled. His lips were so messed up it was going to be a while before he was easy to understand again.

"I'd love to chitchat with you, Myra, but you know how it is." Walt held out the duffel to her.

"I guess you're about to tell this town that your establishment has gone bankrupt," Claude said.

"I couldn't keep the doors open another month as it was," Walt said. "Sweet Myra here simply provided me with a way for something good to come out of a highly embarrassing and distasteful business failure. Namely, that I walk away with something in my pockets."

"Is there anybody else in here?" Ernest walked past the counter and stuck his nose and the Thompson into each of the two back rooms.

"Just me," Walt said. "Are we through?"

Myra took the money from him, and then she showed him her little revolver. She held it right under his nose. "Where's the rest of the money?"

Walt gave her a fake smile. "It's all there, the whole twenty thousand. You can count it if you want to."

"I don't mean what's in the duffel bag. I mean your cut," she said.

"You'd cheat family?"

Myra smiled as thinly as he had. "Well, I'd like to see you profit, truly I would, but you know how it is."

"Please rethink things," Walt said.

"Oh, Uncle Walt, I've thought about this plenty," she said. "And don't expect me to feel bad about it. If I remember what my mother said about you, I'm sure you've been embezzling from this operation for a long time. I'd guess that the twenty thousand you say is your cut is more like two or three times that. You thought we'd be glad to walk away from here with what you've offered, and then you'd tell the police that we took more than twenty grand — a whole lot more."

"You've got me all wrong."

"It's going to take more than twenty grand if you want us to clean up your books for you."

"I don't suppose we can just call this whole thing off?" Walt delivered the joke poorly, probably due to the fact that he was mad, even though he tried to hide it.

"Are you going to cough up some more dough, or do I have to let Ernest here do his thing?" she asked.

"Myra, that's your uncle," Claude said.

She scoffed at the thought. "Uncle Walt here isn't anything more than what he appears. I remember a time when he held the upper hand on me, and he wasn't exactly merciful."

Walt eyed Ernest even more distastefully than he had Claude, but he wasn't scared, not even when he should have been. "I'll tell you once, Myra. Don't cross me."

"Ernest, why don't you stick your chopper in Uncle Walt's mouth and march him back to his safe," she said.

Ernest had only taken one step when Dink started pounding on the front door. "We've got coppers out here!"

They looked at Walt, and his smile wasn't faked anymore. It was positively smug. "I'll ask you one last time, Myra, do you want to rethink things?"

Myra went to the front door and unlocked it. Dink stuck one leg in the doorway and nodded down the street. "There's a county patrol car parked at the corner. The fellow behind the wheel is watching me."

"I'm guessing that they're working for you?" Myra threw back over her shoulder.

"Yes, and if it makes you feel better, they work much more cheaply than you." Walt leaned back against the counter and folded his arms across his chest.

"You're a nervy little devil, aren't you?" Ernest seemed as perplexed by Uncle Walt as Claude was.

"I plan, and I plan well," Walt said. "Did you think I didn't consider that a bunch of thieves might try and double-cross me?"

"There's another county patrol car down the street the other way," Dink said. He was holding his shotgun out from under his coat, plainly visible. "This deal is looking worse by the minute."

"What's to stop me from shooting you?" Ernest asked.

"While your intelligence might be debatable, I'm going to give you the benefit of the doubt and assume you realize that if you kill me the good sheriff of this county and his deputies are going to kill you in turn."

"I hate crooked cops," Dink said.

Myra had grown quiet, considering the ramifications of the latest developments in her little plan.

"How do we know they'll let us go?" Claude asked.

"You'll have to trust me," Walt said.

"Honor among thieves, eh?" Claude asked.

"There's no such thing," Myra said. "Put him in front of us and march him out the door."

"What about the rest of the money?" Ernest asked.

"Uncle Walt's got the trump card on us. We'll have to settle for what we've got."

Ernest took hold of Walt's arm and passed him off to Dink at the door, who in turn, poked his twelve gauge in the crooked banker's back. Claude could see the Chevy through the doorway. All the doors were still open and Bull was nervously revving the engine. They marched to the car with Walt and Dink and his shotgun in front. Dink held Walt at the back bumper while Claude and Myra jumped in the front seat beside Bull. Ernest took the backseat on the passenger side and closed his door and reached one arm out the window. Dink backed Walt into him, and soon as the exchange was made, he ran around and got in the backseat on the opposite side. Ernest held Walt on the running board with the Thompson shoved between his shoulder blades.

"You boys stay calm, and they won't risk shooting me." Walt's voice was beginning to sound not so brave.

Bull made a U-turn and headed south, and the car in that direction moved to block them. The other patrol car tucked in right behind them.

"But they can damned sure follow us." Bull gunned the engine and swerved left off of the street and under the canopy of the abandoned filling station. The Chevy's tires squalled and the car fishtailed wildly as they detoured around the patrol car in the middle of the street.

"Fucking coppers!" Dink shouted as he let off a round from his shotgun at the windshield of the patrol car.

Claude propped his Colt automatic on the side view mirror, but didn't want to shoot at any cop, not even crooked ones.

Bull skidded back out onto the street, and Dink hung out the window and continued to bang away at the two patrol cars behind them. Claude could hear his empty hulls bouncing off the roof of the car.

"What's that?" Myra pointed out the windshield at the immense black cloud on the western horizon.

"That's a hell of a storm," Bull said.

Bull's words didn't begin to describe the awful darkness that swallowed up the horizon. Nothing was going right for them. It was turning out to be a black day indeed.

Chapter Thirteen

"A huge cloud of black topsoil swooped down upon Laverne in the manner of a heavy cloud flattening out upon the earth and spread absolute darkness the like of which has never been experienced by most Harper County folk."
— The Leader Tribune, *Laverne, Oklahoma, April 18, 1935*

The dust storm was so bad that in a matter of seconds it blotted out the sun. It was barely noon, but it felt like midnight. Bull flipped on the headlights as the storm hit the car like a wave. It wasn't just wind; it was dirt — black, choking dust and dirt. The headlights were only a weak glow at the end of the Chevy's hood, and barely penetrated the cloud that surrounded them. Claude listened to the metallic grate of the blowing grit blasting the paint off the car with every gust of wind.

"For God's sake, let me go," Walt pleaded. He held one forearm up over his face, either to protect it from the biting wind, or simply because he couldn't bear to look at the highway passing just beneath his feet.

The patrol cars were only fifty yards behind them, but they soon disappeared in the blackness of the storm. Claude looked back and couldn't even see their headlights. Dink slipped back into the car, choking and wiping at his eyes. Sand was already building up on the rubber seals around the windshield and back glass.

"Roll your windows up," Myra said, coughing up dust.

"I can't," Ernest shouted, "not without letting go of your uncle."

Myra was struggling to make out the road ahead. "Our turn shouldn't be far from here."

"I'm going to stick to the highway," Bull said. "Those local boys probably know these back roads better than you do anyway."

"There's our turn." She pointed out something to their right, and apparently pretty close from her excited voice.

"Too late, I'm sticking to the highway," Bull said.

"I think those coppers gave up," Dink said. "Don't you think you ought to slow down?

I can barely see the hood ornament," she said.

"I'll take my chances." Bull growled like a bear and gunned the engine, asking for more speed.

Claude kept one hand on the dash, bracing for an impact he was sure was about to pop up out of the darkness. His heart was throbbing like a piston in his chest, and despite the danger, he was finding that he loved high-speed pursuits. Death might be inches from the front bumper, but he felt more alive than ever.

The car bounced violently and slid sideways, and something banged against the bottom of the floorboard.

"I thought you were going to stay on the highway," Myra said.

"I thought I was," Bull said.

"Slow down."

"I am." He was still doing sixty.

Claude saw the blur of a sign pass his window. They were still on some kind of a road.

They drove blindly for what seemed like an eternity. Walt kept screaming, and it was loud enough to be heard above the wind.

"My face, my face." It sounded like he was crying.

"I can't hold onto him much longer,"

Ernest said. "All the skin's about peeled off my hand."

Ernest was covered in dust, like the rest of the car. His eyes looked even stranger peeking out of the grime coating his face.

"Stop, please stop," Walt pleaded.

"I guess we've hauled him far enough," Bull said.

"Is that a house ahead?" Myra squinted into the storm.

"I think it's a barn," Bull answered.

"He can hide out there until this thing blows over," she said.

Bull slid the car to a stop. "You get off here, Uncle Walt."

Ernest gave Walt a shove, and the little banker staggered two steps and turned around in a confused circle. He stared into Ernest's window with watering eyes and his face red and abraded in places that looked like raw meat.

"You'd better kill me," Walt shouted in the wind.

"So long, Uncle Walt," Myra said. "I wish I could say I was sorry."

Claude was shocked at Myra's treatment of her own family. They had just robbed and kidnapped the man, and she was the same girl who braided little flower bracelets and cried over sad ballads. He felt it safe to say that she was full of contradictions.

"To hell with you, Myra. I'll be laughing when the buzzards are chewing on your slutty bones," Walt said.

"Buzzards?" Ernest asked. "I'll show you what you can do with your fucking birds."

Claude saw the look on Ernest's face, even through the dust and darkness. He saw the lifting of the Thompson and lunged over the back of his seat. He managed to get his left arm around Ernest's throat at the same moment the machine gun sprayed a burst into Walt's chest. Claude didn't see the banker fall into the ditch, because he was dragged into the back of the car, fighting to keep his chokehold. Ernest put both his feet against the inside of the door and shoved backwards. Claude was pushed over Dink's lap and his head smashed against the far window. He grabbed madly with his free hand for the pistol in his waistband while Ernest kept bucking and smashing him against the door.

Something clipped Claude hard on his left ear. Ernest's arms were flailing wildly, but after another blow to the head Claude realized that it was Dink slugging him.

"Finish that son of a bitch," Bull said.

Claude didn't have time to ponder whom Bull was talking about. Somehow, the door behind him flew open and he lost his grip on Ernest. Falling backwards out of the car, Claude landed on his shoulder blades on the driver's side with his feet still in Dink's lap. His hand found his pistol and he pumped two rounds up into the open door.

Somebody grunted and cursed, and there were two blinding flashes from the inside of the car and something punched Claude hard in the ribs. He couldn't hang onto his pistol. There was another flash, and he was feather light and spinning and falling into the storm.

"That'll help our profit margin" were the last faint words Claude heard before he gave in to the weariness pulling his body down and closed his eyes and shut his mind to the world, the pain fading as the Chevy disappeared into the dust.

Sometime later — maybe an eternity — he dreamed that he was dead. He had to be dead, because somebody was burying him. He could taste the grit in his mouth, wicking away all the moisture there until he couldn't even swallow. The powder packed in so tightly and rapidly that he couldn't spit it out or push it away with his thick tongue. It tickled his ears and filled his eyes until they grated in their sockets. He felt the hot, loose-grained sand pouring through his wiggling fingers. There was a weight on his chest and legs that he couldn't lift, and he was sure that he was almost entombed far below the ground. He arched his chest and strained against the load of earth. His body moved slowly while the world spun and he gasped for breath, blowing hot soil from his mouth and lungs. He rolled to his side, freed one arm, and reached as high as he could for the edge of his grave. His fingers found nothing. The wind howled, and he stared up at the dim white light shining down into his tomb. He waited for it to disappear, as shovelful by shovelful, the light steadily faded.

CHAPTER FOURTEEN

"Woman of shame who
played a hard game."
— Bonnie Parker, "The Fate of Tiger Rose"

Myra kept telling herself she wasn't going to cry. She reminded herself that she was one hard woman, and nothing about life could surprise her or hurt her. People came and went, and all that mattered was looking out for Number One. And if you didn't know who Number One was, you were probably one of those getting beat down. Nobody was doing anybody any favors in the real world, and you had to look out for yourself.

She clamped down on silly sentiment and the little soft spot she kept somewhere deep inside her, but she felt as if the hard shell she hid herself in was cracking like frozen glass, splintering and popping and spider-webbing all around her. She hated that feeling. She'd been a fool to let herself get hurt again, and that was nothing more than weakness. Weak people ended up hungry, beaten, raped, robbed, lied to, and hurt in ways that went beyond imagining. Nobody was ever going to hurt her again.

But they had — a damned fool country boy who wore his heart on his sleeve. She was just as much a fool for letting him get to her with all his pretty words and mooning eyes. He hadn't looked like someone who could hurt her, but maybe that was why she let down her guard. She'd been telling herself for weeks that his kind was always the victim, but it hadn't done her any good. In the end, she was just as weak as he.

The ceiling fan wobbled and clicked crazily, and barely managed to stir the air in the hot, sultry room. The single little window was open, but the curtains hung still and heavy. Myra could see the glow of the neon motel sign through them, the word "vacancy" in glowing red and blinking off and on with a maddening rhythm. The room was stiflingly breathless.

Normally, gin took the edge off, and made it easy to forget. But after three glasses, she only felt bitter. She leaned over her glass at the cheap little table beside her bed and listened to the sound of laughter coming from the room beside hers. Ernest and Dink were celebrating, and she hated them for it. They'd gunned Claude down without a thought for what they'd taken from the world, like setting fire to a pretty picture and not even missing it.

One more glass of gin, and she wasn't going to remember Claude anymore. She wasn't going to remember his cocky smile, the way he stood, or the silly look on his face when he looked at any kind of a gun. The booze would give her willpower. She wouldn't think of him looking up into the car stubbornly while Dink shot the life out of him. She wouldn't think of him squirming in the dust and dying on the side of the road, or of the way his hands felt on the side of her face. No, she wouldn't. There was no profit in memories; nothing but hurt in loving. Claude was dead or dying, and there was nothing she could do about it. As soon as they got back to Dallas she was going to take her cut of the money and go north where it wasn't so hot, and maybe where it even rained sometimes. She was going to rent a little house and sit in her kitchen and drink gin and listen to good music, far away from cons and murderers, and men who pawed at her. Nobody was going to hurt her, not with enough money in her purse, and not if she found a good enough place to hide. Money could buy anything.

She thought of the cash in the duffel bag under her bed, and calculated how far her cut of it would take her. Not far enough, and not as far as she wanted to go. She walked to the window and studied their car. It had a full tank of gas, but Bull had the keys.

The Diamond Joes and Bulls of the world knew how to get what they wanted. They just took it, as if thick skulls and brute arms gave them that right. There were some like Uncle Walt who hid their meanness behind a smile, and thought all the world was there for a remorseless sort to savage. Myra knew she had been born with different weapons. Enough lipstick and a good leg would trick any man, and a bright girl with sense enough to keep her smarts hidden could go far if she was brave enough to gamble.

"Here's to you, Claude Miller." She raised her glass — one last glass and toast to forget him. "My sweet Boy Scout."

She let the empty glass drop to the floor and went to the bathroom and washed and repainted her face. She studied herself in the mirror, and smacked her red lips and blew a kiss at the stranger who looked back at her. "Not bad, doll. Not bad at all."

She gathered the money and her little suitcase and went out the door without another look back. There was really nothing new about her. She was going to take what she wanted.

"Do you reckon he's dead?" a man's voice asked.

"No, but it's a wonder he's alive. Somebody has shot him twice, and he's breathed enough dust to kill most men," a woman said. "Help me dig him out."

"Is he a Mexican?"

"Looks like an Indian to me."

"I don't know, Mother. I'd say he's a Mexican."

"Why, he isn't much older than our Paul." There was the sound of a clucking tongue and then the grunting effort of two people struggling with a load.

"What about that other one over there? Why, it's Walter Neal."

"Dead. He's shot a lot more than two times. He's got holes in him the size of a quarter," the male voice said.

"His face doesn't look like he died peaceful."

"No. I imagine it hurt getting shot like

that, or maybe the Devil's already got Walter counting money."

"Well, we'd best load him too. You take his feet. The Indian was almost more than I could help you lift," the female voice said. "You may swear you're still in your prime, but my back is talking to me this morning. I'm getting to be an old woman whether I like it or not."

"They kind of look like ghosts covered in dust like that."

"We don't look much better."

"Mother, I never expected to find two bodies going to the barn in the morning."

"I don't think anybody ever expects something like this," she said. "Turn the windshield wipers on. I can't see anything."

"There's so much dirt blown over the road we'll be lucky to get back to the house without getting stuck."

"Dan, that young man is going to die if we can't help him."

"Getting to town might be touch and go. I'm not sure we're not in for another dust storm."

"I wish we had a telephone in the house."

"Looks to me like he may already be dead."

"He's still twitching."

"I don't think so, Mother. That's just him

bouncing around on the pickup bed."

"I think I see the sun."

"Do you mean that little glow over there? That's just the house lights."

Chapter Fifteen

"Look at me. I'm all shot to hell here."
— Doc Barker after his failed
prison break from Alcatraz

"Myra?" Claude called out sleepily.

"I don't know who Myra is, but she isn't here," a man's voice said.

Claude opened his eyes and found himself in a strange room. He had a terrible headache and struggled to orient himself. His shirt was gone, and he was wrapped from his armpits to his waist in white bandages that looked like ripped-up sheets. He looked down at his feet to make sure he hadn't lost his cowboy boots. Whoever had stuck him in the bed hadn't bothered to take them off.

Something stabbed him in the lungs when he tried to roll over onto his side in the sagging feather mattress that he lay on, and he gasped. A shadow flitted before him. He squinted his raw eyes at the silhouette standing before the window. Whoever it was moved, and blinding sunlight flooded the room.

When Claude finally lifted his hand from his eyes he considered the elderly man sitting in the parlor chair across from him with a battered .22 rifle cradled in his left elbow. Claude recognized it as a Savage bolt-action, Model 23A Sporter. A good, solid little gun.

"You just take it easy," the man said.

"I guess it's safe to assume the .22 is to keep pointed at me?"

"What? This old thing? I shoot rabbits out of the garden with it, back when we had a garden."

"You must think I'm dangerous."

The man considered that. "Let's just say I've got the gun to keep things polite between us."

"Is it all right if I sit up?"

"You just go ahead if you feel up to it."

Claude tried to rise, but the pain in his ribs was so bad he almost vomited. When that passed, he tried to roll off of the bed far enough to get his feet on the floor. That hurt equally bad, and maybe even worse. He decided to stay in bed for the time being.

"Are you a farmer?" Claude asked.

"I was before it quit raining," the man answered. "Are you a killer?"

"No. What makes you think that?"

"So, you didn't kill Walter?"

"He's dead?" Claude remembered the long burst from Ernest's machine gun.

"He is. Did the same folks that tried to kill you plug Walter?"

"Wouldn't do any good to tell you. They're long gone by now." Claude realized that Myra was gone too.

"If I was an optimist I'd say you were working for Walter and got caught up in one of his shenanigans," the man said.

"And if you were a pessimist?"

"I'd say you were part of the bunch that killed Walter, but they decided to double-cross you while they had the chance."

"You some kind of detective?"

"I'm not stupid," the old man said. "I found three different kinds of cartridge brass buried around you and Walter."

"Maybe a three-armed man did the shooting."

"Maybe, but I found this in your hand." He held up Claude's .32 automatic. "I don't think you look like a bank teller, and I don't think Walter was hiring bodyguards. Although, Walter was always a little shady."

"Who do you think I am?" Claude asked.

"I'm pretty sure you're one kind of outlaw or another." The old man pushed his wire-rimmed glasses back up his nose and tilted his head forward to peer out the upper half of the bifocal lenses as if to reappraise his wounded captive. "Are you a Mexican?"

"Choctaw."

"Well, I hate to tell my wife she was right."

"What are you going to do with me?"

"As soon as I'm sure that another dust storm isn't coming I'm going to have her drive into town and fetch the Law."

"I can wait a day. I'm in no hurry to go to jail."

The old man laughed. "A day? You've slept longer than that already. I bet my wife you wouldn't even wake up this morning. Fact is, I thought you were dead when I first came back in here to open your window shade."

"I hate to disappoint you."

"Thought you might like a little sunshine. That black sky can make a man gloomy. I think all the top soil in Ochiltree County got picked up off the fields by the wind and carried over here."

"Don't put yourself out on my account."

"If my wife comes in here with some food or something, you be nice and polite like

241

you are now. You hear me? For some damned reason you remind my wife of our son Paul that was killed in the war, even though you're an Indian."

"Was he a Mexican?"

"Now, don't you go to getting sassy on me," the old man said. "You don't seem like too bad of a sort for an outlaw."

"They come in all shapes and sizes," Claude said.

"Never ordered one."

"Well, you've got one."

The old man looked at the bandages wrapped around Claude's middle. "You're lucky you're alive. My wife and I don't know anything about doctoring. I think the bullet busted a couple of your ribs and then ricocheted clean out of you."

"I don't feel lucky."

"You're either lucky or have the constitution of an ox."

Claude thought back to his fight with Ernest and Dink. "Was I shot three times? I remember three gunshots."

"Not that we could find, but somebody did knot up your head pretty good."

"It feels like it." Claude gingerly probed around his skull until his fingers felt the knot and blood-matted hair above his left ear.

"You need a doctor. I picked a piece or two of bone out of your side, and you bled like a stuck pig. Besides that, your eyes look funny."

"I might surprise you. You just step aside and watch me walk out of here."

"Sorry, son. I'll let the Law tend to you. There's no telling what you've done, even if you weren't the one that killed Walter."

"They give murderers the electric chair, don't they?"

"Any jury that really knew Walter would probably just give you life in prison, but a death sentence is a possibility if you're guilty."

"I knew it could come to this, but I never thought it would."

"We've got time if you want to tell me some stories from your life of crime. Me and the wife don't have much company out here," the old man said. "By the way, I'm Dan."

"Hello, Dan. Pardon me if I keep my name to myself."

"Suit yourself."

Claude rolled over gingerly and faced the wall.

"You get you some more sleep. I'll just be sitting over here in my chair," Dan said.

Claude closed his eyes and wondered

where Myra was, and if she was okay. But his greatest worry was that she was fine and not missing him one bit. He had to consider the fact that Diamond Joe's crew had intended to eliminate him all along. And that led to the question whether Myra knew about their plan or not — or was in on it. Wasn't it she who warned him not to trust anyone? The cynic in him remembered that she had been willing to rob her own uncle, and even kidnap him. The thought that she might have been in on double-crossing him hurt worse than his wounds. He shoved back his doubts, and told himself Myra would never do such a thing.

He drifted off, but woke himself several times thrashing and jerking and sweating in his sleep, and causing his wounds to hurt. He fought Dallas gunmen and phantom thugs in his nightmares, and dreamed other crazy things that seemed so real as to not be dreams at all. And he dreamed of worse things — terrible things.

His tortured mind twisted his sleep so that somehow he was sitting in a church pew surrounded by strangers inside a great canvas tent. The fevered crowd with sweaty faces was staring at something rapturous, and Claude looked to the front of the tent. The hell and damnation Pentecostal evangelist in his black, starch-smeared, paper-thin and iron-fried suit, and his white hair as wild as Moses shouted to his congregation. His eyes like a rabid dog's found Claude in the crowd. He spat white froth with every word, and he beat on his black Bible like it was a stone tablet he'd carried down the mountain himself.

"The Lord knows ye, boy, like he knows every bird in the sky and every leaf on every tree upon the turning of the earth," the preacher's words thundered in Claude's mind. He couldn't look away from the thick, yellow-nailed finger accusing him and pointing at him like a sword that was about to run him through.

"He sees you in your every hour, and there will come a day when you shall be judged. The reward of the just man is heaven, but the wages of sin, I say the wages of sin, are hell and damnation. Weak is the flesh. Pluck out your eye if it tempts you, cut out your heart if it's impure. Beg for forgiveness, for one day, we will all face the Master. Signs, and more signs, babies starving and crops dead in the fields, wars and rumors of wars, famine and plague. I tell you, it isn't a depression, but the end. The day comes soon when He will smite all the iniquity from this earth and sweep the sinner into the boiling, hissing crack of hell."

Claude felt the earth moving beneath him. He broke away from the preacher's eyes and watched the earth between his feet slowly crack open. He could see the lava-red glow of hellfire, and the smell of sulfur gagged him. He wanted to run, but his legs refused to answer to his will. The great, bubbling maw opened until it swallowed him up, and he felt the flames searing his skin even before he started to fall.

CHAPTER SIXTEEN

"Banks are an almost irresistible attraction for that element of our society which seeks unearned money."
— J. Edgar Hoover

Claude woke up shortly before nightfall, and Farmer Dan's wife brought him a pitcher of water and several pieces of fried chicken. His head wasn't hurting as bad as it had been, and he managed to sit on the edge of his bed with only a few hard twinges from his sore ribs. He was sore and stiff all over, and felt like he had been run over by a truck. Despite his aches and pains, he ate the whole platter and drank the pitcher dry while the old couple watched him silently.

"That was good," he said sheepishly. "Thanks."

"You're welcome," the woman said. "I wish I had some buttermilk for you, but we sold our milk cow."

"That'd be spoiling me," Claude said.

The plump woman rocked in her chair and chuckled.

"Can you walk?" Dan asked.

Claude kept one arm against his wounded side and braced the other hand on the edge of the mattress. Dan picked up his rifle, but Claude ignored him and stood gingerly to his feet. As long as he didn't straighten all the way up or move quickly his ribs didn't hurt too bad. His head swam a little, but got better the longer he stood there. He took a few tentative steps while Dan kept his gun on him.

"Don't worry. I'm not up to running yet," Claude said.

"I'll watch you just the same. I'd say you're a dangerous man, regardless of your youth." Dan held the .22 one-handed, using his free hand to scratch behind the bib of his overalls. He then proceeded to scratch a couple of other places on his body.

Claude noticed that the woman was scratching too. "Ya'll eat up with something?"

Dan pointed to a great red whelp on his elbow, and then pulled back his collar to show the scaly rash on his neck. "It's the dust. Gives you the itch. We've tried just about every kind of salve on it, but rubbing down with axle grease before you go to bed and then a bath in the morning seems to work best. Folks around here've been wrapping their kids up in rags to go to school, covered up with just their little eyes showing like one of those Egyptian mummies you hear about. Teacher told me that all the grease on them has stained the finish on her desks and chairs."

Claude realized he was scratching at his own leg while he paced tentatively across the room and back. "How come all this dirt is blowing around?"

"If you plow a field until it's bare, and then it doesn't rain, you're going to have plenty of dust," Dan said. "I reckon we've about plowed ourselves all the way down to Hades."

The sound of car doors slamming drew all their attention.

"You can just keep on walking," Dan said. "That'd be the sheriff and the ambulance that just pulled up to the house."

"Dan, do we have to?" the woman asked.

"We already talked it out." Dan gave her a hug with his free arm.

"I feel sorry for you, son," she said. "I'm hope you didn't have anything to do with killing poor Walter. Were you framed? I've read all about people being at the wrong place at the wrong time."

"You've got the last part right," Claude said.

"Lord, woman, you've been listening to those radio shows too much," Dan said.

"It's just that he seems like a sweet boy," she said.

"You go down the stairs, and then this sweet boy and I will come behind you."

Dan waited until he couldn't hear her on the creaking wooden stairway any longer, and then he motioned with his rifle. "Go ahead."

Claude took the steps gently, pausing a few times to wince against the pain in his side. He was a long time making it out the front door. As he passed through the living room he noticed that the room was bare of furniture. The well-worn hardwood floor was missing even so much as a single rug. The weak, weird sunlight coming through the curtainless windows highlighted the coating of dust on the floor.

He stopped on the front porch. There were two patrol cars and an ambulance in the yard, but there was also a hearse. Two men were already slipping Uncle Walt into a body bag. The old couple had left the corpse in the bed of their pickup until help arrived. At the sight of Claude standing on the porch, the two county lawmen started across the yard with their guns in their hands.

"Where's Sheriff Donley?" Dan asked.

"He's gone to Perryton to comfort his mother," one of the deputies said.

Both of the deputies were giving Claude hard looks. One of them grabbed his arms and wrenched them behind him. Claude's knees buckled with pain, and it was all he could do to keep from crying out.

"Go easy. He's got some broken ribs," Dan's wife said from inside the house.

The deputy squeezed the handcuffs closed until they pinched the skin on Claude's wrists. "I put them on him real loose, ma'am."

The deputies started Claude toward one of the patrol cars. The one behind him wasn't a patient sort, and he gave Claude a shove in the back of the ribs with the barrel of his shotgun. Claude thought he could feel bones grinding together. The ambulance driver had gotten back into his vehicle.

The sun was indeed shining, but feebly, as if it had somehow gotten farther away than its normal place in the sky. There was a haze of gray over everything, even the air itself. The yard was covered in dirt, so dry as to be more like powder, with only an occasional clump of brown grass poking through. There were several different colors of dirt — some sand and streaks of black topsoil, as if the wind had blown soil from all across the country and set it down on that Godforsaken place. The front end of a tractor was barely visible under a drift, and the blown dirt had piled halfway up the west side of the house. Claude wondered if all that had happened in one storm, or if he were looking at years of catastrophe. The farmhouse and barn looked strangely out of place in such an apocalypse.

Claude noticed a one-ton International truck with stock panels mounted on the flatbed. All manner of household items and furniture were lashed on the back of it until the pile teetered well above the sides of the livestock racks. Pots and pans and other curious and miscellaneous items were hung or tied on the sides of the truck until it looked more like a mad peddler's display or a carnival wagon.

"Dan, it looks like you and the missus are leaving." Claude craned his neck around and purposefully smiled when he said it. The deputies were glaring at him, and it did him good to irritate them a little with his nonchalance.

"Going to California," Dan called out.

"My nephew's out there, and he wrote and told us he's found work picking fruit."

"I hear California is a paradise."

Dan hugged his portly wife closer to him, and tried to offset her worried frown with a halfhearted smile. "California doesn't want any more Okies coming out there, and there are rumors that they're stopping immigrants at the state line. But I reckon we'll make out."

"Well, maybe it rains there once in a while. There's that."

"That's right. Anywhere's bound to be better," Dan said it as if he'd read that in a Bible, or maybe deciphered it from ruins written in the drifting dust. "Anything's better than sitting around and waiting to choke."

"Enough small talk. Get your ass in the car." The deputy gave Claude another jab with the shotgun that knocked him against the side of the patrol car, wheezing for air.

"Aren't you going to take him to the hospital in the ambulance?" Dan asked.

"He doesn't look that bad to me," the deputy holding open the back door of the patrol car said. "Sheriff Donley gave us specific instructions to bring him to the jail if he could walk."

Claude bent into the backseat of the car

faster than he should have. He gasped in pain and tried to reposition himself while the deputy shut the door. Every breath hurt.

"Will you take him to the hospital after the sheriff talks to him?" the woman called out.

The deputy driving Claude paused with one leg in his car. "I promise you, ma'am. We're going to take care of him."

Claude watched as the mortician's crew slid the black body bag onto a stretcher and into the back of the hearse. After they had slammed the rear door shut, he noticed that somebody had written "wash me" in the dust coating it.

The deputy donned a pair of aviator sunglasses and adjusted his rearview mirror until he could see Claude. "You aren't going to the hospital, Injun. You're going to meet Sheriff Donley."

"Sounds absolutely fun," Claude said. "Is there going to be lemonade?"

"Keep chattering, Injun. I'm going to enjoy interrogating you."

"Why, Deputy, have we gotten off on the wrong foot?"

"You're going to wish your buddies had killed you before too long," the deputy sneered. "That banker you boys murdered was Sheriff Donley's brother."

Claude leaned his head back and closed his eyes.

Claude got to meet Sheriff Donley that evening. He wasn't much bigger than his brother Walt, but he was a whole hell of a lot meaner.

The beating didn't hurt so badly, not after the first hour. A man's pain receptors kind of got dull after a while. Neither of the deputies battering on Claude was especially good at what they were doing, and both of them were out of shape. After the initial fun wore off, they would punch him a few times or slap him around some, and then go lean against the wall heaving while the sheriff asked him all sorts of questions — mainly what his name was, who shot Walt, how much money did they steal, and who else was with him.

"Playing tough isn't go to get you anywhere," Sheriff Donley said. "We can do this all night long."

Sheriff Donley had a big belly and his arms were crossed and resting on it. He sat in a folding metal chair, facing Claude and the jail's two cells. Occasionally, he wiped at the sweat on his balding head with a red handkerchief. Claude couldn't see the sheriff out of one eye, and only dimly out of the other. Still, what he had seen before they started roughing him up convinced him that the sheriff was an exceptionally sweaty man. It wasn't that hot in the little jail, and his deputies were doing all the work.

"Your money is long gone," Claude muttered through his swollen lips. He had managed to duck around a bit, but he was still pretty sure they had broken his nose and at least one of his jaw teeth.

"You let me worry about that," the sheriff said.

"The only thing I'm worrying about is whether your deputies are going to have a stroke before they kill me."

The deputy that had driven him to the jail was the bigger of the two, and also the meanest. He must have loved his sunglasses, for he'd kept them on, even in the dark back room. He punched Claude hard. Claude wasn't dodging and twisting like he had been, not with his hands cuffed behind the chair, and after the long beating he'd endured. One of the punches caught him squarely on the gunshot wound. He felt the broken ends of his ribs grinding together again, and wheezed for air and cursed such cowards. And Sunglasses's punch hurt even worse because of the big diamond ring he was wearing, the same one that he pulled off of Claude's finger.

"Hold on," the sheriff said. "We don't want to kill him before he talks."

Claude's chin hung against his chest. He needed air, but it felt like his ribs were cutting into his insides every time he breathed. He coughed and blood splattered his knees. It might have been from his lips and mouth, but he felt as if something was torn loose inside him.

He raised his head defiantly at Sheriff Donley. "Why don't you take your brother's cut of the loot and call things even."

"It isn't about the money, and you've failed to consider that I've already got Walt's cut," Sheriff Donley said. "I'm going to make sure your cronies are caught. Call it having my cake and eating it too."

"I'm sorry about your brother."

The sheriff waved a hand to dismiss the thought. "I never really cared for him, but he did make us some money from time to time."

"I can tell you're a real sentimental sort," Claude said.

The sheriff leaned forward with his elbows on his knees. His face was only two feet from Claude's. "It's the fact that you disrespected me in my own backyard that bothers me. You don't come here and shoot my brother. You don't come here and double-cross me. This is my county, and I'm not a man to be taken lightly."

The shorter of the two deputies held up a carpenter's hammer. "Sheriff, do you want me to tap on his knees a little bit? Maybe take off his shoes and see how much he loves his toes?"

The sheriff waited until Claude was looking at him instead of the hammer. "Listen, things are fixing to get rough. I'm going to start from the top again, and you better answer quickly."

Claude spat blood on the floor and tried to grin. In truth, he was scared to death and hurting like he'd never hurt before. He couldn't keep up the brave act much longer, nor could he take another blow. He believed the sheriff when he said the deputies were just getting warmed up.

"Do you think that little slut niece of mine wouldn't give you up in a heartbeat if it would save her bacon or put cash in her pocket? Believe me, Myra would rat on you in a second," Sheriff Donley said.

Claude had already sworn to himself that he wasn't going to give up Myra's name. "I don't know anybody named Myra."

"Are you dumb? Do you think I'm dumb? Did you know Myra shot her own daddy?"

Claude kept his head down to hide his surprise.

"She shot him with his own gun while he was passed out drunk. You ever see what a twenty gauge will do to a man's head?"

Claude remembered Murder Mike's blood drifting on the water.

"She killed the only parent she had left, and ran off and left her little sisters to the state. What kind of woman does that?"

"I don't know any Myra," Claude said.

"Last chance, or I'm going to turn Cecil here loose on you with his hammer," the sheriff said. "What's your name?"

"Claude."

"Claude who?"

"Miller."

Sheriff Donley thought about that, and seemed to believe him. "Who else was with you besides Myra."

Claude hesitated, partially because he didn't want to tell, and partially because the sheriff wouldn't believe him if he answered too quickly. He didn't mind giving away Diamond Joe's crew. Putting Sheriff Donley on their trail would serve them right, but that might lead the cops to Myra. No matter what she'd done in the past, he couldn't bring himself to believe that she had been a party to shooting him and leaving him for dead.

"I'm waiting." Sheriff Donley looked to the deputy with the hammer.

"Hold on. Let me see, there was Bobby Hammers, Slick Wilson, and Joe Peters," Claude said.

The sheriff mopped his brow and dabbed at his fat neck with his handkerchief. "Use your hammer, Cecil."

"Wait." Claude's mind wasn't working right. The beatings had him confused and he must have bungled his lies.

"I can tell you're lying, Claude. You aren't very good at it," Sheriff Donley said.

"Alright, I'll tell the truth. Just give me time to think." Claude hated himself for caving in and for the fear that the sheriff had brought over him. His daddy would have looked the fat sheriff in the eye and laughed at him.

"Too late," Sheriff Donley said. "Don't get too carried away with that hammer, Cecil. I don't care if you cripple him, but I want him to be able to talk."

"We're just going to play 'this little piggy,' that's all." Deputy Cecil hefted his hammer and winked at the sheriff.

Sheriff Donley stood. "I'm going out for a

while. I don't want blood splattered on my khakis."

"We'll have him singing like a little bird by the time you get back." Sunglasses stepped in behind Claude's chair and held him by the upper arms.

Sheriff Donley paused just outside the room, listening expectantly for the sound of the hammer striking flesh. He'd been the sheriff of Lipscomb County for twelve years, and nobody disrespected him. Those pussies over in Ochiltree County would play by the rules when it came to prisoners, but he prided himself on being an old-time lawman. Crooks didn't deserve anything better than they gave their victims. The Indian was going to suffer until he talked, and then he was going to suffer some more. The state boys or the feds wouldn't ask too many questions if his prisoner was roughed up a little resisting arrest. Cecil was taking too long, and Sheriff Donley closed the door leading to the jail cells and walked out of his office. He would go down and make an appearance at the church house for the Sunday evening services. It never hurt for his constituents to think that he was a good man. There was another election coming, and he intended to keep his badge.

He turned on the radio in the corner until

Jimmie Rodgers was coming through loud and clear. "I'm gonna buy me a pistol just as long as I'm tall." He'd never really cared for the Singing Brakeman, but the hillbilly yodeling and moaning might provide some cover if the interrogation got a little noisy.

CHAPTER SEVENTEEN

"Don't give me a reason to kill you."
— Baby Face Nelson

Deputy Cecil was smiling as he walked toward Claude patting the hammer in the palm of his hand. Claude involuntarily curled his toes in his boots and promised himself he wasn't going to scream.

Deputy Sunglasses behind Claude put him in a headlock while Cecil knelt and pulled off his right boot and sock. Claude's legs were tied to the chair just below his knees, and he couldn't even kick the deputy about to smash his toes. The concrete floor was as cold as a tombstone against his bare foot.

Deputy Cecil pitched Claude's boot against the bars of the cell behind him, and picked up his hammer off the floor. "It's only fair that I tell you that this is going to hurt."

"You can beg if you want to," Sunglasses said.

"I'll even let you pick which toe I smash first." Deputy Cecil slowly passed the hammer over Claude's toes. "We can save your favorite until last."

"Kiss my ass." Claude tried not to watch, but the deputy behind him forced his head down.

"You just don't play well with others," Deputy Cecil said. "I'm going to have to put that on your report card."

"Dang, Cecil, you beat all. How do you think of all that funny stuff?" The one holding Claude was obviously having a good time. "You ought to be on the radio."

"He's a regular riot," Claude said.

"Eeny, meeny, miney, mo, catch a nigger by his toe." Deputy Cecil was showing off and moving the hammer slowly from one toe to another. "If he hollers make him pay, fifty dollars every day."

"Eww, that pinky toe is going to hurt." Sunglasses strained to hold Claude still.

"If I was you, I'd go ahead and scream." Deputy Cecil kept a watch on Claude's face while he reared far back with his hammer.

"You little bastard, you drop that hammer or it'll be the last thing you do." Myra was standing in the doorway between the front office and the cells. One of the duo had left his shotgun leaning against the wall there, and she had it pointed at the back of Deputy Cecil's head.

"You came back for me," Claude managed to say, despite not being sure she was really even there, and not some figment of his imagination.

"I wasn't sure, but I thought you might be too hardheaded to die."

Deputy Cecil dropped the hammer on the floor.

"Now you pitch your pistol back my way," she said. "Easy, you just stay where you're at."

Deputy Cecil slowly unsnapped his holster and took the butt of his revolver between two fingers. Myra put the barrel of her shotgun against the back of his head, just in case he had ideas of being a hero. Sunglasses let go of Claude and backed away.

"You stop where you are, Four-Eyes, and do the same." Myra kept the shotgun against Deputy Cecil's head, but focused her attention on the other deputy. "You look like you might do something stupid, like make me shoot both of you."

Neither of the deputies liked being disarmed by a little blonde in heels and a dress, but they weren't willing to argue with the shotgun. She seemed to know how to use it. Both of their pistols slid across the floor to her feet.

"Good boys, now you take the cuffs off my man."

Deputy Cecil untied Claude's legs while Sunglasses freed his hands. Claude fell over and caught himself with his elbows on his knees. He couldn't see well, but he did notice Deputy Cecil's feet.

"Have you got any idea what to do with these lawmen?" she asked.

"Lock them up." Claude was hurting too badly to think.

"You heard the man," she said. "Open up that cell."

"Hold on a minute," Claude said. "Let me catch my breath."

"Take your time, lover." Myra leaned against the doorjamb with one lovely hip cocked with the butt of the shotgun resting on it.

Claude grabbed the hammer and brought it down on the toe of Deputy Cecil's right boot. The little deputy screamed and Claude hit him again on the knee of the other leg. That was enough to drop him to the floor slobbering and convulsing like he was having an epileptic fit. Claude managed to stand and turn around. Sunglasses was giving the hammer in Claude's fist all his attention.

"Give me my ring."

Sunglasses tugged the diamond from his finger and pitched it to Claude.

"Do you want to beg?" Claude threw the hammer and hit him in the chest with a hard thump.

Both the deputies were down on the floor, but Deputy Cecil seemed to be hurting the worst. He cried and he cursed so much that Claude wanted to hit him again.

"How's that for funny?" Claude wheezed.

"Are you all right?" Myra asked.

"I'm as right as rain." Claude tried to straighten up and pushed his hair back out of his face. "Don't I look it?"

"I've seen you look better."

"If you'll give me that shotgun I'll make sure that sheriff doesn't bother you while you get these boys locked up." Claude held out a hand for the gun.

Myra gave it to him, along with a peck on the cheek. "If I thought that nose of yours wouldn't heal I'd shoot the both of them. They've positively ruined your good looks."

"It's my sweet disposition that you love."

Myra reached down and picked up a pistol in both hands. She let her eyes wander down below Claude's belt. "Among other things."

Claude staggered into the office while Myra kicked Sunglasses in the butt. "Get up and drag your sorry friend into that cell."

"You're going to pay for this, bitch," Deputy Cecil spat.

Myra laughed. "You just keep crying. Maybe one day you can tell your children that you met Claude Miller and Myra Hooser, and how you survived it."

"I've never heard of either of you," Sunglasses said while he dragged Deputy Cecil to the cell.

Myra slammed the door shut on them. "I've got two pistols, a bag full of money, and Claude Miller that says I'm going to be famous."

"You're just a cheap thief and a kidnapper," Deputy Cecil said.

"Sugar, I had me an epiphany last night," Myra said. "You've got to take what you want in life, because good things don't come around often."

Claude stopped inside the front office and peered around with the one swollen eye he could still see out of. He switched off the radio, and turned back around in time to catch Sheriff Donley walking through the front door.

"You have yourself a seat," Claude motioned to the chair at the sheriff's desk.

Sheriff Donley eyed the black eye of the shotgun's bore and kept both his hands well away from the pistol on his hip. He took a seat as he was told.

"If I was any kind of an outlaw I'd blow a hole in you right now," Claude said.

Myra stepped up beside him and handed him his missing boot. "Figured you'd want this."

"Thanks. I'd hate to lose my Tony Lamas," Claude said.

"They're going to need a polishing," Myra said. "You've bled all over them."

Claude noticed that Sheriff Donley was wearing a pair of brand-new boots. "What size do you wear, fat man?"

"Size ten," the lawman stuttered.

"Shuck 'em off, and make it quick," Claude said.

Claude stood watch as Myra pulled the sheriff's pistol from his holster while he took off his boots. She already had two guns, so she tucked the Colt Police Positive in her purse — a dependable gun in Claude's opinion, if a bit small-framed.

"I sometimes wonder just how many guns you keep in that purse," Claude said.

"Wouldn't you like to know," she said. "A

girl never can tell when she'll need to freshen up."

The sheriff pitched his boots across the floor, and Claude hooked a finger through their pull holes. He studied them with a frown. "Well, they aren't Tonys."

"Tony Lamas? I wouldn't wear such cheap boots. Those are handmade by a boy here in town, and cost me fifty dollars." The crooked sheriff was scared, but he obviously set store by his boots.

"You'd best shut up, before I change my mind about what to do with you." Claude was surprised at the number of people who didn't know anything about cowboy boots. Roy Burkhalter back home wouldn't wear Tony Lamas if they weren't the best.

"Just what are you going to do with this old boar hog?" Myra asked.

"Why, Myra, do you know you're talking absolutely countrified?" Claude asked.

"You're rubbing off on me."

"You call me Sheriff Donley. You can kill me, but this is still my county."

Claude shoved his shotgun barrel over the man's nose. It was a Winchester Model 12 with a vent rib and a twenty-eight-inch barrel with a modified choke. It was a tad too long and too heavy to hold one-handed like he was, and he was disappointed that a county sheriff would know so little about guns that he would choose such a poor weapon for police work or gunfighting. The shotgun was more suited for shooting doves and quail than criminals, but the man didn't know anything about boots either.

"I'll call you what I please," Claude said. "I've known a *real* sheriff, and you don't remind me of him at all. I'd say you wouldn't make a patch on the seat of his britches."

Claude went over and retrieved his .32 from the sheriff's desk, and he had to stop and lean against the wall after he'd shoved it in his back pocket. "Help me get this old goat out the door. I'm about to give out."

Myra marched Sheriff Donley in front of her out the door. Claude followed and was shocked at what he saw. He had assumed that the jail was located in the county seat, but there was no town at all. A few homes, a church, and a scattering of meager business buildings surrounded what might be called a town square — if there had been a town. A giant rock courthouse sat in the center of the square, out of place in the desolate middle of nowhere. Not a single soul was moving on the street, but he could hear piano music coming from the church. He looked back at the tiny stone jail with its whitewashed rock walls.

"Quite a metropolis, isn't it?" Myra asked.

"And I thought Antlers was small."

"There's our ride." She pointed out an Indian motorcycle with a sidecar.

"Is that the best you could do?" Claude dubiously eyed the pretty maroon motorcycle with its chief's head logo on the gas tank. He missed his brand-new Ford terribly. He doubted he'd ever get back to Dallas to drive it again.

"I never claimed to be a car thief. Your friend Bull and his cronies had the keys to the Chevy, and I thought I did pretty good getting away with the money," she said.

"How much did you get away with?"

"All of it."

"They trusted you with the money?"

"Yep, and they thought I would leave you for dead."

"They don't know you like I do," Claude said.

"I'm not sure how to take that."

"Have you got a pen or pencil?" he asked.

Myra tucked one pistol under her arm and dug impatiently in her purse. She scowled at the jail, not wanting to go back and find a writing instrument. "What do you want with a pen?"

"I just need one."

Myra held up a tube of red lipstick. "This'll have to do."

"Got a piece of paper?"

She sighed. "I think they beat half your brains out."

"I feel the urge to write."

They drove away from Lipscomb, Texas, on the motorcycle with Myra driving and Claude riding in the sidecar. The goggles Myra gave him kept the dust and bugs out of his eyes, but he tried to sleep instead of watching the road. Myra went way too fast, and her driving was atrociously terrifying.

The members of the First Unity Church walking home from their evening services found their sheriff tied to the flagpole on the courthouse lawn. He was in a foul mood to say the least. The red lipstick that someone had painted his lips with may have caused a portion of his aggravation, but the note on his neck was probably what had him upset most. Whoever had left Sheriff Donley there had hung a brown grocery bag around his neck with a piece of twine. Written on it in the same red lipstick, front and back, was a note informing all of his involvement in the robbery of the Booker bank, as well as his dead brother's and the deputies' roles in the theft. All present, including a schoolteacher and a seminary graduate agreed that the penmanship, despite the writing tool, was impressive and written in a decidedly feminine hand. However, Claude's poor grammar and choppy sentences were quickly pointed out.

Sheriff Donley demanded that he be released from the flagpole, and the crowd readily agreed. They took him over to the jail and locked him up with his two deputies. While the testimony of a pair of bank robbers would usually be taken with a grain of salt, especially a crude note written in lipstick, most of the community had long since had their fill of their overbearing sheriff, and the note left hanging from the sheriff's neck fit with about everything else they suspected.

Later that night, somebody accidentally made a phone call to someone in Booker who coincidentally had once had a large amount of money deposited in his local bank. Naturally, he called a few more of his friends who were slightly perturbed with their dead banker and his sheriff brother. It seemed that there were several victims of Sheriff Donley's violent, heavy-handed ways and past crooked dealings who were also waiting for a chance to get even. Before long, all kinds of people were upset and

274

headed for Lipscomb.

Sheriff Donley looked out the window of his little cell and watched the circle of headlights formed in front of the jail. He first assumed his constituents had come to their senses and were there to release him. That thought was short-lived, to say the least. As he watched the shadows passing between his window and the headlights, he observed some uncomfortable things. Despite his own estimation of his intelligence, he had misjudged things badly. Many of his visitors were carrying guns, a few of them had clubs, and one stooped old shadow had a long coil of rope — the right length to reach a high limb on one of the cottonwood trees on the courthouse lawn.

"You sons of bitches better go home, or I'll see you all locked up," Sheriff Donley shouted. "I'm still sheriff, and I at least deserve a fair trial."

"Shut up, Sheriff," Sunglasses said, although he didn't feel cocky enough to wear his sunglasses right then, not with the mob pouring into the jail.

Deputy Cecil wasn't saying anything either. Both of the deputies huddled far back in their cell. Maybe the mob would go to work on the sheriff first. Perhaps they were cowards, but it might be safe to say that both of them showed far more wisdom than Sheriff Donley when it came to the mood of their visitors.

"You come on in here. I'll show you how I got to be sheriff." Sheriff Donley made two fists, but he too was backed into a corner, as far from the bars as he could.

In the end, none of the mob listened to him as he shouted about justice and legal treatment of prisoners. He tried to lie, but the mob wasn't having it. He did prove to have some courage, if only that of a cornered, cowering dog lashing out and snarling. However, calloused hands strengthened by plows and other hard work took hold of him anyway. They jerked him out of his cell like he was no sheriff at all, rudely and insistently. Normally, the men of Lipscomb County were nice, God-fearing, hard-working folks, but righteous people can get pretty indignant when they find out their elected officers are on the take, especially during a depression. To say the least, they badgered poor Sheriff Donley out of office, and from his grunts and groans and pleas for mercy, the entire proceedings were painful.

CHAPTER EIGHTEEN

"I had to fight all my life to survive. They were all against me, but I beat them and left them in the ditch."

— Ty Cobb

Claude's ribs were knitting slowly, painfully, if at all, and not helped one bit by the fact that the motorcycle rode rougher than a bucking horse. That was the only thing he could compare the Indian's suspension to, even though his only experience with horses were childhood memories of riding his grandfather's gentle plow horses in from the field. It didn't matter if he drove or if he rode in the sidecar, the infernal contraption seemed bound and determined to beat him to pieces.

With little more than a pair of goggles apiece as their chief equipment, traveling the dirt roads and unpaved highways was like being in the middle of another dust storm. For four hours straight, they drove through the night, heading east at a steady forty miles an hour, regardless of potholes, ruts, and ditches. The lights of oil derricks speckled the prairie far into the dark horizon, the occasional flare of burning natural gas winking in the distance like stars floating on water. They passed within inches of deer standing in the bar ditches, only seeing them at the last minute when their eyes glowed white in the glare of the motorcycle's light. Raccoons and jackrabbits and coyotes passed before them, silently padding away from the roaring engine. Owls and other night birds lifted off the road and passed dark shadows across the face of the moon. Claude and Myra were like two nocturnal souls themselves, floating through the blackness, their world contained within the beam of the motorcycle's weak headlight, and their past screened from them by the veil of dust lifting in their wake.

Claude assumed they were lost, but he didn't tell Myra so. They stole twenty cents' worth of gas from a little filling station west of Enid, Oklahoma. He sat in the sidecar with his pistol aimed at the front door of the place while she pumped the petrol. It wasn't long before they figured out that the owners were nowhere around. He managed to hobble over to the soda machine and bust it open while she jimmied the station's front door and helped herself to the meager contents on the shelves. By midnight, they were once again headed east, fortified for the rest of their journey with two RC Colas and a pair of chocolate moon pies. The filling station's owners were going to be a little perturbed when they found their soda machine was busted and their place of business burglarized, but the hundred dollars Claude left under a rock at the foot of the gas pump was bound to soothe their hurt feelings. Myra thought it a foolish gesture, but didn't argue about it too much. She was getting used to her Boy Scout's ways.

Come daylight, they began passing trucks carrying roughnecks and other oilfield workers. They were brawny, shirtless men in overalls, darkened by sun and grease and drilling mud ground into their skin. They tipped their metal, Panama hardhats to Myra or waved and lifted a cigarette or a lunchbox in salute — men of the country with reckless eyes and a tough set to their jaws.

She assured him they were somewhere north of Tulsa. He couldn't argue with her assertion, as neither one of them had a map. They soon passed a CCC crew working to build a small dam for what the government conservationists called a watershed lake. There must have been a hundred men in the work crew, and every one of them was thin and solemn, the kind that looked like they needed a job. The new Civilian Conservation Corps was supposedly putting all sorts of men to work, and the radio and newspapers bragged about the program. Be that as it may, Claude thought that only the government would have men building lakes in the middle of a drought. Granted, the countryside they were passing through was a little greener than Booker, Texas, but it was still going to be a hell of a long time before the new reservoir filled up.

Later, they spotted a little town in the distance. Myra left Claude under a railroad trestle while she went to get them breakfast and a few other supplies. He was too battered not to cause unwanted questions. She returned with a sack full of burgers and fries, a jug of sweet iced tea, and a white shirt and a pair of khaki dungarees to replace Claude's ragged, bloody clothes.

They left the highway, and after a few miles of county road found a little spot on a creek bank to have a picnic. Although the water wasn't swift running and clear — it was a little on the muddy side — it looked cool and refreshing after dust storms and eight hours on the road in the July heat. Myra decided to go for a swim and a bath after their meal.

Claude knew he could use a bath himself, but he wanted nothing so much as to lie on the creek bank and take a long nap in the shade. He was sure he looked like hell and smelled worse, but the gunshot wound and the beating had taken much out of him. It looked like too far of a walk to the water.

Myra stepped out of her dress, and he lazily watched as her silk slip slid off her hips to the grass in a soft pile. She looked like a pale ghost wading into the water, and he imagined her white, soft flesh against his dark skin.

She turned to face him once she was waist-deep in the water. "You like watching me, don't you?"

"You didn't even look around before you shucked off your clothes." He rose and began undressing, gingerly unwinding the bandages where the blood had pasted them to his ribs.

"There's nobody around, just you and me," she said.

"Yeah, but you didn't even look to see if there was."

She arched one eyebrow seductively. "You

don't seem bashful yourself."

Claude glanced down at his growing member, and hustled into the water. She ducked under and resurfaced with her head thrown back to keep her hair behind her. He was entranced by the tiny rivulets of water running off her breasts and between them, and dripping off and circling around the hard pinkness of her nipples. He pulled her close, not even wincing when she pressed into his battered ribs. Her mouth was salty and hot. The light feeling in his stomach and the quiver in his loins that he always felt when she was around was worse than ever.

She pulled her head back from him far enough to look up at his face. "Did you bring your pistol in the water?"

"I can't help it if you make my sticker peck out."

"You're such a romantic sort, you silver-tongued devil." She tried to frown, but couldn't hold in her laughter. His boyish honesty was his most endearing trait, and she needed that more than anything. No lies just love, simple love, or lust, or what-ever was between them that felt so real.

Myra washed his hair with a little bottle of shampoo from her sack of supplies, and fended off his advances long enough to get him to wash hers. She wiped the crusted blood and grime from his face with gentle fingertips while his strong hands massaged and worked the lather into her scalp. They floated in the sun, listening to the muffled cries of tree frogs and crickets with water filling their ears as if in a womb. They laughed and made love in the water, and then again on the creek bank under the shade of an enormous sycamore tree. The sunlight shone down through the leaves overhead casting her skin in mottled shadows, and he lazily ran his hand up the shallow crease of her back. They lay like that for more than an hour, him napping while she rested her cheek against his chest and listened to the strong, steady thump of his heart. She traced a finger gently around the puckered bullet wound in his side, and hummed a song her mother used to sing.

"Where do you want to run to?" she asked when he finally opened his eyes.

He yawned and wrinkled his eyebrows. "Where do you want to go?"

She rolled over on her back and laced her fingers together between her breasts, staring up into the canopy of the tree. "Maybe Kansas City. No, that's not far enough. I want to go somewhere with water and a cool breeze."

He ran one hand through the brown grass beside him, listening to it scratch against his palm. "I suggest we buy a car. What you want must be a long way from here, and I don't know if I can take any more of your motorcycle."

"How about we go up to one of the Great Lakes? They've got guest lodges there on the edge of the water, kind of like hotels where people stay all summer. We could swim all day, maybe even buy a boat and dance in the ballroom at night."

"You mean like up in Minnesota or Michigan?"

Myra shrugged. "I guess."

"You've been up there?" Anyplace outside of Oklahoma seemed like a long way off to him. He tried to remember geography class, and to picture the place she was talking about.

"No, but I saw a brochure once. The pictures looked nice."

"I hear it snows an awful lot up there."

She hugged herself and mimicked a chill. "I'm tired of sweating. I want to go someplace where I can snuggle up beside a fireplace in a fur robe."

"It'd be kind of cold swimming in weather like that."

She whacked his arm with the back of her

hand and tried to act perturbed. "Try to have a little imagination."

He smiled to let her know he'd been joking and hugged her close again. "What would we do all winter while we waited for the ice to melt so we could go out in our boat?"

"We've got a ridiculous amount of money to make sure we have plenty of time to find out."

"I'm listening."

She noticed that his smile was strained and his voice wasn't as enthusiastic as it should have been. "You don't want to go, do you?"

"I want to, but I can't."

Instantly, thoughts of what a fool she'd been were running through her mind. He didn't want any part of her dream, just to crawl on her like some damned bull. Why did she expect him to be any different than the rest of the men she'd known?

He took her chin and kept her from turning away from him. "It's not that I don't want to go north with you. I can't, not yet."

Angry words started to form on her lips, but she remembered the Boy Scout she was talking to and tried to fight back her doubts. "Are you foolish enough to think you can get revenge on Bull's crew?"

The muscles in his jaw flexed, the way they did when he was clenching his teeth and about to get stubborn. "Did they plan to kill me all along, or was it a spur of the moment thing?"

She was tempted to lie, just one little white, harmless fib that would see them both soon sitting in the middle of some cool, clear dream, watching the sun come up and holding hands like the world was born that very morning. "I heard them bragging about how they planned it. The timing was just a moment of opportunity."

He sat up and wrapped his arms around his knees. "I don't like being stabbed in the back, or shot either. A man's got to stand up for himself."

"Remember, we're the ones who got away with the money," she said. "Let bygones be bygones. That much money ought to make it easy to forget."

"Not for me."

"Bull and his crew aren't exactly push-overs." She took hold of him by the elbow. "You'd risk getting yourself killed and losing me?"

"Maybe I could forget revenge, but there are other things."

"What things?"

"Unless I've misjudged him, Diamond Joe

isn't going to take this lying down," he said. "It won't just be about his ten percent, it'll be the fact we robbed his goons. He's going to come looking for us, and soon."

"Bull thought you were dead, and he'll tell Diamond Joe that," she said. "I'm the one he thinks robbed him."

"It's only a matter of time before he finds out we're together with his money. That deal back in the Panhandle will ensure that. The Law has our names now, and the newspapers will be next."

"We'll go so far he'll never find us. He isn't anything outside of Dallas." She said it a little louder than necessary, as if trying to convince herself.

Claude pulled away from her and started tugging on his new pants and rewinding his bandages. "Maybe not, but he might think I'll go back home. I don't want to bring that on my family."

"Your father's the sheriff, right? Diamond Joe may be hard, but he isn't foolish enough to go into another state and bother a cop."

"I wouldn't bet on that. He didn't strike me as the sort to let anything get in the way of business, or to forget somebody that crossed him," he said. "And there are a lot of reasons in that bag yonder to make him bold — about twenty thousand dollars' worth of reasons."

"Maybe he'll show up in Antlers and ask around a bit for you, but I can't see him being so silly as to bother your family."

"Would you want Ernest around your mother?" he asked. "You've seen the way he looks at women."

Myra stood up and started to dress. Claude was surprised to see tears rolling down her cheeks. He'd never seen her cry.

"I know how bad you want to get away from all the things chasing you." He tried to hold her, but she jerked away.

She threw her clothes against the tree and flopped back down with her head bowed, refusing to look at him.

"Myra," he said softly, "I don't want to hurt you. I'd go about anywhere with you just because you asked, but I can't run off thinking that my family might not be safe because of what I've done."

She waved him off and scoffed in a long, ragged breath. "That isn't why I'm crying."

Claude didn't even want to venture a guess what had her so wrought up, and he felt helpless because she was crying and he didn't know what to say to make her feel better. "Myra, don't worry. I'm not bragging, but I think I'm better with a gun than about anybody living. I don't even have to

288

practice; it just comes natural to me, like breathing. I promise you, I can handle Bull and his boys, and Diamond Joe if it comes to that. Nothing's going to stop us from going wherever you want, but it's going to take a little longer to get there."

"Now you're looking all sad," she said.

"I don't like to see you cry."

"I wish I was as good as you." She bowed her head again.

"Don't worry about that. I've seen you shoot and you aren't half bad. But let me shoot Diamond Joe."

She wiped at her tears with the back of her hand and looked up at him as if daring him to make fun of her for crying. "I'm not talking about guns. You're always saying about how wicked you are, but you really aren't."

"I've killed one man, committed armed robbery twice, and knocked over a filling station."

She managed a weak laugh. "I hear the court gives ten to fifteen for grand theft moon pie."

"There's the Myra I know."

"You're good Claude, more than you know. You mistake the little bit of bad in you that everyone has for what you're really made of."

"You're good too. Somebody bad wouldn't have come back for me."

She shook her head. "Not like you. You're worrying about your family, and I was ready to leave mine."

"What family?" He hated that his question might bring up her uncle Walt.

"I've got two baby sisters, and one of them lives in Dallas."

"I thought they were in an orphanage."

"They used to be, but the next oldest to me, Shirley, works in a cathouse down there."

"And you think I'll turn my nose up at that? For Pete's sake, I'm a crook."

"Well, maybe you ought to judge me. I wanted to run away with the money so bad that I've been telling myself that she's in no danger, even when that isn't true."

"How old is she?"

"Seventeen."

"You can't live her life for her. I don't know much, but I've already seen a lot of things worse than working in a cathouse."

"What about working in a cathouse that Diamond Joe owns?"

"I thought he stuck to gambling and fencing stolen stuff."

"And whores." Myra practically spat the word.

"Does he know she's your sister?"

"He hired both of us at the same time." She was looking at him again like she was daring him.

"Do you think he'll lean on her to find out where you're at?" he asked.

She paused for a moment to give that some thought. "Diamond Joe doesn't let his men rough up women unless he absolutely has to, but like you said, there's enough money in that bag to give him reason. And he might send Ernest around to question her."

"We'll figure something out."

"Don't try to act like it doesn't bother you that I was a whore."

"I'm not exactly a shining example. I guess if you can love a half-breed bank robber and a high-school dropout, then I won't be bothered by a little thing like that."

"You don't know anything about me," she said.

"I know enough."

"What makes you think I love you? I've never said it."

"Say it now."

"Sit down." She patted the ground beside her. "I'm going to tell you a story, and then you can decide if there's any good in me."

"I already know . . ."

She put a hand on his mouth to quiet him. "I was born on a little farm in Kansas. My mother should have been put in an asylum instead of left to raise three girls. Maybe she wasn't always so crazy, but she got that way. Dad knew how to farm, but he knew how to drink whiskey too. And not just whiskey, toward the end he'd drink rubbing alcohol or aftershave if he was short of money. I was fifteen when Mother ran off. I'd already seen what the beating had done to her, and I promised myself I was going to run away the first chance I got. Mother wasn't the steadiest sort, but she got that part right."

She paused to get her composure. Claude felt the need in her, and had sense enough to wait her out.

"Only I wasn't brave enough. He beat me once or twice a week, bad. I told myself I'd run, but the next morning he would act nice and promise me things were going to be better. I was fool enough to believe him, or maybe, like I said, I was just a coward.

"And then the beatings got worse. The rain quit coming, his drinking got worse, and there was never anything to eat. I think every time he looked at me he was reminded of Mother, and why she ran off. The beatings got so bad that I'd send my sisters to hide in the barn until after he got home and wore himself out hurting me. Sometimes he used his fists, and other times it was worse. I ran out of stories to explain my bruises to my teachers, so I quit school." She began crying again, quietly, rocking back and forth and clutching her thin shoulders.

"Wasn't there anybody you could go to for help?" He wrapped his arms around her.

"I went to Uncle Walt." She sniffled and straightened her back and put on a different face that Claude had seen before — the hard Myra, the one who wasn't going to let anybody hurt her ever again. "Do you know what that son of a bitch did?"

He waited again.

"He tried to rape me. Laughed when I got away from his filthy, groping hands and said nobody was going to believe a little piece of white trash like me if I told what he'd done."

"Well, he won't be laughing anymore."

"I did a bad thing after that."

"You ran off and left your sisters?"

"Not just that. Worse." She shoved her bangs out of her face and stuck out her lower lip and blew air up her face, gathering herself. "I waited until Dad was passed out drunk at the kitchen table, and then I told the girls to go down the road to the neighbors' house. Lord, I swore I'd never talk about what I did."

"You don't have to tell me if you don't want to. Nothing you can tell me is going to make me love you any less."

"No, I'm going to tell you." She buried her face in his chest. "But it's like living it all over again."

"My mother says talking about hurt is sometimes the only way to get rid of it," he said.

"I killed him. I took his shotgun and killed him, and then burned him up in the house."

"Nothing but pure and simple self-defense."

"I didn't do it for me. Don't you understand? He could use a board or a strap, or put his cigarettes out on me. I could take it all. It got worse if I screamed, and I didn't even cry after a while." Both her fists were clenched in her lap, and her face had changed again to one Claude hadn't seen before, sadder than he could recall.

"I told myself that I might be too big of a coward to run, but I wasn't going to see my sisters go through what I did."

"You shouldn't have had to shoot your daddy, but nobody who knows the truth would blame you for it."

"They didn't do it, just me. What kind of

girl can shoot her own father, no matter how bad he was?"

"So you ran off to Dallas, and the state took care of your sisters?"

"The orphanage had to be better than where they had been living."

"Do your sisters know what you did for them?"

"Some folks believed that Dad got drunk and caught the house on fire, and some thought I killed him. But my sisters suspected the truth. And if they didn't, when Shirley came down to Dallas, I told her."

"What about the youngest?"

"A foster family took her in. She writes me letters now and again telling me how good she's doing in school."

"I'd say they owe you."

"They don't owe me. We've all paid enough."

"You still haven't said it." Claude took her chin in his hand one more time.

"What?"

"That you love me."

"You want to hear that even after all I've told you?"

"I do."

"You're crazy. I've known it since I first laid eyes on you back on that river," she said.

"Say it."

"I love you." She pulled him to her and they held each other for a long time, until the sun was low in the western sky and casting their shadows out onto the muddy water — thinner, wispier versions of themselves, but showing none of the scars.

Claude finally let go of her and pulled on his boots and tucked the tail of his new white shirt into his pants. He held up one foot and then the other, studying the cowboy boots. "These boots are growing on me, even though they aren't Tony Lamas."

"You and your boots and guns." Myra shook her head.

"I like cars too, fast ones," he said. "And I like pretty blondes who carry pistols with their lipstick."

"Like I said, you're crazy." She smiled at him while she dressed.

He went to the motorcycle and rested his foot on the kick-starter, knowing it was going to hurt his ribs like hell to turn the motor over. "Are you coming?"

"Where are we going?" She climbed into the sidecar.

"South, that's all. We'll make things up as we go along."

"Are you planning on giving the money back to Diamond Joe?"

"I'll give him his cut if it comes to that."

"That money's ours, but I don't think he'd settle for that if you offered it to him."

"He'll have to."

"What about Bull and Dink and Ernest?"

"They better hope they don't show up around me, that's all I'll say." He put the motorcycle in gear.

"Are you talking about going back to Antlers?" she asked. "We can have Diamond Joe meet us anywhere. We can leave his money somewhere and tell him where we left it."

"I don't think he'll settle for that. We're going to settle in at a little place I know and make sure he finds us," Claude said. "The Sheriff used to tell me that the soldier who knows the battleground the best has a big advantage."

"How's Diamond Joe going to find us?"

"Why, we'll just send him a message."

The motorcycle was soon a rope of dust worming its way south. For what Claude planned, there was no need to drive so fast, but neither he nor Myra noticed their speed. They were both young enough to think they could outrun life.

CHAPTER NINETEEN

*"Ten thousand red-headed Texas Rangers
is the only thing needed to clean up
Chicago with its racketeers and
gangsters."*
— Kingfisher Weekly Free Press,
Kingfisher, Oklahoma, March 12, 1931

Sheriff Miller remained quiet and all but motionless during the interrogation, and let Sergeant Jones do most of the talking. The two deputies behind the cell's bars wouldn't look into his calm, unreadable stare. It was obvious he made them nervous. Neither of them had any clue how much effort he was putting into sitting so still in the uncomfortable wooden chair he'd been provided. He wanted to readjust his position to ease his stiff back, or maybe even to get up and walk around. However, he'd found long before that a hard stare and a disturbing quiet rattled most prisoners more than threatening them did, especially little weasels like the two he was looking at.

"Are you sure he said his name was Claude Miller?" Sergeant Jones asked for the second time while he brushed a spot of dust from his slacks and admired the high sheen of his polished cowboy boots.

Sunglasses, although he wasn't wearing his tinted optics anymore, picked at the lint on the blanket covering his cot. "That's what he said his name was."

"Who killed the banker?"

"The Claude kid claimed he didn't, but I wouldn't trust him any farther than I can throw a bull by the tail," Deputy Cecil said. "It was definitely one of his gang."

"Tell me again what the blonde looked like." Sergeant Jones ignored the pair's frustration, even though he'd been asking them questions all day, except for a lunch break.

Cecil sat up on his own cot and put a hand gingerly to the bandages wrapping his head and extending below his jaw. Both of his eyes were black and blue and rotten yellow with bruises like the rest of his face. He could barely talk for the gauze packed into his left jaw. "We've told you a dozen times that her name is Myra Belle Hooser. She's Sheriff Donley's niece."

299

"Let me get this straight," Sergeant Jones said. "This Myra showed up and held a gun on you while Claude beat the crap out of you and threw you in a cell."

"No, that mob did most of our damage, but Claude did smash Cecil's pinky toe with a hammer and broke my collar bone." Somebody had given Sunglasses a broken nose.

"Claude snuck a hammer into his cell?" Sheriff Miller finally asked.

Both of the deputies were shocked that the mean lawman finally spoke. It was easy to see that he would rather take them somewhere and beat out of them what he wanted.

"Did you hear what Sheriff Miller said?" Sergeant Jones asked.

The two deputies looked at each other as if hoping the other had a suitable lie. Finally, Sunglasses said, "Cecil was going to hang a picture on the wall, you know, to help with prisoner morale. He must have left the hammer lying here in front of the cells."

Deputy Cecil reached his pointer finger into his mouth and pulled out a bloody wad of gauze and pitched it on the floor. He ran his tongue around in the empty sockets where two of his jaw teeth had once been.

"That sumbitch tortured me. You ever see what the corrugated face on a framing hammer will do to a man's toe?"

"Did he knock out your teeth with the hammer?" Sheriff Miller asked.

"No, those damned farmers did that to me," Deputy Cecil said. "It's a good thing I knew most of them, or I might have killed one or two of them."

"If there hadn't been so many of them, I'd say we could have fended them off," Sunglasses mumbled. "We put up a pretty good fight."

"The sheriff over in Ochiltree County told me that when he first got to the jail, there was a metal folding chair sitting right over yonder with blood all over it and a pair of handcuffs still shackled to it," Sergeant Jones said. "You sure you boys didn't rough Claude up a bit before his girlfriend showed up?"

Sunglasses wasn't quite as stupid as he looked, or at least he was quick to form a lie. "No, that's where that Claude handcuffed Cecil here and smashed his toe. I reckon he would've gotten to me eventually, but then Sheriff Donley showed back up and they locked us in a cell and went to tend to him."

"How come you arrested Claude if you

were all in on the same robbery?" Sergeant Jones asked.

"That note they left on Sheriff Donley was a damned lie," Deputy Cecil said. "We were officers of the law doing our duty."

"So, let me get this straight. You say that Claude had been shot by his own gang. He knew that Sheriff Donley had stepped out of the room for a while, but he took the time to torture you before he made his escape?" Sheriff Miller asked.

"That's what we're telling you. Although, we shot a bunch at the gang during their getaway out of Booker. One of our bullets might have hit the kid."

"Is there any chance that your rounds hit the banker by accident?" Sheriff Miller already knew that the banker had been killed by several .45 ACP bullets at close range, and not .38 police rounds. The coroner's report stated that there were powder burns on the body and two bullets were still inside the victim. However, the more lies he caught the deputies in, the more he rattled them.

Sunglasses immediately regretted suggesting he had fired his gun. "We made sure that we shot wide of Walt."

"How much money did Claude and Myra get away with? The bank's ledger books suggest an awful lot of missing money," Sergeant Jones said.

"The courts might go easier on a man that would tell the truth and help us out," Sheriff Miller added.

"We don't have anything to tell. You talk to Sheriff Donley and he'll vouch for us," Sunglasses said.

"Sheriff Donley isn't going to be talking to anybody for a while," Sergeant Jones said. "Last I heard, he was in a body cast with his jaw wired up and drinking soup through a straw."

Deputy Cecil cast a cautious look at the door leading into the front office. "Have they appointed an interim sheriff yet? I don't want to spend another night here with just that old postmaster standing night watch. I can't prove it, but I'm pretty sure he was one of them that broke in here and beat on us."

"Seems like a nice enough man to me, and there's a few other folks that are volunteering to watch over you two," Sergeant Jones said. "I hear there are some that feel like they missed out on things."

"Are you going to stand by and see two fellow lawmen abused?" Deputy Cecil asked, but got choked up and his voice sounded more like the squeak of a sick chicken.

"There's nothing I can do for you," Sergeant Jones said. "Maybe I could help if you were to lend me a hand with this case, but . . ."

The deputies glanced at each other again, but through silent agreement turned their faces back to the floor.

"Seems like we're done here, Sheriff Miller," Sergeant Jones said.

Sheriff Miller rose and left the room with Sergeant Jones on his heels.

"We need to see the doctor," Sunglasses called after them. "Cecil here's pissing blood, and I need something for my pain. I know my rights, and you can't treat prisoners like this."

"What do you think?" Sergeant Jones asked when they were outside.

Sheriff Miller jerked a thumb back over his shoulder at the jail. "If those two showed up on my porch I wouldn't give them a glass of water."

"They're dumb enough that, given time, I think they'll talk."

Sheriff Miller shoved his Stetson back on his head with one thumb while he looked around the courtyard. "That isn't helping us right now. What about Sheriff Donley?"

"He's sulled up, busted up, and letting his

lawyer do all the talking."

"And Claude's got a three-day head start on us, and we don't have a clue which way he went," Sheriff Miller said. "How do you think it all went down?"

"Just about like the note left on Sheriff Donley said, as far as the robbery and jailbreak went. I'd say that Claude was either wounded in the getaway and left for dead with the banker, or maybe shot by the gang themselves and left behind," Sergeant Jones said. "Either way, Claude was double-crossed and Myra came back for him. Looks like the gang has split up."

"It's hard to believe that Claude would be in on a murder."

Sergeant Jones gave him a cautious look. "Maybe this was a bad idea. You ought to go home."

Sheriff Miller took off his hat and ran a finger around the sweatband inside the crown to wipe off the sweat. "No, I'm in it for as long as you'll have me."

Sergeant Jones pointed at Sheriff Miller's hip. "Maybe I'm nosy, but how come you don't wear your gun?"

Sheriff Miller patted his waist on the right side where a gun belt and a service revolver should have hung. "I've been a sheriff for going on three terms, and I've only belted my pistol on five or six times."

"Don't you think that's a little chancy for a man in our line of work? You don't even carry a pair of handcuffs."

"I trust that I can judge when I need to strap a gun on. Most folks in my part of the world don't trust a man swaggering around with his hand on the butt of his pistol. They'll immediately clam up when you need them to talk, or assume you're some little man with a chip on his shoulder who got his lunch money taken from him back in school," Sheriff Miller said. "That's my philosophy."

"I'd hate for you to misjudge when you need to wear your pistol."

"There's always a chance of that, but I didn't pin on a badge thinking I was going to live forever. You were over there. You know that."

"Yeah," Sergeant Jones said. "How many men have you shot? Not in the war, but in the line of duty as a peace officer."

"One, that hobo killer," Sheriff Miller said. "What about you?"

"Not a one."

"You've been lucky. I've known a lot of cops who never even drew their gun in all the years they worked. I'd say that might be something to be proud of."

Sergeant Jones scoffed. "You'd think different if you were a Ranger. Old Lone Wolf Gonzaulles has been in more gunfights than Wild Bill Hickok, and he's on his way to making captain. Frank Hamer supposedly has a graveyard he started all by himself, and he was a captain when he retired."

"That's nothing to be proud of."

"You aren't a Ranger. I haven't shot anybody, and you'll notice I'm nothing but a sergeant."

"That's some outfit you work for," Sheriff Miller said wryly.

"I'm not looking to shoot anybody, but you've got to get in the newspapers if you want to move up in the service. Texas likes her heroes, especially if they shoot enough bad guys."

"How are you going to move up if your governor is going to do away with all you Rangers?"

Sergeant Jones spat, even though he was far too clean-cut to chew tobacco. "It's going to be a sad day for Texas when there aren't Rangers anymore."

"There won't be as many spotless white shirts with creases you can shave with when you Rangers are gone, I'll say that," Sheriff Miller said.

"What's that supposed to mean? I get the

impression sometimes that you don't think much of the Texas Rangers."

Sheriff Miller held up a placating hand. "I'm just envious of you. I don't know how you keep a white shirt that clean."

"You wear that khaki uniform if you want to. I'm still a single man, and no woman is going to notice a man wearing a getup like yours," Sergeant Jones said.

"Well, if that governor fires all you Texas Star packers I'd say it would be just about as sad as Tom Mix retiring his horse, Tony, and his silver saddle."

"Why Sheriff, I'd have never taken you for a man that would spend a nickel to watch Tom Mix at the theater," Sergeant Jones said.

"My boy's crazy about him," Sheriff Miller grumbled. "What have we got so far?"

Sergeant Jones started to tease him a little more to get even for his poking fun at the Rangers, but thought better of it. The Rangers were indeed becoming a flashy, well-dressed bunch, and it wouldn't do to tick off Sheriff Miller. Gun or no gun, there was something about the man that demanded some respect, even if he wasn't a Ranger.

"The farmer and his wife that found Claude and the dead banker left for California, and nobody's heard from them since.

The highway patrol is looking for them in every motel and roadside camp, but no luck so far," Sergeant Jones said. "It's a shame Claude didn't mention who was with him during the robbery in his little note."

"Claude's not a rat."

"But you've got to admit that your kid's got a little style to him. That note was a cute piece of work."

"That's Claude's problem. He's always been a little bit of a show-off," Sheriff Miller said. "The people I talked to around Booker all swore that there was no way the farmer or his wife would be in on the heist. What else?"

"One of the descriptions of the bank robbers by the witnesses, and mind you that's a few old people sitting in a café a hundred yards from the bank, sounds like a man I might recognize. His name is Ernest Peacock. He did a little stint in the state asylum and I once questioned him over a missing girl found dead over east at Tyler. He's a real loon, but we never could tie him to the murder, or anything else. The word on the street is that none of the whores in Dallas will have anything to do with him, he's that creepy," Sergeant Jones said. "The driver of the car was supposedly a big, wide man. That may be Bull McDonald, a tough, bullheaded Irishman that used to bounce at some of the clubs and speakeasies around Dallas. He's also Diamond Joe's collection man when someone needs a little strong-arming. I've even heard that he played professional baseball back in his younger day, until he beat up a teammate with a baseball bat and got blackballed from the game."

"What about the other man with them?"

"Don't know. He was little, that's all the witnesses said. Could be any number of crooks. I swear, you shake a tree anywhere in Dallas and somebody you ought to arrest will fall out," Sergeant Jones said.

"What about this Myra?"

The Ranger pulled out a little tablet from his hip pocket, and flipped a couple of pages until he found what he wanted. "Myra Belle Hooser. A few years back there were some Kansas cops who suspected her of killing her father, a drunk and a no-good. She ran off, and they never could gather enough evidence to bother with trying to run her down."

"What's her tie to Diamond Joe?"

"Maybe something, maybe nothing," Sergeant Jones said. "You know, lots of these bad men like to have a floozy along with them, just like they want expensive suits and shiny cars."

"What do you suspect?"

"My contacts back in Dallas tell me that she might have worked for Diamond Joe, once upon a time."

"So we're headed back there?" Sheriff Miller asked.

"My gut tells me we stand a better chance there than chasing up and down the roads waiting for them to rob something else."

"If they double-crossed Claude, I don't think he'll go back to Dallas," Sheriff Miller said. "Or maybe he will."

"He and his little blonde gun moll aren't going to get their cut of the money back if Diamond Joe and his goons are involved," Sergeant Jones said.

"That won't be what Claude will be looking to settle," Sheriff Miller said. "That boy never could forget a wrong done him. He's as stubborn as a mule, and talking him out of anything is like arguing with a fence post."

"Kind of stubborn like a certain sheriff I know, huh?" Sergeant Jones asked.

Sheriff Miller scowled and squinted at the sun hitting him in the face, or maybe it was because he never had liked Texas. There was always too much bragging about the state, despite the fact that it looked just as poor and ragged as anywhere else. "I guess we ought to pay Diamond Joe a visit."

CHAPTER TWENTY

*"Remember the first rule of
gunfighting . . . have a gun."*
— Jeff Cooper

Late in the evening, Claude and Myra
topped a hill and spied two cop cars blocking the highway a mile to the east. They
made a U-turn and backtracked until they
found a county farm road that might route
them around the roadblock. They drove
three miles south and then headed east
again. After a few more miles, the road
intersected a highway, and they pulled onto
it, once again headed south. The police may
or may not have been looking for them, but
it appeared that they had given the coppers
the slip. They drove cautiously, however,
stopping often where the terrain gave them
a high vantage point. It didn't help them,
because at dusk they rounded a curve in
the road where it crossed a timbered creek

bottom and ran right into another road-block.

It was only one highway patrolman, and Myra spun the motorcycle around in the highway before he even recognized he ought to get in his car and give chase. She was smart enough to know that she was never going to outrun a patrol car on the motor-cycle. She slid the Indian to a stop at a gate in a barbwire fence on the side of the highway, over a little hill and out of sight of the patrol car that was surely coming after them. Claude opened the gate, and then dove back into his seat as she gunned the motorcycle across the prairie.

The tall native grass hissed against the bottom of the sidecar as she drove wide-open on their new cross-country route. The motorcycle was bouncing so that Claude was hard-pressed to keep from being thrown clear, much less get his legs tucked inside the sidecar. A siren squalled behind them, and he look back to see the patrol car slid-ing sideways through the gate. Myra gave the motorcycle the last bit of throttle she had as they topped a little sharp-combed rise in the prairie. Claude had a sickening falling sensation as they sailed through the air. The Indian's suspension creaked and popped when it struck the ground on the far side, and Myra grunted with the impact.

The ground in front of them ran smooth for almost a mile, but another fence loomed only a hundred yards away. Myra slid to a stop at the last minute, her front tire stopping only inches from the six-strand fence with its sharp-tipped barbwire that would cut you in two if you hit it on a motorcycle at fifty miles an hour. Claude leapt back out of the sidecar and took hold of a small creosote fence post and began to wobble the top of it back and forth, trying to loosen it in the ground.

The patrol car came over the same little ridge they had just jumped with its siren still howling. Its motor revved wildly when its wheels left the ground. Claude and Myra watched as the car sailed through the air some sixty feet before its nose buried into the ground. Sheet metal crumpled and its front bumper flew free. The rough landing must have jostled the patrolman from his seat, for he lost control of the car and it fishtailed wildly from one side to another before it rolled over two and a half times and came to a stop on its top, teetering and rocking for a moment like a child's toy thrown down and left behind.

The fence post was old and rotten, and much of its base was burned away by prairie fires over the years. It gave way with a crack when Claude gave it one last push. The old, rusty wire was no longer strung as tight as it once had been, and he managed to mash the fence down with the broken post. He stood on it while Myra drove over the downed section.

They traveled for miles in that manner, a wild, cross-country race. Claude found a pair of pliers in the motorcycle's little toolbox, and he cut their way through one fence after another. They feared that the cops would encircle them, and be waiting whenever and wherever they could find a road again. The sun went down and they idled quietly through the burnt summer grass, watching for car lights or carbide headlights on a manhunt party in the distance. They had no hope that the cops weren't slowly closing in on them, and could almost feel a noose tightening around them, choking away any chance of escape.

A light did finally show to the north, headed their way, but it was a highball freight train coming down the Frisco line. They left the motorcycle sitting in the middle of the railroad tracks with its headlight pointed at the coming train. Claude knew there was no way he and Myra could jump on a train running sixty-five miles an hour in the dark. They hid in the grass and listened to the engineer honk his horn at the light he could see on the tracks ahead of him. He tried to slow his train, but the nighttime freight was a priority, limited-stop run, and he was going too fast to shut down in time. The locomotive struck the motorcycle, skidding it down the track in a shower of sparks for a hundred yards before coming to a stop.

While the engineer and the brakeman got off to study the damage and to look for bodies, Claude took Myra by the hand and they slipped along the side of the train until they found a half-empty boxcar with a door that slid easily open. He lifted her into the car and climbed up behind her, sliding the cargo door shut behind them. They huddled in a corner and waited while the train crew cleared the tracks of debris. They could hear panicked discussion among the crew, and it was plain that the trainmen thought they might have killed some drunk who parked his motorcycle on the tracks. Finally, they gave up the search for a body.

The train shuddered and crept up to speed. Claude crawled over to the door and opened it a crack. The boxcar's wheels clanked and rattled beneath him as he watched the line of car headlights headed toward the tracks in the distance. It looked as if they were getting away from a posse at the very last minute. He wished the train would go faster.

Fearing that policemen would be waiting in towns along the line, they thought it best to get off the train before the search for them had time to organize itself any farther. Both of them agreed that the policemen must have been looking for the stolen motorcycle, or else a dragnet had been set up when they fled Texas and they had only been lucky avoiding it during their first night of flight.

The train slowed to pass through the next town. From the number of house lights, it wasn't much of a town at all. Claude and Myra perched at the lip of the open door and watched the ground flying away beneath them. They leapt together and hit the ground bouncing and then rolling. They brushed themselves off and licked their wounds and eyed the silhouettes of the town with some apprehension. Myra had only a few scrapes and bruises. Claude had those too, plus his ribs felt like he had busted them all over again.

They walked down the tracks away from town, set on cutting a wide circle around its edge until they could find a car to steal.

They passed beneath a water tower, and Myra noticed the white, chalked symbols and other graffiti almost glowing in the weak lights of town.

"Some of those are hobo symbols," Claude said. "They've got all kinds of code pictures to let them know what towns are dangerous, where food can be begged, or warning others of mean cops and biting dogs."

A railroad bull was coming down the side of another train parked on a siding, holding his lantern high and searching the inside of the boxcars for hobos.

"We'd better get moving," Claude said.

They saw the glow of a campfire burning about a mile north of town, and made their way toward it, tired and hungry and willing to take risks for food and perhaps shelter for the night if they were lucky. As they came closer, they recognized the shanties and makeshift lean-tos of a hobo jungle. Every town of any size seemed to have one, and especially any town that had a railroad running through it. Whoever had come up with the term "jungle" had it right. One and all, they were nothing more than hard-scrabble, refuse-littered villages of cast-off junk formed into the primitive dwellings of vagrants traveling the rails.

"Come on, hobos shouldn't give us any

319

trouble," Claude said. "Most of them don't like the Law any more than we do."

There were several scruffy, unshaven men in tattered clothes huddled around a fire. They were burning worn-out car tires, and black smoke drifted across the orange glow of the fire, giving the camp a hellish look. None of the hobos seemed shocked when their new visitors walked into the light.

"You boys wouldn't happen to have a bite to eat, would you?" Claude asked.

The hobos looked at him like he was crazy.

"Oh sure," one of them said. "We've got lobster tail, caviar, or a porterhouse steak with the best house wine, white or red."

Other than a bottle of booze that they were sharing, there was no sign of food. None of them looked like they were getting regular meals, or bathing often either. With the weird light, they might have been Satan's minions in the inferno, but none of them seemed to have the energy to dance in the flames.

"You ought to get you a bindle stick," a little freckle-faced fellow in an antique derby hat and a patched shirt said. He pointed at the duffel bag Myra was carrying. The rest of the hobos beside him didn't even try to conceal the naked speculation in their eyes.

"What's a bindle stick?" She set the bag down on the ground and used it for a seat.

"Just wrap your belongings in a sheet or any old hunk of cloth, and cut you a stick to carry your bundle over your shoulder," the freckle-faced hobo said. "You two must be new to traveling."

"From the look of his face, they must have come close to greasing the tracks," a large, black-whiskered brute across the fire said. He reminded Myra of Bluto in the Popeye comic strip in the newspapers.

"He means that you look like you almost got killed by a train," the freckle-faced man said. The fire made his eyes twinkle like a leprechaun's.

"Have you got the Law after you?" Bluto asked.

Several of the hobos mumbled and growled and stared into the night as if expecting the cops to come that very instant.

"We've had a good deal here in this little country town. The cops don't bother us too much if we mind our manners," Bluto added.

"We'll be gone in the morning," Claude said. After looking the hobos over, he wanted to be on his way right then, but Myra looked like she couldn't go any farther.

"Nobody's going to give you their shanty," Bluto said.

"We'll make out," Claude said.

"What've you got in that little suitcase?" Bluto asked, and it was apparent that several more of them also wanted to know.

"None of your business," Claude said.

Bluto spit in both his palms and started around the fire. "I'm making it my business."

The man outweighed him by thirty pounds, if not more, and Claude's ribs throbbed at the thought of being battered again.

Bluto cocked his meat hooks and reared back with his right fist to finish the matter with one mighty blow, but Claude drew his .32 out of his waistband and pressed the end of the barrel against Bluto's forehead. The tough hobo froze with his fist raised and staring intently at the pistol between his eyes. To Claude, he kind of looked like the cross-eyed woman back in Louisiana.

"That's our bag, and I'd take offense to anyone who thought otherwise," Claude said quietly.

Bluto nodded his head very slowly, the pistol moving up and down in time with his chin. Claude let him back away. The brute let out a sigh, as if he'd been holding his breath. He stared at Claude, a little shaky, but his eyes were as cold as a dead man's skin. Thwarted for the moment maybe, but he was recalculating his approach. Claude was sure the tough hadn't learned his lesson, and knew he wasn't going to get much sleep that night trying to keep one eye open. Bluto and most of the other hobos left the fire, whispering amongst themselves and throwing glances back at Myra's bag.

"You're quick with that rod." The freckle-faced hobo was still smiling at them across the fire. "Maybe the quickest I've ever seen, and I've ridden the rails from Bangor to San Diego."

"We aren't looking for trouble, just a place to lay our head and let things cool off a little," Claude said.

"No trouble, eh? I thought there for a moment that you were going to send Rufus to the bone orchard."

"He was looking for trouble and almost found more than he could stand."

"I believe you, but I think we all better be getting out of here in the morning. I've got a feeling the bulls will be showing up and raiding this jungle." The little hobo cut his eyes around him, searching the darkness warily.

"Maybe we ought to get out tonight,"

Myra said.

"You're safe enough for now. There's other hobos sleeping farther away, and they'll sound the warning if the bulls show up."

Freckle-face saw that they didn't quite believe him. "Pick up your bag of money and come along with me and I'll show you my luxurious abode."

Myra put a hand on the duffel bag unconsciously. "What makes you think we've got money?"

The little leprechaun smiled. "Nobody clutches their bindle like that unless they've got money or food, and you're too hungry to have any food."

Claude thought the little hobo was too smart for them to trust him. "We'll just fend for ourselves."

The hobo spread his arms wide. "And what would I want with your money when I'm the king of this?"

Claude and Myra followed him through the maze of tarp tents and men wrapped in old newspapers and sleeping inside barrels and wooden shipping crates. They ducked down into a little gully and followed its course in the dark for several yards before climbing up its bank and coming to a large bois d'arc tree with low-hanging limbs.

"Watch out for the thorns," the hobo said.

"They're big and sharp enough to poke through a good work boot."

They ducked under the limbs and found the hobo's shelter, which was simply a pile of discarded fence posts and dead limbs leaned up against the tree trunk with a thick layer of leaves covering it. The hobo led the way into his makeshift tepee and they squatted on the floor while he lit a fire outside the doorway. The flames crackled and leapt up, and the little man looked even more like a leprechaun with his red beard and pug nose illuminated by the flames and shadows dancing on the walls of the shelter.

"There's a lady I've found who'll give a man a little food if he does some chores for her or mends a thing or two," the hobo said.

"Won't the cops arrest you for panhandling?" Myra asked.

"Some will, some won't. Most of these coppers look the other way, or put you on the next train at the worst," the hobo said. "Although the railroad bulls on this line can be bad."

"Do you mean the conductor?"

"It differs from line to line, but whoever is hired to throw hobos off the train."

"Whatever you're cooking smells good," Myra said.

"I hope you don't mind eating bullets.

That's all I've had since the laying house across town figured out I was robbing eggs and sicked their bulldog on me." He laughed deeply and loud. "I'm pretty quick on my feet, but that pug-faced bone polisher about caught me."

"Bullets?" Claude asked.

The hobo quit stirring the contents of the little tin can that served as his cooking pot. He tipped it and held it before Claude. "Beans."

"It must be hard to live like this," Myra said.

The hobo shrugged. "I like traveling and seeing new places."

"You don't talk like a lot of the hobos I've met." Some of the hobos Claude had visited with back home were mentally unstable, or lazy and dishonest to a fault. The Sheriff regularly locked them up in jail, and then hauled them to the edge of town every Monday morning.

"There are all kinds of hobos, and there are getting to be more and more with the times being what they are. Take me. I'm a trained tool and die maker. The factory I worked for went bankrupt and left me without a job."

"I'm sorry," Myra said.

"Don't be. There's still work out there for

a man willing to hunt it, but I probably would have eventually quit my job if the company had kept me on. I never did like working just to keep a roof over my head and bullets in my belly. Seems like a waste of a perfectly good life. Live to be a hundred and spend all your time working just so you can sleep six hours at night and get up and do it all over again."

"I'd say you have to work pretty hard just to stay alive roaming the country like you do," Claude said.

"But I do what I want, and go where I want," the hobo said. "I don't need the booze like some do, and I'm smart enough to read the signs and find places where my lifestyle works."

"You mean the symbols like we saw written on the water tank?" Myra asked.

"If a wily man knows how to read them he can travel from coast to coast and keep himself fed and out of trouble. They're not just warnings, but also directions to food and shelter and information on the townspeople you're about to wander amongst."

Claude heard something in the night and listened intently to hear it again.

"Don't worry about Rufus. He's a buzzard, but he's mostly a bully and he won't risk getting shot to bother you again," the hobo said.

"A buzzard?" Myra asked.

"If you're going to ride the rails you'd better catch yourself up on the lingo," the hobo said. "A buzzard is a hobo who steals from other hobos, or bullies them, or mugs them instead of scavenging for his own comforts."

"He comes around again and I'm going to make him food for the buzzards," Claude said.

"I used to think I'd like a rod to pack around behind my belt, but I've come to think in my later years that I'd rather trust to my eyes and my two legs to get me out of a jam."

"To each his own," Claude said.

They ate about three spoonfuls of beans apiece. Despite the meager meal, the hobo patted his belly like he had just eaten a fine, three-course meal. He leaned over and pointed at a stack of newspapers against the wall. "Just help yourselves to these California blankets should you take the chill in the wee hours. This little shebang I've built isn't insulated too good."

The hobo put out his fire. The night was too hot for one, and none of them wanted anyone stalking his camp with the firelight for a beacon. Claude leaned back against the wall of the hut and Myra laid her head on his chest and went almost instantly to sleep. The hobo was soon snoring too, but Claude swore he was going to stay awake and stand guard. An hour later he too fell asleep.

When he awoke the next morning the hobo was gone, but their money was still with them. He shook Myra awake and they left a hundred dollars and a spare pistol buried under the leaves that the old vagrant used for a mattress. They followed the gully back to the train tracks, avoiding the hobo jungle. The railroad depot house was a short distance up the tracks, and there was a telegraph room in one end of it.

The train depot was nothing more than a one-room bungalow along the railroad tracks, with dull white paint and a sagging roof. A hardwood plank porch ran the length of its front. Somebody inside the station was picking a guitar and trying to yodel like Jimmie Rodgers. The sound carried plainly through the clapboard-sided walls.

"I'm going to go inside and see if I can tend to a little chore," Claude said. "You hang around out here and keep an eye out for anybody coming around."

"What are we going to do for a car?" Myra asked.

"Keep your eye out for one of those too."

Myra leaned against the corner of the depot and smoked a Lucky Strike. She listened to the heels of his cowboy boots thumping on the oak planks of the loading dock, and continuing even after he passed through the front door under the sign that read "Depot & Telegraph Office, St. Louis--San Francisco Railroad, Chelsea, Oklahoma." At one time the sign had been rather pretty, hand-painted and gilded in gold and green letters with pinstriping and scrollwork around the edges. But the years and the weather had faded the paint, and the wood bees and woodpeckers had bored holes in it.

Claude dubiously studied the middle-aged fellow behind the battered desk. The smiling man had his feet propped up on a shipping crate and a Kalamazoo guitar lying across his thighs. Despite the goofy little company cap he wore, Claude noticed the man's Levi's were tucked into a pair of good-looking cowboy boots.

"Are those Tony Lamas?"

The telegraph agent nodded. "It doesn't get much better than a pair of Tonys and a John B. Stetson hat."

The man showed such good sense, Claude probably wouldn't have believed that he was a telegraph agent if it hadn't been for the silly cap and the patch on his company shirt. He leaned forward to read the patch. "Orvon? You play and sing pretty good."

"People call me Gene," the telegraph agent said. "And if I have my way, I'm not going to be sitting in this joint forever pecking like a woodpecker on that telegraph and straining my back unloading freight."

"Doesn't look like such a bad gig to me," Claude said. "That stove should keep you warm in the winter, and I don't see too many people bothering you."

Gene patted the guitar in his lap. "I'm counting on this thing to get me out of here. I'm already playing three nights a week as far away as Oklahoma City."

"The singing telegrapher, huh?"

"Laugh if you want to, but Will Rogers himself was by here not long ago. Flew in on an airplane, if you can believe that. Had that one-eyed Indian pilot Wiley Post with him," Gene said. "He told me I ought to go New York and try to sing for a living. Said I was plenty good enough."

"He's pretty famous. I guess if he got rich with a rope and his wit, maybe you can ride that guitar of yours someplace." Claude didn't let on like he knew his leg was being pulled.

The telegraph agent obviously had lofty

expectations, and felt the need to brag a little. There was no reason Claude could see why anyone would land an airplane anywhere near the little town. He'd only seen two of the flying machines in his entire life, but he knew they only used the expensive toys for warfare, or flying across the ocean so they could have some footage of Charles Lindbergh to show off in the theaters before a movie. Those films swore that aviation was the coming thing. But folks back home said the winged contraptions were never going to amount to anything, because it was a lot farther to the ground compared to an automobile.

Gene pointed cautiously at Claude's waist. "My guitar beats the dickens out of your instrument of choice."

Claude looked down and realized that he had forgotten to cover his .32 with his shirt. "I wouldn't recommend it."

"Well, you know what my day job is," Gene said. "What's your line of work, if you don't mind my asking?"

"Claude Miller's my name, and I rob banks for my living." Claude was finding that there were times when being a desperado sounded pretty good. Not many people could say they robbed banks.

"Must keep you busy, finding ones that

aren't closed or have got any money."

"Sometimes, you might say I'm in the bank foreclosure business myself," Claude said.

Gene eased his guitar to the side and held both his hands up and smiled. "I'll let you know before you stick me up that there isn't ten dollars in the cash box."

Claude laughed. "You can put your hands down. I just want to send a message to Dallas."

Gene had a winning smile, but it was plain to see that he was a little nervous. There was a slight quiver in his hands.

"Don't worry, Gene. I'm even going to pay you for the message." Claude laid a ten-dollar bill on the desk. "You keep the change."

"I just send telegraphs up and down the railroad line to keep the trains running right," Gene said. "Unless there's something that needs sent to another station, I can't help you."

"I thought you could send a message anywhere from a telegraph station."

"Not my company. I'm just here to do railroad business, although I occasionally do some friend a favor and send a message down the line to another depot."

"I need to send a message to a café in Dallas."

"You must be thinking of Western Union, they deliver messages like that. We don't have the runners, even if I sent a message to Dallas."

"You haven't got a telephone have you?" Claude asked.

"Hanging over there on the wall, but it's broken," Gene said. "There's a hobo camp up the track a bit, and they keep tearing down our telegraph and phone wires to try and sell them for scrap. The Law has run them off a time or two, but they keep coming back. It'll scare the dickens of you to walk out to meet the train in the dark and see four or five men bailing out of the boxcars."

"You ever ride the rails?" Claude asked.

"No, although I once thought about it. Might give me some songs."

Claude stared out the window. "They tell me there are hobo camps from here to California."

"And at every train stop I hear there are men begging to chop firewood or hoe your garden for a meal to get them a little farther down the line," Gene said. "What's it like out there on the road?"

"You can see a bit of everything," Claude

said, and then pointed to his bruised and swollen face. "And you can run into anything."

"I wish I could help you with your message."

"I guess I'm out of luck," Claude said.

"Is that a .45 behind your belt?" Gene asked.

"It's a .32 Colt."

"Sorry, I don't know much about guns. Never could hit what I was aiming at when I had one," Gene said.

Claude patted his pistol. "That's all right, Gene. I don't know much about guitars."

They both laughed, although Gene's sounded a little strained.

"I'm too tired to smash up your telegraph machine," Claude said. "Can I trust you not to squeal?"

"I'll keep quiet. You've got my word."

Claude debated whether or not to take the time to carry off the telegraph. "I'm going to take a chance and trust you, Gene, but I'd hate to have to come back here."

"No offense, but I'd hate for you to come back here too," Gene said. "As far as this goes, I didn't ever even see you. Remember, you've got the gun, and I've got the guitar."

"Work on that yodeling some, Gene." Claude started out the door. "Jimmie Rodgers has got it all over you."

"What about your ten dollars?"

Claude paused. "Use it to help buy yourself a ticket out of here. The road isn't so bad if you don't mind something different."

Myra was waiting anxiously for him. "What were you doing in there? Were you trying to send a message to Dallas?"

"Tried, but no luck." Claude found himself in a good mood for some unknown reason.

"What are you grinning about?" she asked. "Do you think it's funny sending for Diamond Joe and daring him not to kill you?"

"I told you, I didn't get to send a message. We'll have to find a phone or a Western Union office."

"Well, what's so funny?"

Claude gave her a reassuring pat on the arm and nodded his head toward the depot building. "There's a danged telegraph agent in there that thinks he's going to be the next Tex Ritter. Says he's pals with Will Rogers."

"I can't believe you found somebody crazier than you."

Claude laughed. "What was it his name patch said? Oh yeah, Autry. Mr. Orvon Autry, but he likes to be called Gene."

"Gene Autry? Lord, who's gonna put a guy with a name like that on the radio?"

"He doesn't sing half bad, but if I was him I wouldn't quit my day job," Claude said.

They were both still giggling when they walked away. Gene carried his guitar to the open door and watched them leave. He halfheartedly played and sang a few verses of "Frankie and Johnnie" while he considered his most recent visitors. He soon lost his enthusiasm for the song, and considered that he should start writing his own stuff.

He'd earned a quick ten dollars, but it was the scariest money he'd ever made. That kid was a smiling sort, but it was a dangerous, gunman's smile. Gene swore that it was going to be his last day in the telegraphing business, because it was high time he found a new line of work. The company didn't pay him enough to sit in the office alone with the kind of people wandering around the countryside. Will Rogers had told him that New York was where he should go, and he'd even been considering California.

He locked up the shop, even though it was early morning. He started home with his guitar, careful to avoid the camp of hobos and vagrants between the station and his house. Most of them were harmless and hungry sorts, but there were some that had a smile like Claude Miller.

Across town, Claude and Myra found a

Buick sedan parked outside a mechanic's garage with the keys left in it. It had a full tank of gas and ran a smooth eighty miles an hour without straining the motor too much.

CHAPTER TWENTY-ONE

*"Never trust an automatic pistol
or a DA's deal."*
— John Dillinger

"That's a funny name for a town, but then again, I can't pronounce half of the place names in your mountains," Myra said, standing on the second-floor balcony of the hotel and reading the sign on the depot house across the street.

"Talihina. It means 'iron road' or 'hard rock road' in Choctaw," Claude said. "Most of the towns around here have Choctaw names, because this was the land the government traded them for a little while before it decided that it wanted this real estate too."

She rubbed her lower back. "I'd say those Choctaws had been riding our motorcycle when they named this place."

The afternoon heat was worse than oppressive, and you could almost cut the humidity with a knife. There were a number of people sitting on white wicker chairs in the shade of the balcony fanning themselves, sipping iced tea, and waiting for the next train to arrive to pass the hottest part of the day.

"Are you clear on what I want you to tell Diamond Joe?" he asked.

"Yeah, yeah, I got it," she said.

"Remember, just his cut, and he's not to bring Bull and the boys with him or we skedaddle with all the money."

"I told you I've got it."

They went downstairs together, but separated in the lobby. Myra went to use the phone while Claude walked out onto the street. He looked back through the open lobby door and saw Myra with the phone to her ear. From the frown on her face he assumed the call wasn't going well, but there was no way to make that kind of conversation friendly.

"Well, big boy, you've done it now. Your fat's in the fire for sure," he said to himself.

He paralleled the railroad tracks until he hit Main Street, and turned and passed along the sidewalk beneath the high red brick buildings until he saw a general store with the word "hardware" stenciled on one of the large front windows. He ducked inside the building and instantly found relief from the heat in the dark, cavernous room underneath rows of ceiling fans. He thought the little town must have been booming, considering the large array of merchandise. There was everything from household wares and clothing, to hardware and a few groceries. He wandered the aisles until a rack of rifles along one wall caught his eye. An elderly man wearing a black shop apron left the cash register near one of the front doors and walked over to him. The rifles stood on their butts in a wooden rack, with the shelves below it stacked with various ammunition. Claude resisted the urge to handle every one of the rifles, and focused his attention on the glass display case that was the gun counter. Six or seven brand new pistols lay there, and he squatted down and put his face close to the glass.

The storekeeper unlocked the back of the cabinet and paused with his hand inside. "Which one would you like to see?"

"I want to see that pair of .45's." Claude stood and watched the hand in the glass pluck the automatics, one at a time, from the green felt they lay on.

"Just like the Army boys use, but blued instead of a Parkerized finish." The shopkeeper set both of the pistols down on the glass countertop with a little clack.

Claude took up one of the pistols in his right hand, aiming it at the eye of a mounted deer head on the wall above the gun rack. The checkered cocobolo grips felt good in his palm. He racked the slide and dry-fired the gun, and then racked it again, liking the sound of steel sliding on polished steel.

"Doesn't get any better than a Colt." The storekeeper readjusted his glasses and tilted his head to focus on the rearing stallion medallion on the grip of the automatic still lying on the countertop.

"No, sir, it doesn't."

The shopkeeper clucked his tongue and shook his head gravely. "Fine pistols, but I'm a revolver man myself. Never trust a woman or an automatic when you're in a bind."

"I learned with a government .45," Claude said.

"Nobody learns with a .45. Too much recoil."

"I did."

"If firepower is what you're after, what about this .38 Super?" The shopkeeper pointed to a nickel-plated Colt 1911 that looked identical to the .45's. "Same gun, but the caliber has a hell of a lot more velocity."

Any kind of gun interested Claude, but he shook his head. "Yeah, but it ain't a .45."

The storekeeper could tell he'd made Claude a little testy. "Which one of them do you like?"

"I want both of them." Claude hefted a .45 in each hand.

"What are you going to do with two of them?" The storekeeper couldn't hide the fact that he thought he was dealing with a foolish kid.

"I need one for each hand," Claude said with a straight face.

"Kid, nobody but Tom Mix shoots with both hands, and if he wasn't on the movie screen you'd be surprised where his shots went when he slings those six-shooters around."

Claude's jaw clamped down like a steel trap. "I'm not as good with my left hand as I am my right, but I shoot tolerable well with it."

"Are you meaning to tell me you can shoot with two guns at once?"

"That's what I said. Do you want to sell me the pistols or not?"

The mention of money brightened the storekeeper's expression. "That's a lot of money."

Claude reached in his pocket for his roll of money with a rubber band around it. "I've been saving."

A big smile spread across the storekeeper's face. He pulled out a stub of pencil and started to write a price down on the ticket.

"I'll give you sixty dollars for the pair," Claude said.

"Seventy dollars."

"Seventy dollars, and you throw in three boxes of shells."

They ended up making a deal for seventy-seven dollars for the pistols, four boxes of ammunition, and a spare clip for each of the guns. The storekeeper threw in a pair of surplus Army flap holsters to sweeten the deal.

Claude turned his back, not wanting the storekeeper to see how much money he had while he skinned the price of the pistols off his gambler's roll. It wouldn't do to be seen flashing money around, not with the Law looking for him.

Claude handed over the price of the guns and shook open the brown paper sack the storekeeper provided.

"Hey, Pete, come over here and meet this kid," the storekeeper said to somebody behind Claude.

A uniformed policeman walked up to the counter and studied Claude's purchases. Claude tried to act casual, and smiled even though he was sweating buckshot.

"Pete, this kid says he can shoot with a pistol in each hand just like those two-gun cowboys at the theater," the storekeeper said.

The policeman leaned against the counter with the same condescending look on his face as the storekeeper had. "No kidding? Where are you from, kid?"

"Tulsa." Claude realized that he was getting better at lying. He hardly even stuttered. "I came down here to do a little camping and fishing with some family and friends."

"Uh huh," the cop said. "What's your name?"

"Henry Smith." The name came quick, but Claude wasn't especially proud of his alias. All he knew was that most outlaws on the lamb used Smith or Jones as a last name, at least they did it that way in the books he'd read.

"Are you a fighter?" The cop was studying Claude's face. "Looks like you tangled with somebody tougher than you."

Claude touched his swollen nose. "If I was a fighter I wouldn't look like this. I should have led with my left instead of my face."

"But you're a trick shooter?" The cop whirled a set of keys on a belt chain around and around and shoved his uniform cap back on his head.

"I can usually hit what I'm aiming at," Claude said.

"How about we go out back and do a little target practice?" The cop winked at the storekeeper.

It was plain to Claude that the man expected him to come up with some excuse so that he didn't have to prove what an awful pistol shot he was. He knew the smart thing was to swallow his pride and get away from the cop, but he couldn't. What was it that his mother said? "Pride goeth before a fall"?

"Cartridges are expensive," he said.

The cop turned to the storekeeper. "How about it, Harold? Can you donate a box of shells to see what this kid can do?"

The storekeeper took another box of ammo from the shelf. He shouted to the woman helping a customer at the register. "I'll be back in a half hour."

Claude remembered how the Sheriff always said guns weren't toys, and a real man didn't show off with firearms. He took one look at the cocky, smug look on the cop's face and decided to be as big a fool as ever.

They went out the back door of the store, down an alley, and followed fifty yards of street to a little dry streambed.

The cop carried a wooden tray of empty Coke bottles he'd picked up at the back of the store. He threw one of them on the far bank of the branch, about ten yards from Claude. "Hit that, Bat Masterson."

Claude loaded two magazines from the cartridge box that the storekeeper offered and shoved one in each of the pistols. He racked a round into one, safetied it, and shoved it behind his belt on his left side. He loaded the pistol in his right hand and busted the bottle with only a glance at it, never even raising the weapon to arm's length.

"Are you some kind of gangster?" the cop asked.

Claude's heart made a ragged beat.

"Just a lucky shot," the storekeeper said.

They pitched two more bottles across the stream. Claude quickly raised his pistol to eye level, but simply pointed instead of lining up the sights. Both bottles exploded as quickly as he could pull the trigger.

"That's shooting," the storekeeper said.

The cop was frowning. He threw another

two bottles out and took a shot at one of them with his Colt Official Police. The .38 Special revolver bucked in his fist and his bullet cut the dirt too high and a foot past the bottle. He took steady aim, holding the pistol with both hands, and busted the bottle with his second shot. He passed the gun to the storekeeper who hit another bottle with three shots and a fair amount of squinting and adjusting his glasses. When they were through they both looked to Claude.

"Let's see that two-gun work," Officer Pete said.

A cop car pulled up behind them, and the officer in it shouted out the window, "What are you doing, Pete? I thought somebody was robbing the bank."

Claude couldn't help but glance at the brick bank building on the corner two blocks behind them.

"Get out and come see this," Pete said.

The newest arrival got out of his car and ambled over. Claude was glad it was so hot, because the way he was sweating wasn't going to seem suspicious. He cursed himself for being such a damned fool.

"This kid is some kind of trick shooter." Pete had a bottle in each hand.

Claude tried to calm himself. There was

no way the situation was going to get any worse. Surely, the little town didn't have more than two cops on duty. "Throw them up in the air."

"What?" Officer Pete asked.

"Throw them high," Claude said.

Pete chucked one bottle, and his fellow cop threw the other at the same time. Claude watched the twinkling glass tumble through the air high overhead. He waited with both pistols hanging at his sides until the bottles reached the apex of their flight. He looked down the barrel of his right gun and busted the first one and pivoted slightly and shot the second bottle with his left gun almost leisurely.

"Hot damned! That's shooting," Pete said.

"Amen," the other cop said.

"What'd you say your name was, kid?" Officer Pete asked.

"Henry Smith." Claude hoped that was the name he'd used the first time. A fellow had to keep up with the stories he told.

"How much practice did it take to shoot like that?" the storekeeper asked.

"I used to shoot a little with my daddy." Claude didn't mention that the practice had helped, but that he'd been able to shoot well since the first time the Sheriff put a pistol in his hands.

"I bet your father is a fine shot," the storekeeper said.

Claude didn't like where the conversation was heading. He decided to tell one more lie to keep from telling another. "He was a trick shooter for Buffalo Bill's wild west show back in the day. You ever hear of Two Gun Kelly?"

All three of his audience looked puzzled, but nodded their heads. Claude was glad that the city didn't hire well-read policemen.

"What else can you do?" the storekeeper asked.

Claude noticed the officer who had just arrived was crumpling an empty cigarette package in his hands. "Put that up over yonder on that tree."

The cop went over and balanced the empty little box on the limb of an elm sapling about five feet off the ground and fifteen yards away. He trotted back and stood behind Claude with the other two.

Claude tucked the .45 behind his belt with the other one. He turned at the hip and made sure the three of them were watching, then drew both guns and knocked the cigarette package off the tree with his first shot. He fired a second time with his left hand, and the package jerked sideways in its fall. He still had plenty of fodder left in the magazines of both guns, so he emptied them as fast as he could pull the triggers. Bark flew off the little tree until there was a white spot of raw inner bark about the size of a grown man's hand. Claude pushed both slide releases on the empty pistols and started putting them back into their boxes while the storekeeper went to investigate his target.

"He hit it both times." The storekeeper walked back and handed the cigarette package to Pete, who gave it a long look. The other cop looked over his shoulder.

"He shot it the second time out of the air as it was falling," Pete said.

"That's about the best shooting I've ever seen." The other cop was studying the white circle on the tree chewed away by Claude's bullets.

"How about you teach us how to do that?" Pete asked.

"Not me," the second cop said, "at least not that fast-draw part. The last time I tried that I like to have shot my toe off."

Their bragging on him had warmed Claude to both of the cops, but the break in the action reminded him that he needed to get out of there. "I'm supposed to meet some family down on Kiamichi River for a little camping trip."

Both the cops looked disappointed. "You ought to go have some lunch with us. We'd like to introduce you around."

"Who's your family?" the storekeeper asked.

"Oh, they're all from Tulsa. You wouldn't know them," Claude said.

"Lots of folks come down here in the mountains to hunt and fish," Pete said.

"Not much outdoor life to be found in the city," Claude agreed.

"You stop by the next time you're through here. I'd be proud to shoot with you again," Pete said.

"Will do. I've always liked to shoot," Claude said.

The storekeeper shook Claude's hand and didn't seem at all put out by the fact that they'd shot up his cartridges and seven cents' worth of penny-a-return bottles. Both the cops had to shake hands with Claude also.

"What do you do for a living, Henry?" Pete asked.

One last lie, Claude thought. No, he wouldn't lie. "I'm in the bank business."

"Your family got a bank up in Tulsa?" Pete asked.

"Oh, I'm an inspector. I travel around to

352

different banks and check to see if they have the money they're supposed to have," Claude said.

"Well, somebody ought to keep an eye on them," the storekeeper said.

"So long, boys." Claude started back toward Main Street.

"Don't tell anybody we let you shoot guns in town," Pete said. "It wouldn't do for it to look like we're playing favorites."

"Will do," Claude said.

"You watch yourself going camping. There are some bad folks traveling the roads," the second cop said.

"You don't have a clue," Claude said under his breath.

He made it to Main Street with his pistols boxed and in a sack tucked under his arm, along with his other purchases. He turned the corner leisurely, but lengthened his stride once he was out of sight of the lawmen. It was only a short walk back to the hotel.

Myra was gone when he got there, and he laid out his purchases on the bed. He went downstairs and borrowed a roll of masking tape from the clerk. He came back up and tied down the grip safeties on both the pistols with several wraps. The thumb safeties would still keep the guns from going off in his holster, and the jury rigging he'd done to the grip safeties would ensure the pistols would fire even if he got a bad grip.

Next, he took his pocketknife and modified the leather Army holsters. He slotted them so they would both ride butt forward high on each hip and cut off the large flaps that buttoned over the top of the pistols. He took the pistols in and out of them several times, whittling the holsters away until they suited him. He ran his belt through them, and back through his belt loops. He holstered the automatics, and a couple of practice draws in the dresser mirror convinced him that his leatherwork suited him.

There was a cut-off piece of board propping one of the room's windows open, and he used it for a mallet to drive the back sights off the pistols with his pocketknife for a punch. He drew the guns a few more times, satisfied that they slid much more smoothly from the leather without the danger of hanging up. He shoved a loaded magazine into both pistols, chambered a round in each, and holstered them with the hammers cocked and the thumb safeties on — cocked and locked like the military carried them, but with the grip safeties taped down.

Myra walked in the room with two big

paper sacks in her hands. She put down her load and studied the pistols on Claude's hips. "New toys?"

As hot as it was, Claude hated to put on his jacket, but he needed it to cover his guns. He buttoned the jacket and studied himself in the mirror again to see if his pistols showed. "We've got to get out of here."

"So soon? Look at the shirts I bought you." She bent over to reach into one of the sacks.

"You can show them to me later. I just talked to two cops down the street, and they might come back around," he said.

"Did they act suspicious?" she asked.

Claude didn't want to tell her what a braggart and a fool he'd been. She would never be that stupid. "They had plenty of questions."

She stuffed their little suitcase full and handed it to Claude without another word. They paid their hotel bill and loaded their belongings into the Buick and left town looking for cops following them. They did pass Officer Pete on traffic watch at the edge of town, but he simply waved at them.

"What did Diamond Joe say?" Claude asked.

"He wasn't any too happy, but he agreed

355

to meet us. And no funny stuff," she said.

"Sounds like a plan."

"A crazy plan," she said.

"Do we ever have any other kind?"

Officer Pete watched the Buick disappear headed south. He'd liked the kid, and wished he would come back and show off a little more of his shooting skills. Nothing much ever happened in town.

An hour later he walked into the police station and the other cop informed him that the highway patrol had just called and said to be on the lookout for a stolen Buick carrying a little blonde girl and a teenaged Indian boy. Both were to be considered armed and dangerous. Officer Pete could vouch for both claims.

Chapter Twenty-Two

*"If you hold a cat by the tail you learn
things you cannot learn any other way."*
— Mark Twain

Sergeant Jones parked the car behind a
black Cadillac in an alley alongside the
diner, and climbed out from behind the
steering wheel, eyeing the seedy little joint
with disdain. He stopped at the entrance
and waited for Sheriff Miller who was just
shutting his car door.

"I notice you're wearing your gun," Sergeant Jones said.

"Yeah." Sheriff Miller looked down at the
single-action Colt .44-40 riding high on his
hip in a basket-stamped pancake holster as
if he'd just noticed it was there.

"How come you don't carry an automatic?" Sergeant Jones patted the 1911 on
his hip.

"Carried one in the war, but I don't trust

'em not to jam," Sheriff Miller said. "And your 1911 doesn't carry but one more round than my wheel gun does."

"Yeah, but I can reload a hell of a lot faster. And I can hold my automatic on somebody and stuff a fresh clip in with a round still in the chamber and without lowering it."

Sheriff Miller smiled. "If six bullets won't do the trick, I'm probably dead anyway."

Sergeant Jones eyed the seven-and-a-half-inch-barreled Colt dubiously. "Alright, but wouldn't a shorter barrel be a little better for police work?"

"I like to hit what I'm aiming at," Sheriff Miller said. "And besides, this hunk of steel comes in handy when you need to smack somebody over the head. Old Joe Leflore taught me how to buffalo a man to keep from shooting him."

"Fair enough, but . . ."

Sheriff Miller sighed. "I've shot machine guns and threw hand grenades and had cannons shot at me, and don't think I need any of them to do my job. Let's just say I'm set in my ways, and leave it at that."

Sergeant Jones led the way into the diner, and Sheriff Miller stepped wide of him as soon as they passed through the door. He did that naturally without thinking, letting his eyes get used to the darkness of the room while he surveyed it.

The only visible inhabitant of the establishment was a waitress standing behind the counter talking to someone through the order hole in the wall, probably the cook. She rested her hand on her outthrust, aproned hip, smacking her gum while she looked her latest customers over.

"Cocked and locked and loaded for bear, isn't she?" Sergeant Jones walked up to the counter and leaned against one of the swiveling stools with round, red vinyl cushions, and shiny metal bands. He started to flip back his jacket to reveal his badge.

"What are you hungry for, Ranger?" the waitress asked, and then stuck her face up to the hole in the wall. "Hey, Cookie, we've got one of those cowboy cops out here."

Sergeant Jones started to say something, but took a breath instead. He looked to Sheriff Miller and shrugged. "I'll have a strawberry milkshake. What about you?"

"I thought you Rangers only drank beer or whiskey. Kind of ruins your image to hear you ordering ice cream," Sheriff Miller said.

"Like you said, you're not up with the times."

Sheriff Miller shook his head at the waitress. "I'll pass."

She was in no hurry to process their order and waited until she'd blown a bubble with her gum before flouncing down to the ice-cream cooler.

"Milkshake or not, you must look like a sure-enough Texas Ranger," Sheriff Miller said. "She recognized you for what you are the second you walked through the door."

"I don't know if the ability to spot cops is bred into criminals, or a learned technique."

"If a coyote or a mountain lion chews up your old hound dog, you can guarantee he'll remember the mauling and growl the next time he sniffs their trail," Sheriff Miller said.

The waitress finally brought Sergeant Jones his milkshake after staring at the ceiling and letting the blender beat against the stainless-steel mixing cup for a prolonged time.

"That'll be a nickel," she said, shifting her pink bubble gum through the gap of a missing tooth on the left side of her mouth. She looked thirty-five, but was probably ten years younger. The ash on her cigarette had grown so long that it threatened to drop into the Ranger's milkshake, but she didn't seem to notice or care.

Sergeant Jones slapped some change down on the counter, but kept his hand over it when she reached for it. He showed the badge on his chest with his other hand so that she could see the Texas Star centered in the middle of what supposedly had once been a silver peso, but was now nothing more than a nickel-coated disk.

"Now that I've got my milkshake I want you to go get your boss for me," he said.

"You're wanting to talk to the cook?" She was still sassy, but it was starting to fade under Sergeant Jones's hard stare.

"You go tell Diamond Joe that I want to talk to him," he said. "And don't bother to tell me he's not here, because I saw his Cadillac parked in the alley."

She started to give him some more lip, but must have thought better of it. She swished her hips to the back of the diner, stopping to spit her gum in a corner trash can before disappearing into a back room.

Unlike Claude and Myra, the two lawmen weren't invited into the back room. Diamond Joe walked out to the counter beside Sergeant Jones.

"What can I do for you, Sergeant?" the crime boss asked. "I thought they still had you working down at Eagle Pass."

"You know better."

"I thought maybe you'd drank too much tequila down there and drowned in the Rio Grande."

"Ignore Joe here. He's just sore that I've arrested a couple of his goons," Sergeant Jones said over his shoulder to his partner.

"And who are you?" Diamond Joe turned to Sheriff Miller.

"Sheriff Jim Miller."

"I don't see a badge on you."

Sheriff Miller didn't bother to dig out the Texas badge they had given him saying he was a deputy of something or another. He simply looked Diamond Joe over from his wing-tip shoes and expensive suit, to the old scars on his knuckles and face. He didn't like what he saw. Diamond Joe was just another crook, no matter how dangerous he was. Rattlesnakes were dangerous too, but not especially impressive when you were used to seeing them all the time.

"If you ever see my badge, you won't like it," Sheriff Miller said.

Diamond Joe grunted and looked back at the Ranger. "Sergeant, I don't think the sheriff here likes me."

"He isn't the talker I am," Sergeant Jones said. "You wouldn't know anything about a robbery over in Calcasieu Parish, Louisiana, would you? Maybe another one up at Booker, Texas?"

Diamond Joe put a hand on his heart and tried to look big-eyed and shocked. "Me?

362

You know gambling is my game."

"What about Bull? Have you still got him around? I'd like to talk to him."

"He's in and out. I'll tell him you're looking for him."

"I bet you will. What about Ernest Peacock or Myra Hooser?"

"Didn't she used to be a working girl over at Crabby Alice's?" Diamond Joe gave a sly smile.

"So you haven't seen her?"

"Great little tits and a cute ass, but she isn't my type. I'll spend two bucks to dip my wick in a working Mollie sometimes, but I don't mistake them for girlfriends," Diamond Joe said. "What about you? Do you pay for your pussy up front, or have you got a wife who bills you monthly?"

"I don't consort with prostitutes."

Diamond Joe let his eyes drift down to the sergeant's crippled leg. "I see you're still a gimp. The war, huh? I didn't know you were hurt so bad, but don't worry, lots of boys over there came back with your kind of wounds. A hero like you ought not listen to those that will say you're less than a man because you've got a chronic case of limp dick."

Sergeant Jones frowned and paused long enough to gain control of his temper.

"You're pushing it, Joe."

Joe raised both palms in a mock gesture of peace. "I didn't mean to insult you. I was just saying that your condition is nothing to be ashamed of. With the leaps and bounds modern medicine is making there may be hope for a cure for you if you didn't get your balls shot off."

"Keep talking, wiseass," Sergeant Jones said through gritted teeth. "I don't suppose you've seen a young Indian named Claude Miller."

Diamond Joe looked up at his forehead and frowned as if he were concentrating. "What's he look like?"

"Like an Indian. He's about six feet tall, seventeen years old."

"Feathered headdress? Breechcloth? Cigar and tomahawk? I saw him down in front of the tobacco shop." It was obvious that Diamond Joe had no fear of either of them, and was enjoying jerking their chains.

"I've got a sneaking suspicion somebody here in town helped my bank robbers out. Maybe they're even paying him off," Sergeant Jones said.

Diamond Joe kept a poker face. "I'd say you've got an overactive imagination, but if not, I hope you catch this kingpin you're looking for."

"What if we were to go into that back room? Who might we find back there?" Sheriff Miller asked.

Diamond Joe's cool showed a little hint of breaking. "My lawyer would chew your ass up."

"Easy, Sheriff. Diamond Joe is a slimeball, but he wouldn't be baiting you if there was anything back there to see," Sergeant Jones said.

"What about those pistols he's wearing under his coat?" Sheriff Miller asked. "I think I recall you saying Crystal Joe here is a convicted felon."

"It's Diamond Joe, and I haven't ever been convicted of a felony." Diamond Joe had all his attention on Sheriff Miller. "I'm not wearing pistols, but if I was, you wouldn't like seeing them."

Sheriff Miller surprised Sergeant Jones and smiled. "Maybe I was wrong."

Diamond Joe smiled back smugly, sensing weakness.

Sheriff Miller patted his flat stomach at the same spot where he thought Diamond Joe was carrying two pistols in his belt. He straightened his lean, fit frame and stood a little taller, even though he was six foot one in his socks. "I must've been mistaken about that bulge at your waistline. It's easy for a fellow to pack a little on around the middle when you get to your age."

Diamond Joe's eye narrowed and his breathing deepened and slowed at the hint that he was fat. "I don't think I'm going to like you either."

Sergeant Jones saw that they were getting nowhere with the thug. "Come on, Sheriff. This milkshake tastes like it was made with clabbered milk."

"Maybe you ought to call the health department," Sheriff Miller said following Sergeant Jones toward the front door.

"Yeah, the fire marshal might want to check out this joint. A slum like this might burn down and hurt somebody." Sergeant Jones immediately caught on and joined the fun. "And wasn't that Cadillac outside improperly parked?"

"Go ahead. I've been harassed by better cops than you two." Diamond Joe hooked one elbow on the counter and crossed his ankles.

"See you later, Joe," Sergeant Jones said in the doorway.

"Hey, Sheriff. You ought to ask for a raise so you can buy something besides that antique you're carrying on your hip," Diamond Joe said.

Sheriff Miller turned slowly and stood

shadowed in the light coming through the front windows. "It's always been good enough."

Diamond Joe shrugged and held out his hands in a peace offering. "I didn't mean anything. I was just saying that getting that hog leg out of its holster can't be easy. You know, some men's hands get slower with age."

"Be seeing you," Sheriff Miller said.

"I won't mind at all," Diamond Joe said.

Outside in their car, Sheriff Miller said, "I don't think I'm going to like him."

Sergeant Jones pulled the shifter into low gear and let off the clutch. The car lurched and banged into the Cadillac in front of them. "Oops."

Sheriff Miller was impressed when he saw the bow in the Caddy's rear bumper as they backed away. "Sergeant, I think you've got a little old school in you after all."

Just for kicks, the Ranger slammed into the Caddy one more time. "I just can't seem to get the hang of this shifter. I keep looking for reverse and finding first gear."

"Happens to the best of us. Wish we had a bulldozer," Sheriff Miller said.

They stopped off at a little Italian eatery for lunch and Sergeant Jones went to borrow the restaurant's telephone while Sheriff

Miller rolled his meatballs around his plate with his fork and thought about Claude and his wife back home.

"Hurry up and finish your food." Sergeant Jones returned and flopped down in his chair. "We've got an airplane waiting for us at Love Field in an hour."

Sheriff Miller wiped his chin with his napkin and tried to hide the horror he was feeling. He didn't like heights at all. "What the hell do we need an airplane for?"

From his smile, Sergeant Jones was obviously proud of his announcement. "The Oklahoma City boys just relayed a call they received from some cops in the northeastern corner of the state. It seems like a blonde and a young Indian on a motorcycle and sidecar ran two roadblocks yesterday. And then they were spotted three hours south this morning in a stolen Buick."

"Claude's headed back home, but what's that got to do with an airplane?"

"A friend of mine bought an old surplus biplane that he barnstorms with. He's offered to fly us to Oklahoma. We can cover some country and see if we can spot that Buick from a bird's-eye view. The Oklahoma boys are already setting up more roadblocks."

Sheriff Miller shook his head and shoved

back from the table. "Not me."

"Do you want to get there while they still might be around, or take most of a day driving?"

Sheriff Miller shook his finger at Sergeant Jones. "You new cops are gonna run old dogs like me out of business."

Sergeant Jones could already tell that Sheriff Miller was going to fly with him. "You aren't much older than me, if any. What are you? Forty?"

"I feel older than that."

Sergeant Jones was excited to get to the landing strip, and didn't bother finishing his meal. "Times are changing."

"Yeah, but I don't have to like it."

An hour later they were both high over Dallas and flying north in a creaking, popping hunk of linen canvas, wood, tubing, and cables. The pilot had assured them that the Curtiss JN-4D "Jenny" trainer was perfectly safe, but it was hard for Sheriff Miller to trust a man to know anything about airplanes when he wore bib overhauls and talked like he came straight out of the cotton fields. Sergeant Jones tried to assure him that aviation was still a recently new thing, and that everybody was still learning about it. Needless to say, when Sheriff Miller considered how high they were off of the ground, he wasn't at all comforted by the Ranger's assertions. In fact, flying in a worn-out training plane that was more than a decade behind the times piloted by a farmer seeking a new career scared him to death.

The Jenny had only two seats, one for the pilot and one for a passenger. Despite their pilot mumbling something about the plane being nose-heavy with an extra man, the two passengers crowded into the front seat. Even though he didn't know a thing about airplanes, it bothered Sheriff Miller that he couldn't see what the pilot was doing behind him. If something were going wrong he was sure he would have some warning if he could only see the man on the controls.

The lawmen's shoulders barely stuck out of the hole in the fuselage, and they held their cowboy hats smashed against their heads while their pilot pointed out the landscape below them. Sheriff Miller didn't look down. The fuel fumes and smoke from the laboring engine burned his eyes, and his stomach threatened to give back the spaghetti he had eaten. There was no way he was going to be able to help spot Claude, because he couldn't let go of his hat without it blowing off, and his other hand had a death grip on the edge of the cockpit preventing him from adjusting his goggles well enough to see anyway. However, he could see the watch on his wrist, and he passed the time counting off the minutes until he was sure the sputtering, whining contraption was going to crash and kill them all.

CHAPTER TWENTY-THREE

*"I never killed anyone
who didn't need killing."*
— John Wesley Hardin

Diamond Joe shuffled his cards and scowled at them for an hour. He was used to cops coming around and showing off their badges and looking for payoffs, but the two who had just left his diner had gotten under his skin, especially the sheriff. The Ranger he could take. The drugstore cowboy bore watching, but he didn't have that irritating something about him. That sheriff now, he grated on a man like sandpaper.

Diamond Joe didn't like anybody smart-talking him. He'd scrapped his way up from nothing on the streets, and he demanded respect. There was no doubt the sheriff had belittled him, even when he wasn't saying so directly. Nobody talked like that to him. He vowed that if the county John Law came around again he was going to show him why that was. It wasn't like he hadn't lined out a smart-aleck cop before. Granted, he was younger then and it got him a week in jail and a suspended sentence for resisting arrest, but it had been worth it to smack a copper.

What was making him even madder was the call he'd gotten from Myra. The little bitch thought she could cross him and then bargain with him. She offered him his cut of the bank loot if he would play by her rules. Who in the hell did she think she was? And that Indian kid, he should have killed him when he first walked into the diner. His cut hell, he was going to Oklahoma and get that and more. Twenty grand was worth the trip, and shooting Claude would be a bonus. Little Myra needed to be taught a lesson as well. He was too soft on dames sometimes, and they tried to take advantage of his generosity.

Bull came into the back room of the diner about the time Diamond Joe was really getting himself worked up. Dink and Ernest followed him. Dink wore a bandage where Claude had shot off the last two fingers on his right hand, and Ernest looked like he had been run over by a train. Their injuries seemed to have put them in a foul mood, or perhaps it was the loss of all the money Myra ran off with.

"Sit down," Diamond Joe said.

"What's up, boss?" Bull took a chair beside Dink across the table from their boss.

"We've got a little trip to take." Diamond Joe laid out the phone call he'd gotten from Myra, and the fact that Claude was still alive.

"That little bitch," Dink said. "I told Bull not to trust her with the money. Ask him if you don't believe me."

Bull set his elbows on the table and leaned forward. He looked like he was about to punch Dink. "Shut up, you ignorant midget."

Dink saw that he had gone too far. "Sorry, boss. My hand hurts like hell and it's making me snappy."

"I thought you said you killed Claude," Diamond Joe said.

Bull leaned back in his chair. "He looked dead to me when we left him."

"Yeah, I thought he was dead as hell," Dink added.

Diamond Joe looked at Ernest who hadn't taken a seat, but was instead standing at the pinup girl calendar staring at Jean Harlow, the Platinum Blonde, in her bathing suit. At least he wasn't rubbing his crotch like he often did when he was lost in thought. If a crazy man weren't useful for some jobs, he would have killed Ernest a long time before.

"What about you, Ernest? I'd think I could trust you to kill a man," Diamond Joe said.

It took Ernest a second or two to forget the calendar. "I was choking and there was a storm, dust everywhere. We couldn't even see him good."

"Dink shot him twice at point-blank range," Bull added. "The cops were on our tail, and I didn't wait around to see him take his last breath."

"Well, the fucker isn't dead, and Myra called me offering my ten percent of the take if I meet her up in Oklahoma," Diamond Joe said.

"Let's go," Ernest said.

"We'll put a marble hat on him this time," Dink added.

"Maybe I should go by myself," Diamond Joe said. "If you want something done right, you've got to do it yourself."

"What about us? We've got a bigger stake in what Myra stole from us than you do," Bull said. "You aren't thinking about cutting us out, are you?"

"Myra told me not to bring you boys, or she and Claude would disappear with all the money," Diamond Joe said.

"What makes you think they'll even show up at the meeting place?" Bull asked.

"Myra's scared we'll bother her sister if she doesn't."

"Shirley?" Ernest jerked as if just then coming to consciousness.

"Leave Shirley alone unless I tell you otherwise. She's our money in the bank, but I don't think we're going to need her," Diamond Joe said. "Myra will make sure she and Claude show up with the money as long as there's a chance we could harm Shirley."

"Yeah, Shirley never did anything to us. She's always been square," Bull said.

"She gave me the crabs," Dink said.

"She's the only one that would give you anything," Bull said. "How are we going to work this thing?"

"Simple, we're going to meet them," Diamond Joe said.

"They'll have somebody watching the meeting place. What's to keep them from running when they see you've brought us along?" Dink asked.

"We could bring Shirley along with us as a hostage. That'd make them turn loose of the money," Ernest said.

"We don't need Shirley," Diamond Joe said.

"Either way, we're getting our cut," Dink said.

"You dumb ass, we're going to get all the money and a piece of Claude's hide." Diamond Joe leaned back in his chair and laced his fingers together and stretched his arms out in front of him. His joints cracked like pistol shots. "Leave the planning to me. There's always a way to get what you want."

"I want another crack at Claude," Dink said.

"Myra needs taught a lesson too," Ernest threw in.

Diamond Joe nodded to all of them. "You boys will get to have your fun, I promise you. Get your suitcases packed. Those two owe me twenty grand worth of trouble and I mean to make them pay."

Bull nodded, but looked suspicious. "We'll get the money back."

"And then some," Dink said with a malicious grin.

Ernest went back to his apartment. It was only a short walk from the diner, but he took the long way around to avoid the city park. There were always pigeons there. People threw them bread, attracting hordes of the flapping, fluttering, and cooing creatures. The thought of birds quickened his step, and he kept his eyes on the sidewalk.

Two kids playing on the stairwell noticed him, and fled with their toys. All the children in the neighborhood talked about Mr. Creepy.

Once inside his single room on the third floor, he locked the doorknob and the deadbolt on his apartment door. He also closed the two other hasps and latches he'd installed himself, dropping a pin through each of them to bar anyone opening the door from the outside. When he was sure that he had the privacy he needed, he went to the refrigerator. A chain was wrapped around the appliance with the ends secured together by a padlock. He selected the correct key from the large key ring in his pocket and unlocked it.

The box fan set in the open window provided little relief from the almost suffocating summer heat. His clothes were already heavy with sweat and sticking to him. No matter how hard he tried to banish them, the birds were fluttering around in his head, and the room swam before his eyes like heat waves in a mirage. A full six-pack of beer rested on the top shelf of the refrigerator, and he took a bottle and downed it in two long slugs, hoping to quench his fever and dull the throbbing headache that had been plaguing him for weeks. He pitched the empty bottle into the sink and reached for the gallon pickle jar on the bottom shelf.

He sat the jar on the floor beside his chair with the yellowed cushioning sticking out of holes and tears in the stained, flower-print fabric. The steamer trunk was the only furniture in the room other than his bed and chair, and he knelt in front of it with the tiny brass skeleton key that opened the lock. He anxiously tilted back the lid. A layer of magazines covered the top tray, and he stacked them on the floor to the side.

He took the lightened wooden tray from the trunk and carried it over to his chair. He sat down with it across his lap and began to browse through his collection, holding them, one at a time, and remembering. The pearl necklace and the tube of lipstick were nice, but the pair of panties that was his latest trophy excited him most. It hadn't been that long ago, and if the room was quiet he could still hear her moaning and begging for mercy.

He felt himself growing hard, and he tossed the panties back in the tray and set it on the floor. He unbuckled his belt while he groped for the jar beside the chair. He held it up before him and watched the pickled little hands floating behind the glass. The formaldehyde made them even whiter, and tiny bits of skin twinkled and swirled around the jar like snowflakes.

And the glass felt so cold. The hands waved at him when he moved the jar, and he watched one twist on its axis, the ruby ring still on one of its fingers.

He held onto his memories while he took hold of himself. His fist hurt It, but he knew he needed to be punished. He was a bad boy. Two eyes stared at him out of the jar, bird eyes. He knew the parrot wasn't really looking at him from the other side of the glass, but he closed his own eyes anyway. The friction his fist created brought tears to his eyes.

"Mother!" he cried.

He imagined all those cold, dead hands clutching him, holding him and laughing. The parrot watched him, and had been watching him all those times with Mother and those other girls.

"Myra," he moaned.

No parrot eyes, poke them out. No watching him while the white cold hands held It. No biting It off with their sharp beaks. Mother said never tell. Poke their eyes out.

"Myra." He felt the hot, slick grease in his palm, and the blood.

"I'm sorry, Mother."

An hour later he rose from his chair and put the tray back in the trunk and the jar in the refrigerator. He went to lie on his bed, his head clear for the moment. He closed his eyes and tried to sleep. He had a trip to take.

CHAPTER TWENTY-FOUR

"We never buried any treasure. We needed all the money we collected for our own uses, or to lend to supposed friends."
— Emmett Dalton, Kansas City Star,
April 28, 1931

"We'd best be going," Claude said to the old Indian.

Minnow Charlie clucked his tongue against his gums and winked at Myra. "You bring Myra around here anytime."

Myra had only gotten to talk to the ancient Choctaw for half an hour sitting on his couch under the trees, but that was more than enough time to learn that he was a flirty, randy old devil with a wandering eye. That was surprising in a man who lacked the energy to sleep in his own house, or to button the fly of his overalls. But he had a sweet smile, however toothless it was.

"You'd just have her building minnow traps," Claude said.

"You two go on. Nobody's going to come by here without me or Betty seeing them. I'll send one of my grandsons up to warn you if anybody comes pilfering around," Charlie said.

Claude's maternal grandfather had died when he was young, and Minnow Charlie had sort of adopted him for his sidekick when he was in grade school. Or maybe it was the other way around and Claude had adopted him. Either way, it was Charlie who had taught him the woodlands and the river bottoms as much as the sheriff. The old man showed him how to build fish and minnow traps and how to make a good fishing pole out of a cured stalk of switch cane. Before Charlie had gotten so old and decrepit the two of them had walked the mountains and talked of how the Choctaws used to live before they took up the ways of the white man.

"I guess you know the Sheriff's down in Texas looking for you," Charlie said.

"He doesn't have any jurisdiction down there."

"He's working with the Texas Rangers."

Claude turned to Myra. "I guess we're on our way to being famous if the Rangers are after us."

"You are going to break his heart, and your mother's too," Charlie said.

Claude didn't think Charlie was really judging him, just worried about his parents. A man that thought he could talk to the spirits every time he got a little whiskey in him and liked to sit in a sweat lodge and chant to the sky was bound to be open-minded.

"So long, Charlie. Keep your eyes peeled." Claude knew that if anybody could be trusted it was Charlie. He realized then that he was getting as cautious and as cagey as Myra.

They left the Buick hidden in Charlie's barn. They walked along a dirt road, and then ducked off onto a faint trace of rutted earth winding through the timber. The mountainside they headed toward was dark green with pine timber and rose some fourteen hundred feet above them. They could see where loggers had left the woods dotted with yellow-topped stumps and the ground was grooved where their mules had skidded logs to little cleared landings where they could be loaded onto trucks and wagons. Soon, they left even that trace of civilization behind and nothing was left but the old trail made when Charlie's parents had taken their land allotment back before the turn of the century. Saplings and other brush had overtaken the trace. After a brief hike, the bottom of the draw, or canyon, turned out to be a small hollow surrounded by the mountain at its back and the tips of two ridges squeezing in from either side. The trail opened up again and Myra spotted the tiny log cabin set in the middle of a grove of post oaks.

"Home sweet home, at least for the time being," Claude said.

"You really know how to put a girl up in a swanky joint to impress her."

Charlie had abandoned his family home many years before to move closer to the river, but he had kept the old cabin in fairly good shape. He used it for a hunting camp in the fall.

The small logs were dovetailed tightly together at the ends, and chinked with blue clay. The windows were glass, but a thick coating of dust and pollen blocked them from peering inside. They sat their groceries on the covered front porch and pushed in the rough-sawn door hanging from wrought-iron hinges. They walked into the single room on top of the puncheon floor of old, yellowed pine logs hacked flat with an adze and broad ax. A sandstone fireplace took up most of one wall, and a rusty bedstead took up the other end of the room. The back wall was covered in crude shelves and traps and bits of rope and canvas hanging from dowels. A countertop and sink ran under the front window with a couple of overhead cabinets.

"Room service is a little lacking, but the bed is great." Claude pounded the feather mattress with his hand and a cloud of dust flew up.

"Who's doing the cooking?"

"I can't cook, and besides, I'm an invalid." Claude made a show of holding his mending ribs.

They walked out onto the porch and studied the trail leading back the way they had come. Two blue jays fussed and flew through the treetops above them, and a squirrel barked somewhere close by.

"Are you sure we're safe here?" Myra asked.

"As safe as we can get, considering what we've started. I think we can lay low here until it's time to meet them. Nobody saw us arrive, except for Charlie, and no city boys are going to find us here."

Myra considered that. "Diamond Joe won't settle for just his cut, and he's going to bring all of them with him, no matter what you had me tell him."

"Did he say that?"

"No, but I could tell from his tone."

Claude leaned against one of the cedar porch posts and tried to plan. He thought he had things worked out where they might get out alive, but he was smart enough to know that once the fireworks started somebody was bound to get burned.

"What'd you tell him?"

She sighed. "How many times do I have to repeat it?"

"Just once more."

"I told him that we would meet him on the iron bridge over Kiamichi River at seven o'clock on the first of the month with his cut, but no more. And I told him not to bring Bull and the rest of them with him. If he did, we were going to run again with all the money, and he was out of luck."

"What about your sister?"

"He promised he would leave her alone if he got his money," she said.

"Do you believe him?"

"He may keep an eye on her, but I think he'll leave her alone once we're gone out of the country. Keep in mind, though, we can't trust him where we're concerned."

"I've planned it that way," he said grimly.

"Why don't you get us some help so we

387

aren't so outnumbered? You've got friends here. Have some of them cover us on the bridge."

Claude shook his head and the stubborn set to his jaw was immediate. "Yeah, I've got friends, but I'm not dragging them into this deal."

"Diamond Joe will bring along anybody he wants to."

He put an arm over her shoulder. "Are you scared?"

"Terrified."

"We've got one thing going for us, and that's the fact that if Diamond Joe kills us he isn't ever going to get all the money," he said.

"He's planning how he can have his cake and eat it too."

"The waiting's going to be the worst part." She paced the length of the porch and back. "I'm already jittery."

Claude went into the yard to start a fire, because it was too hot to cook lunch in the cabin. Myra raised the windows to take advantage of what little breeze there was, and started sweeping the floor and knocking cobwebs out of the corners with a broom she found. Some house wrens had built a nest in one corner of the ceiling, just above the wall in the rafters, but she spared the tiny brown birds' nest from the wrath of her broom. She kind of liked their little high-pitched chirps and the way they hopped around the room fussing at her as if it was their cabin she invaded.

Both of them hadn't had a proper breakfast, and Myra decided she would try her culinary skills over a campfire, however meager their grocery supplies might be. She tried to stay upwind of the fire to heat up a can of beans, but ended up with burning eyes and her clothes smelling like smoke.

Claude took up the duffel bag of money and a tin bucket. "I'm going up to the spring to get us some water, and to see if I can find a good place to hide this cash."

"Did you leave us some spending money in case we need to go to town?"

"There's a thousand in your purse on the bed," he said. "Do you want to go with me?"

She started to rise, but willed herself not to. "No, I trust you."

He disappeared into the timber and was gone for an hour.

The cabin was still too hot to sleep in by nightfall, so they dragged the feather bed out onto the porch. They could see a slice of the night sky overhead just off the eave of the roof, and Myra spotted a falling star.

Somewhere down in the river bottom, a hound bawled and they listened to him continue to bark as he trailed his quarry in the dark.

"Some hunter's about to tree himself a coon," Claude said wistfully. "The hide won't be worth much of anything this time of year, too hot for good fur, but I'm wishing maybe I could go to that hound when he finally trees that old coon. Just for fun and old time's sake."

"You're such a hillbilly," Myra said. "You don't have to go with me when this is over. I wouldn't want to lose you, but I don't want to take you where you won't be happy either."

"No, I quit this country already. I want to live the rest of my life where there are paved streets and shiny cars. I want to dance and eat food I've never tried, and watch baseball games and go to movies. I want to sleep in fine hotels and walk under buildings that reach the sky with all the people crowding the streets headed for places I might not ever visit."

"I don't know how you can love it here and still want all of that," she said.

"I'll have to let go of it for something new."

"We've got a lot of money, but it won't last forever," she said.

"We'll get more when we have to. You've got the brains and I've got the gun hand."

"I thought you'd decided you didn't want to be an outlaw."

"We'll do it our way, with no killers and crazies riding along with us. We'll stick to banks, or maybe a train. I'd like to try that."

She rolled over and kissed his cheek. "It will be a new start for both of us."

"I'm going to go see my mother one last time in the morning," he said. "Do you want to come with me?"

"I don't know how that would work out. The only thing she knows about me is that I started her son on a life of crime. And do you think it's safe to leave here when there are so many probably looking for us?"

"Worry about that tomorrow. Let's just listen to that hound." He closed his eyes.

"I'll go with you," she whispered.

CHAPTER TWENTY-FIVE

"He was a desperate man, this Floyd. But he was pretty pleasant to me all the time we were together. Floyd made no threats. He told me to do what he asked and we would get along all right. But I don't think any ten men can capture him alive. We got to be plumb good friends."
— Missouri Sheriff Jack Killingsworth, a Pretty Boy Floyd kidnap victim

The lawmen's pilot circled three times until he was sure that there wasn't any traffic on the south end of town. He had informed Sheriff Miller that his barnstorming performance name was Crash, and the moniker didn't exactly give any comfort. But there was nothing much either of the lawmen could do about that at the moment. Crash lined up on Main Street, and throttled back on the engine. It was more than a little windy, and the plane crabbed from side to side. Sheriff Miller was sure that they were going to smack an electricity pole or scrape the roof off some building.

The Jenny's front wheels bounced several times on the pavement, the first one really hard and high, before remaining for good on the ground. The plane zipped down the road, showing no signs of slowing, even though the ninety-horsepower motor was only idling. Sheriff Miller gritted his teeth and watched as they approached the business section of town. A delivery truck driver rounded the corner at an intersection in front of them and pulled up onto the sidewalk honking his horn at them and shaking his fist. The Jenny's wingtips seemed like they were barely clearing the red brick buildings on either side of the street.

After over a hundred yards, Sheriff Miller was sure the plane should have stopped long before then. Two men crammed into a seat made for one left little wiggling room, but he managed to crane his neck around far enough to see the pilot. But Crash wasn't in his seat. He was running alongside the fuselage.

Sheriff Miller looked up front again long enough to see the crowd of traffic stopped in the intersection not fifty yards in front of them. The plane had slowed to less than ten miles per hour, but it looked like it was going to take a wreck to stop their momentum. He looked back again in time to see Crash dodge the tail section and grab a hold of the left-hand elevator.

"Jump out and give me a hand!" he shouted as he dug in his heels and pulled back for all he was worth.

Sheriff Miller had never jumped out of a plane, but he had been wanting to for hours. Plus, it looked like they were about to run over a policeman standing in the middle of the street in front of his patrol car and waving his arms.

Both of the lawmen tried to climb out of their seat simultaneously, but only managed to poke each other in the eyes and elbow each other in the head. Fitting two grown men, one at a time, into the hole in the fuselage had been difficult when they took off from Dallas. Climbing out at the same time under duress was like driving a square peg into a round hole, to say the least.

Crash's farm-grown muscles were barely enough to halt the plane less than a foot in front of the hood of the patrol car. The policeman had rolled underneath a wagon-load of potatoes to keep from being squashed. The team of horses, spooked by the charging plane, threatened to throw a runaway and crush the cop anyway.

Sheriff Miller managed to extricate himself from the plane, stepping on Sergeant Jones to do so. He leaped to the ground and looked at the crowd of mad, accusing faces surrounding him. He was glad he had somehow kept his hat on. He felt a little more dignified and official that way. Obviously, the crowd of citizens wasn't accustomed to the pitfalls and dangers of flying airplanes, much less used to having one land on their main street. The look on some of their faces reminded him of the mob he'd faced at the bank.

Crash walked to the front of the plane and checked his prop, seemingly unaware that he had almost killed a policeman and caused a traffic pileup.

"What's the matter with your brakes?" Sheriff Miller asked.

"Ain't no brakes. You've just gotta holler 'whoa' until she stops," Crash said, lifting his goggles and spitting a stream of chewing tobacco. He looked around at the crowd and seemed unbothered by the attention he was getting. "The show's over, folks."

Sergeant Jones rolled over the edge of the fuselage and almost fell when his feet hit the ground. He staggered back down the street and gathered up his hat that Sheriff

Miller had knocked off his head.

"What the hell do you think you're doing?" Officer Pete, the same cop that had shot pistols with Claude, rolled out from under the wagon an instant before the plane backfired and the horses tore off down the street with the wagon rattling behind them.

The wagon driver had left his seat long before, and there was nothing to check the team's speed. The tailgate flew open when the wagon caught the curb of the sidewalk, and potatoes began to bounce out of the bed. The team raced out of sight, a trail of spuds marking their course.

Sergeant Jones made it back to Sheriff Miller's side as the policeman stood to his feet. He stuck out the left side of his chest and pointed at his badge. "Sergeant L. T. Jones, Texas Rangers. We were in pursuit of a gang of criminals and ran out of gas."

Sheriff Miller dug around in his pocket for his own badge, glad that he had it. There were those in the crowd that looked like they wanted to whip somebody, especially the man that owned the wagon.

"You can't land an airplane in the middle of town." The policeman sounded tough, but it was plain that he was impressed by the Ranger's badge.

"Emergency," Sergeant Jones said. "We

need your help."

"Get these cars out of here, and you over there, back your truck up so we can pull this plane out of the way," Officer Pete said.

It took several minutes to get the tangle of cars on their way. Most of the crowd that wasn't mad, at least wanted to gawk. Somebody shouted down the street that the runaway team had been stopped with no harm to the wagon, and the owner was appeased with a promise from Sergeant Jones that Texas would pay for the damaged potatoes if a bill for them were sent to the state capital. Crash was passing out business cards and promising the townspeople that he could put on a better show for them in the future for a small fee and a cut of the gate. The mood had quickly gone from a lynch mob to a circus atmosphere. A couple of children rode in the pilot's cockpit as the plane was towed back to a filling station at the south end of town. A newspaperman dogged Crash's heels wanting an interview and photos.

Officer Pete was more impressed by lawmen riding planes in the line of duty than he was by the pilot. He walked between Sergeant Jones and Sheriff Miller. He calmed enough to recognize Sheriff Miller, the head of law enforcement in the adjoining county, and a man whom he'd met in the line of work before and read about in the newspapers. "Hello, Sheriff Miller."

"Sorry to upset your town, Officer," Sheriff Miller said.

"Who are you boys after, if you don't mind my asking?"

"Two bank robbers in a Buick, Claude Miller and Myra Hooser," Sergeant Jones threw in. He wasn't used to being upstaged by county lawmen, even if they were war heroes. That didn't happen down in Texas where school children learned the names of famous Rangers in history classes.

"They wouldn't happen to be an Indian kid and a blonde girl, would they?" Officer Pete asked. He had already made the connection between Claude's and Sheriff Miller's last names. Antlers was less than an hour south of Talihina, and Sheriff Miller's son's robberies were common knowledge.

"That's our bank robbers," Sergeant Jones said. "I'm assuming that they've already been through here."

"Just left town yesterday afternoon." Officer Pete told them that the couple had been spotted by the local hardware store owner, but didn't mention Claude's shooting exhibition, or his participation in the event.

"Claude's headed back home, just like I

told you," Sheriff Miller said.

"Let's get that plane back in the air," Sergeant Jones said.

Sheriff Miller wanted nothing to do with the plane, but he could see no way around having to fly in it again. It would take him two hours to get to Antlers by car, and he wasn't about to have Sergeant Jones beat him there and muddy up the waters before he had a chance to look around.

By the time they got to the filling station Crash had the airplane pulled up to the gas pump and was topping off the tank. They pushed through the crowd around him.

"How long before we can take off?" Sergeant Jones asked.

Crash rubbed his eyes and then looked to his plane. "That motor wasn't running just right before we landed, and I could use a little time here to tune her up and to make sure she gees and haws like she's supposed to."

"What's the matter with your eyes?" Sheriff Miller asked.

"I broke my glasses yesterday, and they're watering something awful."

"Your glasses?" Sheriff Miller asked incredulously.

"Yeah, you boys were in such a hurry to get up here that I didn't have time to get any new ones."

"Just how bad are your eyes?" Sergeant Jones asked.

"Not too bad. The glasses the doctor gave me help, and I don't need much magnification." Crash held a thumb and forefinger up about a quarter inch apart to show the thickness of the lenses he wore.

"And they gave you a license with eyes like that?" Sheriff Miller asked.

"License?" Crash asked. "Didn't have the money to apply for one of those after I paid for the plane. I sold my car and my plow mule to rake up the two hundred dollars to buy old Jenny, not counting the twenty dollars I put into fixing her up. Her motor was fine, but I had to do a little patching on the wings and some welding on the axle housings."

"Are you a welder too?" Sheriff Miller asked.

"Not really, but it turned out all right."

"How long have you had this plane?" The newspaperman paused his pencil on his little tablet. He studied the hand-painted logo on the tail of the plane.

The logo was supposed to read, "Crash Abbot, Stunt Pilot Extraordinaire," but somebody had badly misspelled the last word. However, none of the crowd seemed to notice. Below Crash's billing was the word "Jenny" with a pair of red lip marks beside it, as if a woman had kissed the fuselage.

"Jenny, that's what you call it?" the newspaperman asked.

"Yeah, that's her name. I bought her from a man up in Topeka a month ago." Crash made sure his white silk scarf was wrapped properly around his neck and that his leather aviator cap was straight on his head. He leaned against the plane on one straightened arm and posed for the newspaperman to take his picture.

"Who taught you to fly?" The newspaperman was full of questions, and Crash's landing was easy front-page stuff.

Crash scoffed. "I flew it around for a couple of days up in Kansas with the fellow I bought it from and then flew it home by myself. Taking off ain't hard to get the hang of, but that landing deal can be a little touchy."

"No kidding," Sheriff Miller said.

"He told me if I got lost flying, to circle a town's water tower and read the name on it and check it against my road map. Spent a lot of time circling water towers, but I made it home," Crash said. "Wife and kids thought I'd never make it."

"Sergeant Jones, remind me to whip your ass when we get to Antlers," Sheriff Miller said. "And that's off the record, Newspaperman."

Sergeant Jones played innocent. "What? I didn't know. Honest I didn't. He told me he was a professional stunt pilot."

"That I can believe, at least the stunt part," Officer Pete said.

"Well, Crash, can you get us to Antlers?" Sergeant Jones asked.

"Give me five minutes and I'll have us ready to go," Crash said.

"Will those things run on car gasoline?" Sheriff Miller asked.

"You bet. My old Jenny's got a V-eight in her, and she'll burn about anything short of kerosene and pine knots. Just gotta watch out for water in your fuel. Old Jenny don't like that. Makes her a little cantankerous."

"You said you were a barnstormer. Did you ever fly through the middle of a barn like I've seen on the movies?" the newspaperman asked.

Crash scratched his head and smiled. "I did it once, but it was an accident."

"You flew this plane through a barn hallway and came out the other side?" The newspaperman's pencil was going wild on his tablet.

"No, that ain't exactly how it went. I flew into that barn, but I didn't exactly fly out. Fact is, the barn kind of snuck up on me. But I patched old Jenny up. Folks that saw her after the wreck said there was no way she was going to fly again, but I fixed her, and me with no airplane mechanic experience whatsoever."

"Was it foggy or dark?" The newspaperman had already decided it wouldn't hurt to add a little color to the story, no matter what the pilot told him.

Crash seemed a little put out with having to do so much remembering. "Was a clear day, but what got me was the fact I wasn't expecting a barn."

Sheriff Miller had a Coke and some peanuts while he avoided hearing his pilot's shortcomings and the plane's past mechanical breakages. He waited for Crash to service the plane, and tried not to notice when the pilot borrowed some baling wire and a hammer. It was probably only a minor, cosmetic thing on the plane that needed attention. Nothing to worry about. Crash was bound to know something about airplane maintenance, or not.

Soon, the plane was towed out onto the highway and pointed south with Crash in the pilot's seat and waving for them to come on.

"You know we're liable to die," Sheriff Miller said to the Ranger.

"You scared?" Sergeant Jones asked.

"To death," Sheriff Miller said. "And that's off the record too."

"Contact," Crash shouted.

The newspaperman set up his camera to catch the takeoff. Half the town gathered behind him and stared at the sky with their eyes shielded with their hands. Officer Pete gave the prop a crank while Crash leaned his head out to look alongside the fuselage and between the upper and lower wings. The motor coughed little black clouds and then a bigger one when the policeman spun it again.

The third spin was the charm, and the V-8 backfired and then sputtered to life. Crash played with his fuel lever until the mixture wasn't so rich and the engine smoothed out, at least a little.

"Is that engine supposed to sound like that?" the newspaperman asked Officer Pete.

The policeman didn't want to admit what he didn't know about airplanes, at least not to a man who was always pointing out the police department's faults in his weekly editorials. "He's just getting it warmed up."

The plane slowly built speed down the highway until the south wind lifted its wings and carried them airborne. Crash circled the crowd once, waving back at them. Sheriff Miller didn't notice the fond farewell. It was too far to the ground to be looking down and waving. The motor backfired again and almost died before Crash managed to get it under control. It felt as if the plane dropped ten feet in an instant before it leveled out again.

"Is the motor supposed to sound like that?" Sheriff Miller asked Sergeant Jones beside him.

The Ranger shrugged and tried to keep his cowboy hat from blowing off.

"Nothing to worry about. Just a little water in the gas," Crash shouted into the wind.

Chapter Twenty-Six

"When you put down the good things you ought to have done, and leave out the bad ones you did do — well, that's memoirs."
— Will Rogers

"Are airplanes supposed to sound like that?" Claude shaded his eyes and watched the airplane pass overhead through the tree-tops.

"What's all that black smoke? I think it might be on fire," Myra said beside him.

"Whoever's flying that plane doesn't know a dang thing about engines. He's either got a bad spark plug or his plug wires crossed. Maybe even a bad set of points." Claude started back along the trail, watching the plane barely skimming over the top of the timber on the next mountain ridge. "A man would have to be crazy to fly with that pilot."

They had decided to leave the Buick hidden and walk to his parents' home. It was only about three miles as the crow flew if you followed the river, but Claude decided to walk the foot of the mountain to avoid any chance of meeting travelers along the county road. The slope was steep, with lots of green briars to snag skin and loose rocks under the leaf bed to turn an ankle. Claude's long legs took the terrain at a quick pace, and he seemed a little impatient with Myra's stumbling and dragging behind.

"I swear you're part mountain goat," she said.

He helped her across a rocky gully and over a fallen log. "Ridge-runner, born and raised."

"I don't know why the government bothered to take this awful, rocky country from you Indians," she said.

"Give it time. It'll grow on you." He smashed an enormous horsefly against her shoulder, leaving a bright red spot of blood on her sleeve.

"Oh, I'm loving it more every minute."

"Keep your eye out for rattlesnakes and copperheads. They like rocky ledges like this," he said.

"Poisonous snakes? That's absolutely adorable. I see now why you miss home so much."

Their path brought them to the end of a narrow ridge overlooking the Millers' farm. Claude stopped them at the edge of a little fenced-in pasture behind the house where the milk cow stood in a clump of bitter weeds. They walked up the fence until they could see in front of the house. No cars were parked there, but he waited for a long time before advancing any farther. Western swing music on the radio was blaring out of the open windows of the little house, and it sounded as if several people were inside. The floorboards creaked and thumped, and footsteps scuffed on the hardwood floor.

"Come on." Claude took her hand and started for the front porch.

"Are you sure there isn't any Law around?" Myra asked.

"Momma listens to Bob Wills and the Texas Playboys every day at lunchtime. She wouldn't have the music so loud if the Sheriff were home."

"What's all that noise? Sounds like two or three people walking around in there," she said.

"Momma likes to dance. She's always asking the Sheriff to take her honky-tonking at Cain's Ballroom up to Tulsa where the Playboys broadcast from."

Claude led her up onto the front porch

and peered into the screen door. Myra could see a slim, middle-aged Indian woman scooting around the kitchen floor and swaying to the fiddle music reeling out of the little radio on a side table. She was oblivious to being watched, and Myra couldn't help but stare. She herself loved to dance, but had to admit the older woman was graceful, and beautiful.

Claude rapped on the wooden frame of the screen door with his knuckles. "Hello, Momma."

Mary Miller jumped like she had stepped on a snake. She turned to the front door with a hand on her heart and her eyes wide. Claude led Myra inside. Mary glanced from him to her, and back again. She was already blushing, but hid it by stepping across the room and wrapping her arms around her son.

"I feared you were dead," Mary said. "You've scared your father and I half to death."

"No, Momma, I'm still kicking," Claude said.

Mary looked over Claude's shoulder at Myra. Her face was unreadable, but there was a little hint of acid in her tone. "And who have you brought with you, son?"

Claude extracted himself from his mother's hug and stepped aside for Myra, as if introducing her on some stage. "Momma, this is Myra Belle Hooser. Myra, this is my mother, Mary."

"Are you the woman that took my Claude off robbing banks?" Mary asked without blinking.

"You get right to the point, don't you Mrs. Miller?" Myra let a little of the cat in her surface, if only to give her time to figure out how best to proceed with Claude's mother.

"I do where my son is concerned."

"I think a lot of him too," Myra said, trying her best to hold Mary's gaze. She didn't want to offend the woman, but she wasn't going to be the first to look away either.

"Don't make trouble, Momma. I love Myra, and that's that." Claude laid his hand on his mother's forearm.

Myra could see that Mary wanted to say more, but she turned away and motioned them to sit at the kitchen table while she turned off the radio and slipped on a pair of shoes sitting by the door leading into the rest of the house.

"Excuse me for my dancing. I get lonesome when Jim is gone, and the music makes the day go by." Mary opened the icebox and began to chip at the block of ice there with a pick. Claude and Myra took seats beside each other and listened to the sound of the little chips and frozen flakes ricocheting off the inside of the galvanized box. Myra had never seen her chip ice, but she was certain the woman was putting a little more power into her blows than was necessary.

Mary made three tall glasses of iced tea before sitting across the table from them. She kept her knees together, sitting only on the front two thirds of the chair. Myra studied her stiff posture and the dainty way she handled the tea glass in her hand. She remembered her mother acting like that when strangers were around, or when she was sitting across from someone she didn't like. She was sure that the woman was putting on an act, and wanted to make clear to the little floozy who had run off with her son that she was a lady.

"I used to listen to Bob Wills down in Dallas when he was still with the Light Crust Doughboys. I was listening to the radio when he won the Texas fiddling championship," Myra said. She felt foolish for mentioning music to a woman who was obviously thinking she was a white-trash slut.

There was a clock ticking somewhere in the house, and Mary let it count off half a minute while she ignored Myra and stared at Claude. Finally, she turned to Myra and smiled. Myra knew the smile was forced, but considered it a start.

"I like Bob's music much better since he's added the trumpet and all the other instruments. It kind of makes his songs swing, if that's the word for it." Mary looked a little embarrassed. "You kids probably think that hillbilly music is for us old folks."

"Not at all," Myra said. "I like all kinds of music, although Louis Armstrong is my favorite."

"I listen to colored music all the time," Mary said.

"Jazz," Myra said.

"Don't think anything about Momma. She likes jazz too, but she isn't up with the lingo," Claude said. "Momma's church says jazz is the Devil's music, and they're always carrying on about colored music. That kind of songs lead to vulgar dancing and such, and the lyrics are scandalous, according to those old birds that Momma quilts with. You know, singing about wild women and boozing. The hillbillies on the radio can sing about all the cheating and killing and whiskey they want, and preachers don't seem to mind."

"Claude, don't be disrespectful of the

church. You were raised a good Baptist boy," Mary said.

"I've tried, Momma, but the Word just didn't stick on me like it did you."

"There will come a day. Remember Paul, when he was still Saul, was a terrible man before God struck him down with a bolt of lightning on the road to Damascus," Mary said.

"I know it's hard for you to accept, but maybe I'm not ever going to be like you and the Sheriff," Claude said.

"Don't call your father 'the Sheriff,' " Mary said.

"Just habit, I guess."

Mary reached across the table and laid both her hands on Claude's. "There's good in you, son. I know it."

"There's bad too."

Mary looked down at the tabletop and closed her eyes as if she was praying. "We've all got an angel on one shoulder and the Devil on the other. Why must you always listen to the Devil?"

"He must hang on tighter."

"I don't suppose you've come back to turn yourself in, have you?"

"No, I just stopped by to introduce you to Myra and to say my good-byes," Claude said.

"The Law is looking for you all over. Where are you going to go?"

Claude gave her his warmest smile. "We're going far away where nobody is going to find us."

Mary looked back to Myra. "Are you two married?"

Myra tried not to squirm in her chair, nor to look at Claude either. She was sure she hadn't blushed since she was a baby, but she felt the warmth rising in her face. She realized then that she would marry Claude if he asked her. "No, ma'am, we're not."

"Where are you from?"

"Kansas."

"Do you love my Claude like he says he loves you?" Mary asked.

Myra looked at him. "I do."

"And you two realize that you're never going to have a real life robbing folks and running and hiding from the Law?"

Claude saw that Myra wasn't going to answer. "Not a life like you and the Sheriff have, but Momma, I promise you I've been living. More than I ever did before I left here."

"You're still so young," Mary said. "Don't go and ruin your lives before they even get started. You two turn yourselves in and your father will try and get the court to go easy

414

on you."

"There's no turning back now, no taking back what I've done. I've heard the Sheriff talk about prisons, and I won't be locked up," Claude said.

"Money doesn't make you a man, and neither does a gun. Do you want people to remember you as a thief and maybe a killer?"

"I know I've shamed you, that's why I'm leaving for good. I won't come back to Oklahoma, so you and the Sheriff just disown me. Write me off like I never was."

"Claude, you'll always be my son, and you're always welcome here if it's safe for you." Mary gripped his hands like he was about to leave that very second.

"Momma, I've learned a few things, and the first one is the most important of all. There's good folks out there that aren't as good as you think, and bad folks that aren't near as bad as you would think. Maybe you could settle for me being somewhere in the middle."

Mary dabbed at the corner of her eyes. "I raised you, so I know I'm wasting my time trying to change your mind."

"I won't change my mind." Even though there was finality in Claude's words, his tone was soft.

"Well then, promise me one thing." Mary looked at both of them. "Swear to me that you'll take care of each other, and that you'll run off and lay low until all this cools down and people forget about you."

Claude and Myra looked at each other and nodded.

"I'm not saying what I'll do with my life, but I'll be with Myra as long as she'll have me," Claude said.

"And that goes for me too," Myra said.

Mary looked at Myra, and her smile was genuine, if full of hurt. "Was your hair blonde before you put the peroxide to it?"

Myra bit her tongue and decided not to snap at such a personal and perhaps rude question. "Yes, ma'am, but I like it even paler. Platinum is what they call it out in the big cities."

Mary took one of her hands off Claude's and held it out for Myra. When she had both of them by the hand she bowed her head. "Lord, watch over these, your children and mine. Bless them and show them the way."

Myra hadn't prayed since she was a little girl, and it had been even longer since someone prayed for her. She couldn't say why, but she fought back tears.

Mary noticed how the prayer had touched

the girl. "You really ought to let your hair be its natural color and get rid of some of the makeup. You're a very beautiful girl."

Myra usually would have been offended at any woman hinting that she looked like a tramp. She'd smacked more than one broad for that. But somehow, the words felt sweeter than they should have. She could only nod, feeling like a little girl. Memories of her own mother came pouring back, of the years before the bad times, before her father started drinking, the weather went bad, and the circus came to town.

"Thank you," Myra whispered, rolling her eyes and feeling silly for her gratitude for such a simple little compliment about her natural beauty from a woman she didn't even know.

Mary rose and took her apron from the counter. "I bet you two are starved. I'll rustle you up a little something to eat."

Claude hesitated over the thought of his mother's cooking. "We'd best be going. Somebody might have seen us walk up, or show up and catch us here."

"Were you going to leave without seeing your father?" Mary asked.

"I heard he's in Texas."

"Would you have even talked to him if he was here?"

"I don't know what I would say to him," Claude said. "Maybe it's best that I leave it at that."

"Your father is just as worried about you as I am. Neither one of us understands you, and that's harder on him."

"Yeah, but you don't have a badge."

"He only wants what's best for you, same as I do."

"He doesn't have to worry. We'll be gone for good as soon as I tend to a little deal tomorrow," Claude said.

"You're going to do what you want, but I don't think you have a clue how bad of shape you're in. Your names are all over the newspapers ever since ya'll robbed that Texas bank and Myra busted you out of jail. They're making out like you and Myra are some kind of Bonnie and Clyde. They say she's the ringleader, like Ma Barker's gang, and that you're a laughing gunman who's killed two men that folks know of, and maybe more."

"I only killed one."

"No matter, the newspapers are laying off that banker's murder on you."

"The Law can't think that. I left them a note."

"The newspapers don't care about the truth. They just want a good story. There have been so many cops killed by outlaws lately, that the Law is liable to shoot you on sight," Mary said. "Haven't you been keeping up with the news? J. Edgar Hoover's Bureau men killed John Dillinger. Caught him coming out of the theater and shot him down on the streets like a mangy dog."

"Now, Momma. I admit that I'm a wanted man, but the Bureau of Investigation isn't looking for me."

"To hell they aren't." Deputy Burke somehow had appeared in the door. "Three of those federal cops came into town this morning looking for you. Seems like robbing a bank is a federal crime now that the government's insuring all the banks."

"Hello, Burke." Claude stood up.

"Easy, Claude. I'm not going to try and arrest you. Your mother has too many kitchen knives handy if I did."

Claude sat back down, but made sure to move his chair far enough from the table where he wouldn't get his guns hung up. "Have a seat, Burke. Normally, I'd say it was good to see you. I'm just home visiting, but I'll be gone for good tomorrow."

"Want a cup of coffee?" Mary asked Burke.

"No thanks, I've drank too much this morning already. It's got me all jittery."

Burke continued to stand in the doorway, despite the invitation to sit down. He studied the way Claude was sitting. "You've gotten scary since I saw you last."

"There won't be any trouble between you and I," Claude said.

Deputy Burke was Claude's favorite of all the Sheriff's friends. Burke used to occasionally give him a lift home from school, and sometimes even stopped on the river bridge to let him shoot turtles with his service revolver. Claude always had to promise that he wouldn't tell the Sheriff they were wasting county ammunition target practicing.

Burke was also remembering how the kid could shoot. He noticed the pair of pistols Claude was wearing. "Isn't it a little dangerous to tie your grip safeties down? You might shoot yourself in the leg if one of your thumb safeties got knocked off."

Claude shrugged. "It's a risk I'll take. I might need to be fast."

Burke looked to Mary. "The Sheriff called and asked me to check on you."

Mary thought the world of Burke. Jim had been different after he came home from the war, and Burke seemed to understand him more than she sometimes did. Burke had gone to war too, but he seemed no different for the experience, just his same old happy, witty self. It galled her that her husband often felt it easier to tell his deputy some things, but that was the way it was. Jim was getting better at talking to her, and in the meantime, Burke would always try and help interpret him.

"Did he say he when he would be home?" she asked.

"He's on his way from Dallas." Burke watched to see Claude's reaction. "He's riding an airplane home."

"The Sheriff in an airplane?" Claude asked.

"He absolutely hates heights," Mary said. Jim didn't like her to say he was scared of heights. He always claimed he just didn't like them.

"Seems like I'm drawing a crowd," Claude said.

"You got spotted up in the Osage country, and then again yesterday in Talihina," Burke said.

"We'd better get going." Claude took Myra's hand.

"Claude, maybe it isn't my place to tell you, but . . ." Burke paused to mull over what he was about to say. "You ever notice how songs about bandits and outlaws never have happy endings?"

Claude's ribs twinged as he stood and he put a hand to them. "I hear you."

"Looks like you ducked when you should have zigzagged. That can be a regular occurrence when a man gets shot at for a living," Burke said. "I'd suggest you settle down somewhere else and find yourself a new line of work. Maybe California. Everyone else seems to be going there."

"The Sheriff says there isn't anything out there but communists and more starving Okies," Claude said.

Burke did have one good point, and Claude began immediately thinking about how he could keep from getting shot anymore.

Claude hugged his mother good-bye. "Don't cry, Momma. We'll be fine."

"I'll cry if I want to," Mary said, and then hugged Myra too. "You take care of him, and I'll never say another harsh word about you."

"I will," Myra said.

Claude nodded at Burke and led Myra out the door.

Burke looked across the table at Mary when they were gone. "The Sheriff would have a fit if he knew I let them walk."

"Thank you, Burke," Mary said. "He's a good boy, just confused."

Burke didn't say anything and looked at the door. He too had a soft spot for the kid, but one look at him sitting in the kitchen was enough. Claude was a hundred percent outlaw, and probably always had been.

He said good-bye to Mary and went to his patrol car. His own wife was fixing lunch for him, and he didn't want to be late. They were expecting their first child soon, and her recent moody spells didn't make her very tolerant where tardiness and inattentiveness were concerned. He pondered about children on his drive home, and the thought of having his own scared him to death.

CHAPTER TWENTY-SEVEN

"May God have mercy upon my enemies,
because I won't."
— General George S. Patton

"Sheriff, you look like you've been in a wreck," one of the federal agents said. They had walked into the office unannounced and highly unexpected.

Sheriff Miller readjusted his smashed Stetson on his head. One of his eyes was bloodshot where a tree limb had poked it, giving him a decidedly grumpy look. He looked across the office at his pilot. "Wasn't a wreck, just an emergency landing. Isn't that what you called it, Crash?"

Crash sat in the far corner of the room, and didn't say anything. A minor error in landing the plane and a little case of whiplash had the Sheriff positively cranky.

The fed didn't have a clue what the sheriff was talking about. He had only used the term as a figure of speech to describe the sheriff's appearance. The local peace officer looked as if he had been in a fight. His clothes were torn and soiled, and his hat looked like he had sat on it.

"And besides, planes are perfectly safe, aren't they, Sergeant Jones?" Sheriff Miller asked.

Sergeant Jones was reticent to respond, partially because he had a headache, and partially because he was afraid that if he answered, Sheriff Miller would continue to harangue him over his choice of transportation and pilots.

In addition, he found it highly uncomfortable that the Bureau agents had caught him not looking his best. Any reasonable person would agree that it was to be expected that crawling out of a smashed airplane would result in a laundry bill, but he would have liked to have the time to clean himself up before taking visitors. His belief had always been that first impressions were everything, and good clothes were at least half of that battle. The feds were never going to understand that he usually wasn't so unkempt.

Their arrival was poor timing indeed, considering what he looked like. His white shirt wasn't white anymore, having succumbed to all manner of stains, and a broken oil line had totally ruined the professional effect of his khaki slacks. On the bright side, his hat wasn't as smashed and disreputable looking as Sheriff Miller's, but that was simply because it had blown off his head and was lost. Sadly, the last time he had seen that particular hunk of beaver felt it was tumbling through the sky on its way to its own crash landing in the timber somewhere within a mile radius of the landing sight. He could only assume it survived the fall, but he was going to greatly miss his gray Stetson. His last girlfriend had always admired how he looked in that hat.

"Did I ever tell you how much I dislike airplanes?" Sheriff Miller asked.

Sergeant Jones felt that point had been made clear to him while they limped two miles to town. In his own opinion, he thought Crash had done a decent job landing with the engine dead, even if the field he had chosen to land in wasn't as long as he thought, and given the fact that he was missing his glasses. The wreck appeared a lot worse than it actually was when they had untangled themselves and looked back at the damage. Perhaps the sight of the mangled airplane shaped Sheriff Miller's sour account of the landing — "carnage" was what he called what was left of Old Jenny.

The Bureau agent cleared his throat and tried to get the conversation back on topic. He was a man with a mission, and didn't care what was going on between the local lawman and the Ranger. "I understand that you and Sergeant Jones have been actively pursuing the bank robbers, Claude Miller and Myra Hooser."

"We have," Sheriff Miller said.

"Like us, have you come to believe that Claude may currently be in this vicinity?"

"What makes you think Claude is in Antlers?" Sheriff Miller asked while he continued to scowl at Crash and Sergeant Jones.

The other two Bureau of Investigation agents remained quiet, content to stare out the windows while the one in the most expensive suit continued to do the talking. He told them his name was Agent Gurvis, or something like that — the name didn't stick. He had a Yankee accent, and the summer heat seemed to greatly affect him. The efforts he made to mop the sweat off his forehead and neck with a bath towel he had procured were in vain, if not decidedly comical. The agent obviously came from a place where it didn't get nearly as hot.

"The Texas Rangers office, the Oklahoma Highway Patrol, and the Oklahoma Bureau of Criminal Identification and Investigation suggest that he may be headed here," the portly agent said.

"That's a God-awful name that only a bureaucrat could love. Down here we just call them the state crime bureau," Sheriff Miller said.

The agent had let one side of his hair grow extremely long, and he realized that it was hanging limply above his shoulder instead of where it was supposed to be. He raked at his hair with his fingers where the sweat and humidity had caused it to lose its style and fall from grace. He managed to reposition it, folding it up over the top of his head, the length sufficient to make at least two coils covering his bald dome.

"I trust that you are now recusing yourself from this case, Sheriff, given your ties to Claude Miller. I would also ask that any of your deputies that you might assign as my aides also be given the opportunity to sit this one out should they feel conflicted about arresting your son," the agent said.

"Like hell, I am."

"I outrank you, Sheriff."

"Not in my county you don't."

The agent held up his badge, although

he'd already shown it upon entering the room. "I also have a letter in my pocket from Director Hoover stating my authority in these types of cases. Should you have any questions you may call the Bureau, or your state capital."

"Your director didn't elect me. But the people of this county did, and they expect me to do my job," Sheriff Miller said. "And until they tell me different, I'm the sheriff of Push County."

The fed was smart enough to realize the argument was getting him nowhere. "Well then, we'll proceed with the investigation and manhunt on our own. The Oklahoma Highway Patrol will be working with me. I understand you're a decorated soldier and have an exceptional record as a sheriff, but you're too close to one of the suspects. Should you want, I can leave one of my agents here with you to keep you updated on the portions of our operations that may be of a personal interest to you, but which do not compromise the capture of Miller and Hooser."

"Take your agent with you," Sheriff Miller said. "I'd think you boys had enough to do in Chicago and New York without coming down here."

"Bank robbery is a federal crime, and so

is harboring and abetting a fugitive."

"I'll arrest myself if I slip up."

"Good day, Sheriff. Sergeant Jones, you are welcome to join us. The Rangers have a solid reputation, and frankly, I could use your help." The fed took his men and left.

"If anybody is going to catch Claude in this county it will be me," Sheriff Miller said to nobody in particular.

"I'm going down the street to see if I can find somebody to haul my plane into town," Crash said.

"I just hope you can find all the pieces," Sheriff Miller said.

"Bring back my hat if you find it," Sergeant Jones threw in.

"There'll come a time when everybody will fly," Crash said as he went out the door.

"Like you said, the flying isn't so bad, but I think the landings will sour people on airplanes," Sheriff Miller said.

"That Bureau man sounded pretty sure that Claude was here," Sergeant Jones said after the pilot was gone.

"He's around."

The Ranger wouldn't look Sheriff Miller in the eye, and seemed restless.

"What's on your mind, Sergeant? Spit it out," Sheriff Miller said.

"I hate to say it, but it looks like you've

been cut out of this manhunt," Sergeant Jones said.

The Sheriff nodded slowly, unwilling to tell him any different. "And I guess you're fixing to run after those Bureau boys and volunteer your services?"

"I've got a job to do, and I'd better go where the trail is hot. If Claude is in the area, we should be able to set up roadblocks and keep him here until we can find him."

"Been good working with you." Sheriff Miller held out his right hand.

"I'll keep you filled in every chance I get." Sergeant Jones shook hands and then took up his bag and left the room.

"I thought you said he was a smart lawman." Deputy Burke walked into the room and took a seat at his desk.

"He's a vain fellow, but a pretty good cop. I guess he thinks all that manpower outweighs me knowing the country and my own son," Sheriff Miller said.

"Well, he's mistaken. I just saw Claude out at your house about two hours ago," Burke said.

Sheriff Miller frowned at his deputy. "I guess Claude had the drop on you?"

Burke kept a straight face. "You know he did."

"You are an officer of the law."

"Yeah, but I consider this a family matter."

"Those feds aren't family."

Burke smiled. "They've been trailing around after Claude all morning, but they don't have the nose for this kind of work."

"Seems like Claude is attracting all kinds of company — Texas Rangers, feds, highway patrol, and the state crime bureau," Sheriff Miller said. "They'll have my house staked out within the hour."

"Claude's already gone from there. Said he was leaving the county in a couple of days."

"That might not be quick enough to keep him from getting killed."

"Probably not," Burke said. "The bartender at Baxter's just waved me down on the street and told me three toughs from Dallas were in the bar asking around about where Claude lived."

"Country's getting crowded."

"Gonna be hard to keep this a family business," Burke answered.

Sheriff Miller donned a fresh shirt out of the storage closet, and went to the peg on the wall by the door where his pistol hung. He swung the gun belt around his hips. "Are you coming with me?"

Burke went over and took his shotgun

432

from the rack on the wall. He stuffed the magazine full of buckshot shells and worked the pump to chamber a round. "I'm honored you offered. Wouldn't miss it for the world."

Minnow Charlie's blacksmith shed was piled high with junk. It hadn't been used for anything in many years other than for storage for the odds and ends an eccentric old man liked to collect. Claude did manage to find a little pile of coal, and he started a fire in the forge basin, turning the crank on the blower until he almost had a fire hot enough to work with. He used to play around in the Sheriff's blacksmith shed when he was a boy, back when the Sheriff was still trying to be a farmer. He'd enjoyed heating metal and beating on it with a hammer.

Claude left his fire and studied the hood on the dilapidated, abandoned Model T in Charlie's salvage row of cast-off farm equipment. It was missing its wheels and propped up on wooden blocks with weeds almost engulfing it. But the sheet metal looked solid. He took a little toolbox and went to work dismantling one side of the hood.

Myra sat in the shade with Charlie in front of the house. The blacksmith shop was out of sight of the front yard, but the steady pounding of Claude's hammer battering against an anvil rang for the better part of two hours.

"The Sheriff won't be hiding that boy out at his house," Roy Burkhalter said around his cigar. "Our uppity County Mountie won't have it said that he's harboring criminals."

Diamond Joe listened to the local tough man with some skepticism, and wondered why he was so willing to come along with them. It was true that he seemed to hate the local sheriff, but any man who would join up with a bunch of strangers after an hour's bar conversation wasn't somebody you could put your faith in. Diamond Joe didn't like Roy, but he needed someone who knew the country. Despite the fact that he had offered the man a hundred dollars to guide them to Claude, it was plain that Roy was more talk than he was tough. However, it wouldn't hurt to let him keep on talking and thinking he was impressing the crew.

The five of them were packed into Diamond Joe's Cadillac — Bull and Diamond Joe in the front seat, and Roy crammed in between Dink and Ernest in the back. Bull had stopped the car at a dirt crossroads, looking skeptically in all directions.

"That's a good thing," Bull said. "With all those coppers in town, it wouldn't be safe for us to prowl around the Millers' home."

"That's true," Diamond Joe said, but was making other considerations. Finding out that the Sheriff Miller who'd come into his diner was Claude's father had pleasing possibilities. Even if he didn't run across that smart-aleck sheriff, coming into his county and killing his son would be ample revenge for his disrespect.

"The kid said he'd meet us on the bridge at seven o'clock tomorrow morning. So why don't we find a flophouse to spend the night?"

"Claude will have the upper hand if we meet him at the bridge," Diamond Joe said. "He'll be set for us, and that would give him the advantage. We want to catch him unaware, and then maybe he'll make a mistake."

"That's right. He's liable to have plenty of local help if we wait and meet him at the bridge," Dink added.

"I just want that twenty grand," Bull said.

"Nobody likes the Millers, except maybe a few Indians." Roy acted like he hadn't heard so much money mentioned. "The Sheriff married one of them. Squaw man."

Things weren't going exactly how Roy had planned them. He was used to being a big man, both physically and financially, and he had assumed he would be treated as an equal to Diamond Joe. He admired the man's rings, suit, and overall flash. Surely, they were two men who could understand each other. However, Diamond Joe and his henchmen continually talked around and over him. None of the four Dallas thugs seemed impressed with him, and the new was rapidly wearing off his infatuation with them. And he didn't like sitting in the middle of the backseat. The little man's high-pitched country twang annoyed him to no end, and the one in the mustache smelled horrible. Roy was wishing he'd driven his own Lincoln.

But everything wasn't going badly. It sounded like Claude had gotten a hold of a hell of a lot of money, and Roy liked money. He regretted not bringing along some of his own toughs from down at the cotton gin. The city bad boys didn't know a thing about the woods. If he could guide them to the right place, there was no way Diamond Joe's goons could stand up to a bunch of hill-billies with .30-30 rifles. All Roy needed was a chance to make a phone call down to the cotton gin, or maybe the opportunity to send word there if they should stop and talk to anyone on the road.

Roy had quickly seen the Dallas bunch as a way to get even with the Sheriff when they walked into Baxter's and started asking about Claude. He didn't have anything against Claude, and used to enjoy the kid walking in his footsteps around town and mimicking his mannerisms. But that sheriff daddy of his needed knocked off his high horse. Roy hadn't gone off to war, but he was sure he was just as brave and twice as tough as Sheriff Miller. Had the doctor let him, there was no doubt in his mind that he would have killed plenty of Germans and won a whole slew of medals.

And then there was that Indian wife of his, smug and proud as if she were a white woman. He'd tried to flirt with her over the years, but she liked playing hard to get. His practiced lines that usually made the girls blush and giggle only made her turn up her nose. She looked at him like she was better than him and walked off. Oh, she was a proud one, but he knew she was just another Indian slut. His father had told him they were good to practice on, but not marrying stock. Somebody needed to take her down a peg.

Roy thought if he were lucky, he might

get some revenge, and if he were even luckier, he might come away richer for his troubles.

"Where to?" Bull asked.

"All looks same to me. Nothing but rocks and trees, and more rocks and trees," Dink said.

"I've got an idea where Claude might be," Roy said.

CHAPTER TWENTY-EIGHT

"They'll never take me alive!"
— Alvin "Creepy" Karpis

Claude dressed and rigged his gear before dawn. "I'm going down to Charlie's to make sure his old pickup will run. I'll come back and get you after while."

Myra came wide-awake. The day was at hand, and she didn't want Claude to leave her.

More than that, she didn't want to go to the bridge. Never in her thoughts did she think things would work out. It was a crazy plan, but Claude was determined to go through with it.

"I'm scared," Myra said.

Claude leaned over the feather bed and kissed her on the cheek. "It'll work out all right."

She watched as he disappeared into the gray morning gloom. He was hardly gone before she felt alone.

Claude walked down to Minnow Charlie's house. He surveyed the overgrown and weedy tangle surrounding it that had once grown cotton and corn. He was usually cautious to look around before he walked up to the house, but he was impatient to trade the Buick for Charlie's pickup. He and Myra were going to need something the cops weren't looking for to drive out of the state, provided they survived their meeting with Diamond Joe.

If Claude had studied the terrain a little better he might have seen the men scattered out amongst the junk surrounding Charlie's house. Had he arrived earlier, he might have seen Dink grab Charlie's dog by the collar and cut its throat. As it was, he came around the corner of what had once been the vegetable garden fence and found himself facing Diamond Joe not ten yards away.

"Hello, kid." Diamond Joe already had a pistol in his right hand. "I looked over that bridge, and it seemed like too public of a place for what we've got to settle."

Claude tried to keep a watch on Diamond Joe while he looked for the others that were sure to be with him. He saw Dink wading out of the weeds to his right with a sawed-off Browning Humpback 12 gauge in his hands. Claude noticed the bandage on Dink's right hand. Bull stepped out from behind the shade tree at the corner of the house behind Diamond Joe, and leisurely walked up beside him, the Thompson sub-machine gun dangling at the end of his arm. There was no sign of Ernest, but Claude was truly shocked to see Roy Burkhalter walk out of the blacksmith shed to his left.

"Where's my money?" Diamond Joe said.

Claude kept scanning for Ernest. "I buried it."

"Well, we're going to go get it."

"That ain't the deal. It's your cut and nothing else," Claude said.

"What about my cut?" Bull asked.

"And mine." Dink patted the forearm of the shotgun in his left palm like it was a baseball bat.

"I'm thinking you owe me a little extra." Diamond Joe was grinning like a cat that just caught a mouse. "Like maybe all of it."

"Let's quit fooling around," Roy blurted out.

The cotton gin owner looked a little uncomfortable with the whole setup. He seemed nervous, and Claude noticed that he was scanning the brambles as if he were thinking about running, or maybe looking for something in particular.

"What about it, kid? Do you want to do this the easy way?" Diamond Joe asked.

Claude knew they were going to kill him, whether he showed them where the money was or not. He could hold out on them, but they would torture him until he talked. And there was Myra to think about too. He could pull on them right then, and it might be his best chance. Not that he really had a chance. The odds of him killing them all were slim to none. But at least he would die shooting, and maybe warn Myra in the process. He told himself to fight on the move, shoot fast, and not to miss a shot.

He quickly decided to shoot Diamond Joe first, and to keep pulling the trigger until he put him down. Something told him he was the most dangerous. Bull should come next, as he had the trench sweeper. It was going to take some lead to put his thick body down — at least two bullets for him. Dink's hand was mangled, and anyway, he was liable to be jumpy and miss his first shot, even with the automatic shotgun. He would be third. Claude would probably be dead before he could get to Roy, but he was going to leave him for last if he survived that long. He was a little surprised that the man he'd admired for so long was acting so scared, but it was evident that Roy had no stomach for a fight.

Ernest was the joker in the deck, and Claude needed to know where he was. Claude was sure he was nearby, and his back felt vulnerable with the crazy man slipping around out of sight. He stalled for time while he tried to locate Ernest.

Myra went to the spring at daylight to bring back a bucket of water. She sloshed most of it on her leg lugging the heavy load back to the cabin, but managed to make it onto the porch with half a bucket full. She set it down and went into the cabin to get the coffeepot. Claude would want his morning java when he got back. She crossed the room and her hand had just taken hold of the pot when she heard the gunshots in the distance. She whirled to run outside, but stopped dead still. Ernest was sitting in a chair underneath the front window. She had passed within inches of him when she walked through the door.

"Ernest, what are you doing here?" Myra looked frantically for her purse. She spotted it on the window ledge above his head. She wondered if that was where she had left it, or if Ernest was smart enough to seek it out because that was where she kept her pistol.

Ernest didn't say anything. His face was

almost blank, except for the wild gleam of his eyes. She considered running for the door, but was sure he would grab her as she passed. She needed to play it cool and bide her time until an opportunity presented itself.

A crow cawed somewhere outside, and Ernest ducked his head and winced. He looked to the ceiling, scanning every inch of it as if something were about to swoop down upon him. Myra noticed for the first time that his pants were unbuttoned, and that he had his tool in his hand. She backed against the wall with the coffeepot held like a weapon.

Ernest rose and started toward her. "I want you to hold It."

She stared at his swollen member, not because of its size or because she had never seen one. What had her almost ready to scream were the scabs and scars that knotted his penis, as if it had been mangled in a meat grinder. Infected pus and blood oozed out between his fingers.

"I said to hold It in your hand." Ernest stopped just in front of her, and his breath was like rancid, rotten grease.

She yelled at the top of her lungs hoping Claude was nearby. She tried to run past the madman, swinging the coffeepot at his head as she did. He easily ducked the blow and shoved her hard against the wall. He punched her in the temple as she rebounded back toward him. She saw black spots dancing before her eyes, and her legs turned to rubber. She caught herself against the fireplace and lunged for her purse. He hammered his fist between her shoulder blades and she hit the floor wheezing for air. He took her by the hair and dragged her back into the middle of the room. She tried to yell again for help, but he rolled her onto her back and slapped her viciously across the face.

Ernest was babbling gibberish and kept hold of her head while he fumbled for his cock and kneeled beside her. She clawed at his eyes and he let go of her hair and caught her flailing right wrist and shoved her hand toward his crotch.

"Oh, Mother." His head was tilted back with his eyes closed in ecstasy, and tears rolled down his cheeks. "Hold me, Mother. I need you to hold It."

Myra's left hand bumped something metal on the floor beside her and she groped for it madly. Her fingers closed around it, and even half blind, she recognized the feel of it for the handle to the graniteware coffeepot she had used as a weapon earlier. She must have clung to it so fiercely that she had broken it loose.

She reared her arm back high above her head and stabbed the handle down into Ernest's crotch. He howled and let go of her, and she crabbed backwards, her hands and feet slipping and hindering her speed. She backed herself into the far corner of the room from the front door and watched him coming for her. There was a knife in his hand, and it was wickedly long and needle-pointed.

"My, what beautiful hands you have," he said.

He passed below the house wrens' nest and the pair of little birds launched themselves from the rafters. They ducked and dived at his head and scolded him. He covered his face with both hands, and screamed. He whirled and staggered around the room batting at the birds. Myra ran, grabbing her purse as she lunged through the door.

She could hear him running behind her, but her legs failed her and she tripped and fell headfirst off the porch. She rolled over onto her back in time to see him stagger out the door with both his hands outstretched and reaching for her. She knew

446

she was going to die, or even worse, but her throat was too dry to scream.

CHAPTER TWENTY-NINE

"I never hold a grudge. As soon as I get even with the son of a bitch, I forget it."
— W. C. Fields

"I don't like what I see on your face," Diamond Joe said. "If I didn't know better, I'd swear you're thinking about pulling your pistols."

"Just take us to the money, and I promise you I'll make it painless and shoot you in the face," Dink said.

"Why are you always threatening to shoot people in the face?" Bull asked. "Why not the head or the heart, or somewhere else?"

Dink shrugged. "I don't know. It just sounds meaner."

"You're all alone, kid," Diamond Joe said.

"I wouldn't say he's by himself," Sheriff Miller's voice boomed in the morning air. He stepped out of the woods at the end of their line, ten long steps off Dink's left shoulder. His Peacemaker was pointed at Dink's head.

"Not at all." Burke poked his shotgun around the corner of the house directly behind Bull and Diamond Joe.

"I guess we've got a Mexican standoff," Diamond Joe said.

"Stand-off, hell. You try and turn around and I'm going to shoot *you* in the face," Burke said.

"Calm down, gentlemen. I'm sure none of us wants to die," Diamond Joe said.

"Lay down your guns, and it'll end there," Sheriff Miller said. "That goes for you too, Claude. You're all under arrest."

Bull was itching to try and swing around with his Thompson, but he was smart enough to know Burke would bust him in the back with buckshot if he so much as twitched. Normally, Dink was the jumpy one, but he had Sheriff Miller's pistol practically in his ear and looked about to mess his britches.

"We aren't wanted for anything." Diamond Joe said it like he was out for a Sunday stroll.

"I just heard you admit to being a part of the Booker robbery, and caught you about to kill my son," Sheriff Miller said.

"And the odds are getting longer against

you." Sergeant Jones came around the corner of the house behind Burke and stopped wide of him. His fancy .45 was steady in his hand, and he was wearing a new Stetson. He kept reaching up to the brim and readjusting it on his head, as if it didn't fit right or he felt it didn't look proper for his image as a Ranger.

"Hello, Sergeant. I thought you'd decided to sit this one out," the Sheriff said.

"I guessed you might lead me to Claude if I appeared to be out of the hunt," Sergeant Jones said. "I've been tailing you all morning."

"Glad to have you," the Sheriff said. "Looks like you might get famous after all. You can shoot Crystal Joe if he decides to be foolish."

Diamond Joe turned his head enough to take in the new arrival and then sighed. "Put 'em down boys. They've got nothing that will stick, and they've got the drop on us."

"Roy, I'm talking to you too," Sheriff Miller said.

Roy glared at Sheriff Miller. "If things were different I'd . . ."

The morning got different in a hurry.

"Just tell us who to shoot, Roy," somebody called out. Claude could see two heads bobbing around in the overgrown field on the

450

other side of the abandoned garden, screened by the blackberry bushes and head-high weeds.

"Kill 'em all!" Roy shouted and ducked around the corner of the house.

Like Claude, the Sheriff had turned slightly to spot his new adversaries. Bull saw the opportunity and dropped to one knee, swinging his Thompson in a slow arc toward Burke or the Ranger behind him. He got on the trigger before he lined his gun up, and the submachine gun chattered and a stream of brass hulls lofted through the air. Sergeant Jones took a bullet and fell to the ground with his pistol going off harmlessly into the air over his head. Burke's shotgun belched and Bull jerked with the impact of a load of 00 buckshot hitting him in the chest. Bull's gun arm went wild, and the second load of buckshot turned him halfway around and caused him to trigger a burst down the line of his friends. One of the bullets struck Dink in the leg just as Sheriff Miller's .44 shot off the top of his head. The little bandit tipped over like a limp noodle.

Claude was only dimly aware of all of that. He only had eyes for Diamond Joe. The bad man's pistol swung up unbelievably fast. Claude drew his right-hand .45 and shot

Diamond Joe twice in the belly an instant before a bullet struck him in the center of the chest. He staggered back, watching the crime boss fall to his knees. Diamond Joe's pistol bucked in his fist again, but Claude didn't hear the report. There were too many guns going off in one continuous, ear-busting roar. He felt another bullet hit him like a battering ram and he staggered backward and pulled the trigger on his .45 as rapidly as he could. Diamond Joe's body jerked with every bullet. It was as if the barrage had propped his body up, for when Claude's magazine ran dry the gangster's neck whipped forward and he toppled onto his face, dead before he hit the ground.

The Texas Ranger was down on the ground behind Diamond Joe's body and firing wildly at the gunmen in the blackberry thicket. A bullet flew past Claude's left ear, and he wasn't sure if it belonged to the Ranger, or if somebody was shooting at him from the brambles. He holstered his gun and reached for the other with his left hand. Roy was hidden behind the corner of the house with only his pistol sticking out. He blindly banged away at Burke on the other corner. Claude snapped two shots from the hip at him. He didn't see if his marksmanship was any good, for he spotted a tall man standing in the weeds to his left with a lever-action Winchester pointing his way. The rifle recoiled before Claude could bring his .45 to bear on him, and out of the corner of his eye he saw the Sheriff stagger.

Claude raised his pistol to eye level and pumped three rounds in the rifleman's direction, none of them hitting home. He struggled to take finer aim, but somebody shot the rifleman before he could. Another bullet ripped into Claude's stomach, and the force of the projectile was so great it knocked him on the ground. He fired from a sitting position at the other rifleman thirty yards into the thicket. All he could see of the man was a straw hat and a wobbling rifle.

The Sheriff hobbled to his side and his fist leapt high with the recoil of his .44. For some reason, he favored black-powder cartridges, and a little cloud of gun smoke hung around him. When his pistol dropped back on target the Sheriff fired again, just as Claude touched off his last shot. The man in the blackberry bushes disappeared.

The scene quieted for an instant before Burke shouted from where he was leaned against the wall of the house. He pointed frantically at Roy Burkhalter running through the bushes.

"Are you all right, Burke?" Sheriff Miller asked.

"Just a little flesh nick, but it's bleeding like a stuck pig." Burke shouted back.

Claude and Sheriff Miller caught glimpses of Roy's head bobbing along as he repeatedly leapt and lunged to avoid becoming entangled in the thorns and vines. His crashing and cursing could be plainly heard for a long time until he disappeared into the thicket altogether. Before Sheriff Miller could help Claude to his feet, a gun boomed, and then again.

"I don't think whoever that is was shooting at us." Claude couldn't catch his wind, and he was breathing in ragged gasps.

Sheriff Miller braced Claude's shoulder to steady him. "It might not be over yet. I think I recognized one of those men out there in the thicket. He worked for Roy down at the cotton gin, and maybe there's more of Roy's boys out there trying to line us up in their rifle sights."

Claude noticed the blood on the Sheriff's right thigh. "Are you all right?"

The Sheriff glanced at his leg disdainfully while he thumbed the empty hulls from his Colt. "I think it was a ricochet. Hurts like hell, but it's just a crease."

Claude holstered his pistols. "We'd better

tie your belt around that leg to stop the bleeding."

Sheriff Miller brushed him away. "Boy, I saw you hit twice, and maybe more."

Claude felt as if he were about to pass out. It was like his chest was in a vice. He ripped open the front of his shirt, and tore at his chest. Sheriff Miller watched as Claude unbuckled the chunk of hammered steel that covered his torso under his shirt and threw it on the ground at their feet. Both of them stepped forward and examined the two dents in the improvised body armor where bullets had punched into it.

"Didn't know you were such a craftsman," Sheriff Miller said.

"It's just two chunks of car hood riveted together in layers and bent to fit." There were angry red welts on his torso that would soon be ugly bruises where the bullets had impacted the chest plate. But his breathing was already getting easier. He spied a fourth bullet dimple on the right side of his armor, about where it would have covered the wound to his ribs. The bullet had punched through the outer layer of sheet metal completely, and the inner layer was driven in at least a half inch. Claude touched his ribs and found that the blow had caused his old bullet wound to bleed again.

"If that one had had just a little more umph, I'd say it would have done for you," Sheriff Miller said.

Claude agreed. The metal looked like it had stretched all it could. It must have been that blow that had knocked the air from him, or perhaps the deformed metal pressing against his tender ribs had kept him from breathing deeply enough. He tried to remember when the bullet might have hit him, and who might have shot him from that angle.

"It must have been Roy who shot me while he was running off," Claude said.

"Maybe. Roy never was one to attack from the front," Sheriff Miller said.

Claude realized what a fool he'd been to look up to Roy Burkhalter.

"Are you two going to hug and kiss?" Burke came limping up with his shotgun butt jabbed into the ground for a crutch.

"We were out here getting shot at while you were hiding behind cover," Sheriff Miller said.

"Piss on you." Burke turned around enough so that they could see the blood on the back of his Levi's. "That damned Roy shot me in the ass. I can still feel the bullet in it."

Sheriff Miller noticed that the spot of

blood seeping through Burke's blue jeans was actually just below his ass, but the wound was close enough. "It's a good thing Roy always packed a pocket pistol, or he might have shot your brains out."

Burke gave him a dirty look and then turned his backside to Claude. "Roy didn't ruin my good looks, did he?"

"I never knew Roy was such a marksman to hit your scrawny ass," Sheriff Miller said.

"I can see I'm not going to get any sympathy around here." Burke hobbled over to where Bull lay, and studied the effects of his buckshot. He went from man to man like that, checking to see if their victims were as dead as they looked.

"I had to shoot that big son of a bitch with the machine gun three times before he'd quit trying to kill me," Burke said. "They must raise 'em bitter where he comes from."

All three of them noticed the fallen Ranger at the same time. They walked over to his body where it lay twisted painfully on the ground with a hand laid over the bloody gunshot wound in his chest. Another neat, little hole, looking more like a large blood blister than a bullet wound, was beneath his left eye. The back of his head stained the grass beneath him.

"A .30-30 will make a mess of a man,"

Burke said. "Was he married?"

"He never mentioned a wife. All he talked about was the Rangers," Sheriff Miller said.

"It's a shame." Burke shook his head somberly.

"It would have miffed him to know how close he came to grabbing some headlines," Sheriff Miller said. "He was pretty fond of the notion of gunfights."

Burke could tell that the Sheriff had liked the Ranger, despite his dry observation of the man's ambitious nature. "I guess the newspapers might think he shot most of this Dallas bunch single-handedly. Somebody might tell it to them that way."

Sheriff Miller narrowed his eyes and considered what Burke had said. "He'd like being a hero."

"Legendary Rangers," Burke mumbled.

"One riot, one Ranger," Sheriff Miller responded just as quietly.

Claude studied the carnage. Four dead men, and maybe more out in the blackberry bushes, was a lot of dying to happen in the matter of seconds. He listened to the lawmen's nervous banter, and figured that it was their way of coping. Shooting people and getting shot at in return had a way of unsettling you.

The sound of somebody busting through

the thicket got all of their attention. Claude reached in his pocket and found a fresh magazine for his right-hand .45. He racked a round home and stepped to where the trail through the berry bushes came out into the open. He waited with the pistol leveled on the trail, and Sheriff Miller stepped up beside him.

"Just let the little ones by you, and I'll take them," Burke said from behind them.

Claude waited for whatever menace was about to show itself. He had to admit, it felt good to be standing by the Sheriff.

"I think I shaded you on that last fellow with the rifle," Claude said.

"Like hell you did. That was my bullet that put him down," Sheriff Miller said.

"I don't know. It's natural for a man to get a little slower with age."

"It's going to be a long time before I'm old enough that you can shade me. This isn't child's play, you know."

"I know that, Sheriff."

Sheriff Miller turned his head enough to put one eye on his son. "Yeah, I reckon you do at that."

Their argument was short-lived, for whoever was coming along the trail was close. They readied themselves with their feet braced and their fingers light on their triggers.

"Hold on there," Minnow Charlie called out.

The old Indian appeared out of the brambles with Betty Ludlow in tow. Charlie had a .35 Remington semiauto carbine resting nonchalantly on his shoulder.

Sheriff Miller lowered his pistol. "What are you two youngsters doing prowling around the brush?"

Betty simply chuckled and blushed. Despite their age difference, she had always found the Sheriff handsome.

"I heard my dog yelp like somebody had killed him, right after I'd seen a covey of quail spook up out of the grass. I figured something was wrong, so I snuck out the back door with my rifle and went to Betty's cabin," Charlie said.

"Was that you shooting about a minute ago?" Claude asked loudly to make sure the old Indian could hear him. Charlie had once been a fine rifle shot and deer hunter, but Claude thought him far too blind and tottery to hit anything anymore.

Charlie smiled, evidently pleased about something. "Fellow came running up to Betty's door with a gun in his hand. He didn't see me."

Claude noticed for the first time that Charlie was smoking a cigar. He rarely smoked, and when he did it was usually a corncob pipe.

"When did you take to stogies?" Claude asked.

Charlie pulled the cigar from his mouth and stared at it as if he were seeing it for the first time. "Roy always bragged that his cigars cost two bits apiece and came on a boat all the way from Cuba. I took one out of his pocket and thought I'd see what all his fuss was about. I think he overpaid."

"Roy was always as counterfeit as a three-dollar bill," Burke said. "Somebody else is going to have to drag his body over here. I'm plumb tuckered out."

Sheriff Miller turned to Claude and held out his left hand. "Hand over your guns."

Claude took a step back and met the Sheriff's hard stare. "I'm not going in with you."

"Son, you've messed up, but maybe it's not too late to set things right."

"Myra and I are getting out of here. Don't you worry, cause we won't be coming back to bother you."

Sheriff Miller took two deep breaths. "The court might go easy on you, considering your age. Don't throw your future away over

461

some wild girl. There's nothing but hardship in the kind of life you've been living."

"I like making love to Myra, and the feel of a gun in my hand," Claude said.

"There's more to life than just rutting and robbing," the Sheriff replied.

"You can't live my life for me. I'm asking you, just this once, let me go my own way, even if it isn't your way."

Sheriff Miller reached for the badge on his shirt. He unpinned it and pitched it to Burke. "There you go, Deputy, I guess you've got a new job. I'm officially resigning as sheriff."

Claude wasn't sure what was happening. He watched the two men carefully.

Burke studied the shiny little shield in his palm. "Are you positive? I wasn't bucking for a promotion."

"I've had enough of this, and I've suddenly found that I can't do my job anymore," Sheriff Miller said.

"Nobody would know you let me go," Claude said.

"I would." Sheriff Miller pointed at Burke. "I guess whether you go or not depends on our new sheriff."

Burke pocketed the badge. "I was wounded in action and didn't see Claude escaping, or maybe he wasn't even here at all."

"You hear that?" Sheriff Miller asked.

"Yes, sir." Raw emotion was welling up in Claude and he felt as if he were about to burst. He understood how hard it was for the Sheriff to take off that badge, and realized that he didn't know the man like he thought he did. In fact, he was rethinking a lot of things.

Before he could say anything, they all heard a faint cry in the distance. Sound carried far in the mountains, and Charlie's hunting cabin was less than a half a mile away as the crow flies.

"That sounded like a woman's scream," Burke said.

Claude didn't hear him. He was already running up the trail to the cabin. With a sickening feeling coming over him, he realized where Ernest had gone.

CHAPTER THIRTY

"I intend to live forever, or die trying."
— Groucho Marx

Ernest started down the steps, but the fussy little birds were still fluttering about his head. He paused long enough to swipe at them again, and that gave Myra time to try for her gun. Her nervous hands fumbled at the purse's zipper, and he was practically on top of her by the time her hand reached in and took hold of her pistol. Just as her revolver was clearing her handbag he kicked her in the ribs, rolling her across the ground. The gun flew out of her grasp, and she was on her belly once more, clawing at the leaves that covered the ground and crawling on her hands and knees.

His hands reached up her skirt and tore at her panties. He rolled her over onto her back and fought to spread her legs with his knees. "You won't laugh at me anymore,

Mother. I'm going to give It to you real good."

Myra clubbed at his face with her balled fists, but he seemed impervious to pain, even liked it. She realized that she was crying, and hoped that he would kill her first.

"Hey, you," another voice said.

Ernest looked past Myra's head, and growled like some wild animal and started to rise. A gunshot blasted Myra's eardrums, and Ernest fell lifelessly across her. She struggled under his weight, fighting to get clear of the horror. She dimly recognized another pair of hands helping her move him. She scrambled free and shoved her back against a tree trunk, wiping at the blood on her face and trying to focus on the woman standing before her.

"Easy, Myra," a familiar voice said.

"Is that you, Mrs. Miller?" Myra asked.

Mary Miller set the double-barreled shotgun against the tree and sat beside the girl and hugged her. "Jim sent me up here to look out for you in case you needed it."

Myra leaned around Mary to look at Ernest's lifeless body lying just a few feet away. "Is he dead?"

"He won't bother you anymore." Mary tried not to look at what her shotgun had done to him, even if he was a rabid animal.

Myra let Mary hug her for what seemed like a long time. She cried on the older woman's shoulder until all the fear and hurt emptied out of her. Her heartbeat slowed, but her body was still twitchy and light feeling.

"I need a cigarette. My nerves are shot to pieces," she said.

Mary looked a question at her.

"They're in my purse." Myra still didn't trust her own legs to get up.

Mary went over and picked the purse up off the ground and brought it back. She plucked a pack of cigarettes and a Zippo lighter from inside it.

"You don't mind do you?" Myra's shaky hands broke the first cigarette she tried to take out of the pack, but she managed to get the second one between her lips with only minor damage.

"Not at all," Mary said. "Fact is, I could use one myself."

Mary shook out a cigarette like an old pro and tucked it into the corner of her mouth. She took the Zippo from Myra and lit her cigarette and then her own. She inhaled deeply and then held the cigarette to the side between her fingers with a feminine bend to her wrist. She smiled at Myra and blew a smoke ring that floated between them. "I'd forgotten why I used to smoke these things before I got pregnant the first time."

Myra was shocked. She'd never imagined a lady like Mrs. Miller smoking a Lucky Strike, much less packing a shotgun. She drew on her own cigarette and let the nicotine slowly creep through her body.

"Don't act so shocked. I was young once too," Mary said. "Jim and I sewed our own wild oats once upon a time. We were quite a couple, even if I say so myself."

"I thought I heard gunshots earlier," Myra said.

Mary's eyes told Myra that she was worried about that very thing. "Jim and Burke went to help Claude, and Minnow Charlie's down there too."

"I've got to go see if Claude's all right." Myra got her legs under her and stood up.

Mary ground out her half-finished cigarette with the heel of her shoe and picked up her shotgun. "Seems like men have been worrying me most of my adult life."

"Loving somebody isn't always easy, is it?" Myra asked.

"You've just got to trust that things will work out." Mary smiled and pointed down the trail toward the river.

Claude was coming at a run. He wrapped

both arms around Myra and kissed her forehead while he glanced at Ernest's body, and then at his mother. He whispered to Myra and brushed the leaves from her hair and dabbed at the blood on her face with the sleeve of his shirt.

A tall man in a cowboy hat limped up the trail behind Claude fifteen minutes later. He was wearing a gun like he was born with it on. There wasn't a badge on his uniform shirt, but when he stopped beside Mary, Myra recognized him for the Sheriff just the same. He stood exactly like Claude, and had that same stubborn set to his jaw.

"I guess you're the Sheriff," Myra pushed away from Claude.

"And I guess you're the famous Myra I keep hearing about," Sheriff Miller said. "You can call me Jim. My days as a lawman are through. I can't keep up with the times."

Mary saw how Claude was looking at his father, and hustled Myra away. "Come on, Myra, let's get you cleaned up."

Claude and Sheriff Miller dragged Ernest out of sight, and rested in the shade while the women were in the cabin. They talked of hunting and theorized when it might rain again, all to keep from talking about the trouble between them.

"I noticed you knocked the sights off your

pistols," Sheriff Miller said.

Claude nodded. "Makes my draw a little faster."

"You can't hit anything at more than a few feet like that, and being fast isn't everything."

"I can."

"Well, I guess you can," the Sheriff said quietly. Both of them recognized that they had made some kind of truce, but it felt tenuous at best.

Neither of them knew that Mary kept Myra inside longer than necessary, and periodically peeked out the window to see what her men were doing. Finally, she and Myra went back outside and joined them. Myra was wearing a fresh dress from her suitcase, and she had washed her face and Mary had brushed her hair. She was going to have a bad black eye, but other than that, she was no worse for her wear. She looked her usual, gorgeous self.

Claude took Myra's hand and looked thankfully at his mother. "Momma, I owe you one."

"You can't trust anybody if you can't trust family," Mary said.

Sheriff Miller kept looking down the trail. "The Bureau has agents in town looking for you two, and somebody is liable to have heard all the gunshots. But either way, it won't be long until there are a lot of policemen sniffing around here."

Claude nodded, but hesitated. "Sheriff, I hate that I disappointed you."

"I only wanted the best for you. You quit robbing banks and I'll be as proud of you as ever."

"I can't promise that," Claude said. "I can't promise anything."

"Well then, I'd suggest you be careful, or neither of you two are going to live long enough to give your mother any grandchildren."

Claude didn't want to argue, not when it might be the last time he saw his parents. "We'd best be going."

Sheriff Miller looked off into the timber, avoiding Claude's eyes. "Claude, don't you come back here. You got lucky this time, but don't ever come back. Folks here know your face, and you're a wanted man."

Mary hugged Myra and then Claude. "Maybe when things cool off you can come back to visit us if we're careful."

"No, Momma, the Sheriff's right," Claude said.

"I love you, son," Mary said.

"I love you too, Momma."

Sheriff Miller stood with his hands in his

pockets, looking apart from the rest of them.

"Jim," Mary said with a little hint in her voice.

Sheriff Miller held out his hand. "Claude, I . . ."

Claude waited. "What?"

A cricket sang from inside the cabin while his father felt around for the right words. "You be careful."

Claude shook his hand. "I will, Sheriff."

Myra nodded at Sheriff Miller and then she and Claude walked away hand in hand.

"You're going to regret not telling him what you should have," Mary said when Claude and Myra were out of sight.

"I already do," Sheriff Miller said. "How long do you think they can last?"

Mary leaned against him. "My mother said I would leave you in less than a year."

"What did she know?"

"Exactly."

Sheriff Miller put his arm over her shoulder and led her toward home. He looked back at the cabin once. "Did you notice that they detoured up toward the spring?"

"Yes, but I thought maybe Claude was taking a different route."

"No, my guess would be that he needed to pick up the money he hid there."

"And you didn't try to get him to turn the

money in?"

He smiled at her like he had twenty years earlier. "I figured the two of them could use something to start them out in life."

"I'll never understand you," she said.

"But you love me anyway."

"Yes I do. More than ever."

Neither one of them noticed the little wad of money Myra had slipped into Mary's skirt pocket. But then again, Myra had deft fingers. Not that she ever intended to make her living as a pickpocket, but it didn't hurt for a girl to learn to take care of herself.

The pickup Charlie traded them for the Buick hadn't been driven much in years, and the engine missed and sputtered and threatened to give up the ghost with every mile. The old truck was so worn out that steering it was like herding cats down the road. Claude wasn't sure that the dry-rotted tires would make it where they wanted to go, but he was getting more used to holding his breath and letting the dice roll where they would.

Myra snuggled up against his side on the seat and stared dreamily out the windshield. "Just how far is it to Fort Smith?"

"We'll be getting on the train and headed north in about three hours." He wasn't sure they would make it at all, but that version sounded good. Good dreams were what kept people going.

"What are we going to do after we've spent all our money up north?" She took a packet of money from the duffel bag on the seat beside her, and ruffled the cash with her thumb.

Claude gave her a playful scowl. "Don't go getting the cart before the horse. Let's just live things out one day at a time."

"I'm glad I found you," she said.

"I'd say it was the other way around, but me too."

Playing with money always excited Myra. She pitched the bills back in the duffel and grinned at him and ran the tip of her tongue across her upper lip. One of her hands started caressing his neck and the other one traced a finger up and down his thigh. "All that fighting didn't take the starch out of you, did it?"

He somehow managed to avoid a wreck when she hiked up her skirt and threw her leg over his lap. Kissing her while at the same time guessing where the road lay was an even greater feat of driving, but he managed it with proper enthusiasm.

"You're going to make us crash." His complaint lacked any hint of seriousness.

Myra sat on his lap and locked the fingers of her hands behind his neck and smiled like the imp she was. "You just keep driving, lover. We've got plenty of time to get where we want to go."

He punched the brakes three or four times to get them to work and skidded the truck to a stop in the middle of the road. "You know, somebody's liable to come along and see us."

"I guess they'll get an eyeful then." She slipped her dress off her shoulders and let it fall around her waist.

"There's never a dull moment with you."

"Does that mean you're going to build me a little house with a white picket fence, and make an honest woman out of me?" she asked. "When are we going to start farming and raising kids?"

He didn't really want to talk, and she was making it very difficult for him to think. "None of that yet. I don't want to take the edge off our relationship. I kind of like not knowing what's going to happen next."

ABOUT THE AUTHOR

Some folks are just born to tell tall tales. **Brett Cogburn** was reared in Texas and the mountains of Southeastern Oklahoma. He had the fortune for many years to make his living from the back of a horse, where cowboys still step on frisky broncs on cold mornings, and drag calves to the branding fire on the end of a rope from their saddle horn. Growing up around ranches, livestock auctions, and backwoods hunting camps filled his head with stories, and he never forgot a one. In his own words, "My grandfather taught me to ride a bucking horse, my mother gave me a love of reading, and my father taught me how to shoot straight. Cowboys are just as wild as they ever were, and I've been fortunate enough to know more than a few."

Somewhere during his knockabout years cowboying, training horses, and working in the oil field, he managed to earn a BA in

English and a minor in history. Brett lives with his family on a small ranch in Oklahoma. The West is still teaching him how to write.